In Too Deep

Fiona Quinn

THE WORLD of INIQUUS

UBICUMQUE, QUOTIES. QUIDQUID

Iniquus - /i'ni/kwus/- our strength is unequalled, our tactics unfair—we stretch the law to its breaking point. We do whatever is necessary to bring the enemy down.

The Lynx Series
Alex
Weakest Lynx
Missing Lynx
Chain Lynx
Cuff Lynx

Strike Force
In Too DEEP
JACK Be Quick
InstiGATOR

Uncommon Enemies
WASP
RELIC
DEADLOCK
THORN

Chapter One

Lacey

Thursday Night

Lacey Stuart's muscles tightened as irritation prickled through her nervous system. She gave her phone yet another check. No new messages. A swirl of frustration blew past her lips, as she pushed the phone farther back on the bar. It didn't look like Steve was going to show. Emergencies popped up, she thought, trying to be generous. But really, what could have stopped him from sending a quick text? She slid her thigh farther up her crossed legs, trying not to skate off the ultra-modern, ultra-awkward bar stool made for someone much taller than she. Lacey caught the server's eye and tapped the rim of her empty Cosmo glass, signaling that another one was in order. She decided to take a Lyft back to her apartment after she finished this drink – with or without Steve.

She should probably be worried about Steve. It wasn't like him to stand her up. But honestly, the only thing she felt was aggravation. It had been a long, miserable day at work. All Lacey wanted was to be back in her apartment curled up with a cup of hot tea, and her book. Lacey glanced down at the winter coat she'd thrown across the stool beside hers to save a place for Steve — a good thirty minutes ago. She couldn't understand why he'd been so insistent on meeting her here, and then not been courteous enough to give her a heads-up that he was running late.

As the server set a fresh drink in front of her, Lacey caught scotch-on-the-rocks guy staring at her mouth. Again. She wondered if he had a thing for bright red lipstick or if she had a strand of spinach from her afternoon snack caught in her teeth. Lacey held her hand over her mouth, lowering her head to stare at her lap while her tongue foraged in the crevices and along the gum line, hoping to excavate any residue.

As she raised her eyes, they caught on a man by the door. He was staring at her as if he knew her and was trying to make a decision. She didn't recognize him, but his attention made a tingle of apprehension skitter across her scalp. Lacey hated living with this pervasive paranoia. Fear and hypervigilance had made her find demons in the shadows. After everything that had happened to her last fall, she no longer trusted her ability to tell the difference between some guy checking her out and some guy who meant to hurt her. *I need to find a therapist*, she told herself. Lacey reached out to touch the base of the pink girly drink in front of her. An anchor. A reason for her to be sitting alone at the bar. Her shaking fingers encircled the delicate stem, and she lifted the glass for a sip.

Out of the corner of her eye, Lacey watched the man by the door take another step forward into the room. As his interest pulled her focus back over to him, he tipped his head as if asking her a question. The stranger's eyes didn't move from hers, even as he eased his shoulder against the wall, letting a boisterous girl-group push past him in a cloud of perfume and shiny fabrics.

The man was tall; his sports jacket looked tailored to his athletic body. He bunched his brow into a wrinkled knot as they looked at each other. His face might have been handsome in a rugged Marlboro-man kind of way in his earlier years, but now he was weathered and balding, and there was something vicious about the slash of his mouth and the way he held his shoulders.

Lacey stopped breathing. Vulnerability swept up from her stomach and stuck in her throat. She forced her eyes away from his and scanned the screen on her phone. No, Steve still hadn't texted with a reason for not showing, or a time he'd arrive. She tapped the app to call a car. She glanced at scotch-on-the rocks guy, who dangled his glass from his fingertips in such a way as to hide his attention. But his gaze was firmly on her mouth. Lacey felt threats everywhere. She worked at being reasonable. She was a woman alone in a bar. Of course, she had attracted attention. Though, neither of these men was giving off the usual bar signals – there was no hoping-for-a-hook-up vibe.

These guys seemed a different kind of predatory. And she felt trapped. Panicked.

Lacey leaned into the bar. "Hey there, I think I'm going to take my check, please." She pushed her almost-full glass away from her to signal that she was finished.

As the bartender slid her tab into a leather folder and placed it in front of her, Lacey jerked her credit card from her phone case. She wished she could ask the manager to let her slip out the back door of the kitchen rather than make her skitter past the guy spooking her at the front. While she signed the bottom of the receipt, Lacey peeked past the long layers of her hair over to the man at the entrance. He was fishing in his pocket, then pulled something out.

Lacey jolted as a crack of thunder erupted violently, causing a wave of gasps and startled giggles from around the room. The lights flickered, and Lacey slid off her stool to leave. As her feet touched the ground, the doors crashed open and a group of festively dressed couples surged in, laughing and shaking off the sudden rain. With the noise and commotion as a backdrop, the man made his move. In an instant, he towered in front of her, blocking Lacey's retreat.

"Danika?" he said quietly.

Even though the room was loud, Lacey could hear him clearly. When she heard that name, her joints solidified, and she couldn't move or speak. Her dark brown eyes, heavy with mascara, pulled wide as they filled with shock. Another clap of thunder worked its way across the sky; the sound held Lacey in place, sucking the oxygen from her lungs.

The man bent his head closer to her ear. "Danika, you're in danger." His last word became a sharp sucking sound as he arched backward. His fingers curled into the pewter satin of Lacey's blouse. He pulled her sideways, reeling to the left, hitting the floor first with his shoulder, then with his head, taking her with him.

Lacey tried to scramble up, to pull her skirt back down below her hips, to regain some decorum now that she had flashed the bar with her pink silk panties. But the stranger tightened his grip and locked her to him with a tight fist. "They know who you are. Trust no one. Run." His words bubbled out with red spittle and the visual made Lacey's mind go numb. She worked hard at processing what was happening, but her brain snagged on the red froth at the corners of his lips, and she couldn't think past it.

As the man exhaled the word "run," he unwound his right hand from the fabric of her blouse. He shoved something cold and hard down into her bra. Lacey tried to pull free. She dropped her jaw to scream, but Lacey couldn't make any air pass by her vocal cords, so her mouth hung open and empty.

Someone gripped Lacey's upper arms, lifted her, questioned her, was she all right?

5

All right? Lacey stared down at the stranger, trying to process the fact that he had called her Danika. That he was there to warn her. And now, a red puddle pooled from under his shoulders.

The bartender rolled the man on to his stomach as the well-clad patrons fished out their phones. Lacey prayed that someone was calling 911. But the bright strobe of flashes meant that most were grabbing pictures to post on Instagram and Snapchat to show what dangerous and exciting lives they led. The flashing lights turned the scene into an impressionist's painting where the eye only took in and defined certain aspects, the outline of a leg, the hem of a skirt, the swirl of burgundy leaching across the floor.

Lacey pinned her focus on the knife handle protruding from the man's herringbone jacket. Someone had stabbed into his lungs, and now he was gasping like a trout lugged from the river. *That doesn't belong there*, was all Lacey's shocked mind could manage. She reached down and yanked the blade from the stranger's back. Blood dripped from the sharp edge. Lacey dropped the weapon to the ground in disgust. She held her hands wide and let the wine-colored droplets trickle from the webbing of her fingers.

Hands now pulled Lacey backward, away from the stranger's flailing legs. A linen napkin rubbed over her fingers.

Lacey twisted to see over her shoulder where she found scotch-on-the rocks guy.

"I'm so sorry," he said, dropping the napkin to the floor. "He's a good friend of yours?" His voice was kind and solicitous. With a solid grip, he moved Lacey away from the dying man, around the back of the fascinated crowd, and toward the front door.

It wasn't until she was propelled out of the bar and a shot of cold, wet air hit her face that Lacey registered the dying man's warning. "Trust no one. Run." She hadn't a clue what he could have meant. All she knew was that Scotch-on-the-rocks had tightened his grip and was herding her toward a black car with its back door gaping open.

Lacey set her high heels into the mortar of the rain-slicked brick sidewalk. She snaked her body and protested, but she made no progress in freeing herself. Without forethought, Lacey's knee slammed into the man's groin. He collapsed with a grunt. As he hit the ground, he stretched out a hand, shackling her ankle with an iron grasp. Lacey freaked.

She kicked at his face with her free foot, yelling for help. Swinging her head, she searched the crowd for a hero. She spotted two men clambering from the black sedan and knew she had seconds to get herself free. Lacey aimed her stiletto at her captor's chest. He blocked it with his free arm. Releasing her ankle, he reached into his jacket. Lacey felt sure he was going for a gun.

Her scream should have cut through the bar patrons' glee at tonight's horrific adventure, should have brought someone to her rescue. But the scream was masked by an EMS truck, speeding up the street, sirens wailing. Lacey reeled back into the bar and ran as fast as her high heels and tight skirt would allow, pushing people out of the way, clambering past chairs. She had to find another way out–a back exit–some way to escape.

Lacey burst out of the kitchen door, stumbling head long into a pile of black trash bags, lining the alleyway. The downpour stung her upturned face as headlights caught her in their abrupt illumination. Car doors popped open.

Pushing herself up—her shoes left behind—Lacey sprinted down the alley, down the road, down the Metro stairs, and into the late-evening crowd. Away from the men's angry shouting.

***

Sopping wet and garbage streaked, Lacey slid behind a Metro System's construction curtain. She panted behind the plastic yellow fabric, replaying the scene of her alley escape from the second car of scary men.

Lacey was sure she had heard a man bark, "Secret Service." But the dead man had said, "Trust no one."

Was he dead? Lacey had never seen anyone blow blood bubbles before and couldn't imagine coming back from that. It was the stuff of horror flicks and midnight campfire stories – the kind of imagery that ruined sleep for nights, maybe even for years, to come. Lacey lifted her hands, crusty with flaked blood where she had squeezed her fists as she pumped her arms and fled. She rubbed her palms together in disbelief.

It was possible that the man was alive, she tried to reason. Surely someone had gotten to him with medical help in time. If he lived, Lacey would like to talk to him and find out what was going on. And while she wanted the information, she also never wanted to be near that guy again. Ever. But still. . . Lacey's head danced with questions like pointillist dots on a canvas all blending together to paint a picture of absolute terror. Lacey was terrified. This was what the word meant. She had used the word so many times when it was just silly – rollercoasters, and exam grades. Lacey pushed the strands of her damp hair back off her face and bit at her lip to stop its trembling.

Did the man really mean trust no one? Lacey sat on an overturned bucket, propping her elbows on her knees and holding her head, trying hard to calm her shaking. Secret Service seemed like reasonable people to trust. Maybe the police? "They know who you are." Suddenly, Lacey wondered why scary people would know who she was. Her mind slipped to her great uncle, Bartholomew Winslow, who owned the art gallery she managed. He was hiding out at his home in Bali, and wouldn't be coming back to the United States until things settled down – until the arrest warrant went away. Did this have something to do with him and his affiliation with the Assembly? She reached into her blouse to retrieve what the dying man had thrust into her bra.

A flash drive.

She sat there, staring at it.

Chapter Two

Steve

Thursday Night

Steve stood wide-legged in front of the flat screen in Danika's apartment. He posted his fists on his hips. A scowl loosened his cheek muscles. His nostril pulled up into a sneer. The local cable news station must have beaten some kind of record gathering that many talking-heads to comment on the odd murder that just happened in Alexandria, Virginia. Steve wanted to jump through the screen and stop the newscaster from identifying the victim as Leo Bardman. Leo's being there at the restaurant, where Steve himself was supposed to have met Lacey, meant she was in immediate danger. Bigger danger than he had believed her to be in. Shit. He had thought he still had time to keep her safe.

Steve held his breath as a montage of video clips, sent in by excited bystanders, played behind the news anchor's head. All of them included a dark-haired woman in a black skirt and pewter blouse.

11

"God, Lacey, what have I done?" Steve whispered. He pressed his hands together in front of his mouth like a man deep in prayer.

The image switched to Lacey, wrestling for her freedom in front of the restaurant. Steve couldn't believe she was capable of stomping on a man's face. He couldn't fathom how she'd gotten away from a seasoned FBI agent.

Steve had had a heads-up that all hell had broken loose at the bar, and Lacey had run away. But the tightly worded text that popped up from his partner hadn't prepared him for the scenes jostling their way across the television. As he watched Lacey bulldoze her way back into the bar, Steve sent a nervous glance to the bedroom door. If Danika came out now, she'd see WDIU News blow his partner's cover.

The news anchor announced, "Tonight, the FBI are being tight-lipped about their agent who failed to apprehend the mystery woman in the doorway when she escaped his grasp. And though the video tapes show men in dark suits, displaying authoritative-looking badges, and yelling their affiliation, the Secret Service denies having a presence at the scene."

Steve wished the videos had captured those men's faces. They absolutely weren't the Secret Service, and he wanted to know exactly who Pavle had sent after Lacey. He wanted to throttle them. Each and every one.

The anchor continued with, "The city police ask anyone who might recognize the woman to contact them immediately."

As the news panel pushed into over-drive speculating about who was telling the truth and who was covering their rear, Danika moved into the living room. She rubbed a towel over her newly-dyed strawberry-blonde hair. Steve swung away from her and stalked toward the front window in an attempt to hide the perspiration and anxiety on his face.

"Guess what I did." Danika bubbled with glee.

Steve forced his voice to be flat and unemotional. "What's that?"

"I flushed those brown contact lenses down the toilet. We're talking *months* of stinging agony. I hope everyone appreciates how much pain I was in."

Steve grunted his response. He felt Danika focus her dark blue eyes on his back as he parted the venetian blinds. He peeked through the slats with binoculars trained on the entryway to Lacey's apartment across the street, hoping Danika would stay on the other side of the room. Steve wasn't acting his usual calm and cool under fire. His body gave away his stress levels. He needed deodorant, badly. He needed his hands to stop rattling the damned blinds. Where the hell was Lacey?

13

"No sign?" Danika asked. "Where do you think she squirreled herself away?"

Steve cleared his throat. "Here are some better questions: How does she know to stay away?" At least his voice sounded unattached, he congratulated himself. "And why hasn't she called me? This isn't how she'd normally act." He glanced back at Danika. "Could Leo have said something to her? Something that would make her run?"

"Whatever he said before Pavle's guy killed him, Lacey was running right out the back door and into the trap." Danika slid up behind Steve, pressing her body against his back and curving her arms around his stomach. "Our guys should have been in place, not sitting in the car, hiding from the rain. It's their own fault Lacey was able to run out of that alley." Danika balanced her forehead between Steve's shoulder blades, rocking it back and forth. "Leo was so nice. I told him not to cut ties with Pavle."

"That's why he's dead? Serves him right, then. Nobody should be that stupid."

Danika's body stiffened against him.

"But you liked Leo—maybe I should I be offering condolences?" Steve scoffed. "Handing you a tissue?" Steve had been playing the game for a long time. He'd lived deep undercover for years. And in those years, he had learned a very clear lesson - emotions were crap on the job. Dangerous. They screwed everything up. He had to find a way to pull this fiasco out of the toilet. Now. Get himself together. Now. Lacey's life depended on him.

"I think I'm okay, thanks." Danika paused. "It's all turned out though."

Adrenaline shot through Steve's system. "How do you mean?"

"Lacey's been photographed with the knife in her hand. Her prints are on it – the only prints the police will find on it, unless someone else at the bar was stupid enough to pick it up. When the cops eventually find Lacey's body, no one will look beyond her for a culprit to Leo's murder, and we'll be off on our next project. Crisis averted."

Steve ignored the gentle kiss that Danika lay on top of his collar and turned the binoculars to take in the length of the street. "But Pavle doesn't have her yet. He can't kill her if he can't find her."

"Hey." Danika's voice turned defensive. "Pavle said that with all those cell phones filming, they couldn't act. Come on, stop worrying. She'll surface soon, and Pavle will dispose of her."

Steve's body recoiled. He tried to cover his reflex by spinning around and snapping, "What if they don't find her?" Steve wanted Danika to interpret his odd behavior as worry about their con. He thought he might just be pulling it off.

15

Danika tipped her head back so they were eye to eye. "When they get to her, she'll be eliminated; it'll be fine. They can't let her body be found until after next Saturday anyway. Can they? And when the guys do dump her body," she continued, "no one will be able to connect the dots on any of this — not the murder or the cons. It's brilliant."

Steve's lips twitched as he held back the words that would make everything implode. *Get your head on straight. Stay in the game.* He could hear his college football coach's voice yelling at him.

When Steve failed to answer, Danika's mouth tightened into a rigid line, and she ducked her chin as if she were preparing to take a direct punch. "Tell me the truth. Did you develop a thing for that girl?"

Watching Danika's moment of vulnerability, Steve felt himself switch gears. His anxiety settled into his intestines, packed in tightly, uncomfortably, but no longer preventing clear thought. He blew a puff of derision through his nostrils. "Lacey is a job, not an emotion." His voice was impassive. "Screwing her is like changing a light bulb—a chore that needs doing so bigger things can happen."

Danika shifted to study Steve's face. He knew she was looking for any sign that he might be lying, that he had developed a soft spot, that she had reason to be worried about his loyalties. Steve ignored her. He fixed his gaze over her

16

shoulder on the TV where Lacey's DMV picture filled the screen.

"Breaking news, the young woman being sought for questioning by city police investigators has been identified as Lacey Elizabeth Stuart, acquisitions coordinator and acting manager for the Bartholomew Winslow Gallery in Washington, DC. If anyone has any information about this case, or the whereabouts of Ms. Stuart, please contact the authorities immediately."

He moved back to his look-out post. Watching Lacey's building entrance through the lenses, Steve muttered a prayer under his breath that she'd find her way to some good guys before the bad guys got her in their sights.

Chapter Three

Thursday Night

Lacey knelt in front of the TV in her co-worker's otherwise darkened bungalow. She clasped her hands tightly as if beseeching the blonde newscaster to say, "The police want to make sure that Miss Stuart is safe and to tell her what happened tonight." God, she wished she knew what had happened tonight – some kind of explanation.

Instead of offering her support, the news crew left her dangling out there, exposed to the public, looking like she was culpable of some great wrong. But she hadn't done anything wrong. Steve stood her up. Then a man got stabbed. But surely she had nothing to do with either. The man, Leo Bardman, had called her Danika. . .Mistook her for someone else.

Tears filled Lacey's eyes as she listened to the talking-heads, speculating about her responsibility for stabbing

19

Bardman, then running from both the FBI *and* the Secret Service. Shame wrapped around her shoulders and wicked the heat from her body. Whatever happened next, her reputation was destroyed. But that seemed the least of her problems.

With sudden awareness, Lacey scrambled on her hands and knees toward the windows. Keeping her head down below the sill, she drew the drapery shut. Lacey didn't want the blue light of the TV to attract the attention of any of Martha's neighbors. Lacey imagined that Martha had told her neighbors that she'd be gone for a long weekend and asked them to please keep an eye on her place. Martha had gone to visit her mother who was in the hospital, and Lacey had offered to step in and feed Martha's cat, Twinkle Toes. Any kindness Lacey had extended by way of cat-care was now being repaid in that Lacey felt like she had a safe place to gather her thoughts.

Lacey thanked her lucky stars that Martha had decided to leave town on Thursday after work rather than Friday afternoon. That gave Lacey this private place to hide. Her other piece of luck was that Martha's door used a key pad instead of actual keys. Lacey had dropped everything from her hands as she ran from the bar. She had arrived in Martha's living room freezing cold with only the clothes on her back, and bloody feet. *And* the flash drive, Lacey reminded herself. She reached up to her blouse to feel the bulge beneath her breast. What could possibly be on that flash drive? It was obviously something big – something that was life or death.

With her jaw set, Lacey reached toward the coffee table where Martha's work computer had been left recharging. She lifted the lid, and typed in the management password. As she waited for the computer to come to life, Lacey pulled the flash drive from her bra, stuck it into the port, and squeezed her eyes shut. Decision time. By looking at this, whatever *this* was, she'd have a new level of responsibility and knowledge. She was afraid to know what was there, and she was afraid not to know. Would it put her in even greater danger than she was in now? Why was she in danger?

"They know who you are. Trust no one. Run."

Lacey's fingers shook too hard to press the right keys. "Run." She would do just that if only she had the right direction to head.

Her mind jumped back to the bar, and she could smell the man's breath as he leaned down – a yeasty combination of beer and sausage. The scariest part of what the dead man said to her was "Danika." That was the second time someone had mistaken her for this Danika person, whoever she was.

Kneeling before the screen like an acolyte before a prayer candle, the first file that Lacey opened was a series of photographs of oil paintings, beautiful works by some of the best artists in the United States. There was "Magnificent

Dawn" by Chambray, a piece that she had dearly hoped to acquire for her uncle's new exhibit at the end of this month. Next week, actually. But that had fallen through. Understandably. With rumors whipping through the industry that her Uncle Bartholomew was on the run because of art theft, who would chance being in a show at the Bartholomew Winslow Gallery?

Photos of art and the tight grip of the FBI around her ankle, that was an interesting juxtaposition. If the FBI was after her because of art, then this probably had something to do with her Uncle Bartholomew's wrongdoings. Maybe even something he framed her for. Again. Even though Leo Bardman had called her Danika, she thought it was too much of a coincidence that she was associated with the paintings on this flash drive, albeit it was a distant kind of association.

Lacey sat back on her heels, utterly confused. Why would that guy with the FBI be watching her at a bar, or grabbing at her, for that matter? She'd been compliant and forthcoming when they investigated her uncle. If the FBI was trying to find her Uncle Bartholomew, Lacey had already given them all of his addresses and phone numbers. Her name had been completely cleared of any offenses. Deep had made sure of that.

Deep Del Toro's handsome face formed in Lacey's mind. A special operative with Iniquus, Deep had shown up at her gallery when his security company was trying to recover their stolen corporate art collection. Lacey's thoughts snagged on their first meeting. He and his colleague Jane were there, undercover. Jane and Deep had walked through the door, where Lacey was waiting for the interview they had scheduled with her, and as soon as she saw Deep, Lacey's insides dropped like she was on a carnival ride.

There was something magnetic and wonderful about Deep. And it went way beyond his laughing brown eyes and his warrior's body. Something about him made Lacey feel like, as long as she was touching him, she was home. A belonging. He had shaken her world with that meeting. Lacey wished Deep was there with her. He would know exactly what to do. Lacey bit at her lips. Should she call him?

"Trust no one." That phrase cycled through her head. That was just an impossible directive. She'd have to trust someone. Maybe Steve?

Having experienced that draw and sense of connection with Deep, Lacey saw her relationship with Steve in a different light. Up until she had met Deep, Lacey thought that, even though she and Steve had only been going out for a short time, Steve was probably *the one*. He had acted like that was their destiny, talked about it all the time, and Lacey had gone along for the ride.

After she had met Deep, Lacey's feelings for Steve seemed farcical and staged. She had been trying to break things off for months, but the timing always seemed to be wrong. Roadblocks kept popping up. These past few months, dating Steve was like a child playacting at recess. "You be the daddy, and I'll be the mommy . . ." until the bell rang, and the game was over.

Lacey picked up a pen and let it rat-a-tat-tat on the coffee table as she tried to process her situation. Her brain wasn't functioning properly, and she knew it. Images of the night melted and sagged like objects on a Salvador Dali canvas. She grasped at anything that had the semblance of solidity. She needed facts. Facts like the name Leo Bardman. The news people had said the guy stabbed in the bar was named Leo Bardman, and that he was indeed dead.

Lacey reached far back into the closets of her memory and searched around. No. She would probably have remembered that name, because it sounded like it belonged to a Shakespeare-like figure, a poet – and the man who had approached her had seemed antithetical to poetry. Well, the nice kind of poetry – the poetry of Keats or Whitman. Maybe he could have been a Don John in *Much Ado about Nothing*, but that was really beside the point. The point here was—well, she had actually reached two points of conclusion—Lacey had never heard Leo Bardman's name before, and she had no desire at all to reach out to Steve.

Truth be told, thinking about Steve only piqued her sense of resentment. She blamed him, on some level, for being in this situation right now. It was, after all, Steve's idea to meet in the bar before going out for dinner. And it was he who failed to show up. She couldn't imagine ever wanting to speak to Steve again. At that moment, the only person Lacey wanted to talk to was Deep Del Toro.

Lacey typed in her password for Carbonite, which allowed her to pull up files from her personal computer. She searched her downloads for the business card she had scanned in on the day Deep and Jane had stopped by the gallery to gather evidence against her.

There was a lot of evidence to gather too. She was indeed culpable. Her Uncle Bartholomew had her acquire art for a retrospective. It was some grand scheme on her uncle's part to get Iniquus' artwork out of their headquarters and into a storage unit. Why? She had no clue. Absolutely no clue. It made no sense to her at all. Even the FBI had scratched their heads. Iniquus knew. They'd said it was an industry secret that they'd never reveal. Case closed.

Lacey could understand Iniquus's wanting to keep this quiet. Iniquus was a privately-owned company who did specialty contracts for both the US government and private citizens. What exactly that entailed, she hadn't dived in deep enough to ask, but everyone at their headquarters seemed to have come from a military background, and she knew it had something to do with security. That was probably why everything was kept so hush hush. The idea that someone (she) had gone in and removed their corporate art from under their noses wouldn't be great for their reputation.

Lacey sucked in a lung full of oxygen then tried to let it out as smoothly as she could to slow her racing thoughts. She pictured Deep winking encouragement her way as things had gotten tense at Iniquus Headquarters where Deep had stood beside her, literally and figuratively while the case unraveled itself. He made sure that she bore no responsibility and was not held accountable for her role in the fraud that lead to the Iniquus corporate art being removed — *stolen*.

Could she trust Deep? She flung herself backward and stared at the ceiling. Was he the one person she could trust when she was told to trust no one?

In that whole Iniquus fiasco, she had been innocent, Lacey reminded herself, and had been following through blindly on her uncle's orders. Hmm, it seemed that Lacey had been going along blindly for a while now, both in her business life and personal life. It was time she opened her eyes. Was she equally blind about something else going on? Why did Leo Bardman think she was Danika?

I'm all questions, no answers.

A car's engine sounded outside. Heat flowered across Lacey's chest as her fingers and feet went numb. A sharp prickle across her scalp made her pull her body in tightly, trying to make herself small. Listening. *No, the car didn't stop. It drove on past.* Slowly, she uncurled herself and pulled the computer down to the floor next to her. She minimized the picture of Deep's business card. Then she scrolled back through the paintings in the first file on the thumb drive. She shouldn't be afraid of the authorities. She hadn't done anything wrong, Lacey reminded herself. Well, not really. Yes, maybe. But . . .

The dead man had called her Danika.

Unable to make her brain form coherent thoughts, unable to get her legs to hold her body weight, Lacey crawled to the bathroom and turned on the hot water. A bathtub had always been her refuge and thinking spot. And that's what she needed more than anything in that moment - peace and clarity so she could take the right actions. She peeled off her filthy clothes and winced as her feet—bruised and cut from her four-mile, barefooted hike from the Metro to Martha's place—dipped beneath the water.

Lacey lay her head against the lip of the tub and let the pictures flutter through her brain. If only Steve had been there on time, they would have eaten dinner and gone home to hear the news of the murder on TV, and it would have been unremarkable. If Steve had been there, he would have protected her from the scotch-on-the-rocks guy's stares – not a guy on the make, an FBI agent. Questions surfaced and floated in front of her. Leo Bardman had been killed warning her to trust no one. How could she find her way out of this maze if she trusted no one? She was on the run – but why?

Chapter Four

Friday Morning

Lacey pulled Martha's home phone toward her and lay back. The wooden floor pressed against her shoulder blades. It was cold, and it hurt. She liked that. The ache stopped the hysterical giggles from exploding from her chest.

Jittery from her night of high-adrenaline pacing, Lacey was exhausted. Dawn hadn't even scratched at the horizon, but Lacey was ready to go on the offensive. What she needed was to get to the high ground where she could look down at the problem instead of groveling in the ditches – or in a jail cell. And the only way to do it was to show the world that she was just someone standing in the wrong place at the very wrong time.

Lacey's teeth scraped over her lower lip as she plugged the numbers from Deep's business card into Martha's house phone and waited through two rings.

29

"Joseph Del Toro's line. How may I assist you?"

Surprised that a woman had answered, Lacey stalled. "I, um. Good morning, is Deep, I mean Joseph, available to the phone?"

"This is Mr. Del Toro's answering service. May I have your name and message, please?"

Lacey's free hand clutched protectively over her throat. If she gave this woman her name, the woman might contact the police, and Lacey would be on the defensive. That wasn't her strategy.

"Thank you kindly, but no." Lacey gently set the hand piece back in the cradle. Okay. Plan B. The only other person she was willing to call right then was her lawyer. She wrinkled her nose at the thought. Four o'clock in the morning seemed too early to call someone's house—funny how that never crossed her mind as she was reaching out to Deep—but Lacey needed to get going. As each second ticked by, she felt more vulnerable. There weren't many people who knew that Lacey was taking care of Martha's cat, but a few did — Steve and some of her colleagues. Someone might make a call and give this address as Lacey's possible hideout.

She had no way to leave. Lacey had no transportation, no ID, nor money – not even shoes. And she'd look darned conspicuous walking in daylight in her date-night outfit spattered in dried blood. Martha's clothes and shoes were much too big for her.

Lacey dialed her lawyer's number by rote. She had dialed it often enough during the Iniquus art debacle. Unlike Deep, Mr. Reynolds answered on the first ring.

"Hello?" Mr. Reynolds sounded wide awake. There was an effervescence about his voice – something excited and anticipatory that made Lacey's lips seal tightly.

"Lacey? Is that you?"

"Yes, Mr. Reynolds, this is Lacey Stuart."

"I thought I might be expecting your call. I saw you on the news. Are you alright? Were you injured?"

Lacey looked down at her cut feet, and the bruise that encircled her ankle from the FBI agent's grip, but she knew that's not what her lawyer meant. "I'm a little worse for wear, but I wasn't stabbed."

"I called your home phone and cell, but you didn't answer."

Lacey took in a long, faltering breath. "No, I didn't feel safe going home."

"Are you in a safe place now?" Mr. Reynolds asked.

"Yes, though I don't believe I'll be safe here much longer." Lacey lay back on the floor. With her eyes squeezed tightly closed, she pitched into her tale of fear and escape. She was glad Mr. Reynolds just let her ramble without asking too many questions. Her whole grasp on what had happened, what was happening, was tenuous. It all felt very dream-like. Nightmarish. Lacey finished up her story but held back two pieces of information – what Leo Bardman said to her, and that he had given her a flash drive. Why she didn't share that, she didn't know. But something in her brain felt hyper-protective of that information. And since it wasn't really tied to her, Lacey, and was instead tied to some woman named Danika, it really shouldn't matter. Should it?

"The sooner we get your story out in front of the public, the better this is going to be for you," Mr. Reynolds said. "Cases are tried in the court of public opinion, and we know you did nothing wrong. We have to let everyone else know you did nothing wrong, before your reputation is further compromised."

"Yes, thank you. Yes." Lacey's voice was barely a whisper. "People should know that I was a bystander at an unfortunate event, and I was very scared and upset and that's why I acted the way I did."

"I'm going to call the media, and we'll do a press conference," he said.

Lacey's hand was shaking so hard that she had to hold the receiver away from her ear, making Mr. Reynold's voice sound distant and tinny.

"I'll tell the police," he continued, "that after we talk to the press, we'll head down to their precinct so you can answer questions. I'll contact the FBI and let them know we'll be available for their questions, too." Reynolds pushed on. "We'll stage the press conference right out in front of the gallery."

Lacey's voice warbled. "The gallery? I don't think that's a very good idea. I don't want this to hurt the gallery's reputation."

"Imagine it, Lacey, you're standing at a podium on the portico surrounded by those beautiful marble columns. People will see you for who you are — an upstanding citizen from an excellent family, who spends her days dealing with artists and the caliber of people who can afford to collect art. Someone who is beautiful, well-educated, and well-spoken. On the news last night, you seemed—" He stopped to clear his throat. "Well, in the videos, it shows a woman who looked like a wrecking ball. We need to reframe perceptions so people understand that you were afraid for your life and fighting strangers who seemed to have malevolent intentions. You had no idea that when the special agent was reaching in his jacket, it was to pull out his badge. Like you told me, you thought he was pulling a weapon in order to shoot you."

"I see what you're saying. You're probably right." Lacey faltered. "I'll have to go by my house and get some clothes. What I have with me is covered in blood."

"We want to be the ones who come forward. If you go home, there's probably an officer staking out your place. They'll take you in for questioning, and we'll be behind the curve – reactive isn't the way to play this game."

"What should I do, then?"

"I think you and my daughter are about the same size. I can bring you something from her closet."

"Okay, yes, I, um, I haven't any shoes. I lost them when I was running away. I wear a size five."

"If my daughter's not the same size, I'll find some, somehow. I have your number on my caller ID—I'll call you back as soon as I have a time set up, and then I'll come over with the clothes. It'll be soon. So if you could, you need to work on fixing your hair and makeup. I want this on the air while people are getting dressed and watching – not buried somewhere during the day when people are at work. We want the most exposure we can possibly get."

There it was, the glee that she had heard at the beginning of the phone call. "Thank you," she said after a moment of hesitation. Blood had raced to Lacey's face when Mr. Reynolds mentioned caller ID. She hadn't considered that, and was under the assumption that if the call hadn't gone well, she'd still have her location concealed. But people could Google a phone number to find the accompanying address. It didn't take a PI. Well, Mr. Reynolds was her lawyer, and that meant any information was privileged, right?

Chapter Five

Steve

Friday Morning

"**W**hat in the hell is going on?" Steve Finely demanded, slamming the door to Monroe's office in the imposing white stone building on Fourth Street that housed the Washington DC FBI headquarters. It was only zero-six-hundred but already the halls were bustling.

Monroe leaned back in his chair and considered him. "Too much caffeine? Didn't get laid? What's crawled up your ass this morning, Finley?"

Steve glared at Monroe, his nostrils distending as he breathed in deeply, trying to keep his fist from smashing into the guy's unperturbed face. Steve had spent a shit night with Danika, making her believe all his lies about their relationship so his team could stay in the game. And he was terrified for Lacey. Steve was sure that Pavle's assassin hadn't rested last night as he tried to find Lacey and finish his job.

Monroe leaned forward and pressed a button on his phone. "Martin, can you find Higgins and get him in here?"

It didn't take long for the door to snick open. Higgins shuffled into the office. He acknowledged Monroe with a nod and turned tired eyes toward Steve. The bruises on Higgins face showed just how serious Lacey had been about wrenching herself from his grasp.

"Catch Finley up," Monroe ordered. He leaned back into his seat, making the springs screech, ramping up the migraine that lit Steve's head on fire.

Higgins crossed his arms and pressed a shoulder into the industrial grey wall. "She got away from me at the bar."

"Yeah, I got your text. She's not in protective custody, then?" Steve's bottom jaw jutted out, and he stared down at the toes of his boots. They had played a little loose with the pawns in this last game of good guy versus bad. But sacrificing Lacey—a civilian—was not in his DNA, no matter how many bad guys they'd be able to bring down. "I thought maybe you all had caught up to her. *Hoped.* I hoped you had caught up with her." His gaze came up, angry and determined. "Pavle told Danika that Lacey slipped by his guys, too, but that doesn't mean anything. He's a lying piece of shit."

"Near as we can tell, she's in the wind, man," Higgins said. "We're looking, but the trackers were in her shoe, her phone, and her purse. When she ran, she left all three behind. She hasn't gone anywhere in her normal circuit."

Steve's phone vibrated; he snatched it from his pocket and stared down at the screen. When Steve slid it back into his pants, Higgins pointed. "She hasn't contacted you?"

"No. And that's not like her. I had her on my hook pretty good." After a pause, he muttered, "Or so I thought." That wasn't true, and he knew it. It was really Steve who was on Lacey's hook. He loved her. Couldn't imagine his life without her. He had even decided to give up his job in undercover if that was what it would take to be with her. And he was pretty sure that that was what it was going to take - especially once she found out that the bureau had been using her without her consent or knowledge.

Higgins shook his head. "Pavle's assassin is a brazen SOB, stabbing Bardman in front of all those people. And not a single witness is pointing a finger at anyone but Lacey."

"Hmph," Monroe grunted, scratching at his chin.

Steve let his gaze settle on Monroe. "The sting went too far."

"We were protecting her," Monroe said.

"The hell we were. We were never protecting her. We were using her. If we were protecting her, she'd have been put into our witness program months ago. If we were protecting her, we wouldn't have been casting a bigger net. We would have taken down Danika and her friends and been glad that at least some of the scum was off the streets."

"This was our opportunity. These bastards support fucking terror. Because of the Zorics, people are suffering. Dying. Children are in terrible trouble. We had to take the chance."

"The chance is that she'll be killed." Steve realized he was yelling, and worked to rein himself in. "No. Not a chance. A *certainty,* unless we can get to her first."

Monroe squeezed his lids into mere slits. "It was a calculated risk, and we had you on her heels the whole time. If you'd done a better job of getting her to fall for you, you would have been her first phone call asking for help."

"Hell, no." Steve stabbed a finger at Monroe. "You aren't laying this at my feet. I did my job. I followed the directives." He had been ordered to become Lacey's love interest, and he did whatever it took to be just that. Things had gone along fine until last November when she found out her uncle had duped her into stealing Iniquus' art. Something about that episode had instantly changed their relationship. Steve had taken the issue to Monroe, and Monroe had ordered Steve to find a way to stay in the game. So Steve had lied. He told Lacey the doctors found something wrong with his heart, and he needed to undergo testing. Lacey had stayed – he knew she would. She was too kind of a person to break up with a guy whose heart was already broken. But she also refused to have sex with him, telling him she was afraid of his heart condition. He couldn't take that for very long.

He knew, at that point, how much his undercover role had become a reality. He had come to love her, deeply. To get back in her bed, Steve invented a clean bill of health from his doctor, but that good news was followed on the same day with tragedy as he found out his five-year-old nephew had leukemia. Yeah, he was that much of an asshole. He made up a fake nephew and gave him fake cancer just so he could sleep with the girl. That wasn't the only reason, he tried to remind himself. He did what he had to to keep the sting going, save lives, fight the money stream to terror organizations.

Still, things had been different between them. Steve knew for months now that Lacey had left their relationship emotionally but was too bighearted to drop him while he was in crisis

"You didn't follow directives last night." Monroe countered. "You were ordered to be at that bar moving Lacey into protective custody, not leaving her protection to Higgins."

"I called Higgins in because Danika made it impossible for me to take off without raising suspicions." Steve leaned his back against the cool wall, muttering, "Goddam Danika for taking so long at the warehouse." Steve wrapped his hand around the back of his neck. "You know, now that Bardman's dead, I'm thinking Danika wasn't at all surprised by the news,"

Steve said. "Maybe she was ordered to keep me away from the scene so I wouldn't get involved in the murder. Maybe she knew what was going down on Pavle's end and was trying to protect me." He focused on Higgins. "Tell me what happened last night."

"You know, man, it was confusing. At first, I couldn't tell if it was Danika or Lacey sitting there on the stool. I thought maybe communications got the message mixed up, and I was supposed to be trailing Danika. I was trying to catch a look at the girl's lips." Higgins pinched his lower lip and pulled it out. "Before I could decide who I was dealing with, the girl dropped her head, and Bardman comes through the door. He stared at the girl as if *he* was confused, too. When he went up to her, he whispered something in her ear. I didn't hear it, but it made sense to Lacey, because she reacted like she'd been punched in the stomach. Then I see him grabbing her, and I jumped up to get in between them. But the two of them went over onto the floor and the crowd pushed forward. I muscled my way through, reached out to pull her up, and Bardman's holding on to her, whispering in her ear. Then it looked like he shoved something down her blouse."

"You didn't see what it was?" Monroe asked.

Higgins shook his head.

"So where were you the rest of the night?" Steve lifted his chin toward Higgins. "Holding ice on your nut sack?"

"I've been out trying to run Lacey down. Unlike you, I was out in the cold, turning over rocks. Meanwhile you were cozied up in a nice warm bed, screwing Danika. So don't shoot shit at me."

Steve's fists clenched. In his mind, he became defensive. He needed to sleep with Danika to reassure her and keep his foot in the door. He needed to be in the loop in case any news came up about Lacey.

Monroe made a brushing motion with his hand as if to dismiss their bickering as so much garbage that needed clearing from the table. "Quiet. Let me think. Bardman grabs Lacey, whom he might have confused as Danika, and whispers something to her, then, as his last dying act, he shoves something in her blouse?"

Monroe stared at the ceiling; silence engulfed the office.

"Maybe," Higgins said, finally. "That last part I can't say for sure."

"How much interface did Bardman have with Danika?"

"Plenty," Steve said. "When Danika met Bardman there was chemistry. She insisted that Bardman take over as her shadow, so Pavle assigned him as Danika's partner the whole arts con."

"You think they had a something going on between them?" Higgins asked.

"I'm sure I'm not the only one Danika screws. She thinks that having sex with me keeps me on a leash. She's that kind of narcissistic. Of course, she sleeps with anyone who can get her what she wants. Though, Bardman seemed to believe she genuinely cared for him." Steve pressed his thumbs into his temples to stop the thrumming that interrupted his thoughts. "Did they have a side job they were working together? Something besides a romantic relationship? Something that would raise Pavle's hackles? Nah. His organization's too savvy. They wouldn't let Bardman and Danika get away with . . .oh, hell."

"Yup. Let's play that one out." Monroe said. "Say he and Danika step over some boundary, and Bardman gets his hands dirty. He ends up dead." Monroe pointed back and forth between the two men. "I want to know what Bardman said to Lacey and what the heck he handed her."

"If he handed her anything at all," Higgins said.

Monroe ignored the comment. "And get someone to pick Danika up immediately. We don't want another body to process."

Steve grimaced.

"Shit. We were days away from shutting this case." Monroe stretched his hands to the ceiling with a groan, laced his fingers, and posted his hands behind his head. "We need a plan. Come on Finley, what would Lacey do next? Where could she possibly have gone?"

Chapter Six

DEEP

Friday Morning

Deep Del Toro spun his steering wheel next to a parking spot well away from the hubbub up the street and backed his Land Rover Defender behind a bare-branched oak. He took a moment to assess the scene. News vans dotted the street, waiting for Lacey's press conference, where they'd get the scoop on last night's murder. Reporters in their long coats and winter hats shivered through their sound checks, then squared their shoulders and smiled brightly as they taped stay-tuned teasers from the sidewalk, with a back drop of stone buildings.

After his answering service passed him a non-message from Martha's phone at zero-four-hundred, Deep had decided to run a quick safety check on Lacey on his way to the airport. It had to have been Lacey calling for help from her colleague's phone. It's the only thing that made sense. In her crisis, she had reached out to him. And that gave him hope.

47

When Lacey had turned down his invitation to dinner the day they met, walking away from Lacey Stuart had been one of the hardest things he'd ever done. Bar none. But she had said she was dating Steve. And all Deep could do was leave the door open and hope that she'd walk through. Maybe today was that day.

Before he could get over to the address pulled up by his service operator, the radio announced that Lacey Stuart and her lawyer would be holding a press conference at the gallery. Listening to the announcement, Deep's gut contracted. Lacey was making a big mistake exposing herself in public. He had watched the videos of her at the bar on the news and those posted to YouTube and social media sites last night – and what he saw looked professionally orchestrated. Somehow, Lacey had thwarted someone's plan. Professionals didn't like to be thwarted, and they definitely didn't like it when witnesses answered questions. Especially on podiums in the public eye.

Deep wasn't sure what Lacey's lawyer was thinking by allowing her to have a press conference, in such a public setting. Then again, yeah, he did. Lacey's lawyer wanted all that free publicity he was going to get. Reynolds would want the televised images to fit a specific picture painted of himself. One that mirrored what Reynolds had seen put on by high-dollar lawyers-to-the-stars.

Last November, when Lacey had showed up at Iniquus to shake hands all around and to personally apologize for the role she'd played in the art fiasco, Deep had taken a disliking to Reynolds. Deep had made sure he was by Lacey's side the whole time, keeping an eye out for her. That same protective instinct he felt then had motivated him to come into the city this morning. So what if he missed his flight to Costa Rica for an overdue vacation? He could see that Lacey made it safely to the police station, make sure a few of his buddies over there kept eyes and ears on her, and then take a later flight. After all, the cross-country four-wheeling expedition wasn't headed out until the next morning. He could catch a different flight later in the day, or, if push came to shove, he'd catch up to his friends on the trail. No problem.

Deep opened his rear hatch and reached in his jump bag for the black skull cap that he pulled low over his brows. He yanked a hoodie over his head and zipped it up, then tugged the ties enough so it concealed the sides of his face. He added a winter coat that hid his build. He'd rather not be recognizable — even to Lacey.

Sauntering up the street, in his blue jeans and work boots, Deep blended in with the news crew techs. There was a lot of grumbling going on as they set up their lighting systems. Even though it was coming up on zero-seven-hundred, the sky was dark and heavy. Ice crystals scented the air with a coming storm. The temperature must have dropped thirty degrees in the last hour.

Deep didn't have to think long about why Reynolds had chosen this time of day for the press conference. Reynolds wanted to hit the prime news time. He'd want to get his voice on the radios and television sets before people had focused on something else in their day. Deep stepped over a sluch puddle from last night's rain. His gaze slid along the roof lines. What Reynolds obviously wasn't considering was the tactical disadvantage all this had on Lacey's safety.

Deep took advantage of the buzz and turf selection going on by the TV crews to gauge the area. He tried to figure where he'd initiate his shot if it was his job to take down a combatant. The columns that curved along the portico and the overhanging roof of the gallery offered her some protection. But certainly not enough.

Deep wished he'd had a better heads-up so he could have been first-on-scene and done a thermal search of the area. But he guessed his surprise at the choices Reynolds was making would have been the same for any would-be bad guys – someone trying to harm Lacey would be scrambling to get into place the same as he was. Chances were that the bad guys wouldn't even try. They might let this opportunity pass on by rather than stick their necks out so publicly. That was his hope, anyway.

Deep edged forward through the crowd, his brain moving with the precision trained into him as a Marine Raider. His eyes swept from cover to cover as he planned possible escape routes, choke points, and blind spots. He scrutinized the people's faces to see who belonged to which group and if anyone stood out as being alone, like he was. It was hard to interpret nervousness or hidden weapons on days like today when people hunkered down and shivered with their hands thrust deeply into their pockets. It put him at an uncomfortable disadvantage.

At the top of the hour, Lacey and Reynolds emerged from the building. Reynolds looked like he was playing his role to perfection with his long, black wool coat and carefully tucked silk scarf. His arm reached in a fatherly way around Lacey's back as he steered her toward the podium.

Lacey wore a suit that bagged over her petite, athletic body. The overly-bright colored winter coat looked like she'd pulled it from someone else's closet. Which might very well be the case, Deep reminded himself. Lacey probably hadn't gone home since the murder took place. She seemed so small and pale standing there. She lifted her chin and let her gaze travel around the crowd, looking people in the eyes with the conviction of an innocent woman. Though, she still had a vulnerability about her that tugged at his heart.

51

By the time Reynolds stepped up to the podium, Deep had maneuvered his way to the front of the crowd, just to the side, where he had a good view of the platform. Deep rounded past a sound engineer holding a long-handled microphone boom.

"Ladies and gentlemen, thank you for coming out on such an inclement morning." Reynolds stopped speaking to allow the news crews jostling to come to a standstill and for quiet to descend.

Lacey offered up a plastic smile, her teeth chattering. Nerves or cold? Deep tried to decide. That's when he spotted the red dot of a laser scope dancing near her hairline. Even before his conscious brain was able to recognize and interpret the meaning, Deep pushed into the balls of his feet, launching himself towards her. On muscular legs, he propelled forward as the dot slid down toward the center of the T-zone where a bullet would instantly kill Lacey.

As the point of light settled between her eyebrows, Deep's feet left the ground. He wrapped his arms around Lacey's waist, forcing her backwards with the full weight and power of his go-mode.

Before they hit the ground, Deep rolled with Lacey in his arms so that it was his body that crashed onto the stone flooring.

There was a collective intake of breath before a woman's scream cracked the air as if it were glass. The sound glistened the area with shards that ballooned out into the frozen morning, suspending time, then tinkled to the ground. Shouts and chaos followed.

Deep never stopped his forward momentum. As soon as his back touched down, he kept turning until he was on his knees with Lacey between his legs, his body shielding hers. He looked down to see her face — gray and fixed with her mouth agape. Her brows lifted toward her scalp and her lids peeled back, showing the whites of her sclera all the way around her dark brown irises. He instantly recognized that her brain had shut down. She was frozen with fear.

From behind the column, Deep leapt to his feet, reached down and grabbed Lacey's wrist. Then he reached his other hand between her thighs, and hoisted her over his shoulder in a rescue carry. His eyes caught on Reynolds hunkered behind the podium with his hands wrapped protectively over his head. The news people climbed over each other trying to get out of the confined area, dumping their equipment in their haste. A man squatted over a woman lying on the ground, blood spurting from her wound.

Deep plastered himself against the building where the shot had originated. He sucked in a lung full of air and ran full out down the sidewalk to his car, where he dumped Lacey onto the passenger seat.

He was extending the seat belt to strap her in when her foot shot out and caught him in the diaphragm. Deep's lungs deflated, forcing him to take a knee while his body fought to get his respiratory system back in rhythm. He pushed back away from Lacey's second kick, then yanked back his hoodie and pulled off the cap to reveal his face to her. It took a second. Suddenly, she pushed out of the car, wrapping her arms tightly around him.

"Oh my God, Deep. What have I done? I'm so, so sorry."

Deep tried to use his arms to create a pocket of air around him while his chest spasmed from her kick. He couldn't manage speaking yet. Instead, he folded her arms across her chest and pushed her into the car. He made his way slowly around to the driver's side with a fist countering the jumps of his diaphragm. With or without oxygen, this was a dangerous spot, and Deep had to get Lacey to safety.

Chapter Seven

Friday

Lacey's fingers knotted tightly in her lap. She had squeezed them bloodless. "I'm so sorry I kicked you, I didn't know who you were."

Deep had the car in drive and was steering with one hand, his other hand working the gear shift. With an intense focus, Deep searched his mirrors, taking sudden turns and switching lanes. Lacey had never seen Deep like this – it was intimidating, and she felt very small as she curled into the seat beside him.

Finally, Deep closed his mouth, and Lacey thought he might be breathing normally again.

"Can you speak yet?" she whispered.

"I'm good. Are you doing okay?" He sent her a brief but thorough once over.

The blood that had filled her brain with pressure as she had dangled from Deep's shoulders was finally flowing back down into her body, and Lacey was left feeling dizzy and disoriented. "Why did you tackle me and carry me like that?"

Deep glanced at her then changed lanes to drive between two semis effectively hiding them from view as they sped along the highway. "You didn't hear the gunfire?"

Lacey's face drained of color, and she felt the interior of the car whirling around her. "Gunfire?"

Deep reached a hand over behind her neck and pushed her head down between her knees. "At this rate, one of us is going to pass out before we get somewhere safe. Hang on."

Lacey fought off a swoosh of nausea as grey clouds filled her head and distorted her vision. She put her hands on the floor board and wished that Deep would stop driving like a maniac. She just wanted to be still for a minute and figure out what was going on. As her head cleared she pulled herself back up to sitting.

Deep lifted his hips and tugged his phone from the pocket of his jeans. Lacey had heard it vibrating since he had thrust his keys into the ignition. Whoever was on the other end of the line was darned persistent. Deep jetted his car off the ramp and onto a different highway. He tapped the screen for speaker phone, then said, "Deep here."

"Holy moly! Tell me that wasn't you downtown dodging bullets at that gallery."

"Hey, Lynx."

That was Jane. Lacey recognized Deep's teammates voice immediately. Bullets at the gallery — "Oh my God, that really happened?" she asked. It wasn't that she had disbelieved him – it's just that it was so farfetched.

"Deep, it *was* you down there," Jane's voice came over the speakers, "I knew it. You're all over the news. You were the last thing the cameras caught before all hell broke loose, and the crews ran for their lives. Was that Lacey I heard in the car with you?"

"Yup. I thought, you know, she turned me down for dinner last time I asked, so this time I went for the Neanderthal approach." Deep sent Lacey a devilish wink.

Was he really flirting with her after such a near miss?

"Cute. Were either of you hurt?" Jane's voice was colored with worry.

Deep raised an eyebrow at Lacey, and she scanned her body. She wasn't sure if she was hurt or not. She felt sore and nauseated and a little bit like she wasn't fully pieced together. And she had lost her shoes—again. She offered Deep a tight-lipped smile.

"Lacey's fine. I might have some internal bleeding." Deep rubbed a hand over his chest with a grin on his face. All Lacey could do was stare at him with her eyes stretched wide. He seemed perfectly fine, perfectly at ease with the fact that someone had just shot a bullet in his direction. He actually seemed to be having fun.

"Internal bleeding?" Jane chuckled. "If that's all, I won't worry. Okay, so you're not in Costa Rica. Instead, you're saving a damsel in distress. Now that you have her, what are you going to do with her?"

Lacey pressed her hands over her throat.

"Well, funny you should bring that up," Deep said.

"She can't come on Iniquus campus. And Striker's house isn't habitable yet," Jane continued.

"Yeah about that . . ." Deep paused, watching his rearview mirror. Lacey turned to look out the back window. A van was moving up with a little too much conviction, but it didn't follow their car when Deep veered across three lanes and took an off ramp. Lacey spun back around and grabbed at the armrest, sucking in a lungful of air.

"Oh no," Jane suddenly moaned out. "They pronounced her dead. The reporter who took the ricochet, it sliced through her carotid, and she bled out. Shit."

Dead. A reporter from the press conference was dead. Lacey repeated the words in her head, trying to make them make sense. Words were so funny right now. Lacey could hear them. Recognize them. But when they were strung together into thoughts that were being passed back and forth between Jane and Deep, it was like listening to a foreign language. She just couldn't make them mean anything. It made her panicky. It made her vulnerable. *When you can't think, you have no power.* That much she understood. Lacey turned her face to the side window and let tears roll down her cheeks. She could taste them, hot and salty, as they pooled in the crevices beside her lips.

"Please, tell me you're headed for the police station," Jane was saying.

"For some reason I don't think that's the best move. That shot was professional. I'm not sure who's playing on what team, if you know what I mean."

"Gotcha. How about Dave Murphy? I'm sure this case hasn't landed in his lap, but if you wanted to talk to a detective with whom you already have rapport, and who you know is as clean as they come –"

Lacey silently listened to the teammates work through a strategy and thought how oddly heavy she felt. Like her borrowed coat had been made of lead.

"Actually, we're almost thinking along the same thought line."

"So you'll go to Dave?" Jane asked.

"Well maybe not so much Dave as maybe your neighborhood. I was kind of hoping I could use your house while I try to figure out why a sniper was aiming between Lacey's eyes."

"Deep," Jane said, and then paused. "Yeah, I'm not sure about that. If Lacey's got a target on her back, I don't want her anywhere near my neighbors. I don't want any more evil finding their way into my neighborhood."

"No one would be able to trace her there. I swear. We'll use the back entrance, and she'll go dark. I mean, you'll have to give your neighbors a heads up that I'm staying there, possibly for a few days, but you wouldn't have to mention Lacey. She'll be a shadow."

"Are you sure you can manage her?"

"If I can't, then I won't stay there, I promise." Deep flicked on his blinker and turned onto a new road.

Lacey felt his eyes on her, so she turned toward him.

"Lacey and I haven't had a chance to talk yet, so I don't know what she wants or needs. I want to get her somewhere quiet so she can think and make her decisions."

Quiet. Yes, that's what she needed. Just some quiet. Just some space so her brain could function again, and she could come out of this funk.

"There must be a reason you don't want to use one of the Iniquus safe houses," Jane said.

"Well, yeah. If the police or FBI hires Iniquus to find her, I'd have to hand her over. No matter what Lacey wants."

"Deep, if Iniquus gets a contract to find her, I'll have to tell them you picked her up and where you are."

"That's true, but you'd have to know Iniquus had the contract, and with the rest of our team down range, and you in the Puzzle Room by yourself, no one's going to hand you this case. One of the joys of 'need-to-know'. You won't need to know, and people will think I'm on vacation."

"I don't know that that's true. I mean, you were playing superman on TV."

"Lynx, what did you see on the screen? Did they show my face?" This was the first time Lacey had heard anything like concern in Deep's voice.

"No."

"Then how'd you know it was me?"

"I guess I just knew," Jane said. "I mean. Lacey was obviously in trouble from what was on the news last night. I didn't really think you'd be able to stay away from her. And then that 'diving into the fray' bit is kind of your signature move."

Deep pulled to a stop in an alleyway. "So, your house?"

"Okay. You can stay there. But Lacey goes dark. And any signs of interest, you get her out of there."

"Understood," Deep replied.

"Where are you now?"

"I pulled up to your garage. I'll put the code in so I can hide my car."

"I'll let the neighbors know you're staying there. Call me if you need me. Love you. Stay safe."

When Jane said 'Love you,' to Deep, Lacey tucked those words into her pocket to think about later. There were a lot of things from that conversation she had filed away. A lot of questions that she needed to ask once she had gotten her balance back - like why would a professional try to shoot her? And why were there questions about the police being safe?

Deep stuck his phone into his pocket.

"That was Jane." Lacey thought her words were slurring a little, like a drunkard.

"She was only Jane when we were undercover, trying to find the Iniquus art. Her name is Lexi Sobado, she's engaged to my good friend, Striker Rheas." Deep seemed to get that Lacey was struggling. He spoke slowly, clearly. He seemed to be reminding her of some information that she already knew but had forgotten. "Lexi and I work on the same team at Iniquus. She goes by the call name Lynx, like I go by the call name Deep."

"When we met, you said your mom gave you that nickname," Lacey said. "'Still waters run deep' is what you said."

62

"It doesn't matter where you get a call name, only that you have one." Deep popped his door open and went to open the garage.

Lacey watched him move to the keypad and enter a code. Frustration gave way to anger, though she tried to wrestle those feelings down. When Deep got back in the car, Lacey was pinching her nose, considering him. "Did your mom or did your mom not give you the name 'Deep'?"

"She did not. I received that name on assignment, and, no, I won't tell you how or why." He raised his eyebrows for emphasis.

She had to be able to trust this man. But how could she trust him if he didn't tell her the truth about something as simple as his name? "What else have you lied to me about?" Her voice was smooth and low but there was something in there that made her feel like she was challenging him.

"Probably everything out of my mouth when I was undercover on the art case was a lie. And not a single thing, when I'm not on a case, has been or will be a lie. I'm not a liar, Lacey."

She nodded, but she wasn't sure she believed him. "So Jane, I mean Lynx, is going to let me stay here at her house?"

Deep pulled his door shut and rolled silently into the garage. The automatic garage door closed behind them. They sat in the dark with only pinpricks of light to show any illumination. "Lacey, you have some highly skilled people after you. I think you need to keep your head down until you've made some decisions. I'm not going to tell you what to do, but I'll offer you my professional opinion if you want it."

"The person who shot at me—you called him a sniper. Why?" Lacey whispered. She felt calmer here in the dark. Safer.

Lacey heard Deep shifting beside her. "The shot was taken from a rooftop using a high-powered rifle. Not some random guy in the crowd. They had to find their way on to the rooftop, quickly and stealthily, and they used a red dot to hit a specific part of your brain."

"Which part?" Her eyes stretched wide in the darkness.

"The part that makes sure you never get up or speak again."

The seriousness in his voice sent a tremor through Lacey's body. "Lynx said a reporter died. But how?" People went their whole lives with no one dying near them, and now Lacey had gotten two people killed for being near her in less that twelve hours.

"The bullet ricocheted off the building, or maybe a chunk of marble hit her."

A storm cloud of silence filled the car. Deep seemed to wait for Lacey to take the lead.

"Lynx told you I had to go dark if I were to stay here. That's operative speak. What does it mean exactly?" Lacey found herself whispering.

"You have to understand that Lynx's neighbors are family to her. She's worried that by giving you a safe place to stay, your presence would attract the people who are after you. You might put her family at risk. There are lots of little kids who live around here. We absolutely can't let the people who are after you find their way here. So there can be no sign you're around. You can't use the phone. You can't use the Internet. You can't even stand in a window and look out. If you go anywhere, you'll be in disguise, and you'll move out the back door to the garage and away from the area. No contact. Period. If you feel like that's too much, then I'll think of something else. Maybe get you into a motel room in Maryland. Or maybe you'd prefer that I talk to some of my contacts and get you into a protection program until everything is straightened out?"

Deep stopped talking, thank goodness. He had handed her a whole headful of information. It felt like all of the decisions that needed to be made were pushing against the inside of her skull, crowding outward until the seams and cells strained with the pressure. But even in her confusion and feelings of overwhelm, Lacey was grateful that Deep was trying to make sure that what happened to her next was her own decision.

"I'm so tired." Lacey's voice was barely audible. "I haven't slept since Wednesday. I don't think I can hold a rational thought right now. Perhaps I could take a nap, and then I might think clearer."

"Sounds like a plan. First your disguise, then we'll go inside."

Deep got out and flicked on an overhead light before moving around to Lacey's side of the car. He reached in the back seat where he had thrown his coat. As Lacey clambered out to stand beside him, she saw Deep take in her stockinged feet. She curled her toes on the cold cement.

"Let's get you covered up and inside where you'll be warm."

Lacey shrugged out of the chartreuse-colored coat that Reynolds had brought to her that morning. To be frank, it was a hideous color that screamed for attention. Attention was not welcome. Now that she had been seen wearing it on the news, anyone who might spot her as she made her way to the house would instantly recognize her. Lacey replaced the monstrosity with Deep's hat and hoodie. As she zipped up, she blanched and groped the bottom of her left breast, feeling for the flash drive, then quickly pulled the zipper the rest of the way up, hopping from foot to foot. Deep grabbed a pair of rain boots from beside the door, handing them off to Lacey. He found the spare key hanging behind the oil collection pan, and walked her to the house.

"Lynx bought this duplex and renovated it while her husband, Angel, was deployed to Afghanistan. It was supposed to be a surprise for him when he returned home," he said as he stuck the key in the lock and turned the knob. "Unfortunately, his return trip was in a casket, and Angel never saw what a beautiful job she did." Deep pushed the door wide, letting Lacey walk in in front of him. "Are you hungry?" he asked as they moved into the kitchen.

Lacey shook her head.

She moved through the neat-as-a-pin kitchen, and into the dining room. From the architectural detailing, Lacey could tell that Lynx's home had been built at the turn of the century in the shotgun style, the bottom floor lined up — kitchen, dining room, and living room. Deep put his hand on her back, steered Lacey to the stairs, and showed her to the guest bedroom.

The rooms upstairs were lined up just like downstairs, the front guest room, a bathroom, the second guest room, and then the master suite. Deep directed Lacey to the center bedroom. "This one doesn't have any windows, and from a security point of view, is the least likely to draw attention."

Lacey took in the butter yellow room with bright-colored quilt smoothed across the double bed. She stepped forward and ran her hand over its surface, remarking that it had been handstitched.

Deep leaned against the door jamb, but didn't follow her into the room. "Lynx's Kitchen Grandmother, Nana Kate, made that quilt for Lynx when she was recovering from an accident," Deep said. "You want to wait here for a second? I'll grab a pair of Lynx's sweats and socks."

"You don't think she'd mind?"

From the hall, Deep called back toward her, "Lynx spent her own share of time holed up in a safehouse. I'm sure she'd want you comfortable."

Lacey nodded her acknowledgement at her own reflection in the mirror, too tired to call anything back to Deep. She looked like a stranger, disheveled and thoroughly overwhelmed; her shoulders drooped like they bore a tremendous weight.

When he came back, Deep carried towels along with the borrowed clothes. "You'll find toiletries under the sink, so help yourself. Lynx keeps things stocked for guests, so you should be set. Here's a change of clothes. We'll figure out how to get some more things in for you if you decide you want to stay here. Why don't you take a nice long soak? I bet it'll make you feel better."

Lacey reached out her hands to accept his pile as she moved passed him into the hall. Just before she turned to shut the bathroom door, Deep propped himself in the doorframe.

"Oh, and Lacey, while you're in there, you might want to decide whether you trust me enough to tell me what you've got hidden in your bra."

Chapter Eight

Friday Afternoon

Lacey woke slowly, stretching out and letting her eyes blink open. It took her a moment to remember where she was. With no windows in the room to add light, she was depending on the ambient glow from the hallway to create outlines of the chest of drawers and lamp. She glanced over at the digital clock on the side table. It said three o'clock. Lacey hoped that meant in the afternoon. Feeling like she had rolled down a mountainside, Lacey's muscles stiffened and protested as she shifted her weight. She heard voices talking quietly downstairs, but she couldn't quite make out what they were saying.

The aroma of something savory cooking wafted up from the kitchen, and Lacey's stomach growled. She realized that the last time she had had anything to eat was her spinach salad snack on Thursday, twenty-four hours ago.

Steve never made it to the bar to meet her for dinner. Lacey was still mad at him for that. Still blamed him for leaving her alone while all hell broke loose. *Though, he's probably out of his mind with worry*, she thought. People were probably flooding his social media accounts with questions and copies of video since yesterday evening. He'd know that that guy Bardman had died from his stab wound, and the reporter had died from the ricochet. Lacey squeezed her lids tight. This simply wasn't something she knew how to navigate.

Everything she had tried to create for so long and with such determination seemed to be falling to pieces.

Who found themselves in crazy messes like this? Drug dealers. Bad people doing overtly bad things. But that didn't describe her. She was as vanilla as ice cream - as straight and narrow as they come. The worst she'd ever done was run a stop sign. Well, that wasn't entirely true, Lacey reminded herself. She chewed on her thumbnail.

She should call Steve and let him know that she was safe. Was she safe? Well, at least she should let him know she was alive. No, wait. Deep said she couldn't use the phone.

Lacey's stomach wouldn't let her stand there contemplating. It insisted she go find something to eat. She pulled on the fuzzy house socks that Deep had provided, pushed her hair back behind her ears, and headed for the stairs.

The voices she had heard speaking in a low back and forth stopped as she walked through the dining room. Lacey found Deep standing in the doorway. "There she is, fresh from a wrestling match with a mountain lion," he said with a grin.

Lacey ran her fingers through her hair, and adjusted the sweatshirt down around her hips.

"Stop teasing her." Lynx came into view. She was taller than Lacey by a good four or five inches, with long blond hair and bright blue eyes. Lynx flashed her a friendly smile, but Lacey read deep worry in her eyes. "Welcome to my home. Come on in and sit down. I've got some food in the oven. It'll be ready in a few minutes. How about something to drink in the meantime?" Lynx asked as she moved to open the fridge. "I haven't been staying here lately, so I brought in some groceries. Let's see milk, orange juice, some different kinds of soda?" She peeked from behind the door. "Or maybe you'd prefer some tea or coffee?"

"Coffee, thank you." Lacey said on an exhale. By the back door, Lacey spotted a grey camo duffel bag that hadn't been there before.

Deep followed her gaze. "Lynx brought my go-bag, so now I can brush my teeth."

"You can brush your teeth, too." Lynx moved to the coffee maker, while Deep held a chair for Lacey, and Lacey gratefully sank onto the seat. "You'll find what you need under the guest bathroom sink."

"Yes, thank you kindly. Deep showed me."

Lacey wasn't sure that her *Emily Post's Etiquette for the Modern Age* covered this kind of situation. What do you say to someone who puts you up in their home while you're on the run from the police, the FBI, and maybe even the Secret Service?

Lynx brought over a pile of dinner dishes to set the table. "You know they have the word 'brunch' for a meal served between breakfast and lunch. We really should have a better American word for something between lunch and dinner. 'Tea' seems wrong, since I don't have finger sandwiches."

Lacey didn't answer. She was staring vacantly out the kitchen window at the grey sky spitting ice at the panes.

"Are you feeling okay?" Deep asked.

"Overwhelmed." Lacey blinked long eyelashes at him. "But physically I'm fine."

"The news showed Deep landing on you, then tossing you over his shoulder." Lynx grinned at Deep. "If you need a chiropractor, I've got the name of a good one."

"That was on the news, then?" Lacey's eyes rounded with dismay.

"Since the newscaster was killed, they've been looping it all day long," Lynx said.

74

Lacey nodded, then brushed the tears from her eyelashes. That bullet had been meant for her. It seemed anywhere she stood was a disaster area. She didn't want to put Lynx or Deep in danger. She didn't want Lynx's neighborhood kids in harm's way. She needed to decide. She either trusted these people, and she was truthful with them, or she didn't trust them, and she needed to leave.

Lynx put some cream and sugar on the table, then poured coffee in a mug and brought it over. "You want some, Deep?"

"Thanks," he said, leaning forward. "You know, Lacey, sometimes it's good to think out loud. You can hear the holes in your arguments."

Lacey reached under the sweatshirt to find the flash drive nestled against the underwire of her bra. She dropped it on the table as if it were too hot for her to keep ahold of. "When the man in the bar, Leo Bardman, was stabbed, he grabbed me and shoved this into my bra."

Deep canted his head. "I saw him putting something in your blouse on one of the videos. Did you know this guy?"

Lynx pulled open a drawer then walked over with a pair of nitrile gloves for Deep. She pulled a pair on her own hands.

"I'd never seen him before." Lacey shook her head for emphasis.

"So you were in the bar," Lynx said, picking up the flash drive and turning it over. "A guy approaches you. He's been stabbed in the back, and he gives you this?"

"And he said, 'Trust no one. Run.'" Lacey added.

"Sounds like good advice," Deep said. "Have you looked at what's on here?"

"Art," Lacey said. "I only opened the first file, and it was full of pictures of art."

"Art, like paintings?" Deep asked.

"Yes, and oddly, they're all paintings I know. I was supposed to be curating a show in the gallery this month. But, as you both know, my uncle pulled that scam on Iniquus, and while people don't know that there was a kerfuffle specifically with your company – well, sometimes the rumors are worse than the actuality. I can't clear anything up since I signed papers with Iniquus to never disclose what happened." Lacey blushed hotly. "Not a kerfuffle a crime. But since that time, all of the artists' agents snatched their clients back out. No artists. No show."

"When did you work on the show?" Lynx asked.

"I never actually made any headway. Last September, I learned we were to host a show. Then Uncle Bartholomew put it on hold. In November, when he moved to Bali, he said the January show was cancelled. But during the interim, I researched the artists. And like I said, I recognize all of the pieces from my list."

"So this wasn't some random guy who happened to be standing near you in the bar. You were actually the person that he had tracked. And his last act was giving you this?" Lynx asked.

"That seems to be so." Lacey's mouth tugged down at the corners. She dipped her head to sip at the coffee, hoping to warm herself up. Fear hung icicles from her ribs. She couldn't stop shaking.

Silence filled the kitchen. When Lacey looked up, Lynx and Deep seemed to be having a whole conversation with their eyes. Lynx caught Lacey's gaze on her, raised her brows at Deep, and stood up to pull a lasagna from the oven.

"It's not Thursday," Lynx said cryptically. "But Deep likes to eat Italian every night." She set the lasagna on top of the stove, then reached in to pull out the loaf of garlic bread that made Lacey's mouth water.

Deep stood to open a bottle of red wine and poured for three without even asking, while Lynx produced a salad and a bowl of red grapes.

Lynx raised her glass. "Here's to a good puzzle that we can put together with ease."

"Here, here," Deep said, then took a sip.

Lacey couldn't understand their attitude. Not at all. She dragged her napkin across her lap, dropped her chin to her chest as if in prayer, and squeezed her eyes tight against her distress.

"Lacey." Deep's voice pulled her gaze up to find warm brown eyes framed with thick lashes that gave an endearing, almost boyish, sweetness to his face. The kindness she saw there made her heart skip forward two beats too fast. "We're going to help you the best we can. And we're damned good at our jobs."

Lacey nodded with a stuttering inhale.

Fortified from their early dinner and relaxed a bit by the glass of wine, they sat in front of the computer with Deep at the keyboard, flanked by the women.

"So, let's see here," Deep said as he pulled open the first file. He flipped quickly through the images.

"And these are all familiar to you — the artists and the tableaux themselves?" Lynx asked.

"Yes, they were all on my acquisitions list." Lacey knotted her arms under her breasts.

Deep moved to the second file. "You haven't opened this one yet?"

Lacey shook her head.

It was another series of pictures with dates and time stamps. These pictures chronicled Lacey's days — there were photos of her at the gym, the park, work, dinner . . . There she was with Steve. And there they were again; she was standing on her toes to kiss him.

Someone had been following her – stalking her. Her whole body buzzed as her nerves lit up. All Lacey could do as Deep scrolled forward was shake her head. "I don't understand. I don't understand," she muttered.

Lynx reached behind Deep to touch Lacey's shoulder. Lacey knew it was meant to be a supportive gesture, but Lacey had to brace herself so she wouldn't jerk away. It was if she was holding all of the sensations that her body could possibly contain, and Lynx's touch overwhelmed Lacey's coping ability. Lacey would do everything in her power never to feel this way again.

Deep pressed the keys to pull up the third file. This one held copies of emailed correspondence with artists' agents. Contracts with the agents, caterers, engravers, and with shipping and storage companies – it was as if the art show was completely planned and on schedule for next week. And her name and signature was on each and every one. As if she was moving forward on-task with a show that she knew wasn't going to happen.

"No. No. No." Lacey moaned as Deep flipped through the pages. "This is exactly what happened with the Iniquus art."

"Not exactly, Lacey," Lynx said. "When you were collecting the Iniquus art and putting it in storage for transport, you were hands-on arranging all of the details and following through with your uncle's directives."

"Yes, that's right," Lacey agreed.

"You told us that this show was called off because no one trusted your gallery. Your uncle never came back from his trip to Bali, after the Iniquus art theft was exposed. Right?"

"That's right. He left me in charge of running the gallery the best I could."

"Do you have proof that these agents pulled back from the show?" Deep asked.

"You mean their letters telling us to take a flying leap? Why yes, they're on my computer. Do you want me to access them? I can get there through Carbonite."

"No not now," Deep said. "If the FBI has your computer, they could be waiting for you to log on so they can follow the information back to this one."

"They can do that?"

"They have some pretty wonderful capabilities," Lynx said. "Right now, we don't want them combing our area. So let's hold off. It's not important to see those emails right this second."

"They can trace a computer?" Lacey's brow furrowed. "Huh. Well, hopefully it won't matter."

"What's that?" Deep asked.

"Well, I accessed my computer through Martha's work computer at her house. I was looking up the business card you gave me. I had scanned it into my downloads file. I called you earlier this morning, before I contacted my lawyer, but it was your service that responded."

"Well, I knew you called me. My answering service gave me the phone number and address of where you'd called from. Of course, the name they gave me was Martha Schwartz, but I was pretty sure it was you. I was swinging by Martha's house on my way out of town when I heard the radio station announce your press conference."

"Wow. That's pretty scary," Lacey said. "Not that you were coming to check on me, thank you for that, but that you had all that information when all I did was hang up on the woman."

"Another reason why I thought it was you," Deep said.

"What I find the most bizarre about these three files are all the third-party photos of you. Did you know you were being photographed?" Lynx bumped Deep's shoulder with hers and flicked her finger toward the screen.

"No. I never saw anyone with a camera. But I guess anyone on a phone could have taken these."

Deep scrolled back over to the pictures of Lacey. Lynx stood and tapped her hip into him. He got up and switched chairs with her. They obviously had been working closely together for a long time; they seemed like two wheels on one bicycle. But Lacey didn't feel like she was a third wheel. More like she was the cart being dragged along behind them.

"Lacey, who's this guy in the photos?"

"Steve Adamic, he used to be my boyfriend." Lacey's lips had trouble forming the word boyfriend and she wondered, as she said it, why her answer felt like a lie. She also noticed she had used the past tense. That at least felt truthful.

Lynx continued to flip through the photos. Without taking her eye off the screen, she said, "Lacey start at the beginning and tell me the story. Was the bar Thursday night a place you go often? What were your plans for the evening?"

"Well," Lacey said. "We were usually pretty quiet, especially on weeknights. Even on the weekends, we cooked in and watched Netflix. Bars weren't really our scene."

"He lives with you?" Lynx asked.

Lacey shot a glance toward Deep. He seemed to be engrossed in the photos. "Not officially, but he was at my place all the time."

"How long have you two known each other?" Lynx asked.

"Not quite five months. We met in September."

"And he started hanging out almost all the time at your house when?" Lynx pulled a pad toward her and drew a couple of bubbles where she filled in Lacey's information.

"Well, I was hurt at the time we met, and he was worried about me. I guess he started staying over almost right away."

Lynx looked up. "Hurt how?"

"I was in a car accident. I swerved when I hit a deer, and I crashed into a tree."

More thought bubbles were drawn on the paper. "So you normally stay in. Why was Thursday night different? Were you celebrating something?"

"No, Steve called and asked me to meet him there for drinks and dinner."

"You sound like you didn't want to go," Lynx said.

"I was tired. I'm finding it pretty stressful trying to run the gallery without my uncle there – trying to save our reputation."

"It wasn't a special occasion? Have you ever been to that restaurant before?" Lynx pushed.

"I've never been there before, and I have no idea why Steve wanted to meet me there. Or for that matter, why he never showed up."

Lynx stalled. "Wait. What? He never showed? How late was he?"

"About forty minutes. I'd given up and was leaving."

"No text? No call?" Deep's brow furrowed.

"Not anything," Lacey said.

Deep focused on Lynx.

"I can call from a secure line back at headquarters," she told him.

"Let's hold off until we can figure out if he's playing on the right team," Deep said.

What that meant, Lacey wasn't sure.

Lynx flipped the notebook page to a clean one. "Do me a favor, would you? Can you write down everything you know about Steve? Full name. Address. Contact numbers. Social media accounts. Where he works? Where he was born? Names of friends and family – that kind of thing."

"But why?" Lacey asked.

"Just turning over rocks," Lynx said.

Deep got up and walked toward the kitchen. Lacey could swear she heard Deep mutter, "To see if there are any snakes hiding underneath."

Lynx went back to the beginning of the photo-journal chronicling Lacey's days. After Lacey finished with her list, she stared out the side window. It was dark already. Suddenly, Lacey's eyes pulled wide. "Oh, no."

Lynx followed her gaze to the window then back to Lacey. "What?" she asked.

"Martha's cat. I'm supposed to feed Twinkle Toes."

"Well, you can't do that. You can't go back to a house where people might be waiting for you," Lynx said.

"The FBI could have traced your computer," Deep agreed as he came back in the room. He handed Lacey a cup of tea. "This should help warm you up."

"No, the FBI can't do that," Lacey insisted, taking the tea and sending Deep a brief smile. "The IP address would merely show the city I'm in. They can't home in on a single address, can they?"

"I can," Deep said. "Well not here on Lynx's ThinkPad. But if I were at Iniquus, I could."

"But Twinkle Toes." And that was it. The last straw. She had been grabbed, bloodied, herded, chased, shot at and bounced on Deep's back down the street. She had found out that she was being stalked and photographed for months on end. Why it was that thinking about Twinkle Toes, alone and hungry back at Martha's house, set off Lacey's crying jag, she wasn't sure.

Lacey pushed her mug onto the notepad and pulled tissue after tissue from the box that Deep held out toward her. He seemed unfazed by her near hysteria. Lacey tried to hide the worst of her splotchy red eyes and mucus-filled nostrils from his view behind her French-manicured nails.

Lynx reached out and moved Lacey's tea toward the center of the table and out of harm's way, allowing Lacey to fold her arms on the table and hunker down to finish her cry. Lynx put a comforting hand on Lacey's back but didn't try to stop Lacey's tears.

"You know, Deep, I could stop by on the way back to the barracks and feed the cat," Lynx offered.

"Oh, no, you won't. Striker would kill me."

"Striker would never know."

"No. But thank you." There was no compromise or wiggle room in the tone Deep used.

Lacey looked up over her tissues as she wiped the last of her tears.

"Do you know anyone else who could take care of the cat?" Deep asked Lacey after she blew her nose in a long, satisfying way into yet another Kleenex.

Lacey couldn't believe that she was comfortable enough with these two veritable strangers that she'd allow them to see her blow her nose. She didn't even let Steve see her do that. She unfolded her legs from under her and stood up. "Well, they'd simply need the door code." Lacey moved to the powder room to throw the Kleenex away, rinse her hands, and run her fingers through her hair to try to regain a touch of her normally lady-like demeanor, but the hiccoughs betrayed her. "I could ask Mary to go over."

"Uh-uh. Lynx will ask Mary to go over from a secured line."

Lacey jotted down Mary's number and the house code on a sticky note and handed it to Lynx.

"And if Mary can't go?" Lynx asked.

"Then send Panther Force." Deep's teasing smile lit up his eyes. "Titus Kane is a softie for furry little kitties."

Lynx snorted as she headed out the door.

Lacey turned to Deep. "What happens next?"

Chapter Nine

Steve

Friday Night

The crisp crackle of cellophane wrappers broadcast large against the otherwise soundless night. Steve hunkered in his car, unwrapping stadium hand warmers. As they came free of their packaging, he shook the contents to create a chemical reaction. He slid one down his shirt and rested two on the tips of his boots to help revive his toes and keep them safe from frostbite. The last one, he held between his hands to keep his trigger finger warm. The weather app on his phone said it had dropped to twelve degrees, and that didn't take into account the wind rocking his car. But he couldn't risk running the engine.

He had pulled his car into a ditch, comfortable that the magnolia tree masked most of its bulk. He still maintained a pretty clear view of Martha's bungalow. He knew Lacey. If she was physically able, she'd show up to feed the cat. Lacey couldn't stand the thought of an animal suffering.

She'd been here the night before. The bureau traced her location down when she'd accessed her computer remotely. Higgins said after that, Lacey made a forty-second phone call to someone named Joseph Del Toro. Higgins was following up on that. The next call went to her lawyer's house. Those were the only calls she made. Lacey hadn't called him, and Steve couldn't fathom it.

Steve thought about all the lies he had been feeding her since she first met him. Almost everything about the case – who he was, what he did for a living, how he spent his days – lies. But he hadn't lied about his feelings. He loved her. He had already decided she was the one he wanted to make a life with. The one to mother his kids and spoil the grandchildren.

But first he had to find her, keep her safe, and explain.

He wasn't sure, after this mess was over, how he could help her to understand what he did or why he'd done it. He knew that trust was going to be an issue. But he truly believed he could build back her trust with time. If she'd give him the chance.

Right now, he needed to figure out what was going on. Who scooped Lacey up at the press conference? Where had he taken her?

His phone vibrated and displayed a number he didn't recognize. "This is Steve."

"It's Higgins. I've got the skinny on your boy Joseph Del Toro."

"Yeah?"

"He's clean as a whistle. Born on Long Island. Lived there through high school, then signed with the Marines. After Parris Island, he trained as a Marine Raider. He deployed three times to the sandbox, has medals all over his chest, and now he's home working as an Iniquus operative on their Strike Force team. Goes by the call name, "Deep". And as it turns out, I've worked a case with him. Good guy. Highly skilled. Tenacious. Fearless."

"Huh."

"She must have met him when her uncle stole the Iniquus art work," Higgins said.

"And when she was in trouble, that's who she called." Steve scrunched down in his seat as a pair of headlights bounced down the road.

"It's who I'd call. She thinks you're a software engineer. What the hell would you do up against big bad men who aren't afraid to stab people in public?"

Steve didn't take the bait. "So did you call Del Toro in for an interview?"

"Iniquus has him listed as on vacation overseas – 'unavailable for emergency deployment.'"

"So that wasn't him grabbing up Lacey at the press conference?"

"Not unless he's got himself a worm hole."

"Call you back, Danika's on my other line." Steve swiped his finger over the phone to pick up the new call. "Hey babe," he said. He watched as a car turned slowly at the corner and was now inching up the street.

"When are you coming home? I've got the munchies, and I want you to bring me something."

"Yeah sure, in the next hour or so. I'm still out here looking for Lacey."

"Oh, you don't need to do that anymore."

Fear grabbed hold of the base of Steve's spine and shook him violently. "Why's that?"

"Pavle picked her up this morning at the news conference."

"I was at the news conference."

"I know. I saw you on TV."

Steve felt the fine hairs on his arms lift as his skin puckered with goose flesh.

"We all saw you. Pavle is pissed as hell that you got your face front and center on the news. He says it was sloppy-ass work. He doesn't need clowns mucking up like that in his organization."

He swallowed hard. "What do you think that means?"

"I don't know, but I'd be kissing his ass if I were you."

"Hang on, I was at the press conference trying to catch hold of Lacey. The sniper was late with his shot. Some guy tackled Lacey, and the bullet ricocheted and hit the woman standing in front of me."

"Right, well, that was Pavle's plan, see? The family staged it so the sniper didn't hit Lacey, but it gave an excuse for his guy to grab her in plain sight instead so she couldn't go talk to the police and so we'd have hold of her."

"So it was Pavle's sniper? You're a hundred percent sure?"

"Who else would have a sniper gunning for Lacey Stuart?"

"This makes no sense. Why would they go through that charade?"

"Did you think someone was trying to kill her?"

"Yes," Steve replied, lifting his binoculars to watch a woman getting out of her car in Martha's driveway. She was too bundled up for Steve to get a good look. She was pretty short – it could be Lacey.

"Did you think that some hero ran in and saved her life?"

"That's the way it looked to me," Steve said, half-paying attention to Danika. If he didn't get a good visual when this person came out, he'd follow her car and call the license in to Higgins.

"But what really happened was Pavle kidnapped her. Isn't that marvelous?" The receiver filled with gleeful laughter. "So now the family can ask her nicely to get the stuff back from her friend, then they can dump her body. Everything's handled."

As the woman walked back out the door, Steve saw a long blond braid hanging down her back. It was the gallery intern, Mary. *Shit.* "The family can ask her nicely to — what? What stuff are we talking about here? Do you know where they're holding Lacey?" Steve pressed his eyelids tight in prayer.

"I'm not sure where they've got her. Pavle didn't say. So you're coming home now? Could you bring me some Nacho-flavored Doritos and some chocolate Ben and Jerry's?"

"Yeah, that's fine, baby." Steve tried not to let his emotions come anywhere near his words. If Danika picked up on anything wrong, he could be the next one in Pavle's assassin's crosshairs. He needed to play the game to stay in the game. He needed to move the ball and move it fast.

He knew that any chance of saving Lacey was thin. And he was terrified about what techniques they might use on her while they tried to get her to talk. Talk about what, though? He'd have to ask Danika in person, when he had her full attention. "I'll swing by the grocery store. I have one quick errand to run first."

"K. Hurry."

As soon as Steve swiped the red button, Higgins was back on the line.

"Steve, man, Monroe wants you in the office ASAP."

"Yeah, alright." Steve reached out to turn the key and crank his engine. He'd be glad to get some warm air blowing. "Did he come up with something?"

"Yeah, our snitch says Pavle's got your name out for a hit."

Steve could feel his heart beat accelerating. His armpits were damp with a sudden sweat. "I just talked to Danika. She'd find some way to warn me if that was true."

"You sure? What was she calling about?"

"Yes, I'm sure. She's got the munchies. It's her time of the month. So everything will go smoother if I stop and pick her up some carbs and chocolate on the way back to the apartment."

"She said that? Bring her back some carbs?"

"Doritos and ice cream, if you need the list."

"And she was calling you from where?"

"The apartment. She wanted me to come home with junk food. What's with these questions, man?"

"Yeah, here's the problem with that scenario. Monroe asked us to pick Danika up, right? Keep the body count down? So we've got our boys out looking. I pulled the short straw, and I've been freezing my ass in the van, watching her place all day. From where I parked, I can keep an eye on Lacey's front door, too. Lacey hasn't come home yet, no one's turned on the lights up there, and the lights are out at Danika's, too. They've been off all day. At Danika's, though, there's voices, male voices speaking what sounds a whole lot like Slovakian, but you'd know better than me. No female voices and nothing coming up as a positive on voice recognition."

"Wait. Let me get this straight. Danika calls me, making me think she's at home, asks me to go back to the apartment right away, and says she needs me to bring munchies. But her lights are off, and you didn't record her talking to me – all you got were male voices. How many?"

"Four, from what I can tell," Higgins said. "They've put on the lights in the front room of the apartment and drew the drapes. I can hear the music from down here. I don't even need to have my headphones on. They've got the place rocking, and ready for your arrival, ice-cream delivery boy. Looks like your time playing with the Zoric family has come to an end, my friend. Monroe called it; they've got their guys waiting for you. You showed your colors at the press conference. There's no way they could overlook that, man. I know it's against your core to walk away, but trying to keep that reporter alive when she was a lost cause sunk your ship, dude. I'll let Monroe know what's going on. I'd head home to your real apartment for tonight. We can gather our task force in the morning and figure out our next move."

"Yeah, man, okay. Shit." Steve had accidentally run a stop sign, and now his rear-view mirror was lit up with red and blue lights. He patted his belt, then remembered he didn't have his

FBI ID on him. Well, this ticket was going to Steve Adamic, anyway. Steve Finley would still have a clean record. "A boy in blue's pulling me over. Are you going to stay there and watch for Danika?" Steve asked. "I don't want her walking into that apartment."

"Yeah, I'll try to grab her before she goes in. We need her testimony, and between you and me? It's feeling like her hours are numbered."

Chapter Ten

Saturday Morning

Lacey woke up not knowing where she was. She cast her eyes around the room, then down at the pink flannel pajamas a couple of sizes too big. *I'm at Lynx's house. I'm safe.*

She slid slowly out from under the warm covers and pulled on Lynx's thick terrycloth robe and a pair of socks before she made her way out of the guestroom. The door to the front room where Deep slept stood wide open. She padded down to take a peek in. His bed was made with precision. Unlike the haphazard way that Steve would toss the covers, Deep's duvet looked like you could bounce a quarter off the top. She smiled.

Deep's room had windows that lined up with the front of the house. Edged with curtains, beautifully embroidered with white on white leaves, the windowpanes were painted with the feathery strokes of blue morning frost backlit by a dove-colored sky. Lacey longed to go over and see what the

99

neighborhood looked like. But she had promised to go dark and live this weird little shadow existence. She couldn't take the chance that someone might see her, recognize her, and bring attention to her from the wrong people. Though who the "right people" were – well, she was still guessing at that.

Lacey moved to the bathroom, where she gave her teeth a quick brush, gave her hair a quick comb, and tried hard not to focus on the dark circles under her eyes. Lacey let her nose lead the way as she followed the rich oily aroma of freshly brewed coffee. As she made her way through the house, Lacey seemed to be the only one there. She wondered where Deep could have gone. When she made it to the kitchen, she discovered it was much colder than the rest of the rooms. She thought she might take her coffee into the dining room, where a cheerful fire snapped.

As she reached up for a mug where she'd seen Lynx place them the day before, Lacey saw Lynx and Deep standing together outside. Lynx had her hands on top of Deep's forearms and Deep had reached his hands underneath to support her elbows. They stood locked together as they talked. Then Lynx released Deep's arms to rise up on her tiptoes and give him a hug. If Lynx kissed him, Lacey decided instantly, she'd walk right out the front door and move on down the street. That thought came as a complete surprise. It was shocking how bitterly jealousy sat on her tongue, and Lacey wondered where those feelings had sprung from. She had no room for jealousy – only gratitude.

Lynx caught Lacey's eye through the frost coated widow and gave her a friendly wave and smile, then she released Deep and moved through the back gates, her prancing black Dobermans cavorting at her heels. Lacey would have liked a chance to have pet Lynx's dogs.

When Deep came inside, his arms were full of bags.

Lacey quickly moved over to shut the door behind him. "What's this?" she asked.

"Lynx went shopping for you. She thought you'd be more comfortable in clothes your own size."

Lacey rifled through the bags. She couldn't believe how well Lynx had chosen things for her. Not simply her size, but her personal style – the one she wore when she was comfortably at home and not dressed for public view. There was even a bag from Victoria's Secret. Okay, that was a little odd. She was grateful, but, hmmm, still . . . Lacey frowned as she looked up to catch Deep's gaze.

"I told you, didn't I, that I first met Lynx when I was guarding her at a safehouse?"

"You mentioned a safehouse, yes."

"So she knows a thing or two about how that can feel. She says she hopes you'll forgive her for any mistakes in picking things out."

"Oh, no. This is all so very kind of her. I'll be sure to tell her how grateful I am when she comes back."

Deep shook his head. "That probably won't happen. Lynx came by this morning to let me know that our boss lent her to Echo Force, one of the other teams at Iniquus. She's headed out of town to look at some evidence and try to lay a trail."

"You said your team is 'down range.' What does that mean exactly?"

"They're off on assignment. I was scheduled for R and R. It's required that we take time off every few months so we've got our head in the game when we're on duty."

"Then you shouldn't be here with me. This is more on-the-job time, right? This is what you do?"

"More or less. My job's pretty diverse." Deep moved to the fridge, where he pulled out the makings of breakfast.

"I'm sorry," Lacey said.

Deep turned to her—his hands full of eggs, cheese, and vegetable—and tipped his head.

"That you're here with me, when you should be relaxing."

The warmth of the smile that Deep sent her way stopped her breath. She gazed at him and thought she had never seen such a gorgeous, capable man in her life. How was it possible that someone like her had found a man not only willing but able to run in front of a speeding bullet to save her? He was the reason her brains were still safely stored in her head. Good things didn't normally come Lacey's way. And while bullets and bad guys definitely weren't good, Deep most definitely was.

Maybe too good. She took in a faltering breath and released it in a sigh.

"Hey, now." He was suddenly by her side, tumbling the food onto the table, and reaching for her hands. "None of that. I'm here because I want to be, okay?"

"Okay," she agreed reluctantly. "Was everything alright outside? Lynx seemed a little upset when you two were speaking." Lacey wished he'd pull her into a hug. She longed to rest her cheek on his chest and listen to his heart beat and feel his arms wrapped protectively around her.

"She's concerned that Iniquus picked up the contract to find you, so she was warning me off making contact with the office. She isn't sure; she didn't hear if any of the teams picked up the assignment, but your name was floating around the halls when she was over there this morning."

"She was already at the office, and then drove here?" Lacey glanced at the wall clock. "It's hard to believe she went to bed at all."

"She didn't." Deep released her hands and went to pull a frying pan from under the counter. "Last night, she was running information on Steve – Lynx only had time to do a cursory investigation, but she says everything checks out."

"You said that with a funny tone." Lacey pulled the lapels of the robe tighter across her chest and dipped her chin under the fabric.

"Yeah, she said that, on paper, Steve's a little too clean. Something seems off to her, but she didn't have time to dig enough to find out why." Deep caught Lacey's eyes, and it felt as if he were trying to drill down and find a truth. Lacey lowered her lashes and looked at her fingers, knotted in her lap.

"Oh, okay," was all Lacey could figure to say.

"She pulled your calendar from October and November. She thought it might be interesting to get a timeline going – where did you go when, and why you thought they took those particular photos. She also said that there is something majorly off about the photos. Something was niggling her about them the whole time she was looking at them. But again, she didn't have time to pin it down."

"Something niggled at her?" Lacey wrinkled her nose.

"Do you know what Lynx does for Iniquus?"

Lacey shook her head.

"She's our Puzzler. It means you hand her a bunch of odd pieces, and she sees how they fit together. It's really kind of nuts how she pulls some of this stuff off. Believe me, if Lynx says there's something there, there's something there. I just wish she was playing on our team while we figure this out. But it looks like it's going to be you and me."

"Are you sure this is a game you want to play?" Lacey whispered. Her voice was colored with hope that honestly felt more like fear.

He sent her a happy grin. "It's been pretty fun so far." He cracked an egg into the mixing bowl. "Are you ready for my famous Frittata Italian?"

***

With breakfast over and dishes cleared, they moved to the dining room, where Deep stoked the fire to make the sparks fly. The smell of hardwood burning was comforting, and for a moment Lacey was back in her grandparents' house on a snow day, drinking hot chocolate and listening to her nana reading from *Charlotte's Web*. She must have been about four years old. It was one of her nicer memories from childhood, and she wished she could live in that picture a while longer.

Deep unrolled a huge tube of white paper across the dining room table. "When Lynx starts a puzzle, she likes to get things out there visually. She says that if you see it, say it, hear it, write it, and think it, it gets more parts of your brain working. And I've found she's right. So I thought we might try this with your photos."

While Deep covered the table with paper, Lacey dashed upstairs to change into a pair of black yoga pants. She pulled a thigh-length sweater, knit from the softest mohair, from one of the shopping bags. She thought the rich plum color made her brown eyes particularly pretty, and found herself hoping Deep would think so, too. She swept her hair into a makeshift bun on the nape of her neck and hurried back down to the dining room, where Deep held a jar of colored markers. He placed them gingerly on top of the credenza, then fished around, looking for something else.

Lacey moved over to stand beside him. The smell of smoke and the outdoors had caught in Deep's sweater. Steve always smelled like men's lemony aftershave, which seemed urban and somehow feminine to her. Really, she should find a way to get word to Steve that she was okay, she thought once again. But the solution to that problem hadn't come to her. And there was that back and forth that had gone on between Deep and Lynx — something about not being sure about what team Steve was playing on. Could he be a bad guy? Could he have set her up somehow? That didn't resonate as right with her – but then again, it didn't resonate as wrong, either. Maybe she should talk that over with Deep?

Lacey felt guilt wash over her. Standing there thinking about Steve made her feel like she was cheating on Deep. Even though it was Steve who had been her boyfriend, and Deep was . . . was what? A guy who risked his life to save hers. A guy who gave up his vacation to dive in front of a bullet. I guy who was so darned cute that he'd made her dreams last night particularly difficult to pull herself from this morning.

Deep glanced up at her from where he'd bent over the drawer. "What?"

"You dove in front of a bullet for me. Who does that?"

"I didn't dive in front of a bullet. I dove *under* a bullet." He smiled. "There's a difference."

It was Lacey's turn to ask, "What?"

"The laser sight was focused on your forehead. You're about five-foot-two, right? So as long as I kept myself down around four feet, I wasn't in much danger."

Lacey didn't know what to do with that. She saw the laughter in Deep's eyes. *This must be gallows humor*, she thought. Probably some kind of soldier coping-mechanism he'd developed in the Middle East. But Lacey didn't find anything funny about the situation at all. And he did too risk himself for her—otherwise he would have stood there and watched her die. "Five-foot-one," she mumbled.

Dear God, she'd nearly died. Someone had aimed a bullet at her head. Lacey reached out to the wall to steady herself. She needed a drink – a double shot of bourbon to defrost her veins. This whole mess made her glacial inside. She couldn't imagine ever feeling warm again.

What she really needed to do was get busy fixing this, figure everything out, and regain control. Control of her life.

Control of her emotions. All of these horrible feelings would go away once she was back in control. Her eye snagged on a printout of her calendar. She picked up the papers.

"Deep?" she asked as he moved back over to the table and lay out the ruler, pens, and markers. "How did Lynx get hold of this information?" She turned the pages so Deep could see.

"They were on your computer."

"But you said not to access my computer because people could track me, and I never gave you my password for Carbonite."

Deep's ears turned pink at the tips. "You know, you were under investigation when we were working through the Iniquus art theft."

Lacey nodded.

"Well we – I—I hacked into your computer, and we have an in-house copy of your hard drive."

Now Lacey understood why his ears had turned red, like a little boy who had been caught in the act of stealing candy. What right did he have? Hack her computer? *Oh, no.* Lacey's hands came up to frame her face as her eyes stretched wide. He had looked through her computer. There were pictures. Her personal, private pictures. Pictures from her childhood that she used to remind herself of how far she'd come. A demarcation of "that was then, and this is now." Pictures that she didn't want to share.

Deep seemed to understand the look she shot him, because he followed up with, "The only thing that I looked at was your email correspondence with Japan. I would never look through a lady's computer. That would be pretty scummy. I mean, I have sisters, and if they ever caught me reading their diaries, well, I'm sure I wouldn't be around today." He smiled with the chuckle of a private joke and shook his head. "You know my family's Italian. We tend to get passionate about things. Living in such a small space, my sisters were definitely passionate about their privacy."

She gripped the turtleneck collar at the top and stretched it up to cover her chin. "But someone else could have gone through it? Seen things?"

"Only my teammates, and believe me, our plates are so full, we're not randomly looking through computer files."

"Now that that case is closed, can you destroy what you have or return it to me?"

"I'll ask Colonel Grant for permission. We'll figure it out. What's on there that you don't want me to see?" He looked out of the corner of his eye at her, and she could swear there was more than a hint of teasing in his smile. But to her there was nothing funny about this. Those pictures should have been safe, and now she felt more exposed than ever. Lacey felt her face warming as she blushed.

Deep was out and out laughing at her. "It must be pretty good, whatever it is. Come on." He patted the chair. "Let's get to work."

Lacey pursed her lips and drew in a breath, trying to let the moment pass. She'd deal with her pictures later. They were the least of her problems at this moment in time.

Deep gestured to the blank paper. "What I think would be helpful is if you use this paper to make a timeline of everything you did from your calendar and recollection, and then switch marker colors and layer on the top of your schedule the dates and times of the photos and what is in the picture."

Lacey put the photocopied schedule in her lap and picked up a blue marker. "Write down what's in the picture on this flash drive? I'll know what's in the picture by where I am on the timeline."

"Look at what's specifically in the picture. Is it you and Steve? Is it you with an obvious location? For example, if someone was taking your picture in front of a business with the name displayed, that might mean that they wanted to put you in that location at a specific time and date. That kind of thing. There's a reason for these pictures, and that's what you're trying to figure out."

"Okay. It might be faster if we worked as a team."

Deep took his place in front of a metal case that looked like it might hold the Presidential launch codes. But when he opened it, Lacey saw it was another computer.

"I'm going to approach the same problem from a different direction." His fingers typed out what she assumed was a code, then he leaned in to the screen. "Optical recognition," he said. There must have been a prompt because then he said, "Deep Del Toro. Iniquus special operations, Strike Force."

Lacey stared at him.

"Lynx brought me my field computer."

Lacey blinked.

"I have some specialized software that might help. When she said there was something off about the pictures, I wondered if maybe it was odd shadows Lynx was picking up on – like maybe these pictures were Photoshopped. I have a program that can tell me if that's the case." He looked up, caught her eye and held there. A slow smile crossed his face, and his chocolate brown eyes warmed. Lacey found herself smiling back, though she couldn't guess what he was thinking. He cleared his throat, and with the smile still on his face, focused back on his computer screen.

Chapter Eleven

Saturday

After about an hour, Deep sat back and said, "well, isn't that interesting?"

Lacey glanced up from her task of putting her calendar onto the time line. "What are you doing now?"

Deep pushed his chair back and Lacey watched him flex his long legs. The material of his jeans wrapped tightly around his thigh muscles then released as he stretched out. "Ever since this morning when I said goodbye to Lynx, I've been concerned about what she saw on the news when I was rescuing you. I can't have my face out there in the public eye – it could compromise future missions. If my face is known, it puts not only me but my teammates at risk and makes an already dangerous job that much more difficult."

Lacey's eyes filled with concern. "Is there anything you can do about it?"

"I've been pulling up the various tapes that've been posted on the web. Now, I'm feeling more secure that Lynx is the only one who could possibly figure out it was me tossing you over my shoulder. There don't seem to be any frames that include any part of my face. This guy, on the other hand. . ."

Deep reached out to tap the screen and still the video that had been playing. He adjusted the metrics, then turned the computer toward Lacey, "This is Steve Adamic, right?"

Lacey's brows pulled in tightly with surprise and confusion as Steve's face filled the screen. Even though he wore a baseball cap that shadowed most his features, Lacey nodded immediately. "Yes, that's him. He was at the press conference?"

"Just a sec." Deep diminished the picture to make it part of the videoed scene. "Come here, I want you to watch this."

Lacey moved over behind Deep. Resting her hands on his shoulders, she bent down until they were cheek to cheek, and she was seeing what he was seeing. He pressed the button, and the screen changed as the camera shot panned over the small park across the street from the gallery entrance. The park was crowded with news equipment and cold people, stomping and huddling to keep warm. Their breaths came out in little clouds that hung in the air. The camera view swung up to take in the steeple of the church that filled the window behind her desk when Lacey was sitting in her office at the gallery. Next it swung down to the portico as the gallery door opened and Mr. Reynolds walked out. Lacey stiffened. She didn't want to see this. She absolutely did not want to see the red dot sliding down her forehead, and Deep diving in to rescue her. Her hands gripped his shoulders.

"Hey, it's okay," Deep said, as he reached out and wrapped his hand around her elbow. He pushed partway onto his feet, lifted and spun his chair so the corner was in front of the table, then pulled her around, seating her on the extra part of the chair between his legs. He reached around her and typed his commands into the keyboard. "I edited out all the parts with you in it. There's no reason to put those images in your head."

Lacey pushed back into his chest, rolling her shoulders forward. Deep tapped enter, then folded her tightly in his arms and held her closely to him. Lacey closed her eyes and let Deep's warmth radiate into her. She lowered her hands to rest them on his thighs and thought how perfectly they fit together. How comforting it was to be here. Safe. Cared for – Lacey felt cared for in a way that she had never experienced before. She had to force her eyes open to see what Deep had wanted to show her.

The camera shot was of the crowd. There was the back of the guy that she had identified as Steve. Why was Steve there hanging out in the crowd of onlookers? He should have been knocking on the gallery door, or, even standing where she'd see him and gain some confidence because he was there supporting her. Something was off. And it became more apparent when the echo of the rifle fire split the air. As she heard the bullet crack through the sky, Lacey jumped and coward against Deep. He used his legs and arms to hold her tighter.

Deep whispered in her ear. "Most people have never heard gunfire in real life. It sounds nothing like it does in the movies, and their brains don't immediately register what the sound means. You only jumped because you knew what was coming. They didn't. See how the crowd stood there, non-reactive." He pointed at the screen where Deep had set the video to move forward in slow-motion. "The thing that created the panic and stampede was not the sound of gunfire, but the sound of this woman's scream when she was hit by a stream of blood." Deep pointed at an Asian woman in a royal blue hat who dove backwards with her hand up protectively. "That's blood from the newscaster's neck." He moved his finger to the redheaded woman whose arms flailed out to the sides. "See how people spin toward the sound of the scream? Now they see the blood and the woman collapsing. That's when their brains put together the pieces, and told them to get out of there. But watch carefully."

Deep moved the video back several frames. "Steve was front and center in the frame of this camera. When the rifle

116

cracked, he squatted and his hand reflexively reached for his hip. That's where a right-handed person would find their holster. His first reaction is to duck and retrieve a gun. His head tips back, and he's scanning along the rooftops. Hang on, this is where the cameraman abandoned his camera."

There was a moment of crazy shots of the sky and buildings until it came to rest, pointed at where the victim collapsed beside Steve. "Okay, watch what he's doing. His finger stabbed into the woman's wound to stop the flow of blood, but he's not looking at her. Do you see how his head is moving? That's the trajectory I took with you on my shoulder. Have you ever heard of something called tunnel vision?"

Lacey shook her head.

"Unless you're trained for stressful situations, and sometimes even *if* you're trained for stressful situations, what can happen is that your brain focuses all of its power on the threat. Someone's holding a weapon on you? All you see is the weapon. You've got your fingers in some woman's neck while her blood geysered around your finger? All most people would be able to focus on was that wound or maybe that woman."

"Oh, God." The sight of the mayhem made Lacey's stomach churn. She pulled Deep's arms tighter around her stomach and leaned her head back into the cup of his neck under his chin.

"Sorry," Deep said, dropping a kiss into her hair.

Lacey stalled. Deep probably didn't realize he'd done that. Though he'd never kissed her before, it felt like an everyday part of their communication. Normal. Right. Lacey felt her cheeks turning pink and with a sigh, she forced herself to refocus on the computer screen.

The next frames showed Steve placing his other hand on top of the first increasing the pressure on the woman's neck. Blood seeped between his fingers. When the blood stopped flowing, Steve pulled out his finger, checked for vitals, pulled back the lid of her eye, and touched her eyeball. He shook his head, wiped his hands on her coat, stood, and almost nonchalantly walked away. With Steve out of the picture, the camera now took in the slack jaw and half-opened eyes of the dead woman and an empty city cul-de-sac.

Deep quickly reached out to tap the screen black.

Shifting his weight to the side, Deep rotated Lacey until she was looking in his eyes. "Lacey, you said Steve was a software engineer. Was he in the military? Did he serve on the frontline?"

"No." She shook her head. What was Deep talking about? Why would he think that?

"Police? ROTC? EMS-Fire?"

"No, are you kidding me? Steve isn't the hero type. He's the geeky, latte-drinking, book-reading type. And to tell you the truth, he's a little bit overboard about germs. If I hadn't

118

seen this video myself, I'd never believe that Steve would stick his finger into that woman's neck."

"Are you okay? Your face is a little grey."

Lacey swiped a hand across her brow. "I'm overcome."

"Do you want me to get you a cup of tea? Maybe lace it with some whiskey?"

"Please, don't let go of me." Lacey leaned her forehead against his chin.

Deep tucked her back into his arms and changed the image of Steve on the screen. Lacey was glad when he moved the conversation to safer grounds.

"He's in good shape."

"Yes," Lacey agreed. "He goes to the gym every day. His father died when he was in his forties — type two diabetes and heart-disease. Steve is fighting his genes."

Deep shook his head from behind her. "No, that's not the reason."

"Why would Steve lie about his dad's health?"

Deep tapped the screen to start the same video again. "No clue. He's trained, though. Very well-trained."

As Lacey watched the scene, she curled her fingers tightly into Deep's knees. Deep rubbed his hands over hers, then loosened her grip.

"I'm sorry," she said with chagrin. For a second, it felt like she was heading over the top of a rollercoaster, grabbing onto whatever might keep her from flying from the cart. Lacey hadn't realized she'd actually grabbed hold of his leg.

Squeezing her shoulders to hold her in place, Deep stood and swung his leg free. He pulled another chair up and sat so their knees were touching, his elbows on his thighs, his hands resting on her legs.

"Lacey, I need you to tell me how you met this guy."

Chapter Twelve

Lacey

Saturday

Lacey's eyes lost their focus as her mind spun backwards in time to when and how she had met Steve. It was that horrible day. She'd been racing down the road, thinking that if she could get home, she could figure this all out. Where should she start the story for Deep? She decided it was best to simply answer his question – how did she meet Steve? Lacey rolled her lips in, and with her chin dipped nearly to her chest, she looked up at Deep through her eyelashes.

His eyes hardened. "That right there. That's why you scare the hell out me."

Lacey lifted her chin and widened her eyes.

"No. You're not going to look at me like you're an angel. No."

"I. . ." Lacey was about to defend herself, but she didn't have a clue what Deep was talking about.

"Lacey, look. I'm not playing games with you. Straight up, here's the way it stands with me. I was working field support for Lynx the day I first saw you. I was eyes and ears and backup if she needed it, but the case was need-to-know. I didn't know why we were at your gallery talking about Iniquus's artwork. All I knew was that when I saw you, everything changed. I never felt that kind of connection with anyone before in my life. And I *know* you felt it, too. That's why I told you my real name and not my call name, something I got raked over the coals for by the Iniquus owners."

Deep's eyes had changed in energy. This must be what Deep looked like on the battlefield. His intensity was almost unbearable, and Lacey wanted to push back in her chair and give herself a cushion of air between them.

"I asked you out for dinner, and you said you were dating Steve. It was like taking a body blow. Physically painful. But I walked away."

"You never tried to call me or change my mind," Lacey pointed out.

"I don't do that, Lacey. You said no. No, to me, is a clear statement. No doesn't mean maybe. No doesn't mean I should try harder or go after you like a predator. I've got sisters. If one of them ever said no to a guy, and he kept pushing? I promise you, if I walked into the picture, it wouldn't go well for him. It's a matter of respect. I trust that you know your mind. You knew how to get in touch with me. And when and if you were going to say yes, you could."

Wow. That was . . . something. What Deep said went against all of her understanding of how men and women interacted. Maybe it had to do with her Georgia upbringing, where girls were taught to flirt and act inaccessible. She'd always been told it was important to make the boys jump through hoops to get to the girl. The boys had to prove to everyone that the girl was a hard-won prize, and therefore valuable. She would look easy and cheap if she said yes the first time a man asked her out. So of course, Lacey would never have said yes to a first request. Besides, she had been in a relationship with Steve. Had been? Yes, that relationship seemed to belong to a different lifetime, one where people didn't shove flash drives down her blouse and die in front of her. No meant no — that was a culture shock to Lacey.

"You called me, Lacey. You had a choice between phoning me or Steve – or the police, or anyone else. You called *me*. Why?"

Pain slid across Lacey's jaw line.

"There." Deep pointed at her. "Say that out loud."

"I wanted to feel safe, and I thought you were safe."

"I am," he said definitively, taking both of her hands in his. "You are safe with me. But Lacey, in order to keep you safe, I have to know everything that's going on. You can't censor or edit the story. I'll miss something. And those little somethings can end up making the difference."

Lacey pulled her hands free and raked her fingers through her hair, fisting her hands around the ends. If she told him, they'd kill her. And if they killed her, they'd kill Deep, too. She hadn't thought through the ramifications of her phone call. Hadn't even realized what they were until this conversation started. But here, she'd sucked him into the vortex that had been spinning her world. Could the murder of Leo Bardman be connected to the horrible day that she and Steve met? It had to. Somehow. Because the dead man had called her Danika.

"Okay, I can see this is going to be a process," Deep said. "We'll take it one step at a time. One thing you can't do, though, is lie. If you can't tell me the truth, I'd rather you be quiet. Can we agree on that much?"

Lacey nodded.

Deep chewed on the inside of his cheek while he considered her, then he rubbed his hands down his thighs and leaned forward. Very quietly, he said, "When I was on the battlefield in Afghanistan, I wasn't afraid of dying. I was a little afraid I'd be injured — lose my legs or my sight. Afraid of what that could mean to the rest of my life. But what I was really afraid of was that, in a moment of personal weakness, I might let my brothers down. That I'd make a mistake that would put them at risk."

Lacey watched his lips forming words. She had wondered since the moment they met what it would be like to kiss Deep's beautiful lips. She pictured him on the battlefield with his mouth pulled tight and grim, worrying about his brothers. And her heart swelled with pain. Thank God he had survived. Had kept his legs and sight. Had come home – the "to be with me" part of that thought was pushed back into the recesses of her brain. It felt too selfish for Lacey to allow it to fully form.

"That's how I'm feeling right now." As he spoke, Deep's brown eyes had darkened to almost black. "Like there's a landmine somewhere near your feet and if I don't spot it first, it's going to be my fault that you trip the wire. And Lacey, I need you to hear this." He paused until she fully focused on his eyes, then he pressed on. "I'm not asking for my feelings to be your feelings. But the very first time I saw you, I felt like you were meant for me. And if there is such thing as an instant connection, a belonging – well, I felt that. Intensely. That conversation is for another time. But I figure if I lay everything out on the table for you to see, then maybe you'll feel like you could do the same." He didn't wait for her to answer. He used raised eyebrows to end that statement then he moved on asking, "What can you tell me about meeting Steve?"

Lacey was a little shell-shocked by Deep's words. It made speaking feel like a new skill, but she worked to make her lips and tongue form words. "I remember driving too fast down a country road. The speed limit was 55, but I was going a lot faster than that. I was headed toward the highway, back toward DC. I slowed for a turn. I remember putting on my blinker, but not stopping at the stop sign. The next thing I knew, Steve was calling my name. I woke up, and Steve had his hands around my throat—he was trying to keep me from hurting my neck. Apparently, I lost control and hit a tree. He said he was travelling behind me when I swerved after I hit a deer."

"This is the story of how you met Steve?"

"Yes."

"He was calling your name? How'd he know your name?"

Lacey shrugged. "I imagine he looked in my wallet or something."

"Okay, go on. He was first on scene after you lost control of your car and crashed."

"Yes, I was scared. My whole body hurt. Every inch of me. My chest. My face – when the airbag shot out, it took the top layers off my face. It was like acid being poured onto my skin. When the paramedics got there, they put a collar on me. Steve held my hand; he didn't leave my side. He even rode in the back of the ambulance when they took me to the hospital."

Lacey watched a cloud pass over Deep's face, but he didn't say anything.

"I didn't have any broken bones or anything, but I had deep bruises and whiplash. I had to wear the collar for six weeks." Lacey leaned over to look in the mug. It was empty, so she swallowed hard, trying to unstick her words.

Deep nodded.

"Steve was wonderful to me after the accident. I don't have any family here to help me." Lacey cleared her throat. "I'm from Georgia, originally. I moved up here for grad school and to work for Uncle Bartholomew. Anyway, Steve was there for me – helped me around the house, did the groceries, you know—the stuff boyfriends do." And now that she was looking back on things with a little perspective, Steve seemed to just move into her life and make himself at home. One minute she was coming back to awareness in her bashed in car and the next she had a live-in boyfriend, readymade, taking care of her like they had been together for a long time. With a little distance and discernment, the speed of their relationship did seem . . . odd.

"We can get an email to him. I can send it through encryption software so it'll be untraceable, but if you say something personal, he'll know it's you. That way, he'll know you're safe. Put his mind to rest." When Lacey said nothing Deep said, "Or your mom and dad. They're probably pretty worried about you. I think I remember you saying you were an only child, so no sisters or brothers, but your parents—we can get word to them."

Lacey shook her head.

"Friends that would be worried?"

"I don't have any of that." Lacey focused on the rug. "It's not that I'm anti-social, it's simply that . . . It seems from the little bit that I know about you, our childhoods were probably night and day. When I left Georgia to go to grad school here in DC and work for my uncle, I wanted to leave that part of my life behind. I needed a fresh start."

"Did you get a fresh start? Do you think any of this has to do with family ties outside of your uncle and the art world? Something you left behind in Georgia?"

"Surely not. It's been years since I had contact with anyone down there. I've been in DC for five years. I was busy with grad school and work, and then just with work. Seems everyone I know is associated with the gallery and my job, besides Steve, of course. I'm not close enough to anyone up here that I think I should reach out to them. Uncle Bartholomew – but he's in Bali and probably has no clue this is going on."

"And Steve?" Deep asked once again.

Lacey lifted her gaze to the window and held it there for a long moment. Bony twigs from a tree branch tapped against the pane like fingers working on a tempo to accompany the whistle of the wind. Cold and bleak. Lacey wanted to go back upstairs and curl herself under the covers of her borrowed bed.

"Do you find it odd how many pictures there are of Steve and me together in those files?" She glanced at Deep briefly, saw his keen eyes on her —thoughtful and intelligent—but he didn't comment.

Lacey knew that he had absorbed all of her words and would process through them. He hadn't missed a thing. She wished in that moment that she did have friends and family who cared about her, who sat on the couch and sobbed as they begged the TV cameras for people to come forward with information. But the truth was, nobody cared. Lacey felt the shame she always felt when people realized she was disposable. That nobody gave two hoots if she lived or not. She preferred that people assumed, like her lawyer Mr. Reynolds did, that she came from a good upstanding family. That she belonged somewhere.

"There are pictures of me alone, and pictures that have me and some strangers, but the only person that I recognize is Steve—no pictures included me with my friends or colleagues. That's kind of curious, don't you think?"

Chapter Thirteen

Steve

Saturday Afternoon

Sprawled in an armchair in Monroe's office, Steve pitched a pencil into the air and caught it time and again. He was listening to the tapes that Higgins had recorded from Danika's apartment the night before. It was all crap. Many of the words the men used seemed to be slang, and Steve didn't understand the meaning behind things like, "Crank man, he's in the tub." Maybe that wasn't what the guy said at all. It was hard to tell between the crackling of the microphones and the guttural accents of the men speaking.

Steve would be glad when the Slovakian translator finished the English transcripts and handed them to him. Though she'd been told to push the pedal down on this assignment, she couldn't be fast enough, from Steve's point of view. Every second counted. He rammed his imagined pictures of Lacey

131

being tortured as far back and as deep down in his mind as he could. If he panicked, he wouldn't be helping her.

Leaning forward to tap the start arrow, again, Steve listened hard. No, he didn't recognize these men by their voices, but it didn't matter. One member of the Zoric family or another – they all worked together as one body. And Pavle Zoric was the brains.

Pavle was the one who'd brought Danika Zoric to the US when she was twelve, when her birth family couldn't afford to feed her anymore. She had earned her keep as a prostitute all the way through high school. After that, she danced and worked hard to lose the remnants of her Slovakian accent. Now, the family found her useful for other things. Most of it had to do with information-gathering and blackmail. Why earn a hundred dollars turning a trick when you can videotape an affair and use it like the proverbial goose laying golden eggs? It had been her idea. And Pavle appreciated her creativity and her business acumen.

Monroe moved into the room and put an uncharacteristically fatherly hand on Steve's shoulder. "I'm sorry you lost her."

Steve froze as he tried to interpret that sentence.

Monroe pulled out a rolling chair, sat down with a thud, and pursed his lips. "Hell of a thing, to stick your fingers into someone's neck. You would have been a hero if you'd saved her. 'Course, if you'd saved her, you'd be on desk duty for the rest of your career. Your face would be too recognizable to use you in the field anymore. As it is, you can't interface with anyone associated with our investigation. Your cover's blown to smithereens."

Steve felt lightheaded and reached up to rub the back of his neck, trying to force some blood into his brain. Monroe was talking about the reporter who took the ricochet at the press conference, not Lacey. Lacey still might be alright. Well, alright in the Zoric family's hands would be stretching it – but maybe alive.

Monroe pulled out his phone, checked the screen, then crammed it back in his pocket. "Higgins catch up with Danika?"

"Not yet," Steve said. "He's gone home to get some shuteye. Last I talked to him, there were men in her apartment. No sound from her. I'm listening to those tapes now – translation should be coming up soon." Steve rubbed a hand over his five o'clock shadow. "When Higgins saw the team leave, he went up to take a look around the apartment, and everything was in place. No signs of trouble. But Danika's keys were on the kitchen table, and her purse was in the bathroom. He found her phone on the bedside table."

"When's the last time *you* got some shuteye?" Monroe asked.

"Not happening until I get Lacey back. Even if you order me home. So don't even go there with me."

"Danika, then. What are the plausible explanations that that's all normal?"

"She doesn't carry her purse unless she's carrying something for work – weapons, what-have-you. Instead she has a coin purse that she keeps in her pocket with her ID and Metro pass. Higgins didn't find that. She has a house key on a chain necklace that she sometimes wears when she wants to be hands-free. She's not as addicted to her phone as some people. Besides, she knows Pavle follows where she goes with the GPS app. I can see her going out to visit a friend, not wanting Pavle to find her, having too much to drink, and crashing on their couch."

"You don't believe that's what happened."

Steve took a minute to explain that Danika had called to let him know that Pavle had Lacey and she was trying to lure him back to her apartment. But Higgins had warned him about the ambush in time.

Monroe tugged at his earlobe. "I think whether she's alive or not at this point depends on the answer to two questions — do they need her anymore? And does her benefit to the family outweigh any drawbacks?"

"What's going on at the warehouse?" Steve asked.

"It's been almost seventy-two hours since anyone turned the lights on. No one's set off the motion-sensor cameras. Their artist hasn't shown up, but he's got to be going in soon. The art show's this week and one canvas still isn't finished."

"Are you putting someone in place to watch?"

"We'll have to depend on the cameras. I haven't got the manpower to cover the warehouse, too. I've already got extra agents in the field trying to hunt down Lacey Stuart, and now we're going to have to try to catch up with Danika Zoric." Monroe got up and shuffled some papers around his desk. "You let yourself get personally involved. It's a risk all of us take in the field. It happens to the best of us." He turned to catch Steve's eye. "So who is it you fell for, Danika or Lacey?"

"Laccy, of course," Steve muttered.

"She's a beautiful girl, smart, on the way to being a big success in her industry – well, before the Iniquus shit happened, anyway. She was exactly what we needed, too – no real ties to anyone but her great uncle, no one to give you the look-over and warn her away. Probably a little lonely, a little needy. She was the perfect cover for an easy sting. Funny how everything just seemed to unfold so perfectly. It's like it was meant to be. I was glad when you joined our task force to pull down the Zoric family. Surprised. But glad. Have we moved forward enough in the case that you can give me some background now? Why is it that the terrorism task force is interested in the Zoric family?"

"I can tell you this much. When I was trying to find the Zorics' weak spot, we landed on Bartholomew Winslow. He was on Pavle's hook."

"Hook? How?"

"Extortion," Steve said. "The specifics I can't share with you right now. We still want this compartmentalized and need to know."

"Understood." Monroe said with a nod.

"You know the name Krokov?"

"Krokov?" Monroe shook his head. "No, I haven't heard his name before."

"He's dead so any part he's playing in this is over. Publicly, Radovan Krokov bought a few paintings from the Bartholomew Winslow Gallery. The CIA mentioned it in their briefing on the Krokov family sent in from their Slovakian station. We found out after Krokov's death that he was actually Winslow's long-time secret lover. This is interesting in that Danika Zoric was working some kind of con either *on* Krokov or *with* him. When she was with Krokov, Danika called herself Lacey Stuart. That was long before Lacey's accident happened. What kind of relationship Danika had with Krokov at his death, I'm not clear. But I do know that Krokov had known

Danika since she was a young teen. She was some kind of olive branch between the families. A peace offering, maybe."

"You mean a *piece* offering?" Monroe asked with derision. "When did Danika start calling herself Lacey Stuart?"

"June of last year. It was when Danika started to help Winslow work on the show, gathering the paintings they wanted to steal." Steve's head was pounding, and he wondered if Monroe might have some Advil or something in his desk drawer. "We discovered that Pavle Zoric gave Winslow that list of paintings he wanted to have collected, and we knew that Winslow was actively trying to set up a show with those pieces so they could be stolen all at once. We brought that to the arts task force, hoping they could take our players off the field. Then we discovered that you guys were already going after the family. But then Lacey was in the car accident. My coming to Lacey's rescue was a huge break—it gave me the idea for the bigger con – more money, more players. I fed the idea to Danika, and she pitched it to Pavle. This turn around meant we were going to be able to take down almost the whole family in a single sting. But to do that, we needed you, and arts and us all working together."

"And it was happenstance that put you on the road behind Lacey Stuart when she had her car accident? Life doesn't happen that way."

"Danika," Steve said. "I still think it was Danika who caused this shit to go down with Lacey that day. And for the life of me, I can't figure out how or why. Especially since Danika saved Lacey's life."

"What's this?" Monroe asked.

"The day of the car accident, I got a call from Danika. She's screaming that Musclav is going to kill some woman and ruin everything. She said I had to stop him. Musclav was going after Lacey, but I caught up with him and told him to leave it alone, that I'd handle Lacey."

"Why would Musclav Zoric be trying to kill Lacey Stuart?"

"I'm sorry, I'm not going to be able to tell you the particulars. Those details are classified with a different program, and you haven't been read in."

"The day of the accident is the day you joined the team." Monroe paused. "When I ordered you to date Lacey, it was so you had an inside track and could keep her safe while the con played out. And I have to admit your con was genius, really. Up until then, the Zorics had kept us at arm's length. Once you stepped up to the plate with the insurance game, things changed. It was an important move. It *had to* happen in order to take the Zorics down." His last words sounded deflated.

Steve thought Monroe was rationalizing. Steve's mom always said that if Steve had to rationalize something, he'd know that he'd done that something wrong. Involving Lacey had definitely been wrong. "Looks like I did a shit job on the protection front."

"What does Lacey know about all of this?"

"Nothing. She didn't remember anything from the accident, only that she was going to Radovan's house to hang some art and woke up stuck in her car. Other than that, she did her thing at the gallery, she dated me, and she talked about getting a puppy when the spring warmed things up." Steve voice cracked as he realized he was talking about Lacey in the past tense. "She led a quiet life. A nice life."

Monroe scowled. "I thought we had the Zoric family all but cuffed and deported. Off our darned streets."

"I think we need to focus on Danika. She's had something up her sleeve." Steve was now pacing manically in the small confines of Monroe's office.

"Is Danika smart enough to outthink Pavle?"

"Street smarts and high IQ make up for a lack of higher education. I'm sure she thought she was smart enough to pull one over on Pavle. I guess if she succeeds in her endgame, that'll tell us who can outthink the other."

Monroe pulled at his eyebrow, a sign that he was in his head moving parts around, trying out theories, rejecting them, and trying out others. "She could be in the wind. She might have had an exit plan if things got iffy."

"Maybe." Steve let his thoughts do what they would, trying to get a sense of whether or not that was a believable scenario. "That doesn't feel right to me," he concluded.

"Sit down already. You're jumping on my nerves," Monroe growled. "What does feel right?"

Steve moved to a chair, but he couldn't stop his leg from jackhammering the floor. He didn't answer Monroe's question. Nothing felt right. Nothing at all. He shook his head. He had nada.

"Yeah," Monroe said. "I'm right back in the ditch with my tires spinning over how Lacey ended up slung over some guy's shoulder and disappearing from view."

"I feel like this all ties into the car accident. I can't figure out, though, what Musclav was trying to accomplish. If he caught Lacey and killed her, the Zorics wouldn't have the art in one location to steal which was the directive from Slovakia. If he killed her, there would be no art to ship home."

Monroe tapped Steve's knee to make him stop jiggling. "How's that?"

"If Lacey were murdered, her Uncle Bartholomew wouldn't have stuck around for his turn at the point of a gun or in a prison cell. He would have done exactly what he did when he was caught stealing from Iniquus – headed for Bali. And the Zoric family? Instead of one hit, they'd have to make a dozen to get the artwork that they needed for their Slovakian family members."

"This whole thing's a powder keg. I think our mistake was not bringing Lacey in and explaining that to her." Monroe pointed a fat finger at Steve. "If she gets in front of a news camera. . ." He shook his head. "She needs to keep her mouth shut."

"I hope she's still alive, and I get the chance to tell her that."

Chapter Fourteen

Lacey

Saturday

Lacey woke up when the persistent beeping of the oven timer sounded. She'd been napping on the living room sofa at Deep's insistence. He said that being a witness to a crime was sort of like being a traveler in a foreign country, where your brain is turned to the highest setting all the time, trying to understand the language, the culture, and the new sights. It was fatiguing, and she needed the extra sleep. Lacey couldn't argue with that. She'd been exhausted ever since the day of her accident way back in September. Her brain, indeed, had needed a little extra sleep.

She stumbled into the kitchen, rubbing her eyes, and punched the timer on the stove as the back door swung open. Without thinking about it, Lacey shuffled into Deep's arms, her cheek nestling into the dampness that clung to his sweater. She closed her eyes and breathed in the scent of wool and

143

wind. Pushing to her toes, Lacey tipped her face back for a kiss. It was only when the electric sizzle of soft lips on hers made its way through her body that Lacey realized what she'd done.

"Oh!" Lacey lowered her heels and looked wide-eyed at Deep.

Deep grinned down at her, his hands still wrapped around her waist. "Hello to you, too. That was a nice welcome home, and all I did was take out the garbage. What happens if I go grocery shopping?" He wiggled his brows.

She knew he was teasing her, but all the same, Lacey's cheeks warmed to bright pink. Deep released her and headed over to the oven to pull out the lasagna he had re-heated.

"Wait. Do that again," Lacey said.

Deep set the pan on top of the stove and turned his gaze on Lacey. "Do what again?"

"Kiss me."

He offered up a slow smile that warmed his eyes. "You have to say the magic words."

"Pretty please?"

"Close enough." Deep grinned and moved in her direction. He wrapped his arms around her waist, and started to lean down.

"No, sorry, not like that."

He stalled.

"Just stand there, okay? Let me kiss you." Lacey watched Deep's face become a complicated jumble of merriment and confusion. But he dropped his hands to his sides as she approached him. She put her hands on his shoulders, pulled herself back up on her toes, and tilted her head. "Put your hands back around my waist," she instructed. "Okay, now kiss me."

And he did.

The second kiss was even better than the first. It was like a switch was turned on in her body, and she tingled down to her toes. He moved her around to deepen the kiss and add a tangle of their tongues, not letting her up until they were both breathless.

"You do that really well," Lacey said. Her hands rested on his chest, and she could feel his accelerated heartbeat. She shook her head a little to clear her thoughts. "But I need you to kiss me again—this time, no tongue. Actually, don't really kiss me. Just lean down – I need to be able to think. I can't think when your lips are on mine."

Now the confusion was gone from his eyes, and they were bright with full-on laughter. "Should my hands be here?"

"Uh huh. Lean down, and hush yourself, would you, please?"

He stood that way for about the count of three, and then he was kissing her again. "Sorry," he said. "I couldn't help myself."

Lacey took a step back. "How tall are you?"

"Six feet even."

"Steve is five-foot-eleven." Her brow was pulled in tight. "Isn't that curious?"

"You've lost me."

Lacey reached out and grabbed Deep's hand so she could pull him into the dining room. She sat in the chair behind Lynx's ThinkPad, where she'd spent the morning cataloguing the photos.

She flipped through a couple of them. "Here, look. I'm kissing, Steve." Excitement painted her words.

Deep gave her a good long look. She thought the smile that she usually found in his chocolate-brown eyes had dimmed. He pulled a chair over so they were thigh to thigh, and he could see the screen from the same angle as she.

Lacey moved forward in the file. "Here, I'm kissing Steve again. Can you do something to put these photos side by side?"

"Sure." Deep turned the computer toward him and his fingers moved over the keyboard.

"Okay, so I'm five-foot-one in bare feet. If I'm wearing heels, they usually add another four inches or so, making me about five-five. Look at the picture on the right. This one seems about right to me. See how when I kissed Steve, I rose up on my toes and tipped my head back? When I do that, he still had to bend his head to kiss me. But look at this one on the left. Same dress. Same heels. But look, in this picture, my heels were flat on the ground, and I'm leaning in with only the slightest tilt in my head. Now look at my dress. See? It comes just under my knee in the right-hand photo. That's where I like my clothes to be cut, but here on this other woman the dress is slightly above her knees. She's the same size around the hips though. We probably have the same dimensions except for our heights."

"You're absolutely right, Lacey. Look, different time of day too," Deep pointed out. "See? Same location, but look in the picture in the right, sun shining in the windows. In the left-hand side, the sun's coming from the opposite direction. There's about four hours' difference in these two shots. Different weather, too. It's easy enough to reset the date and time stamp on a camera. I'd say from the angle of the sun this last one is mid-afternoon. Where were you supposed to be around three?"

Lacey looked down on the schedule she had diagrammed on the white paper table covering. "At the time of the second photograph, I was supposed to be at the gallery for a meeting with my uncle. This is up the street from my apartment, so the wrong side of town."

Deep studied the picture. "The right-hand picture with the female on her toes —"

"That's me."

"Are you sure?"

"Yes, that's why I was experimenting in the kitchen. I'm sure I stood on my toes and tilted back when I kissed Steve."

"Oh, so that's what was happening in the kitchen? I was a lab rat?" Deep sat back and crossed his arms over his chest, making his biceps bulge. "And here I thought my magnetic personality had finally drawn you in."

Lacey's face brightened with her smile, and there was even the tiniest fringe of laughter mixed in.

Deep leaned in and kissed the tip of her nose. "That's the first time you've really smiled since the gallery."

"It's the first time I've honestly smiled since. . ." Her eyes clouded over as she looked past him into the living room like she was seeing ghosts. "Well, in a very long time."

Chapter Fifteen

DEEP

Saturday Evening

"This is pretty amazing," Deep said, staring at his screen. They had each moved back to their computers to try to work through the data, looking for more clues about Lacey's mysterious double. Hoping for understanding.

"What's that?" Lacey uncoiled herself from her twisted pretzel position on her chair and moved to the seat next to his.

"I'm using this face-recognition programming. See here? I'll put up three pictures. A. B. C."

Lacey let her eyes scan over the images.

"This is you on the left. This is the mystery girl on the right. The one in the center is an overlay that points out the differences, so that an operative can look to see if prosthetics are used to change her appearance. The computer analyzed her coloring – eyes, hair, and skin tone. Your eyes and hers are pigmented differently. The mystery woman is wearing colored contact lenses. The computer suggests that she used a hair colorant because her hair doesn't have the variant shades mixed in like yours does. Hers is monochromatic. And you're both wearing makeup in the exact same shades."

"Which means?"

"That she knew your brand and the color name and used the same ones you did. Those differences are probably only visible to computer analysis, though. People aren't that observant. No – that's not accurate. What happens is the brain interprets what it sees within the context of the known. So if one of you were in a room, walked out, and the other woman took your place – the person who saw this happen would read it as the same person even with these subtle variations."

"I would agree with that. Even though it's me in some of those pictures, I looked at all of the photos and I didn't immediately see a difference. Now that I know there are two of us, it's pretty obvious to me. Tell me about photo B."

"The center photo is what you need to pay attention to. Here, where the dotted white line runs along—it shows the geographical differences in the planes of the face. The eye shape is almost identical. The noses are almost the same. Yours is only millimeters shorter, see that?"

"Her lips are fuller, too. Actually, that's the most significant difference."

"Let me magnify this. There, do you see how she's used a lip pencil to shape her lips and make them a little smaller? Not enough that it's obvious. She's good at this, whoever she is."

Lacey rubbed her index finger over her bottom lip. "Hmm."

"What, hmm?" Deep tipped his head.

"The night in the bar. I was sitting on the stool, and I felt trapped. Leo Bardman was looming over by the exit. And the scotch-on-the-rocks guy, the FBI guy who grabbed my ankle, was at the end of the bar, blocking the hall that lead to the bathrooms and the kitchen. The FBI guy was staring at my mouth the whole time. I thought I had spinach in my teeth. That or he was really into red lipstick."

"Always a possibility." Deep winked. "Go through that part for me again. Higgins was there before or after Bardman showed up?"

"Who's Higgins?"

"The FBI guy."

"You know him?" Lacey asked.

"Yeah. Well, I worked a case with him last year. Good guy. I'm trying to figure out what he's got to do with you, though. It's possible he was re-assigned, or was lent to another task force."

"Because normally he . . ."

151

"Works for Violent Gangs. He's not on their Arts Crime team. And from the files on the thumb drive, I'd guess that that's what we're looking at here — some kind of arts con."

"Did you recognize Steve, too?" Lacey asked.

Deep shook his head. "I don't know Steve. Who got there first, did you see? Higgins or Bardman?"

"Higgins was there when I arrived. He already had a drink in his hand. He was sitting alone for the whole time I was waiting for Steve, and I thought that was a little suspicious."

"Suspicious, how? Do you think he was looking for Bardman? Do you think he recognized Bardman when he came in?"

"Higgins? No, he was kind of fixated on me. He was dangling his drink in front of his face to hide the fact that he was staring. It's not unheard of that a guy would stare at me at a bar, but he didn't make any kind of move. He didn't lift his glass in a salute; he didn't order me a drink; he didn't move any closer. He simply sat at the end of the bar alone."

"You were alone – that could have been seen as suspicious, too." Deep countered.

"True, but I was waiting for someone. Do you think that was the case here too? Do you think he was waiting for someone else to show up? Maybe he was off-duty, and when he saw the guy die, Higgins might have thought I had something to do with it, so he tried to hold me for the police? No, that couldn't be it."

"Why's that?"

"You saw Steve in the video. He did first aid on that woman. Wouldn't Higgins's first job be to save that guy somehow? He'd have to prioritize, right? How'd I become the priority?"

"Good questions. I don't know. But you're right. If he was assigned to follow you, *especially* if he was assigned to protect you, then he'd have to stay with you and not get diverted."

Lacey rocked around in her chair as she stared at the computer screen.

Deep checked his watch. "It's getting close to dinner time. Are you hungry?"

"I wish I could —"

Deep put a hand on her arm to get her to stop talking. Footsteps on Lynx's front steps had caught his focus. He signaled for Lacey to be quiet. Then, with hands cuffing her upper arms, he shifted her out of her chair and moved her into the bathroom. He pushed in the lock button and pulled the door quietly shut. He automatically shifted into combat breathing – inhale for four — as he moved to put himself between the person coming through the front door and Lacey. Hold for four — he pulled his Glock from the back of his waistband. His finger lined up with the trigger guard; his elbows tucked tight, ready to punch out and fire if need be. He pointed the barrel in the low ready position. Exhale for four — there was a scrape of the lock, and then a woman burst through the door.

When she saw the gun, she screamed. Her eyes tracked up to Deep's face. "Holy crap, you nearly scared the actual shit out me," Sarah said, her hands on her cheeks.

A grin spread across Deep's face, but his heart still thrummed against his ribs. "Sorry about that, Sarah. I wasn't expecting anyone." He tucked his gun back away.

"It's my fault. Lynx called and said she lent you her house – she said you were working on a project that needed your undivided attention. I forgot you were here. I . . ." She looked back over her shoulder across the street to her house, then back to Deep. "I have no idea why I'm here. You scared the thought right out of my head."

Deep moved over to give her a warm hug. "I'm so sorry." He caught her under the elbow and pulled Sarah farther into the house, shutting the door behind her. "Good to see you, though. How are the kids? Mikey? Ruby?"

"They're a mess, as usual." Sarah grinned. "Are you here by yourself?" Sarah's eyes seemed to focus on the two sets of chairs that where set close to each other on either side of the table each with an open computer. The white paper covered the table with the timeline penned over its length. The notes Deep and Lacey had been jotting weren't readable from that distance, but Deep still moved to block Sarah's line of sight.

"All by myself."

"Good, then come to dinner tomorrow night. I'll make spaghetti and invite everyone over. Justin and Manny will be really glad to see you. Jilly-Bean still hero-worships you. It would mean a lot to her to see you."

"That's such a tempting invitation, thank you. But this assignment's got my full attention. It's time-sensitive. I have to stay fully focused on it. But when it's over, I'm going to take you up on a neighborhood spaghetti feast."

"Okay. Just let me know." Sarah turned to leave.

"Uh, Sarah?" Deep caught her elbow. "Did you need something from Lexi's house?"

Sarah threw her hands in the air. "Flour. I told Mikey I'd bake him cookies if he could be quiet while the baby was sleeping. Who would think he'd be able to follow through? I'm all out of flour, though."

"Wait here, and I'll go get the bag for you." Deep moved toward the kitchen. He turned back as he made his way through the dining room arch to make sure Sarah understood that "wait here" meant she shouldn't wander around looking at anything. Sarah kept her focus on the ceiling. She understood enough about what they did at Iniquus that she knew better than to pry. Deep grabbed the blue and white paper sack of

Pillsbury flour, slid it in a plastic grocery bag, and took it in to Sarah.

Sarah kissed him on the cheek and jogged down the front stairs with a backward wave.

Deep went to tap on the bathroom door and let Lacey know it was safe to come out. Wide-eyed, she rolled into his arms and grasped him tightly around the waist. He wrapped his arms around her and felt her body relax into him.

"She scared me to death. I thought it might be that woman from the photographs."

Chapter Sixteen

Sunday Morning

Lacey stood at the bottom of the steps, watching Deep work at his computer like a maestro over a grand piano. He was focused on the screen as his fingers flew over the keyboard. The morning hush was broken by a family outside calling to each other as they got into their car to head to church.

"Do you ever sleep?" Lacey asked as she moved into the room. Deep looked up with a smile. his fingers still tap-tap-tapping.

"I'm a hound on a scent." He reached out a hand and pulled her gently into his lap, then rubbed her hair with his nose. "I'm sorry you didn't sleep very well last night."

"How'd you know?" Lacey lay her cheek against his head and tried to read over the information on his screen.

"You were thrashing around a lot, talking in your sleep. It's pretty typical for people in a safehouse. The anxiety from what

157

landed them there makes recuperative sleep difficult. If you need medication to help, I can get you something."

"We'll see," Lacey said. "What's this you're doing?"

"I was trying to figure out who was in the photos from the flash drive. We know there was you and someone you call Steve Adamic."

"You don't think that's his name?" She turned to look at Deep. He rewarded her with a kiss.

"Probably not. But I don't make any assumptions. We know that there's a guy that you call Steve Adamic. Is that his name? At this point, it's irrelevant. We can tag him, and that's what we care about. There are four other people in the photographs, right?"

"Yes." Lacey twisted back until she was facing his laptop where it rested on a rolling computer table.

He had pulled up a gallery shot showing each of the people on the flash drive. "Using my access to our facial recognition database, I found this one woman here." He pointed. "Her name is Lynda Stamos."

"She's the agent for Reagan O'Neil. One the artists on the flash drive."

"Have you met her?" Deep asked.

"Lynda Stamos? No, not in person. I recognize the name. She was in your database? Does that mean she's broken a law?"

"She's in there because she went to the White House to do a consultation, and they run background checks on all White House visitors."

"Oh." Lacey leaned forward onto her elbows to get a better look, and Deep's hands moved down her back to her hips. Lacey was suddenly aware of how their bodies were lined up.

"So after I realized she was an artists' agent, I wondered if the other three people were, as well."

"Were they?" Lacey twisted around.

Deep caught hold of her and held her still. His eyes dilated to almost all black with a predatory look that he softened with a chuckle and a shake of his head. "If you're going to sit on my lap, you're going to have to sit still."

Lacey felt the air charge with sexual tension and blushed as her body responded, heat spreading across her chest and catching her breath.

Deep held her tightly to him as he stood up. "Are you hungry? I made coffee." With his arm still around her, he moved toward the kitchen.

Deep had changed directions on purpose. Lacey wondered why he hadn't taken advantage of that moment. Maybe she had misheard or misinterpreted what he had said before about how he felt about her. Maybe she misjudged those kitchen kisses. "Not hungry. Antsy."

"I wanted to talk to you about maybe taking a field trip and get you out of the house for a little bit."

"Wait, I was asking about the other three people in the photos?" Lacey reminded him.

"Three of the four are agents for the artists on the list. I was working on number four when you came down. Why don't I make some pancakes while you tell me what had you in knots last night?"

"I was thinking about Steve."

Deep offered up an encouraging nod as he opened the fridge.

"I'm trying to figure out if he's a good guy or a bad guy. Who do you think Steve is in all of this?"

"No flour, I gave it to Sarah yesterday. Omelets?"

"That's fine, anything really. Just a cup of coffee would be lovely."

"You need to eat. It helps your body deal with the stress. Protein." He raised his brows as if he wouldn't take any argument on the fact. Lacey thought that was probably a face his mom used to keep him in line when he was a boy. Deep reached for a bowl and started cracking eggs. "About Steve? I'm afraid to speculate."

"Please do anyway." Lacey went to the cupboard to pull out the dishes and flatware to set the table. And for a moment in time, everything seemed domestic and normal. Happy, even. For a moment, she could almost pretend nothing was wrong.

But then Deep answered her question.

"Clean file could mean nothing at all. Or it could be a good cover. He's well-trained—that's not speculation. He's fit and ready – that's not speculation. Higgins is FBI and was in the bar watching you – that's interesting. Could be that Steve was running late and asked Higgins to serve as his eyes and ears to make sure you were okay. Could be Steve is under Higgins's spotlight and Higgins was waiting for Steve, just like you were. Could be Higgins has nothing to do with Steve, and it was all happenstance. But that last one doesn't feel right. I'm pretty sure, though, that Steve is playing on the good-guy team."

Lacey poured coffee into the mugs. She doctored hers with sugar and milk and set the mug of black coffee by Deep's plate.

Deep wandered over and took a sip. "Thank you." He took another one, then set his mug down and moved back to the counter. "I can't imagine another reason that they'd let a stranger from a car accident jump in the back of the rescue squad – he must have flashed his badge and handed them a story."

"I don't think he's a good guy," Lacey said, her voice flat and angry.

Deep was chopping herbs, a kitchen towel tossed over his shoulder. He paused to turn and take her in. "Why do you say that?"

"He was kissing the fat-lipped girl." Lacey's own lip pouted out like a little girl whose feelings had been stepped on. She didn't want it to be true – but it did hurt her that Steve was kissing someone else. And Lacey wasn't stupid enough to think that Steve would stop with kissing another woman. They were all adults. Obviously, if Steve was intimately involved with someone else at the same time she was dating him, it made her disposable in his eyes. And that feeling took Lacey right back to when she was six-years old, when she became a knick-knack to be shelved and intermittently dusted.

Deep scattered the herbs over the eggs sizzling in the pan.

Lacey talked to his back. "When I first realized there were two of us, I thought this woman might have duped Steve. He thought he was kissing me, when he was really kissing fake-Lacey. But that's naïve. Of course he knew he was kissing someone else. Look at you."

Deep turned and rested his hips against the counter, crossing one ankle over the other. He held his hands out to either side and smiled. "Look at me."

"When you kissed me, your hands knew exactly where to go. Your head knew exactly how far it needed to bend. If suddenly I changed height, even if you missed all of the other

162

subtle things, wouldn't you know that the person you were walking next to was at a different conversational level? When you kissed all of the women in your life, if suddenly they were a different size in your arms, wouldn't you know that?"

"Well, of course. If I played a violin and suddenly I held a viola in my arms, I would need to position my hand differently, change the way I pulled my bow across the strings." Deep stopped and grinned. "You know, you're pretty cute when you get that jealous crinkle under your eyes."

Lacey blinked, trying to change her expression. Deep was right. She had imagined flashes of other women in his arms, beautiful women, intelligent women, fabulous, world-wise women. She knotted her hands tightly in her lap and felt very clearly that she didn't belong in that picture. She belonged in a picture with a latte-drinking software engineer. Someone more white bread and less, oh, Channing Tatum-as-GI Joe-like. Maybe a lawyer. Possibly a director of some well-intentioned nonprofit. But not Deep. He was so much more vibrant and . . . male.

Deep watched her speculatively. "Do you want to share that thought?"

"No, thank you." Lacey reached out for her mug. "When I came downstairs this morning, you said maybe we could leave the house today? Go on a field trip?"

"Yeah. I pulled up the files from your accident with Bambi. It doesn't follow protocol for an accident. The way things stand, I'm surprised your insurance paid out."

"It hasn't. My lawyer's trying to figure things out."

"I'd like for us to go by the spot and see what there is to see. Nice drive in the country. It should be good for you to see some trees and sky."

Lacey gulped in a lung full of air.

Chapter Seventeen

DEEP

Sunday

Deep didn't need Lacey to point to the place where she'd had her accident. The tire marks decorated the roadway like a picture made with his nephew's Spirograph. He reached out to squeeze Lacey's knee, and she held on to his wrist with both hands. He wondered if he made a mistake bringing her here.

"Looks like Mr. Toad's Wild Ride," he said. "This is from your accident?"

She nodded.

"Do you remember spinning around like that?"

Her head shook.

Deep needed to get her talking. The more she talked, the more she could process, and the more she talked, the less she'd get trapped in fear. He wanted her to be able to move through this, maybe get some closure. "Lacey, look behind us. Tell me what was happening before the accident."

Lacey unhooked her seatbelt and flipped around in the seat. "I came up that road."

"Here, let's get out."

Deep unhooked his belt and popped open his door. Before Lacey could right herself, Deep was at her side, helping her jump down. They moved around to stand at the back of the Land Rover.

"Okay, so you were driving up that road, and you said you were speeding. That doesn't seem like something you'd do. I'd guess you're the kind of driver that has a perfect driving record. Maybe even the kind of stickler for minding the speed limit that ticks off the other drivers." He hoped if he poked at her a little, it might get her blood flowing again. Lacey was as white as a sheet.

"What you're really saying is that when you researched me and the accident, you saw that I had had a perfect driving record."

"Well, this is true. I did see that – but it confirmed my suspicions. You're a little tightly wound, you know, Lacey. Breaking a few rules every now and again is human."

Lacey looked down at her shuffling feet. She'd probably missed the teasing tone he'd used. She looked like a child who got caught doing something naughty, even if he was kidding her for the exact opposite reason. "Something made you feel more afraid than the fear you usually experience when you

166

break rules. You said you didn't come to a full stop at the stop sign; you remember putting on your signal, and then you can't remember any more."

Lacey stared at the length of street that she had sped down, then looked at the stop sign. And then she looked up the street at the skid marks. Gripping at her chest, she said, "I remember not being able to breathe. Like I was suffocating. And my heart – my heart had been doing strange things."

"Do you remember why you were frightened, Lacey?" Deep asked gently. "Do you remember someone chasing you in their truck?"

Lacey looked up at him, her eyes wide.

Deep reached for her hand, and they walked to the front of the car. "See here? These are your wheels. But this track here? Those are from a different vehicle. See how they line up? The vehicle behind you hit your back left bumper and spun you. Come on." Deep hoped he wasn't pushing her. She looked awful. But when he started walking, she tucked under his arm and walked with him.

"Three circles, and then the rotation stops. There's a break . . ." He walked farther up the road until he found a tree that had obviously taken one heck of a blow. "And this is where your car stopped. Did Steve ever tell you why he was out this way?"

Lacey shook her head.

Deep's eye caught on the glint of sunlight on a lens. His jaw tightened. And he felt his chest expand, ready for action. He pulled Lacey in to his body and stepped back so a tree on the hill stood between him and the reflection. He peeked back over his shoulder and saw two points of light. Binoculars — not a rifle sight. Still, he didn't want anyone's eyes on Lacey.

"You're trembling," Deep said. "Let's get you back into the car and warmed up. I want to take some pictures before we leave."

He didn't like how quiet she was. He wondered if he had overstepped, bringing her to the place where she'd had such a traumatic event. He had hoped being here might get her talking about things that would give him more clues to work with. Even though he was working to solve her case and make life safe for her again, he still felt selfish.

Last year, he remembered watching Lynx go through the rings of hell when a lunatic was stalking her. He had watched Striker try to navigate the act of managing Lynx as a crime victim living in their safehouse, Lynx's role in solving the crimes, and Striker's own feelings for her. Deep suddenly had a great deal more insight into what a tightrope act that had been for Striker. And now he had to walk a similar tightrope with Lacey.

With the heat blasting out of the vents, Deep grabbed his camera and climbed onto the roof of his Land Rover. While he wanted to take photos of the area in order to study them later, he also wanted to use his zoom lens to figure out who had their eyes on him.

Soon a pale blue mid-century Ford, more rust than paint, chugged its way up the road and pulled over on the opposite shoulder. Deep tapped his elbow against his hip, reassuring himself that his sidearm was ready.

"Howdy," the man said as he jumped down from his cab. Dressed in jean coveralls, a red plaid wool overshirt, and a baseball cap that said NRA, the man tilted back to get a good look at Deep, then spit a stream of tobacco juice into his Budweiser can.

"Hey," Deep said and climbed down from his roof. "You the guy watching us from over in the woods?"

"I was out tracking rabbit for tomorrow morning's hunt. Thought I saw something peculiar happening over here, and decided to come take a look see."

"I'm Dean Huit," Deep said reaching for his wallet, pulling out a card, and handing it over.

"I'm Horace Taylor. It says 'investigator' on here. Whatcha investigating?"

Deep pointed up the road. "My client's insurance company doesn't want to cover her accident. So we're going to end up in court. You wouldn't happen to know anything about the accident here, would you?"

"I reckon I do. But I already told the authorities all about it. You can get hold of the report. That should be all you need." He reached in his pocket, pulled out a bag of Red Man, and packed a little more tobacco back in his cheek. "The lady, she lived through it? They wouldn't tell me – said it had to do with some damned HIPAA privacy crap."

"She survived. It took her a while to get better. Amazing, though. When you look at these road marks you wouldn't think it was possible. Could I ask you, Mr. Taylor, to share with me what you know? Could I tape record it so I can understand what I'm seeing when I get back to my computer with my photos and measurements?"

"Name's Horace, not *Mr.* Taylor." He held Deep's eye like he was taking his measure. "You look to me like a military guy."

"Yes, sir, Marine Raiders. Three tours in Afghanistan."

"Ooh-rah, son. I served in Nam, myself." He rotated his cheeks and jaw and spit into his beer can. "Sure, I'll tell you what I seen. That'd be fine."

Deep pulled out his phone and hung it from his pocket, allowing him to hands-free video record.

Horace pointed back at the stop sign. "I was out ahead of deer season, tracking to figure out where might be good to put my hide. Engines come racing up the road over there. I thought it was some high school kids playing hooky. I was going to get a description of their cars and call it in to the sheriff. You can see pretty far from my hill over there." He turned and pointed. "That's where I was with my binoculars. I never go out the house without 'em. Curious darn thing, that's for sure. I saw a grey car — found out later it was one of them rich cars, an Audi A3—coming up too fast, like I said. But behind it was a truck coming up even faster. Black Chevy Silverado. The faster it came, the faster the girl in the Audi drove until she run out of road. She slowed down to make that there turn, see, and the truck tapped her back bumper. Looked to me like it was aimed and on purpose. Guy brakes his truck in the middle of the road. The girl, her car's making crazy circles down the center. Well you can see – kind of banged along some of the berms. Good darned thing they slowed her down some before she hit the tree. See here? These ain't ditches and hills. They're trenches dug during the Civil War. Some parts still come up to a man's neck. Here, they're eroded down. Some parts of the shoulder are softer than others. Still, if her wheel caught in there, her car would have flipped for sure. Seen it happen time and again. This here's a dangerous stretch of road."

"It's interesting how you can see the spin marks, but then it looks like she straightened out like she regained control but for the curve in the road. If the road had gone straight, she might not have crashed," Deep said.

171

"Yeah, I can see how you might think that – but she never had control of that car. So imagine she's spinning down the road and all that squall from up under her tires trying to grab ahold of the roadway, a buck comes flying out of the woods, and she clips him. He's flat out dead, and she's wrapped around the tree. Blink of an eye."

"Deer in the road, girl in the tree," Deep said, and clicked a picture with his camera.

"You'd think that'd be the end of it. I was getting ready to run to the house and get her some help." He pulled a red bandana from the back of his coveralls pocket and mopped at his face, even though the day was vivid with cold. "The guy in the Silverado slowly rolls up to the deer. He jumps down and for a while I can't see him." Horace turned to point. "I hustled up to that there hill. When I got to that oak, there he was. He's looking up and down the road. He stands right there in front of that holly tree and watches another car come up and park in the road behind him, and they're arguing. The wind was carrying their voices my way. They sounded right heated, but I couldn't make out what they were saying. The big guy — big as in tall, not, you know, muscle-y big – skinny guy but really tall. Good guy for a basketball team. He pulls a pistol out from inside his coat. He walked over to the woman's car and aimed his gun at the woman's head. I thought for sure I was witnessing a murder." Horace spat in his can again. "The other guy—the short one with brown hair—is pushing the gun down and gesturing for him to get back in his truck. The tall guy finally does and takes off down the road. So the brown haired-fella runs over and gets the door open on the back passenger side. It's the only one that isn't bashed in – he crawls over to the front seat. I'm thinking he might be trying to kill her, ya know? I was creeping up on them. I'm a quiet man; I've had my time in the jungles. I had my knife with me. Course, it would have meant a swim through that there gully. If I needed to, I coulda tried to stop him. You know, if the guy were trying to kill her."

"Had you already called 9-1-1?"

"Ain't got cell service in this here part of my land. Things are kinda spotty out this way. But the brown-haired guy must have a different provider, 'cause he was on the phone. He was looking up and down the street like he was trying to give them landmarks. I saw him staring at that historical marker up the road." He pointed up past the tree Lacey had hit. "Probably gave them that as the place they should head. He seemed to be trained in what he was doing; he checked her over. Held his fingers to her neck and the like. She wasn't conscious. He kicked at the door to open it, then gave up and crawled back over the seat. He moved his car to the side of the road, put up flares, and grabbed a first-aid kit. Professional. This wasn't his first rodeo."

Deep nodded. "I really appreciate you telling me this. This is all going to help my client. Did the brown-haired man stay here until rescue arrived?"

"Yeah, he climbed into the back seat. Ambulance came, fire truck, a couple of police cars. She was awake by that time. Guy was keeping her head from moving and helped put on that white collar that they use. He stayed in the car and held the blanket over her while they were cutting her out. Jaws of Life. Pretty amazing invention. Still, it took a while."

"Did the brown-haired man stay and give a report to the police?"

"He took off in the ambulance with her – so I assumed he was off-duty rescue of some kind. Another car pulled up. Some guys got out and pulled credentials from out of their pockets. Even though I could see all this going on through my binoculars, it wasn't like I could head on down and tell them what I saw. With the water there in the gully, ain't a good way for me to make my way down. When I spotted you standing in the road, I had to go get my truck and drive over here. The day of the accident, though, I thought I'd sit tight for the moment. Do my reporting from back at the house."

"Leaving a car out on this turn looks like it might be a hazard. Did they tow the brown-haired man's car?"

"The other car I told you about, the one that had pulled up, one of those guys, he goes and gets in the brown-haired man's car and takes off. That left the driver of the SUV. I didn't get a make or nothing. If it ain't a pickup, I don't really pay the new models no mind. The SUV driver goes over to the cops and shows them his badge – looked like a badge wallet from where I was standing, anyway. There's some talk between them. He's pointing to the deer, then the police officer's on his phone, then everyone packs up and goes home. They didn't do none of the things you're doing, taking pictures . . . and what's that thing in your hand?"

"This does laser measurement. I can put a plastic tent on one end and aim the laser at it, and it will calculate and store the distance. I can put all of this into my computer, where I have software that can analyze distance and speed of the car at impact, things like that. And this camera," Deep lifted the Nikon and held it out to Horace, "is 3D, which is pretty cool. See when you look through the lens, it sets up the photograph so it's not a flat picture but you can see dimensionally."

"Pretty fun toys." They stepped to the side as a car inched past. The man driving waved. "That's the preacher. He's probably headed down the road to talk to Maud. She's newly widowed and in a bad way."

"I'm sorry to hear that. I hope he can bring her some comfort. You know, I really appreciate you coming down and introducing yourself to me. Standing out here in the cold. You

Fiona Quinn

were telling me how the police packed up that day and went away. Do you think that the accident went uninvestigated?"

"I'm not for sure. I went back to the house, and I had to think through what I saw. I wanted to figure out if I could explain it in my head. But it sure did look like someone was chasing that woman – wanted to kill her. So I called the police to make a report, you see?"

Deep rocked back on his heels. "They sent a police officer out to talk to you?"

"Not police. No, sir. FBI."

Deep let his camera hang from its strap and reached up to rub his hand over his head. "Do you remember a name?"

"I got his card back up at the house," Horace said.

"I'd be grateful, sir, if you'd let me take a look at it."

Chapter Eighteen

Lacey

Sunday

Lacey was quiet on the way back to the house. While Horace Taylor had been talking to Deep, she had laid her seat back and waited. She didn't want the man to pay any attention to her. And when Deep got into the car, she didn't want to hear what Horace had said. Deep didn't push her. But she could tell by the way he kept both of his hands on the wheel and his increased vigilance, looking in his mirrors, that what Horace said set off Deep's warning buzzers.

When they got back to Lynx's, Lacey pulled the hood up over her hair, ducked her head, and moved quickly from the garage to the kitchen door and inside. She sat down in the first chair she reached. Her legs were so rubbery they wouldn't hold her weight. She was scared to know what Deep had found out.

Deep came inside and crouched down in front of her. "I need you to watch this. And I need you to hear how close you

177

came to being killed. Whoever Steve is, it looks like he saved your life. Whether he turns out to be a good guy or a bad one, right now, you're breathing because of him."

"The accident?"

"Was more like an on-purpose. Any idea why a guy pulled a gun on you?"

Lacey's jaw set.

Deep leaned forward until their foreheads touched. "Lacey, I'm going to keep telling you this until you can hear me. I've never felt the way I feel about you before with anyone else, ever. I can't imagine these feelings going away. I hope you'll learn to trust that – and me." He lifted his head and looked her in the eyes. "Try really hard to believe me."

Lacey nodded and waited. Inside, she knew that was the preface.

"I hope you can tell me what about that day is scaring you so badly. For everyone's sake, the sooner, the better. There's backstory. I know it, and you know it." He paused, waiting for her to start talking.

She couldn't tell him. Her silence was the only thing that was keeping her alive.

"Lacey, not that I can imagine this is true, but if you've done anything wrong, we can face it together. I know really good lawyers, I . . ."

Lacey rolled her lips in so her mouth formed a straight line. Pushing on his shoulders, Lacey got up and tried to walk away, but Deep caught her wrist. "Take this in the living room and watch it." He pressed his phone into her hand with the video queued up. "I think we both need a little space. I'll check on you in a little while."

An hour had passed. Lacey had watched the video three times. Each time, a few more of Horace's words seeped down through the protective filters her brain had constructed. She figured that tomorrow, she'd try to listen again and hear about the gun pointed at her head and how Steve had knocked it away. How he had crawled over the seat of the crumpled car, and how he stayed with her until she was away and safe. He had kept watch over her ever since. But why? He obviously knew her. Well, maybe not knew *her* but knew something about her before the Silverado hit her car, before the gunman pulled the pistol. Lacey's mind searched back, but she couldn't find a pickup truck anywhere in her memory of that day.

It didn't mean she didn't know why it was chasing her down. And that was her sticking point.

Lacey walked over to the TV and clicked it on. It was tuned to some children's show. She didn't care; she simply wanted noise that came from outside of her head. Something that would drown out the voice that told her what a royal screw-up she was.

Deep seemed to take the blare of the TV as his signal that she was done thinking. He walked in and stared at the screen. "Really?" He quirked his brow at her. "Bubble Puppies?" He picked up the remote and moved over to the couch, where he unceremoniously pulled her to standing so he could lay down its length, and then drew her down to lay in front of him. He tucked the lap blanket over her and wrapped his heavy arm around her torso. Lacey lay perfectly content in his arms. She was glad that the discordant emotions that had bump into each other in the kitchen had smoothed out. Her head was pillowed between his shoulder and bicep. He rested his head on the arm of the sofa, where it was easy for him to bend forward and kiss her hair.

"Comfortable?" he asked.

"Yes, thank you," Lacey said, pushing backward and burrowing a little bit closer.

Deep channel surfed until he got to the weather station.

Lacey tipped her chin up so she could catch his eye. "The weather?"

"What?" he asked. "It's good to know what's blowing our way."

Chapter Nineteen

DEEP

Sunday Evening

Deep wrapped Lacey tightly against him so he wouldn't jostle and wake her, but her hip was grinding painfully into his hard-on, and he needed to shift her to the side. She had fallen asleep almost instantly. And not a delicate lady-like sleep—she was snoring, and his shirt was growing damp where drool dribbled out from her slackened jaw. When he met her at the gallery, he could never imagine Lacey being this comfortable.

She isn't comfortable, he reminded himself. *She's traumatized.* He knew from his work—saving victims from war zones and mass disasters, from hiding witnesses and stealing back hostages—that one of the things that they all seemed to have in common was the sleep of the dead. They swam so deep in their delta waves that nothing brought them back to the surface. And then, as their sleep glided into the

181

shallows, where nightmares could torment them, they'd moan and writhe and talk in their sleep.

"You don't know me." That's what Lacey had been shouting last night. He had heard her in her bed, pitching around with a nightmare. Listened to her muttering under her breath words that he couldn't quite make out. He'd pulled on a pair of sweats to go sit by her bed and hold her hand. But by the time he got to her, she had descended into a different layer of sleep—one that allowed her to breathe steadily—and he didn't want to disturb her. But it was hard to walk out of her room.

He didn't know her. That had been the steady drumbeat pulsing in his mind since the day he first laid eyes on her in the gallery, and fell for her. Hard. He had tried to talk himself out of his feelings. But that was kind of stupid. Feelings weren't something you could wish away, and they sure as heck didn't listen to rational argument. You had them, and you dealt with them. And when they were uncomfortable, you got busy focusing on something else. That technique had gotten him through many a break-up in his past, but it had done nothing to get Lacey out of his blood stream.

He remembered back when they met at the gallery, his first thought was "high maintenance," then she reached out to introduce herself and shook his hand. Her hand was small and soft and absolutely female. When their fingers touched, his heart beat so powerfully that he could hardly speak. Neither one of them let go. He was like that kid with his first crush — completely tossed end over end by her touch. Ever since then, she walked his dreams at night. He found himself playing sappy love songs.

The day Lacey came by Iniquus to apologize for her role in the art theft, he'd hoped that she'd tell him that Steve wasn't in the picture anymore and, yes, she would like to go out to dinner with him, if the invitation was still on the table. But she had turned to him, and held out her hand to say good-bye. It had killed him. This was killing him still.

I don't know her, he reminded himself for the umpteenth time. He bent his head and brushed his lips over her forehead. Last night he'd gone over the photos again and again – the ones he knew were of her. He could easily tell her from the mystery woman. Lacey had a softer, finer mouth, intelligence instead of cunning in her eyes. He had studied the clothes Lacey chose, and they all seemed to have the same kind of armored appearance. Well-tailored from expensive fabrics, she presented as a refined lady. Her jewelry was always large and heavy around her throat like the gorgets the medieval knights wore into battle.

Lynx had picked up on that, too. The clothes she brought to Lacey were mostly jewel-toned sweaters that made Lacey's hair look like sable. The fabrics, though, that Lynx brought were softer and more pliant than the clothes Lacey wore to the office. He thought they suited Lacey better. She had a gentler, kinder spirit than those suits were meant to suggest.

The sweaters Lynx had chosen all had cowl necks or turtlenecks. All of them covered Lacey's throat. When Lacey felt threatened, she'd pull the wool up higher and covered her chin. Lacey wasn't an embattled knight, and she wasn't a damsel in distress. She was a woman playing out of her league. Whether she was a victim, whether she had committed a crime — *that* he didn't know. All he really knew was that even in the heat of the battles he'd waged in Afghanistan, he'd never been this scared before in his life.

Laying there on the couch, with the weatherman in the background, predicting more ice storms, Deep found himself squeezing Lacey a little too tightly.

"I'm sorry," she mumbled, lifting her head, and wiping her wrist across her mouth. "I fell asleep."

"You passed out." He grinned down at her.

She scooted around until she was laying with one leg running alongside of his and the other tossed over him. She stroked a hand down his chest, past his belt, and smiled as it came to rest on his hard-on.

She pushed herself higher to kiss his mouth. It started out with soft pressure, but when a little moan parted her lips, Deep's hormones took over. His fingers tangled into her hair as their tongues danced together. She pushed herself up on top of him, straddling his hips, with her knees bent beneath her.

When she lifted up so she could rock herself along the ridge of his cock, his breath caught. They stared into each other's eyes as she moved. She arched back, letting her breath push from her lungs followed by a groan.

Deep stilled her with his hands on her hips.

She looked back down into his eyes, her focus hazy. Her panting told him to take her. There was nothing he wanted more at that moment. *Nothing.*

Except not to hurt her.

"Lacey." He'd meant for his voice to focus her, but in his head, it sounded more like a benediction. He cleared his throat and tried again. "Lacey." This time it came out more forcibly, and she stilled. "We can't." Deep wasn't able to disguise the regret in his voice.

"Yes, we can." She smiled seductively as she bent to kiss him again, long and soft, a woman's kiss that held a little mewl of need.

His dick pulsed and drew almost all of the blood from his head, making rational thought nearly impossible. He sucked in some air, hoping oxygen would help, as he lifted her off him so she was kneeling with her thighs wide, her hands on her knees, and a look of disbelief on her face. His focus dropped to the sweet spot between her legs where he wanted to play. He dragged his gaze back up to her eyes. "It wouldn't be ethical. You're under my protection."

She tipped her head. "Is that an Iniquus rule?"

"Yes—an important one." He worked to bring conviction into his voice and gain control of the situation. "Someone in danger might make decisions they normally wouldn't make — a kind of psychological duress. I wouldn't make love to someone who had too much to drink for the same reason. They weren't making their decision from a place of clarity."

"Because the person you're guarding is subordinate?"

Good. The more he talked from the rational part of his brain, the more he had a handle on the situation. "Only in terms of dependence. Yes, the people I'm guarding depend on my skills to stay safe. It's not about me being superior. It's about roles. And getting emotionally involved in cases."

"I thought you *were* emotionally involved," Lacey said with a scowl.

Deep let out a wry laugh. "*That* would be a gross understatement."

"So this Iniquus 'don't fuck your subordinates' rule — you remember, don't you, that I'm not a client? I'm . . ." She stalled out.

Did she really just say 'fuck'? His cock pulsed. "What? What are you, Lacey?"

She didn't answer him for a moment. It looked, from where he was sitting—as she twitched her lips to the side—like she was searching for a good word to toss out there.

"I don't share," he filled in for her. "As long as Steve's in the picture, we aren't going to happen."

"Steve's been out of the picture since I chose to call you and not him. And to be honest, he's been fading from the landscape since I met you."

"But all those months — you didn't call me until you were in danger."

"I didn't call you all those months because *I was* in danger, I didn't want you involved. Then, I wasn't thinking, just calling." She wrinkled her brow and looked at him pointedly. "And you didn't call me, either. It was your 'no means no' rule."

Deep caught her words about being in danger and filed them away. He was having trouble keeping his brain in charge as testosterone pumped through his body.

"If you trust a girl's no to mean no," she crossed her arms at her waist and pulled her top off, leaving her breasts on display in white lace and pink ribbons, "why wouldn't you trust a girl's yes to mean yes?" She sent him a seductive smile that clipped the last thread of his restraint. She batted her eyelashes. "What if I were to ask pretty please with sugar and cream on top?" She licked her lips as she rocked forward on the couch, leaning in to kiss him. "Please?"

She twisted until she was in his lap with her arm wrapped around his neck. The "please" became a hum, a siren song. And Deep did the only thing a man in this situation could do. He scooped her up and carried her to his bed to please her.

***

Deep sat with his back against the headboard, looking down at Lacey. He'd been up for a while, but couldn't bring himself to leave her side after the night they'd spent in each other's arms. He couldn't remember ever just lying in bed. Before, when his eyes opened, he was ready to get on with his day. But today, yeah, he wasn't ready yet to break the spell.

The room was dim, with the only light coming from the street lamps. Dawn had not yet crawled up from behind the horizon. The sky was still dark. It was really nice to sit here and watch Lacey relaxed and peaceful in her sleep. The longer she could sleep, the better. He smiled at the fan of silky brown hair that draped over her shoulders. Lacey shifted to wrap an arm around his leg, and Deep reached around to tuck the duvet over her.

As he pulled the warm covers up her back, Deep noticed the tattoo between her shoulder blades. It was as large as a fist

— an intricately rendered Mockingjay symbol, recognizable even in the darkened room. This was not the tattoo of a drunken night on the town. This was planned. From his own tattoos, Deep knew this one was done by a high-dollar artist over several sittings.

She presented as so prim and proper – if he met her and was guessing about her role in life, he'd say she was a lady-who-lunches. Pampered. Entitled. That she was tattooed at all was a surprise. That she'd chosen this one—rather than hearts or butterflies or even ribbons and poetry like he'd seen on the girls he knew who had tattoos—this one had the feel of a soldiers' ink.

It was another puzzle. She was a puzzle.

Whatever was going on for Lacey, she needed to trust him. With that thought, Deep felt the friction of her obstructions rubbing against his nerves. And as he contemplated all of the mysteries that surrounded her, Deep grew angry. He didn't know what to attach this anger to; it was an emotion he rarely experienced. He did know, though, that the energy blowing off his skin like a desert haboob would make everything worse. He needed to burn it off before he spoke to her.

Deep quietly left the bed, grabbed some clothes, and moved to the bathroom, where he set a note against the mirror, letting her know where to find him. He headed down to the basement to run his daily five and do some lifting in Lynx's home gym.

***

As Deep put the weights back on their stand, he felt like he'd screwed his head on straight again. Water moving through the pipes told him that Lacey was in the bath. The thought of her naked body covered in soap bubbles made his cock hard. Once again, his dick was taking over his brain. *This might be a problem.* He moved toward the tiny gym bathroom to take a quick rinse in the shower. A very cold rinse in the shower. There were actually good reasons for Iniquus's 'keep your dick zipped' rules. Deep had blown it by taking Lacey to bed. True, he was emotionally invested before they'd made love. But having had her in his arms like that, it would muddy his perceptions and decisions even further. It would be better if he was at arms' length and fully in his rational mind. But that bridge had been crossed and burned. It couldn't be helped, and didn't even really matter. From the get-go, Deep knew he'd do anything it took to protect her, whatever the threat and whatever her truth.

Chapter Twenty

DEEP

Monday Morning

Coffee on, Deep sat at the computer and worked on his task from yesterday, finding addresses that might turn up more information.

Lacey walked in and dropped a kiss on his lips.

"Good morning." A sappy smile spread across his face.

"Have you been up long?" she asked.

"A couple of hours." He shifted some papers out of his way. "There's fresh java. I thought we could grab breakfast out."

Lacey moved into the kitchen. "You want me to top off your cup?"

"I'm good," he called to her.

"Oh, I'd say you're better than just good," she called back.

That made him laugh. He was still grinning when she made her way back to the dining room with a mug on a salad plate and sat down kitty-corner to him. She curled a knee up to her chest and tucked the other foot under her hip. She looked very small and fragile as she blew ripples across the surface of her coffee, and he felt his protective instincts ramp themselves up. He was going to get to the bottom of this, one way or another, so they could move forward—one way or another.

"How did you get so good at this computer thing? Is that what you have your college degree in? Cyber security or something?" Lacey asked, then took a tentative sip from the mug.

Deep leaned back in his chair, stretching his long legs out in front of him and crossing them at the ankle. He scratched at his over-night stubble. "I went to the University of Hands-on Experience."

Lacey tipped her head as if asking for more information, and Deep decided that she was testing him – seeing how forthcoming he'd be about his past. He'd better serve up some meat, he realized, if he was expecting her to share something from her plate with him afterwards.

"Dad took off and left my mom with five kids — my four sisters and me. I was the filling in the sister sandwich – I have two older sisters and two younger sisters. But we were all born in the same decade, so we were close age-wise and caring-wise. When I graduated from high school, though, I'd had it up to the throat living in a woman's world. So I did the manliest thing I knew."

"You joined the military and became a soldier."

Deep puffed out his chest. "I became a marine. Ooh rah!"

Lacy giggled, and it was the sweetest sound he thought he'd ever heard.

"I imagine that was like diving into a testosterone swamp," she said. "Did you like it? Bootcamp?"

"One of the best decisions I've ever made. It was a good fit for me. Filled in some of the manly shit I'd missed out on when my dad moved on." Deep offered up a lopsided smile. That won him a soft smile in return that warmed Lacey's eyes. And his heart stuttered.

Deep licked his lips. *Keep going,* he told himself. *Tell her the truth and not the bar pick-up lines.* "They sent me for advanced training with the Raiders, then deployed me to Afghanistan for a few go-rounds. Things went bad, and I landed back in the states at the VA hospital for a while. To keep myself sane, I worked on learning new skills, and it seems that hacking computers fits the way my brain's wired. It comes easily to me. When I was released from the hospital, a SEAL I met on a couple of combined efforts, Striker Rheas, helped me get my gig at Iniquus. They put me on Striker's team as technical support – as things improved for me capability-wise, I went back into the field with them."

"Striker Rheas—that's Lynx's fiancé?"

"Right."

"Is that why you have scars on your hip and legs? You left the Marines because you were injured over there?"

When did she see the scars on my hip and legs? "Once a Marine, always a Marine." Deep said it in such an adamant tone that he saw Lacey dip her head like a chastised kid.

"The scars on my legs. . . I turned around one day to find myself standing a little too close to a grenade, which won me a free trip to Europe, then back stateside. They gave me a new femur and hip – stainless steel and Teflon. They're pretty good. My injury's not holding me back from much. It acts like a pretty accurate barometer, and I can still save a beautiful woman from a little red dot." He reached out and brushed Lacey's hair from her eyes and bent in to kiss the tip of her nose, trying to roll back the mistake he'd made with his earlier growl. "But I did retire my position in the Marine Corps."

"I'm so sorry." Her eyes turned red and glassy like she was going to cry, and Deep knew if those tears were for him, he wouldn't be able to take it.

"Don't be. Really. I was one of a handful of lucky soldiers that got picked to play guinea pig with this new-fangled skin gun they were trying out. I'm a walking miracle."

"Say that again - a skin gun?" Lacey put her mug on the plate and wrapped her arms around her posted knee.

"You know that when soldiers are injured in the Middle East, they send them first to Germany and then home."

"Yes, Landstuhl Medical Center," Lacey said.

Deep scratched his cheek and ran his hand over his chin to buy himself a few seconds. He hated talking about that point in his life. "I was pretty badly burned — forty-three percent of my body. My whole left side, up my leg, over my chest and face. I looked pretty horrific. But lucky for me, I had second-degree burns and not third-degree burns. Of course, that would be lucky on any day. But I arrived at Landstuhl the same day as this guy from McGowan Institute for Regenerative Medicine. He had developed this gun that sprays a solution of cells and water onto the damaged skin."

Lacey's brow creased. As she listened intently, she leaned forward and rested her chin on her posted knee.

"The professor and his research fellows came to talk to me. They offered to let me be a test subject. I jumped at the chance."

"What did it do when they sprayed water and cells on your burns?"

"Basically, what these guys were doing was harvesting healthy skin from other parts of my body, and then they used a 'skin gun' to spray my own skin stem cells onto the wound. Sort of like using a paint sprayer. Then they wrapped me up in special bandages that helped support my skin as it regenerated on its own. A couple of weeks later, I looked in the mirror, and I was back to my pretty self." He smiled and stroked a hand over his face and neck.

Lacey craned her neck, scrutinizing him. "All I see is a really hot guy." She smiled and leaned back.

"It was the biggest miracle, Lacey. If you had seen me before – I looked like a monster. I thought that that was going to be my life, walking around freaking people out by how horrible I looked. I didn't want to get shipped home. I didn't want my mom to see me like that, you know? I mean – it would have killed her."

Lacey was frowning at him and shaking her head. He wasn't sure how to interpret that. "The guys I met who got the normal treatment – the grafts that they grow – that takes months, and they got terrible infections and some of them died because of them."

"Why couldn't they use the skin gun on all of the soldiers, even if it was experimental?"

"Some of the wounded had third-degree burns, and the skin-gun technique doesn't work for that yet. But on me, it worked great. It took a few months for the color of my skin to come back to normal and the texture to develop. When you feel my skin, there's not much changed except where they did my leg surgery and sewed up all the holes. I was so blessed. I'm telling you, this skin-gun technology is a miracle. Of course, if you ask my mom, she'll tell you that I got myself back together and almost as good as new because I was wearing the St. Michael's medal she gave me." Deep reached into his shirt and pulled out a chain with a pewter pendant.

Lacey took it in her hands to examine it more closely. "Did you know that St. Michael is the patron saint of artists?"

"Also of bakers and soldiers." Deep grinned. "I told Mom I thought that she would have preferred I became a baker to a soldier. My mom loves going to the bakery. Every Sunday, without fail, we'd go up to Fiorina's after mass to get cannoli and cakes."

"That sounds lovely. Do you still go to mass?" Lacey kissed the medal and stuck it back in his shirt.

"When I'm home. Special occasions. Always on Christmas. My religion is important – a touchstone. My culture."

"Kind of like the background in a painting. It dictates the color and mood, but doesn't really affect the action in the picture?"

"Exactly." Deep leaned back and crossed his arms. "Okay, now it's my turn, why don't you tell me the story behind the Mockingjay symbol on your back? I would think, since you're a fine arts kind of girl, that you would pick something different."

Lacey cocked her head to the side and sent him a one sided smile. "Like what?"

"I don't know, Van Gogh's missing ear? A Monet water lily?"

"You like 19th century art?"

"I'm not much when it comes to knowing about art. Those are the ones I remember from my Western Civ class."

"I see. Well, there's not much to the story. I gave it to myself as an eighteenth birthday gift."

"It's done by someone with a lot of skill. I've seen tattoos done by some amazing artists – yours is one of the best. It looks 3D. That was an expensive birthday gift. I was surprised when I saw it. You didn't strike me as the type of girl who'd get a tattoo."

"Really? What kind of girl did I strike you as?"

"Oh, you know, the kind of girl who likes to have tea parties in her rose garden and throw charity galas for the country-club set." The smile he sent her was to tell her he was teasing – but in reality, he wasn't teasing much. "Why'd you choose there, between your shoulder blades?"

Lacey reached back and touched the spot where her tattoo lay. "It's where I'd reach for an arrow if I were wearing a quiver." She smiled as she mimed pulling the arrow over her back, stringing it on a bow and letting it fly.

"So you identified with the character, Katniss? I haven't read the book. I saw the first movie, though. It was pretty intense. What part of that speaks to you?"

Lacey stalled, as she often did when he asked her things. He'd tried to make it sound like polite conversation. But it felt to Deep like his words caught on the hem of all those layers she had donned to protect herself. He desperately wanted to lift up the edges and peek under the skirts of her armor.

Deep read resignation and anxiety in her eyes, and he felt like an ass. Here he was, pushing her again.

"The book came out when I was a senior in high school, and I was heavily into reading dystopia. In the first book, Katniss Everdeen's dad was killed in a coal mining accident, leaving her mom depressed and unable to provide for her children. It was up to Katniss from a very early age to use her intelligence and her skills to stay safe and alive and maybe even flourish. I thought she was a pretty good role model for me."

"I'm not sure I'm following."

"My dad, he was killed in a skiing accident. If you're a rich guy, that's really the way to go. He was skiing in Vail and lost control. Plowed right into a tree and died on impact."

Deep nodded encouragement her way.

"I was six when Dad died, so I remember everything pretty well. We had a big house–too big—and it was just mom and me. My mom wasn't a very strong woman. She was depressed after Dad's death. She spent most of her days in bed. She didn't want the lights on, or the drapes opened. She didn't want noises around her, like talking. It was rather tomb-like." Lacey chuckled a little, though there was nothing funny about what she was saying.

As Deep listened, he wanted to gather Lacey into his arms and stroke her hair. But he thought if he did anything other than listen, she'd use it as an excuse to stop talking.

Lacey's eyes strayed to the window, so it looked like she was telling her story to the naked branches tapping against the pane. "We were very rich, but Mom fired everyone who worked for us in the house. She didn't like their noise or movement. She kept the gardeners because someone had to cut the lawn. That's about it." Lacey seemed to fold in on herself.

"She was like the mother in *The Hunger Games*?" Deep asked, trying to pull her back into the room and out of her memories.

"Yeah. Incapable. When you're as depressed as my mom was, you forget things. Things like paying the electrical and water bills, buying food and stuff. I understood that she was ill. Her mind wouldn't let her love me. Or take care of me."

Deep reached out his hand to cover Lacey's. "Did she finally get the help that she needed?"

"No, she died. I guess breathing became too much for her, too."

When Deep saw Lacey's body wilt, he knew she was sharing something very private and painful. "How old were you when she passed?" Deep sought out her eyes, but Lacey refused to look at him.

"Almost seventeen. My Uncle Bartholomew became my guardian. He told me to stay put and finish up my senior year, and then go ahead with my plans for college. So I did. I had been running the house for a while, anyway." She paused for a long moment. "It didn't make much difference in the day to day of my life. The day I turned twenty-five and came into my trust fund, I sold the place. I accepted the first offer that came my way, which was about half the market value. Not a sound economic decision, of course. But a huge weight lifted off me as soon as it was out of my hands. I'm so glad I'll never see that house again." She offered up a sad smile. Talking about her house and childhood seemed to drain all of the light and life out of Lacey.

"People had to have intervened on your behalf – someone must have noticed."

"My teachers, eventually. They told me I stank, and I needed to take a bath. But we didn't have any water. They turn it off when you don't pay the bills, no matter how much money you have in the banks. The principal at my prep school ended up contacting my mom's lawyer, and the lawyer hired a CPA to pay our bills. He hired a nanny and a housekeeper."

"But that didn't turn things around?"

"The help made noise, so Mom would fire them. I'd call her lawyer; he'd send in the next wave."

"And the tattoo?"

"Reminds me that I have skills. I can take care of myself. I'll be fine, thank you kindly."

"Do you believe that?" Deep asked.

"Ha! No. I don't believe that at all."

"Why not?"

"Because I don't have the kinds of skillsets I need to get free of this mess."

"But I do," Deep said.

Lacey finally focused on him.

"I *do*," Deep insisted.

Chapter Twenty-One

Lacey

Monday

.

Lacey tucked her hair under a fuzzy hat and wrapped a scarf around her neck and the bottom part of her face, effecting a disguise so she could leave the house. She was glad they were headed out the door. This morning's conversation had been hard to hear and hard to speak.

She kept seeing Deep in a mud hut in the desert, burnt and broken, and screaming in pain. God, it sucked the oxygen right out of her cells, completely deflating her. The image she conjured of that grenade exploding blew enough sand into her consciousness that it masked the shame she felt for being loveless and unlovable as a child. Unwanted. A task for a lawyer to contend with. And really, her story was sad, but Deep's was harrowing. No comparison. It felt selfish for her to harbor any sense of self-pity when he had survived so much worse.

Lacey had been afraid that knowing about her past would make Deep see her as others had – as a nuisance to contend with. An object to be shuffled around. But telling Deep her story didn't seem to change how he looked at her at all. She pinched her cheeks and tried on a smile in the mirror before she headed down the stairs. Since they had missed breakfast, they were going to grab some lunch out. Then they were headed over to the warehouse where the mystery people, the ones who were planning the gallery's art show, stored the paintings. Deep said that he wanted to get a peek inside and see if they could pick up any information that might help them get a clearer picture of what was going on.

Deep had done what he called his "due diligence." He knew the security systems and the schematics of the place. He said he'd go by himself, but he needed her there to sign in with a security guard.

Deep parked the car in the garage, and they walked the two blocks to the warehouse hand in hand. Lacey was pretty nervous as she moved past the steps that she had seen time and again in the pictures on the flash drive. Deep reached out to hold the door for her, and Lacey set her shoulders as she hustled through, and turned left the way Deep had instructed so she could sign the book.

She was a little taken aback when the guard called her by name.

He laughed and winked. "Good thing we have that privacy clause in our contracts. I saw you on the news again this morning. The police are still looking for you."

Lacey's eyes stretched wide.

"I ain't gonna call nobody. The boss would fire me if I did. And I couldn't care less that you killed that guy. You probably had a good reason, huh? He treat you bad?"

Lacey didn't know what to do so she just turned on her heels and walked away.

She and Deep hung out around the corner for a few minutes while Deep used the camera on his phone to watch the guy. The guard kicked back at the desk and was eating a sandwich.

Deep took her by the elbow, and they moved through the spider web of corridors of the climate-controlled warehouse until they reached the unit that was supposedly hers.

Deep left her standing outside the massive metal door while he carefully paced the hall. She had no idea what he was looking for, but his eyes seemed to cover every inch of the space. Arriving back by her side, he unbuttoned one of the pockets that lined the legs of his grey cargo pants. He handed her a pair of blue nitrile gloves, then pulled out a second pair that he tugged onto his hands. Lacey followed suit.

"Okay, Lacey, are you ready?"

Lacey turned her wide-eyed stare toward Deep. *Ready for what?*

"Here's the plan. I want you to put your hand on the wall right here." He moved her over to the wall and stuck her hand where he wanted it. "Don't move from here. I'm going to turn off the lights in the hall, and it's going to be pitch black. Don't be afraid, everything's going to be fine. I just need you to hold still."

"I don't understand."

"There's probably some kind of security system inside the unit that was put in place by the FBI, if they know about this place, or maybe there's internal security put in here by the criminals," Deep whispered in her ear. "Someone's bound to be protecting the interior. I'm going to put on my night-vision goggles from my backpack, go in and look around, and if I find a system, I'll neutralize it. If it's a camera, it might be triggered by movement or heat. Either way, I don't want them to see us. So you're going to hang tight. I'm going to make it safe to go in with the lights on without giving us away. Okay?"

Lacey nodded.

"Now when we go in there, we need to work fast. If someone sees we've taken out their system, they'll probably head right over to get eyes on the problem. We're going to look around quick, and then we're going to leave. I don't want you to say a word until we're out of here, in case they've got bugs planted. I don't have the equipment with me to find those. So take mental notes, and we'll compare our observations when we get safe. Okay?"

Lacey nodded, her eyes growing wider and rounder.

Deep pressed her hand against the wall, then moved down the hall to the switch plate, covered over with a plastic box and locking system. Deep pulled his wallet from the cargo pocket on his leg and picked out what looked like two thin sticks. With a couple of movements at his wrist, the box popped open, and Lacey was plunged into a stygian lake of nothingness.

"You okay?" Deep whispered near her ear, causing her to buck to the side.

How did he get up the hall without her hearing footfalls? "Yes," she breathed out.

"I'm tumbling the lock."

A sharp squeak told Lacey that Deep had gone inside, and she was standing in the hall alone. Standing. Standing. Lacey felt a bubble of hysteria work its way up her throat. This was more than she had bargained for. She put both of her hands on the wall, trying to keep her emotions under control. She couldn't believe the relief that flooded her body as the unit light clicked on and Deep appeared in the doorway.

He gestured her in and reminded her of the plan to be silent by putting his finger to his lips.

She walked into a room that was a mostly empty twenty-foot cube.

Photography lights were set up facing a painting that she recognized right away as Grover Whitlock's *Nude, with Anthurium*. Since Whitlock was still alive, this was one of the moderately priced paintings on the acquisitions list, and was set to sell for forty-four thousand dollars. That's what happens to the value of an artist's work when Forbes puts one of their paintings in his pool house. Lacey didn't actually believe *Anthurium* was worth that price. She didn't even like this piece. It was vulgar, in her opinion.

Deep tapped her shoulder and handed her a tiny video camera. She could see the red record light was already illuminated.

Lacey focused the lens on the artwork, then swung around, where a like-sized canvas was posted on a tripod. She noticed that an artist had already applied a thin coating of gesso to the linen canvas and had begun layering on the colors for the background. They were obviously replicating Whitlock's nude.

Lacey's gaze moved along the floor, where fans oscillated gently and a large dehumidifier hummed. She crept along the wall, where canvas after canvas stood in various stages of drying. The lighting in the room was bright and the heat was turned up high enough that Lacey wanted to ditch her outerwear. She knew Deep wouldn't approve, though. She needed to stay wrapped up and unrecognizable in case anyone came through the door. But the wool from her hat and scarf made her itch as perspiration formed on her head and neck.

Walking back to the workspace, Lacey picked up a clean rag, which she dipped into the can of Ace Artist's White Spirits, then moved over to the enormous expanse of the Chambray-like work. Gently, she rubbed the painting's surface, pulling off some of the pigment. She folded the cloth and put it in her pocket just as Deep's hand landed on her arm.

Lacey turned to him and saw his night vision goggles were positioned on his forehead. He put a finger to his lips, reached for her hand and steered her toward the light switch. With a flick, Lacey was back in complete darkness. She was wholly dependent on Deep's guiding touch as he moved her to the back of the room, toward the stack of boxes she'd seen piled there. Deep pressed on her shoulders, and Lacey folded her body down until she was bunched into as small a package as she could make herself.

Whistling moved up the hall with the steady heel taps of an unhurried gait. The door pushed open, the lights snapped on, and rustling movements filled the space.

Lacey turned her head toward Deep. He was crouched between her and anyone who might move this way; the toes of his work boots were curled under and his weight rested on one knee. Lacey felt her lips sticking to her teeth, and she moved her tongue around to encourage her mouth to produce more saliva.

As the noises from the other side of the boxes settled down to a rhythm, Deep slowly reached his hand out and just as slowly pulled his hand back in. He tapped the screen, then showed Lacey the video of a man painting. She got her best view of the artist when he scrutinized the Whitlock. Deep raised his brows as if asking did she know him. She shook her head in response.

That's when the guy's phone rang.

Chapter Twenty-Two

Monday

"**Y**eah?" The man's voice conveyed his distraction.

"I'm checking on your progress," a voice on the other end of the phone echoed out of the speaker.

"Good. Good. I'm a little behind because I had the flu, but I'm well enough now that I can finish. I'll have all of the canvases ready for the show. Not dry, but ready. When do you want to start moving them?"

"Thursday morning."

"So soon? Why not on Friday? Friday would be better."

"It has to be Thursday. They need to be hung in time for Friday's reception. Everything has to be ready for the agents and photographers. There can be no mess ups. No missing works."

Deep had taken his phone back from Lacey and was recording the call.

"You will make *sure* you can get the paintings done in time. Understood?" the caller said.

"I'm finishing up the last one today. It won't be dry, obviously. You'll have to move it with great care and place it in the dimmest part of your room. But ready nonetheless."

"You're sure?" When the man asked, his voice changed precipitously. Now, menace rose from the phone.

"I'm a professional. I meet my commitments," the artist growled from the other side of the boxes.

"My friend, you and I both know what Lacey Stuart is like when she doesn't get her way. I've been there when things haven't followed her plans. I've seen what she's capable of, and I'm telling you, I want no part of her temper. For your well-being, as well as mine, I need to make sure Ms. Stuart stays happy."

"Don't worry about the show. Everything will be ready, I swear."

Lacey was freaking out as her name projected into the air. The perspiration that had dotted her brow now made her clothes humid. Her tongue sat on her lip as she panted for air.

Deep twisted in his crouched position, reached out, and swept his hand along her cheek. His fingers held her chin, tipping her face until he held her focus. Suddenly, there was nothing for her in the room but his brown eyes, so intensely brown that they were almost black and the defining line between his pupils and irises was not visible. They were intelligent and steady. They were solid and capable. They were home – she could live there in his gaze. If all this crap could fade away, and she could be allowed to live there in his gaze, everything would be okay.

After a moment, she pulled her tongue back in to lay in the bed between her lower teeth. Her lips sealed and her breathing came softly through her nostrils. The claustrophobia that drowned her in her sweat-drenched clothing abated. And her heart, though it still beat thickly, became small enough in its protective cage to allow her veins to carry blood, unimpeded, to her still-tingling extremities.

Deep's eyes clearly asked if she was okay and if he could trust her to keep it together.

Laccy wanted more than anything to be able to impress him with how courageous she could be. *I'm fine. I've got this,* Lacey tried to telegraph back to him.

With Deep poised between her and the old man at the easel, she'd get out of the warehouse today. But the phone call reminded her that her name and likeness was being used in something bigger. Something 2.8 million dollars big, if she multiplied the worth of the original show to match the doubling of the artwork. What would someone do to protect an almost three-million-dollar payday? One of her professors during her undergrad days had been shot leaving campus over the three dollars he had in his wallet. Dead for three dollars. So would anyone's life be safe if they stood in the way of a million times that amount?

***

"It makes sense to me that the FBI would be involved if they thought that there was a crime involving art," Deep said. "They're the ones you called when you thought that someone had stolen the Iniquus pieces from your warehouse last November, so I know you know that art theft falls in their laps."

Deep was navigating through the streets in a less than pleasant part of town. Lacey would have avoided this section if she were driving alone. After the fear she experienced hunkered down behind the boxes, she was almost okay with the street corner thugs that looked speculatively into her window.

The artist had painted for about an hour, and when he went to take a break, they'd used the opportunity to get out of there. They had clomped down the front stairs and started down the street when suddenly Deep had reversed directions and walked her away from where they had parked. "He's on the corner, smoking a cigarette," Deep explained. So they shared a piece of cheesecake at Cutie Pies, sitting in the window where Deep could keep an eye on the guy. Now they were on the road, and Deep was making absurd U-turns and quick lane changes to make absolutely sure they hadn't picked up a tail.

"Not a huge amount of new information. Most of what the guy was saying is already available in the files on the flash drive Bardman gave you."

Lacey sat silently as they drove past an empty park. Icicles hung from the monkey bars and the swings wavered in the wind.

"I've run a search online," Deep said, "and in every case I can find, there are only two choices when it comes to art theft – art is stolen, or art is replicated and sold fraudulently. You saw what I did in the warehouse, Lacey, you've seen the computer files, and you heard the guys' phone conversation. From your background, what do you think could be happening?"

Lacey leaned back in her seat and crossed her legs. "Art thieves are usually motivated to take art because, for the size and weight, it can be very valuable. Some art pieces are worth millions of dollars. It's easy to transport — simply detach the canvas from the frame, roll it up, and stick it in a tube. You could mail it anywhere without raising suspicion. People send mailing tubes all the time with drawings and schematics."

"Wouldn't that damage the painting, though?"

"Yes, but depending on the price of the painting, someone might be willing to inflict damage. For example, have you ever heard of the theft from the Gardner Museum in Boston?"

He shot her a quick look, then did another mirror scan. "Sorry, that doesn't ring a bell."

"Two guys, dressed like cops, showed up at the museum saying they were responding to a call. The museum had two guards on duty. The guard watching the front went ahead and let the uniformed men in through the security door. Then the fake cops had the security guard call the other guy on duty, telling him to come to the front desk. The robbers took the legitimate security guards down to the basement, where they cuffed the poor men to the pipes, and duct taped their heads. The security guards weren't found until the next morning when their relief came in. Meanwhile, the fake cops cut twelve paintings from their frames. They took a box cutter or some such sharp tool and dragged it along the canvases to cut them off the frames. Some of those works were priceless. Nothing was ever located—either the paintings nor the thieves who stole the works."

"What happens to stolen art?" Deep asked. "Seems a hard thing to fence."

"There are a lot of private collectors. People who have secret vaults with their special collections."

"You said that with a sneer."

"Absolutely. A lot of the things in those private collections are there because they're illegal. For example, they might be stolen pieces of national treasure – things that were discovered in archaeological digs and are owned by the people of the nation – pieces of antiquity that should be housed and curated by a museum. Other times, it's art made from the body parts of endangered species—rhino horns and the like. Some of the things might have been stolen during a war – the Nazis, for example, took whatever they wanted from wherever they wanted it. Stolen pieces have been handed down in families. Quietly."

"None of that fits here."

"No, but sometimes, people like a piece of art – they simply don't want to spend the kind of money on it that's being asked on an open market. Or maybe it's not even available on the open market. Megalomaniacs who think their every desire should be fulfilled don't care about such things. Then those people might hire a thief to go in and get it for them."

"How about insurance fraud? Could the pieces be stolen so the owner could collect the money?"

They were back on the highway, and Lacey was starting to recognize the exit signs again. Deep must have deemed it safe to head back to Lynx's house. "Not very likely. High-profile museums have extremely tight security. The Louvre, for example. But for the most part, multi-million-dollar art collections have disproportionately poor security measures in place – there's really very little security protecting art, and that includes the Bartholomew Winslow Gallery, too. Poor security but also very little in the way of insurance.

"What does your security entail at the gallery?" Deep asked. Lacey could tell his mind was buzzing with ideas, and she was impressed that he was still able to listen to her and ask systematic questions. Self-control. She found it very sexy.

"We have a security guard 24/7. But that's really for show. If someone wanted one of our displayed pieces, a retired police officer isn't going to stop them, I'd imagine. We rely on electronics, and the paintings are attached to the wall with a lock."

"But someone could cut them free from their frames like at the Gardner?"

"We have infra-red detection. If someone steps too close, moves a body part past the velvet ropes, then a silent alarm sounds and our off-location security monitors can manipulate the cameras to do a close-up of the action and the person who got too near. The off-site security would notify police, and we can track the bad guy as far as the corner of our block. So we'd have copies of their license plates, probably."

"But those cameras only function if the alarm is set off?"

"Right, we don't run them all the time. There's no point. We really don't have anything other than art that's of value to a thief at the gallery – we don't have cash, for example. The only reason for anyone to eye us as a potential target would be the art."

"So there's no way that your cameras might have caught the face on the sniper?"

"No. No one would have been in our building other than our night security guard. So no one would have set off the alarm that would start the off-site security taping."

"That's too bad. I'd sure like to get a look at his face. Even seeing his rifle would give me a lot of information. So, insurance—you were saying you have very little – so this probably doesn't have anything to do with insurance fraud?"

"If we got an insurance payout, it would go to the artists whose work was stolen. We work on commission. We don't buy and then sell. We show the works, and then take a forty-percent cut of the sale. The agent usually takes fifteen percent, and the artist is left with thirty-five. If a hundred-thousand-dollar painting is stolen pre-sale, and if it were insured, it would only be insured for thirty-five thousand dollars—that's the amount that the artist would be out. The gallery would make no money. The agent would make no money. We all understand this from the beginning. No art? No payday. The owner, in this case the artist, is the one who posts the loss, and the artist would recoup the loss of his share of the payday pie. See?"

"Yes, that makes sense, but how do you come up with that amount? How does the insurance company know what a painting's worth?"

"Exactly the right question. How could they know? 'I'm Joe-anybody, and I painted this picture of my dog smoking a cigar. I think it's a million-dollar masterpiece.' That's not going to wash. Value is developed through expert opinion. It's similar to real estate. A house value is somewhat subjective too – where is the house located? What is the condition of the house? Did someone famous live there, or did something historically important happen there? What's the market doing now? What is a buyer who bought a similar house this month willing to pay? Those kinds of questions. It's really a matter of knowing your market as to what price you put on a piece – and everyone has to agree: the artist, the agent, and the gallery."

"You were making a point about never-before-sold paintings."

"Just that once they've been sold, then they've established a market price. We know what they're worth. And since someone paid a hundred thousand dollars to procure the painting, they'd get the whole amount if they filed an insurance claim. Just like if you crashed your fifty-thousand-dollar car, they don't go back and give you the amount that it was when it was sitting in the factory parking lot before all of the middlemen took their fees."

"Huh, interesting. Did you insure the paintings when you started the collection process?"

"Honestly, I didn't get that far. My uncle gave me the project, then asked me to hold off making any overtures, then he let me know that we wouldn't have any art with which to move forward." Lacey sniffed as she opened the glove compartment and peeked inside. Then she patted her coat pockets.

Deep popped a button on the central console and reached in for a plastic travel pack of tissues. "So fake-Lacey made all of the arrangements?"

"Someone else. Not me, that's for sure." She pulled a tissue from the pack and rubbed her nose, hoping she wasn't catching cold. She really didn't need a fever and misery to add to her problems. "Let's remember what the counterfeiter said. They needed the fakes on display; they needed the agents to be photographed with the fakes, thereby giving them the air of authenticity; and they were doing that on Friday so something could happen Friday night ahead of the Saturday opening show. That's extremely strange. What were they going to do with the originals?"

"Well, we can watch and see. But our presence there today might have shaken things up," Deep said.

"How would they know we were there?"

"You signed your name. The bad guys would know either you or fake-Lacey were there today, if they were to check the logs – a stretch, but it could happen. Also, there were two cameras in the room. When I went in there with the lights off, I moved boxes in front of the lenses, so the camera feed would show black. And even though I moved everything back the way I'd found it, that will probably raise some suspicions. But sometimes, you have to take chances to gather intel. And I think we lucked out on the artist being in there and taking the phone call."

Lacey's body convulsed with a suddenly shiver.

Deep sent her a searching look.

"Someone just walked over my grave."

Chapter Twenty-Three

Steve

Tuesday, Dawn

"Steve, man, I hate to do this to you," Higgins's voice came over his phone. "We need you in the morgue to do a quick identity check from the Zoric case. I'm swinging by to pick you up."

Steve had just fallen asleep, and for the briefest second, thought this was his recurring nightmare.

"Are you there, man?" Higgins's voice picked up in volume, and Steve had no choice but to wake up fully.

"Why do they need me?" There were only two possible victims that would have the bureau pulling him from his bed. Sudden tears blurred his vision.

"They think it's either Danika or Lacey. You're the best person to refine their search."

"Shit." Shit. Shit. Shit. Steve scrubbed shaking hands over his face. A living shit-filled nightmare. *Please, don't let it be Lacey.* "How far are you out? I need to pull on some clothes."

"I'm outside already. And I've got a cup of joe in your cup holder."

Steve couldn't make himself stand up. His body wasn't cooperating. The last thing he wanted to do was go down in the basement of the hospital and pull out a drawer to find Lacey laying there. It was as if his body had decided if it wouldn't stand up and make the trip, if he stayed put, then Lacey would be safe and not artificially preserved in a refrigeration unit.

Safe, Steve reminded himself, wasn't really on the table. If Lacey got scooped up by one of Zoric's professional abductors, then she might be wishing she were dead at that moment. And with Joseph Del Toro out of the country, Steve couldn't imagine another man from Lacey's rather narrow life who had the capacity to sweep in and save the day, like some freaking action hero. In his mind, Steve couldn't find a single scenario that made Lacey okay.

"Look, have them measure the body. Lacey is five-foot one, and Danika is five-foot five," he said.

Higgins cleared his throat. "That's not going to be possible. I'm sorry."

***

"I can tell you she was already dead when the train hit," the medical examiner said as he pulled back the drape to expose the victim's head and shoulders.

Steve looked down at the long brown hair. Her face was bruised and battered. It was one of them, Lacey or Danika, he was pretty sure. Last he had seen, Danika had dyed her hair strawberry-blond. But he knew that had been temporary, since Danika was supposed to host the agents at the pre-opening cocktail party Friday night, acting as Lacey.

Lacey should have been in a safehouse by now. Steve was trying to pull her out the night Bardman was stabbed. They had planned to hide her away where she'd be safe until the bureau scooped up all of the players and put them in jail. He'd failed her. Then Higgins had failed her. And Lacey had run.

"They beat her up a couple of days ago. There was time for her injuries to start healing. Then she was shot. Three rounds in the heart is what we can see from a cursory exam. She's third on the list for autopsy once the rest of the team gets in to the lab and our workday gets underway."

"When did she die?" Higgins asked.

"With this cold snap, it's going to be hard to give a tight timeframe. We'll know better with the autopsy. I'm not going to speculate."

"So she was already dead when they dumped her body on the rail?" Steve asked.

"She was dead when she was found." The medical examiner shoved his hands into his lab coat and rocked back on his heels. "You can read the witness report the police left. It basically says a nurse saw some men dump a woman on the tracks, jump back in their car, and drive away. No descriptions. It was too dark. Only headlights from the car and what they illuminated as they moved the woman. The witness saw the train coming and tried to get to the track in time to save her. The witness was dragging the victim off the tracks when the train came up, and she had to let go of the victim to get away herself. The train cut off the victim's legs above the knees. That's when the witness realized the woman was already dead. The PD are trying to find the legs now. They must have gotten dragged down the track."

Steve stalked over to the corner, grabbed the lip of the trashcan, and vomited up his coffee and a good dose of stomach bile. He moved to the sink to rinse out his mouth. His face was slack as he moved back toward the victim, his eyes drooping with exhaustion and grief. Lacey wasn't okay. Whether this was her or not, she wasn't okay. She was a kind, sweet, amazing girl who happened to be at the wrong place at the wrong time; the great-niece of a really wrong-minded man, and the girlfriend of a freaking asshole. Steve knew that whatever had happened to Lacey, he could have stopped it. *Should* have stopped it. And didn't.

Please don't be Lacey. It was an idiotic prayer; either it was Lacey or it wasn't. Wishful thinking couldn't change one girl's fate for the others. Not that he wished Danika dead. *Shit.*

"Lacey Stuart has brown eyes and Danika Zoric's eyes are navy blue."

The medical examiner shook his head. "Too soon to tell. The victim's eyes are blood shot with broken blood vessels from the blows to her eye sockets, and the pupils are still dilated from her death."

Steve swallowed hard as bile jumped up his throat again. He had to bend over and put his hands on his knees to try to catch his breath. Higgins pat his shoulder, then left his hand there, stabilizing Steve.

With a barely audible whisper, Steve offered, "Lacey had a tattoo of a Mockingjay about four inches wide between her scapulae."

The medical examiner shook his head again. "High caliber exit wounds. Her back is shredded behind her heart."

"I'm sorry," Steve said, his eyes squeezed tight against his tears. "I can't tell you who this is. I don't know who this."

Chapter Twenty-Four

Lacey

Tuesday, Dawn

Sleep that night had been tough for Lacey to catch hold of. It seemed like she had spent hours swirling on the dark waters in that Neverland place on the other side of wakefulness. She must have been making a lot of noise, because Deep left the bed to snap on the hallway light, then went back in to untangle her from the sweat-dampened sheets. Fear was cold, sweaty business.

When he'd straightened her bed clothes and tucked her neatly back in, Deep started to leave again to click off the light.

"Please don't go," she whispered, in the darkness of the windowless room.

"I'm right here." His voice, warm and comforting, came from the side of her bed. Then she felt the mattress sink as he put the weight of his knee down. He climbed under the covers and pulled her tightly against the curve of his body. He stroked her hair, kissed her neck; Lacey had responded by sitting up to wiggle out of her nighty.

Large and strong, with the rub of callouses, Deep's hands made Lacey feel oh so much like silk and femininity. His loving hands stroked over her body; his touch pulled her away from the anxiety that overwhelmed her. There was nothing that she wanted more than Deep's hands on her. Well, that wasn't entirely true. Perhaps there was something she wanted more. And as Deep complied with her body's request, Lacey had giggled against his neck.

The stubble of his nighttime beard rasped past her cheek. "What?" he'd asked.

"Nothing. I was thinking about your call name."

"This is not the reason I earned it," he said, tucking his hand under her thigh and pulling it over his hip.

But Lacey wasn't sure she believed him.

Lacey peeked at the clock. According to the time, the stars were already hiding behind the sun and a new day had begun. She missed waking up and looking out of a window. It was strange to contemplate all the things she'd taken for granted, she thought, as she stretched out in the bed. She was surprised she had slept so soundly this morning. She hadn't even noticed when Deep had gotten up.

Lacey rose to shower and get dressed, choosing a beautiful sapphire sweater that she thought Deep might like on her. Then she twirled her hair into a low-riding bun, letting her long layers frame her face. For the first time in her life, she felt pretty. People had always told her she was a beautiful girl and that she took after her mother. The pictures she had seen of her mom in her twenties, before her dad had died and before the psychotherapeutic medications left her grey and hollow-eyed, were indeed very lovely. But Lacey had never seen the resemblance, and assumed people said that about her because having a lot of money in the bank has a way of making people seem more attractive.

As Lacey headed down the stairs, she hoped Deep hadn't started breakfast yet. She wanted to do something for him this morning, and cooking was about all she could come up with under the circumstances. She gave Deep a finger-wave as she passed through the living room. He glanced up with a smile, but tucked right back down into his computer, where something was pulling his attention.

Deep had hot chocolate already in the pot, and there was a little bowl of marshmallows laid out next to a quiche that he'd warmed from the freezer. He'd already eaten a slice. Lacey wasn't hungry yet, but the cocoa smelled warm and inviting.

She poured two mugs and moved to join Deep in the front room.

"You had a rough night last night," Deep said as she joined him.

"I'm supposed to be dead." Lacey handed Deep a cup of hot cocoa, then sat cross-legged with her back to the brown leather couch. Beneath her stretched hardwood floors that had been scored and stained in various shades to make it look like antique marquetry. The walls that wrapped around them were a beautiful shade of rose terracotta, at once warm and grounding, cheerful and uplifting. This was a magical jewel of a house. Even sucked into her own crisis, Lacey could appreciate the uniqueness and care that went into creating this space. And she felt deep gratitude that Lynx allowed her to be here.

"Many times over, I'm supposed to be dead. I'm actually surprised that I'm still breathing." Lacey's sigh tried to sound like a chuckle.

"How many times over?" Deep asked.

"Three. No, wait." Her eyes lost their focus and landed somewhere near the fringe of the rug. "Four," she whispered. Clearing her throat, she sent a tight-lipped smile Deep's way. "Somebody wanted to shoot me the day I killed the deer, then Leo Bardman was stabbed while he was warning me to run. The FBI was there in the bar in the front on the street. Who knows who was waiting there in the back, and whether they would have caught me if the rain hadn't been falling so hard. They jumped out of their car when I came out the door – so they must have been trying to stay dry. I would have done likewise. It was a terrible storm."

"Right," Deep said. "Then the sniper. That makes three."

"I'm sure the only reason why I'm alive right now is that I'm hiding here in Lynx's beautiful home and no one knows where to find me." Lacey's eye travelled around the room, from the skillfully rendered oil seascape over the mantelpiece signed Gavin Rheas to the thick drapes that hid their movements from the street. "I'm so lucky to be here with you. Thank you." She brought both hands up to her heart.

Deep offered a half-smile, but his eyes showed his mind was pinging.

Lacey picked up the mug of cocoa resting between her bare feet and lay her head back on the sofa cushion, the mug dangling between her posted knees.

"I keep thinking about fake-Lacey and my clothes. There are two ways she could have worn my clothes. One, she or someone had access to my apartment, which would be fairly difficult in that I live in a high-security building that requires a thumbprint scan to access the stairs or elevators. Or, two, Steve gave her my clothes. I was thinking about that possibility. Steve was a little OCD about our laundry. It wasn't like we had a laundry day. For Steve, every day was laundry day. He made jokes about it. I'd take off an outfit and the washable things, my hose and lingerie went right into the washing machine. They weren't even left for the maid to handle. Every day, Steve would take my dresses to the dry-cleaners on the way to work, then he'd pick up our clothes on his way home."

"That's interesting. Same dry-cleaners?"

"Yes, it's across the street and down the block at the Metro station. So it's not a big deal. Steve took the Metro to work anyway."

"What about the shoes? Fake Lacey couldn't possibly have had your size feet."

"I mostly wear neutral-colored pumps. If she had a picture of my shoes, or the brand names, it wouldn't be hard for her to find a look-alike in her size."

"Interesting. I have another question about your dresses. If Steve brought a dress to the cleaners in the morning, would it be the same dress he brought home that night?"

"No, there was a day's lag. It says on the sign 'Same-Day Cleaning,' but that's only if you get it in by a certain time."

"Who said that to you, Steve or the cleaners?"

"Steve."

"And whose name is on the cleaning receipt, yours or Steve's?"

Lacey pursed her lips in concentration as she tried to remember the yellow paper stapled to the plastic garment bags he'd brought home. "I believe it's my name."

"I think we have another fieldtrip to take later."

Lacey's brow bunched, and she set her mug down. With crossed legs, she leaned over looking into the depths where her mini-marshmallows were melting, like she was using the surface to scry the future. "Deep, if they killed me at the news conference, how could they have continued their scam? Wouldn't they need me alive to make that work out?"

"I don't know, sweetheart. I can't guess at what they've got going on."

Hearing Deep call her 'sweetheart' blurred Lacey's vision with tears. She was glad she was looking down, and Deep couldn't see. The endearment twisted her gut with bitter-sweetness. If she weren't in this mess, Deep wouldn't be here with her. He'd be off on his vacation, having fun, resting and relaxing. It made her feel a little less guilty about how things were turning out now that he called her "sweetheart". She swiped at her tears surreptitiously. He had told her a few times now that he believed they belonged together. And she had understood his feelings in a kind of distant, amorphous way. But hearing him call her 'sweetheart' suddenly made his words feel true. Solid. And Lacey's heart expanded with gratitude. When she looked up her tears were shining her cheeks.

Deep tipped his head, concern filling his gaze.

"Those are thankfulness tears," she said with a rueful smile.

Deep suddenly turned his ear toward the front door. He caught Lacey's eye and lifted his chin, pointing toward the bathroom.

Lacey scrambled up, grabbed her mug, and tiptoed to the powder room. She was locking the door when the bell rang.

Chapter Twenty-Five

DEEP

Tuesday Morning

"**D**ave, man, good to see you." Deep spread his arms wide to hug Dave Murphy, one of Lynx's oldest family friends who lived across the street and two doors down. It had been Dave who'd helped Lynx find this house, so he could keep a closer eye on her when she had a psychopath stalking her.

Dave stepped back with a smile. "You're up early."

"I haven't been able sleep past zero-five-hundred hours since boot camp. It's like my drill sergeant moved into my head." Instead of inviting Dave in, Deep put his hand on the door and held it against his shoulder, effectively blocking the detective from peeking in.

Dave gave him a knowing look and nodded. "I just stopped over for a second. I have a message for you from our girl."

"Is everything okay?"

"She's fine, but somebody's not. Falls Church PD brought a body in early this morning that they haven't identified yet. Lexi picked up on it over the police band, and called me first thing this morning. She was afraid it might be a mutual acquaintance of yours. They've put out pictures to the PDs to see if anyone had a name or a missing person file that might make sense. I pulled a few of the images and brought them over. Lexi thought they might be of interest."

"Thanks, I appreciate that. Do they know what happened to the victim?"

"Three shots to the chest, thrown on a train track. PD's got the dogs out looking for her legs." Dave handed Deep a sealed manila envelope. "But everything's okay here? Lexi wants me to text her a thumbs-up. She says to let you know it would probably be a bad idea to contact her directly unless you need their help."

Deep nodded. "Yeah, everything's good. Catching up on some computer stuff. Enjoying a little peace and quiet."

Dave grunted and moved on down the stairs.

Deep went back inside, and with his back to the door he unsealed the envelope and pulled the photos out. Three. One of the victim's face, and either side of her profile. Someone had beat this girl viciously. Still, he could see the victim was a dead-ringer for Lacey. Whatever role Fake-Lacey had played in the scheme, it was now over.

Deep slid the pictures in the envelope, placed them on the dining room table, and strode to the bathroom to give a knock and let Lacey know she could come out.

"Everything okay? Another neighbor inviting you for spaghetti?"

"Lynx got in touch with a friend of hers after she heard some chatter on the police scanners. There was a murder in Northern Virginia, and they're trying to identify the victim."

"Lynx thought it might be me?"

Deep nodded, then realized that he was blocking Lacey from coming out of the bathroom. He knew he'd have to tell her about the other woman, and he didn't want to add this stress in with the rest. For a split second, he considered shoving the envelope into a drawer, but he also knew that Lacey was holding something back. This morning, she had said there had been four attempts to kill her, but only named three. He needed to know about the fourth attempt. He needed to know everything. Honesty and trust on his part might make the difference to Lacey when she was making her choices about whether to trust him with her story. He stepped back.

"Deep, you're scaring me. Who was at the door?"

"Dave Murphy. He's a detective who lives in the neighborhood. He came over with photographs of the victim and to make sure everything was okay. Lynx was asking for a thumbs up."

239

Lacey's gaze darted to the table where the envelope lay. "Is it her? Is it Fake-Lacey? Oh goodness, we can't ever call her that again. It seems so . . . so . . ."

"Disrespectful. I know. It looks like her. But we can't jump to conclusions. The girl was pretty banged up, and it could be another lookalike."

"You don't believe that," Lacey said, walking over and putting her hand on the envelope.

Deep's gut contracted. He didn't want her to see those photos. Knowing that someone was trying to kill you and seeing that they could be successful only added to the level of psychological torture. He didn't think Lacey needed her nerves ratcheted any tighter.

"Is it okay if I don't look at them?" Her brows pulled tightly together, making lines crisscross her forehead.

"It won't inform you in any way. I'd leave it alone. But if you think you need to see them, I'm putting them away here in this drawer." He moved into the room and picked up the envelope, sliding it in one smooth action into a credenza drawer and closing it away.

"Her being dead, if it is the stand-in from those pictures— what does that mean to the scam that's being pulled?"

"I'm not sure. You have to be careful about how you line up your thoughts about crimes and criminals. This isn't a novel plotline."

"I don't understand," Lacey said.

"Come on, let's get our coats on and head over to the dry-cleaners. We can talk in the car."

Going forward, their fact gathering was going to be a little tricky. Deep wished he had a couple of his Iniquus pals at his back. Heading in to the dry-cleaners could be a non-event. But then again, he'd been in enough situations that he knew not to assume anything. He'd have gone himself and left Lacey back at the house, but he wasn't willing to let her out of his sight. Things felt too shaky, especially now that he had stashed the manila envelope with the dead woman's photos in the credenza drawer. Besides, Lacey was the only one who could legitimately pick up her clothes — if there were any there.

He wasn't sure why snagging Lacey's freshly-pressed dress needed to be done. But he felt in his bones that this move was important. And if he learned anything from working with Lynx, it was to follow his gut like a bloodhound on the trail. Home in, put his head down, and go.

The question was, would anyone else know that Lacey might show up at the dry-cleaners—or maybe they might think the other woman would—and be staking it out? The thought might seem a little paranoid, but Deep had seen weirder things go down.

When he was in his room going through his tactical decisions, his plans had come down to winging it. *I have to keep Lacey bundled up as much as possible*, he had thought as he slid a .380 into his ankle holster, and pressed his Glock into the conceal carry pocket on his tactical jacket, his normal level of protection.

When he jogged down the stairs he had a pair of pants and a blouse in his hands from Lynx's closet. He saw Lacey focus in on them.

"What's up with those clothes?" she asked.

"I don't want people to know we're together. Couples don't normally go to the cleaners together and the workers will be used to associating your name with Steve. So I'll follow you into the cleaners as a customer while you do your thing."

Deep put his hand on her back and ushered Lacey out the door. They crossed the backyard quickly with their heads bowed and slid into the garage, separating to get into their respective sides of Deep's car. Deep pulled the door shut and looked over to find Lacey smiling at him. *God, she's beautiful.* Deep felt the full weight of her confidence in him, not just here today, but in the whole mess. While she seemed secure in his abilities, Deep wished she'd be a little more forthcoming, so he could feel the same level of conviction that they'd get this figured out.

They were buckled in and heading down the road when Lacey turned to Deep. "I can't think about this like a novel, you said. What does that mean?"

"A novel, a movie, it's all nice and neat. You know what you're supposed to know, and everything progresses in a linear manner. There might be some red herrings thrown in to take you off the path, but for the most part there's a straight trajectory: a bad person acts, good guy figures out how to stop the bad guy, the bad guy goes to jail. Real life doesn't work that way at all."

Lacey swiveled in her seat, and Deep felt the intensity of her focus without shifting his gaze off the traffic in front of them.

"First off, in real life, if law enforcement gets *some* of their questions answered, they're lucky. If we catch a bad guy, we may have to let them back out on the streets. Sometimes the bad guys are really good at what they do, and we don't find them at all."

"Sometimes they're powerful with friends in the right places, and their criminal behaviors are part of the status quo and brushed under the carpet," Lacey added.

Deep glanced her way, then focused back on his driving. "You're thinking about your Uncle Bartholomew and the Assembly."

"I am."

"Let's revisit that in a minute when we talk about families. I want to explain three very broad groups of criminals. I'm talking in generalities, so you can kind of get a feel for what we're dealing with here. There are crews, families, and gangs."

"Are we dealing with a gang, since Special Agent Higgins was at the bar?"

"You can't jump to conclusions. The guy might have been at the bar for a drink."

"He was staring at my lips the whole time."

"Well, you can't blame a man for that. They're beautiful lips."

Lacey reached out to swat at Deep, then folded her arms across her chest. As he changed lanes, he caught a little smile playing at the corners of her mouth.

"Okay, so a crew is a group of criminals—anything more than someone working as an individual—who come together because they see an opportunity. Usually, crew members are chosen for their skillsets. For example, someone might be good at popping locks, and someone might be good at intimidating security, and someone might be a good driver. There, you put that crew of three together and you've got a quick breaking and entering team. They can get a lot more complex, depending on the job and the dollar amount involved. If we're dealing with a crew, then a criminal picture is harder to put together. They come together, then they blow apart. It's difficult to find them and make the connections. See?"

"Yes, I've got it."

"When you pull a crew together, there's danger because each person is in it for themselves. There's no loyalty. And each person might have their own agenda. You have to remember that criminals, in their minds, know that they are doing something wrong in that they're breaking laws and can be punished. But at the same time, they also think that their actions are justified – they're out there hustling, trying to make a life for themselves. Sometimes they think that they have to bend some rules to overcome where they've come from. Sometimes they feel they get to bend the rules because of who they are or where they come from. "

"Yes, like my Uncle Bartholomew—he was a member of the Assembly. They truly believed that they were God's chosen and that the rules were in place for the everyman. The rules kept the sheep together. But the Assembly, they were above the rules and could act with impunity." Lacey's voice was small, and she looked out the side window instead of at him.

"The Assembly have members in high-ranking places that make sure their members suffered no consequences from their improper actions. That reinforced the idea that they were special – secretively special – but a special part of society."

245

Deep sincerely hoped this didn't hook into the Assembly somehow. Even though Iniquus had been instrumental in exposing the Assembly and their crimes – they still had an enormous amount of political and financial power. Going up against them was like going up against a Moby Dick. A severely wounded Moby Dick – but a monster of a problem all the same.

"The Assembly, though, functioned like a family." Deep glanced quickly her way then over her shoulder as he changed lanes and let the Jaguar asshole blow on by. "A criminal family works like a genetic family. There's the head that steers the members in certain directions. They think longer term and try to position the group in such a way that their tasks are easier and more lucrative. It used to be back in the day that they would have certain gigs."

"Like the Mafia and their protection money and bootlegging?"

"Right, protection – you pay me X amount of dollars each month, and no one burns your store down. Couple that with running drugs, and you can keep a family well-fed. In modern-day crime, the big thing in both gangs and families now is diversification, a broader portfolio, so if things get too hot in one area, they can lean on another."

"And gangs work like families, too, don't they? That's what I've read."

"They have elements of families – all those things I already said but, and this is a big but, they also are in tight. It's not healthy for a gang member to try to pull a private crew together or try to eat a piece of pie without sharing. A family is more like a nuclear family. Sure, Mom and Dad try to steer the kiddos toward the same values and get them to work together. The reality is, the kids like the security of the nest, and they want to fly out and do their own thing at the same time."

"Gangs don't do that?"

"Not if they want any kind of life expectancy."

"And with the art, what do you think we're looking at here—crew, gang, or family?"

"I don't have enough information yet to tell. Even though Higgins's task unit is Violent Gangs – families fall under their roof. So, I'd speculate that this isn't the Crips or Bloods – this doesn't feel like gang activity. It's not a matter of sophistication. Gangs can be highly sophisticated. Here, the education level's too high, and a sniper rifle from the roof isn't really their MO. It's not what families usually do, either. The sniper has me confused. But this seems to be a little too complex for a crew looking for an opportunity – they like things streamlined. In and out. So I'm guessing family."

"A dysfunctional family." Lacey grimaced.

"Could be," Deep said.

"Huh." Lacey pinched at her nose.

"Okay, what was that thought?" Deep asked.

Lacey didn't want to share, so she pointed out the window, "Looks like we're here."

Chapter Twenty-Six

DEEP

Tuesday

Deep was glad when he found a parking spot near the Metro entrance. In the almost non-existent on-street parking of DC this was a real coup, and Deep chose to take it as a good omen. Lacey got out, according to their plan, and started down the stairs to the underground shops to the side of the Metro entrance. Deep waited a beat, then followed after, his eye scanning for nonchalant individuals standing alone anywhere in the corridor.

When he got down the stairs, Lacey was already in the cleaners, apologizing for losing her receipt.

"You haven't been in in almost a week. We were wondering what happened. You're usually here like clockwork."

Lacey offered up a smile, the slightest upward tip at the sides of her mouth, as another person came forward and took Deep's clothes and started a ticket for the items.

"I got behind on a project at work, and it's taken over my life," Lacey said.

"Oh, I thought it might have had something to do with that guy getting killed. Wasn't that you on the news the other day?"

"Same name, different woman," Lacey said with a trace of hesitation.

The worker went away and came back with a suit and blouse. She hung it up on the rod and read the receipt. "You left something in your pocket," she said and moved to a side table where there was a box of junk. After rifling through, the worker came back with a coin purse and compared the numbers, then held it up for Lacey's inspection. "You recognize this?"

"Oh, yes, thank you kindly. I was wondering what happened to that."

"You left twelve dollars in your pocket as well." She used a key dangling from an elastic on her wrist to open the cash register. And began to count out the money for Lacey.

"Thank you, but why don't you keep it? Have lunch on me," Lacey said, lifting the clothes from the rod.

The woman looked up with a frown. Deep walked out of the store.

"Please," Lacey said. "I so appreciate your good service. Have lunch on me." She gave a little wave and headed out the door where Deep was bent over, pretending to tie his bootlace three steps away. Lacey held the change purse by the tag that had been safety-pinned to the hole at the top of the zipper pull and walked right by Deep, up the stairs, and to the car.

Deep pressed the button on his fob to unlock the car and without waiting, Lacey popped in. She flung the clothes in their thin plastic covering onto the back seat and laid the coin purse on her lap while she pulled her buckle into place. Deep climbed in and in a flash, had the motor humming and the car tangling into the DC traffic.

As they pulled up to a stoplight, Deep bent over, popped the glove compartment, and pulled two nitrile gloves from a box he had stored in there, and laid them on Lacey's lap. "You okay?"

"This feels like a present on Christmas morning. Like I was just handed a gift." This time, Lacey's smile was broad and bright and believable.

Deep smiled in return, then crept forward with the traffic, trying to get them to a place that was safe and quiet so they could look at what was left behind.

Lacey pulled on the gloves and sent a questioning glance toward Deep. "Should I?"

"Yeah, go ahead."

Lacey licked her lips and pulled the zipper. Into Lacey's lap tumbled a pocket comb, a tube of lipstick, an ID card with Lacey's name, and a Metro card. Lacey looked down at the stuff and then looked out the window.

Disappointment seemed to wrap around Lacey, but also confusion. Deep let it sit. Sometimes the mind latches onto something that is unconscious – something that needs a moment of quiet to bubble up. He recognized that look from his brothers in combat. They'd stop at a doorway, stall. A sense of something — the mind needed a moment to filter the right piece of information into the right portion of the brain for a thought to form. If it was interrupted, it might never take the required path. And as he knew from battle, that could be deadly. So he moved as little as possible as he got them to a parking garage and waited at the ticket machine with the window still up until she was back in action.

Deep collected their parking ticket and waited for the security arm to rise, allowing them through. Lacey rubbed her thumbs around the insides of the coin purse. She turned it inside out as Deep backed into one of the better-lit spaces. Then she held it out to him so he could see that the lining had been carefully cut and sewn back together. Deep slid his knife from the concealed sleeve pocket in his coat and severed the threads.

He handed it back to Lacey so she could be the one to pull the paper out. She unfolded the sheet and smoothed it over her knee. "Superior Pawn Shop. That's my name, but not my address." Lacey picked up the ID card and flipped it over. "Same address, 2759 East McKinley Avenue. Apartment 511. She lives – lived — directly across the street from me." Lacey held the ID out for Deep.

Deep reached past her and grabbed his own set of gloves from the glove compartment before he took the DMV card. "This is either an official driver's license, or an expert forgery. I'm guessing it's a forgery."

"Why is that?" Lacey twisted around in her seat so she was facing him.

"This card says Lacey Elizabeth Stuart is five-foot five. If your lookalike had gone into the DMV and said her license was lost or stolen, they would have used the characteristic information from the computer. Your height being one of those attributes. She wouldn't have been able to ask them to update the height."

"What does that mean?"

"Well, whoever's running this con is sophisticated for sure, but we knew that already. What's your home address?" Deep pulled out his phone to do a Google search.

"2760 East McKinley Avenue. Apartment 520," Lacey replied.

Deep turned his phone toward her. "She had an apartment right across the street. With a telescope or binoculars, she could probably have seen right into your window. I wonder how long she's been renting there."

Tears filled Lacey's eyes, and she pulled her turtleneck up to cover her mouth. "Someone's been watching me in my place? That's so violating. They could have seen everything, me walking around naked, having sex, eating a bowl of ice cream in front of the TV. I never shut the drapes. I assumed everyone was minding their own business."

Deep's brows suddenly pulled together. He picked up the lipstick case and fiddled with it until the bottom popped off and a button battery and wire slid out.

"Shit." He rolled down his window and tossed the lipstick across the garage. Jammed the car into drive and drove steadily out into traffic, his eye scanning. He felt his awareness expanding, as adrenaline shot through his system.

Lacey trembled beside him. "What's happening, Deep?" Her question came like an oscillating breeze as her words stuttered out from her turning head as she mimicked his movements.

"The lipstick had a tracker. If anyone's watching it, they'll know that it moved."

"What if it's the FBI? Surely the garage has security cameras, and they'd have caught your license plate. They could track your name down."

"Not this car, they can't. This car belongs to an offshore corporation. It can't be traced to me."

"I can't believe I'm running from the FBI. Maybe I shouldn't be."

"That's your call. I'll help you do whatever it is you want to do." Deep's muscles tightened at the thought. He wasn't sure that the FBI was a good choice until they had a better grasp on what was going on.

"If you thought it was a smart move though, you would have told me that. Shouldn't we trust them? I mean – you hear such bad things about the police on TV these days, all of the problems in Chicago and such. People who misuse their jobs. Is that what happens with the FBI, too?"

Deep's muscles became less armor-like and his eyes softened from their predatory sharpness the farther away they drove from the garage. "I've worked hand in hand with the FBI for a long time now. And I only know of two incidents where the agents went bad. I absolutely believe in and depend on the integrity of the special agents."

Lacey frowned. "I can hear a big *but* dangling in your words."

"But something really screwy is happening here. I think they lost control of a mission. Things got out of hand, and somehow you're looking like collateral damage to them. I'll do everything I can to not let that be the case. Bottom line, though, I'll help you go whatever direction it is you want to go. If you think talking to the FBI is in your best interest, then I'd suggest we do it through Iniquus. My company is highly respected, and they'd make sure that no one was playing fast and loose with your safety."

They had driven in silence almost all the way to Maryland when Lacey finally spoke. "If it's okay with you, I'd like to keep my head down and try to figure out a little more of what's happening before I make that kind of decision."

"Alright, if you look back at the photos, they started at the end of September after you were back at work, following your accident. Let's say the accident was the starting point. This is speculation – I'm throwing out an idea, okay?"

"Okay." Lacey gave a vigorous nod.

"Steve seems to be the connector. Something had to start the con off. Steve saved you at the car accident for reasons we don't understand, but there can only be two possibilities. He had no idea who you were, or he had an idea who you were. Right?"

"Yes, I guess."

"If he had no idea who you were, he was trying to stop your murder for a reason that had nothing to do with you personally. In that case, it might be that he saw a resemblance and got some con under way. You were out of work for ten days. That's enough time to get a new ID made and rent an apartment, set things up and move forward."

"And if he did know me?"

"That gets a little more confusing. If he knew you, and he's FBI, say, then he would have saved you because that's his job. Add to that you might have been an asset, someone who somehow played into something that was already underway. When did you get the letters from the people pulling out of the show?"

"My uncle emailed the file to me from Bali."

"They didn't come to you at all?"

"No, to my uncle," she replied.

Deep did a U-turn.

"Where are we going now?"

"I think we need to go pick up whatever our mystery girl left at the pawn shop."

257

Chapter Twenty-Seven

Tuesday

Deep parked the car in Lynx's garage and popped his door open. Lacey had tilted her head back against the headrest and closed her eyes. She hadn't said a word since they'd left the pawn shop.

Deep leaned over and kissed her cheek. "Lacey, we're here."

Lacey didn't want to move. She was exhausted. She couldn't remember a time in her life when she felt like the plug on her cells' energy had been pulled, and she was so thoroughly depleted. Since she had arrived at Lynx's house, she was sleeping at odd intervals and waking up only long enough to discover some other awful new truth, and then she'd be back to sleep again. Asleep, awake, asleep, awake—her body was so confused. *She* was so confused.

"Come on, Lacey, you'll freeze sitting here in the car."

259

Lacey doubted she even had the power to drag herself across the tiny backyard into the house.

"I'll fix you a cup of tea and make some sandwiches. You'll feel better after you eat."

Lacey peeked through her eyelashes at him. "Why do you always try to make things better with food?"

"I'm Italian." Deep winked. He pushed the button on her seat belt, and it retracted. "Come on, up and at 'em." He walked around and opened her door, reaching for her hand. "What you're experiencing now is typical. Your body can only handle so much stress before it says it needs to hibernate. So sandwich, tea, and nap."

Lacey responded with a wide-mouthed yawn that she hid behind her elbow. "How about nap, then sandwich. I'm not sure I have the energy to chew." She let Deep guide her body into the house and up the stairs, where she flopped across the guestroom bed. Deep chuckled as he pulled off her boots and socks and worked at her coat. "You're going to have to help a little bit."

"Alright," Lacey said, not helping at all. Finally, Deep scooped her legs further onto the bed and threw a blanket over the top of her before he quietly shut the door. Lacey was already delicately snoring.

Lacey woke from her nap discombobulated. She lay there staring at the ceiling, filtering through all of the things that had been happening over the last few days. Everything seemed new and terrifying. Not the least of which were her feelings for Deep. They were much too sudden. Much too profound. And yet, he was the only thing that felt solid around her – everything was spinning like a carnival ride, throwing her center of gravity off with its centrifugal force.

Lacey's bladder was what had woken her up, and was now forcing her out of bed. She shuffled to the bathroom. As she was washing her hands, she looked into the mirror, trying to see what Deep saw when he called her beautiful. She wasn't even wearing makeup. Hadn't used a blow dryer or products since the bar scene. Even her gel manicure was giving out. She was a mess. Yet the way he looked at her, well his eyes called her beautiful as much as his words did. She believed his eyes more than his lips. Well, no. That wasn't true; his lips were reverent as they moved over her body. She felt cherished in his hands. This was a really horrible place to be, but for the first time in her life, she didn't feel like she was facing things alone. Someone stood by her side. And it felt . . . strange. Part of her scoffed at the idea and part of her—a small part of her— had hope. Maybe after everything got cleared up, and she was safe . . . *If,* she reminded herself, maybe *if* things got cleared up, and she was safe . . .

Lacey picked up the comb and pulled it through her hair, then started down the stairs to check out their newest piece of information. Now they had a black fur coat from a pawn shop that meant enough to the mystery woman that she sewed the ticket into her coin purse to hide it. Lacey wondered why.

Chapter Twenty-Eight

Steve

Tuesday Evening

Steve sat in Lacey's apartment gripping a tumbler from the bourbon he'd knocked back in one gulp. He punched a fist into his chest to get his lungs going again. He liked the alcoholic flames engulfing his esophagus; he welcomed the pain. Steve reached for the bottle and poured two more fingers, appreciating for a moment the deep amber color magnified by the prisms of Lacey's Waterford crystal. He swirled it twice, then tipped it back. He wanted to get drunk – badly. But this was all he was going to allow himself. A couple belts of whiskey and a shower. Then he'd hit the streets again.

He wasn't sure what he was doing, driving around like he was. But Monroe had told him no contact with the case, and that meant he couldn't tap any of his informants or show his face in any of the places where people might know him as

Steve Adamic. And that made tracking Lacey's movements after the press conference all but impossible.

Today, though, something happened. Someone had gone by the cleaners. His computer had pinged, letting him know one of his trackers was on the move. This was the first ping he'd picked up from either woman since the day Lacey disappeared. He grabbed Higgins, and they hauled it over to a parking garage four blocks from the women's apartments. It could have been either of them. Whichever one of them was still alive. Higgins found the lipstick, with the tracker exposed, thrown in the corner.

The garage was right near the dry-cleaners he had used to pass Lacey's clothes to Danika so she could pose for the pictures. It was a long shot, but he and Higgins went by the cleaners on the off-chance that it was indeed Lacey or Danika who made the tracker move from Point A to Point B.

Yes, the cashier had said, recognizing Steve right away. Lacey Stuart had been there that morning. She had gone into the store alone to pick up her suit. But he and Higgins both knew that didn't necessarily mean anything. If someone had made either woman go in under duress, their handler could have been waiting outside.

"She seemed fine," the cleaner said. "No, not stressed or upset or hurt in any way . . . No not in a hurry. As a matter of fact, she was the nicest she's ever been . . . She was smiling and gave me a tip; told me lunch was on her today."

This whole lipstick thing was nuts. Why the heck would either Lacey or Danika go pick up that suit? It made absolutely no sense to him. His fingers drummed against his glass. He knew the lipstick was at the dry-cleaners because that's where the GPS had positioned it on his map for the last few days. Okay, they search your pockets before they put the clothes into the machines. So they must have handed it back to the woman when she picked up her suit, and then there was movement as the person went from where the cleaners was located to the garage. And someone obviously discovered it. Would Lacey think to look for a tracker? Would Danika?

The color of lipstick didn't tell him if Lacey had left it in the clothes or if Danika had, since both had the exact same lipstick manufacturer and color, and he had wired them with the exact same tracker unit. He was such an idiot. Of course, they had to wear the same color to pull off the photos. But with the trackers floating back and forth between the two women, Steve should have found a way to mark the lipsticks as different. Twenty-twenty hindsight wasn't helpful.

Someone was alive and not visibly hurt. Could it possibly be Lacey? Did he have a chance to right his wrongs? To find her, explain, apologize, and tell her he had never lied about his feelings? He was willing to spend the rest of his life making this up to her. Nothing would make him happier.

Who was alive? The medical examiner was working on it. They didn't have a fingerprint match in the system. They were doing some math to try to estimate the person's height, but that would be unreliable in that people's bone structure was sometimes longer in the torso and sometimes longer in the leg. It was pretty hard to tell with certainty. They still hadn't found her legs. Steve pushed his imagination away from the visual of the hunt and discovery that popped up like a horror flick.

Higgins had told Steve that they had warrants for Lacey's dental records. Steve had brought Lacey's toothbrush to the lab for DNA samples, but if they ended up relying on DNA, that could take months. Years, even. He had also brought a few items that Lacey might have been the only one to have touched. But honestly, it was unlikely they'd find prints. Lacey had hired a housekeeper with OCD because of her thoroughness. This woman attacked Lacey's apartment twice a week like she was in an out-and-out assault against an invading bacterial army. There was nothing that didn't get lifted, scrubbed, and disinfected within an inch of its life. Lacey thought she had hit the jackpot of all housekeepers, and Steve had actually taken a cue from the maid. He claimed to have a little OCD issue of his own, one that had to do with anxiety around germs on clothing. Pavle had thought the move was brilliant. He'd won kudos and deeper entrée with the Zoric family. And sucked Lacey deeper into the world of crime.

Steve tipped back his glass to swallow the very last drop, then carried it to the kitchen sink and rinsed it before putting it, still wet, back on the shelf. Not knowing if Lacey was alive or not was killing him. He lived in a constant state of panic. And he couldn't let it show. If Monroe thought he couldn't handle his emotions, Steve would, rightfully, be completely pulled from the case, even the little he was allowed to do now.

The Zorics were moving forward according to schedule. Higgins was watching them and reporting in as the family set up the rented gallery space, prepping to hang the paintings, and adjusting the lighting. They had already moved in the catering tables and the all-important open bar where Musclav Zoric would be doctoring the drinks. With the addition of a little powder, the arts agents would be pliable and uninterested in the details of the evening, especially when it came to whether the paintings were the originals or not.

Yup, the Zorics acted as if everything that had happened was part of the con and all was going along as planned. If that were true, there was still a chance that the FBI could round them up as one big fat family, and the good guys could stop at least one path that allowed so many people to get hurt. Honestly, it felt like turning off the faucet in the kitchen when Steve knew well enough that under the streets there was a whole piping system with gallons flowing freely and unseen. What was the use of turning off a single faucet? Especially if someone he loved died in the process?

Steve eyed the bourbon again. Then forced himself toward the bathroom, dropping his clothes along the way.

Who was it that was alive, damn it? Lacey never picked up her clothes at the dry cleaner. He didn't even know if that was the dry cleaner she had used before he had insisted on taking over that chore. Had she thought that was odd? Did Lacey go there to try to figure out why he did that? Lacey didn't think in those terms, though. She thought in terms of strokes of paint and pallette colors. She thought in terms of finding beauty in surprising and unexpected places—the rust on a gate, or a mud-stained shoe in the street.

"It's so interesting, Steve. Look at it from this angle, and you have the grey of the cast-away shoe juxtaposed with the bright red leaves the dogwood is casting away, too," she'd say.

"Juxtaposed" was one of her favorite words when Lacey was viewing things through her Lacey-colored glasses. She'd brought the world to him in a whole new way. Surprising. And poignant.

"Poignant." That was another Lacey word. She'd use it when she was crying over articles about elephants that were rescued from circuses or when dogs with the mange were given veterinary care.

"It's so poignant. These poor animals were cast away, and then someone reached out and helped them."

Huh. "Cast away" seemed to be another Lacey phrase. Yeah, she used that one a lot.

Was she alive? Or was she cut open by a medical examiner, weighed, and repackaged in her skin bag, waiting for someone to claim and bury her? Who would even do that? Lacey's only relation was her Uncle Bartholomew. And her uncle would never put himself at risk to come home and make final arrangements for her. Steve thought probably it would fall on him to do it. That winded him. He leaned forward in the shower and sucked and blew air in and out like an old man with respiratory failure.

He imagined himself sitting in the office, talking to an undertaker. What would he do if that became reality? What would she want to have happen? Maybe it was in her will. Maybe it would have to be that shithead Reynolds who would claim her and use the process to make some big show to get himself more time in front of the camera. That was exactly what that guy would do. Just look how he trotted Lacey out in front of the crowd and risked her life for a little celebrity. And that action had killed her.

You don't know that, he tried to talk himself down. But still, there was a sniper and there was an abductor. There was a body.

"A day or two," the medical examiner had said. "We should know by sometime later in the week."

Of course, in a day or two the con would be done. The Zorics would either succeed or not. The Bureau would either succeed or not. But the dead woman would always be dead.

Steve wasn't sure he could survive this feeling until he knew for sure what had happened to Lacey. He turned off the water and rubbed himself dry with a towel. Until they'd definitively IDed the victim, Lacey could still be alive. And if she were alive, she was okay enough to go to the drycleaners. And that meant he might have enough time to find her and save her.

He pulled on a pair of jeans and a turtleneck, yanked on some socks, shoved his feet into his boots, grabbed his jacket and keys, and ran from the apartment. If only he knew where he was running.

Chapter Twenty-Nine

Lacey

Tuesday Night

As Lacey came down the stairs, she was surprised that Deep didn't react. He didn't glance up at her and offer her food. He didn't glance at her at all. But she didn't mind. It gave her time to observe Deep's face when he wasn't being his steady, tender self.

This must be his warrior's glare. His lip snarled back. Disgust painted his face with intensity. She watched his finger tapping the enter button, watched his eyes focus on the screen. Each tap seemed to roil his emotions. Each tap seemed to make his muscles expand like Maori warriors performing the Haka, showing how they'd use their primal ferocity to drive the enemy back into their boats and away from their shores. Yes, that's what glowed in Deep's eyes. Primal ferocity. And it unnerved her. She moved to scamper back up the stairs, but then Deep noticed her.

He quickly shut the lid of the computer, tamped down on the overt waves of aggression, and stood. "There you are. Are you hungry?" His voice was a lower range than usual, but as he directed his words toward her, there was only gentleness and concern.

The laugh that bubbled from Lacey's throat was from nerves. "I knew that would be the first thing out of your mouth. Food. I'm not hungry. Thirsty, though. I'm going to get some water. What can I get you?"

"Water's fine." He scrubbed his hands over his face, further calming the combative energy that swirled around him. He followed her into the kitchen. "The mystery woman was pretty darned smart," Deep started.

Lacey stood on the tips of her toes and stretched for a glass. She could just barely touch one with her fingertips. Deep came up behind her, reached past, and handed two down to her open hands. "Thank you kindly," she said as she moved to the fridge and pressed the button for the ice maker. "Smart, how?"

"She needed something of value to offer to the pawn store, and so she used the coat."

"She needed money?"

"She needed to hide two thumb drives somewhere off-premises is my guess."

"Two more?"

"Yup." Deep took the water from her hands and sat down at the kitchen table.

From her point of view, Deep looked like he was weighing his words carefully. Lacey gingerly sat in the chair opposite him and waited.

"How well do you know your Uncle Bartholomew?"

Lacey's gaze searched over the table, then returned to Deep's. "I'm not sure how to quantify that for you."

"Did you know he slept with other males?"

"Well, yes, I did. But he's not the one who told me. Uncle Bartholomew hasn't come out of the closet. The Assembly doesn't approve of homosexuality. He wouldn't be allowed to remain a member if they knew he was homosexual, so it was a tightly-guarded secret. His lover probably thought I was in the loop, because he mentioned it to me. Mentioned a little more than I could ever want to know, to be honest."

Deep's jaw tightened. "What did he say to you?"

"Oh you know, girlfriend gossip. 'He's so cute,' 'he makes me so hot.'" Lacey gave a shudder. "It's fine to hear from your friends when you're out for a drink, but I didn't need the visuals put in my head about two old wrinkly men with paunch bellies going at it."

"Visuals from words? Only wrinkly old men?"

Lacey stilled. "What's going on, Deep?"

"What's the man's name whom your uncle was seeing?"

"Radovan Krokov. Why?"

"And you met this man in person?"

Lacey's voice tightened down. The last thing she wanted to be talking about right now was Radovan. Poor Radovan. "Yes, but he's passed away now. Why?"

"I'm going to tell you, Lacey, just. . . Let's start somewhere easier first, okay?"

"Yes, alright." She rotated her glass on the table, spinning it faster and faster, until some of the water sloshed out. "You're really scaring me." She got up to grab the dish towel, hanging beside the sink.

"I'm sorry. I don't mean to. One step at a time, okay? First step—while you were asleep, I searched the coat and found the thumb drives sewn into a pouch that attached to the pocket in the lining. It was very clever how it was placed. Like the thumb drive Bardman gave you, there is a purpose behind these, I'm sure. They both hold information. One is very clear and condemning information."

"Like what?" With her spill sopped up, Lacey leaned forward and grasped Deep's hands as if she was going over the ledge, and he was the only thing that could keep her from falling. She had no idea what was coming, but she knew it was going to be bad. And once she heard what Deep had to say, she knew she could never unhear it. She sensed that Deep was preserving some piece of her innocence for a little longer, and while she appreciated that – it also made her feel terrified. Yes, there was that word again. It never seemed far. It was always painted right there in the picture with her.

"Okay, we'll start with the first thumb drive. Mostly, it held some contracts. There were contracts signed by each of the painter's agents lending the various works to the gallery. All of them included the provision that the paintings would be insured until sold or shipped back to the artist."

Lacey blinked. "But that would have cost a fortune. Who signed these contracts?"

"Your uncle."

"I doubt very much that my Uncle Bartholomew would sign something like that. Did he actually take out insurance on them?"

"Yes, but not the kind described in the contracts allowing the paintings to be represented by his gallery."

"An insurance scam? No, he would know just how little insurance we have in place. We really just cross our fingers and hope for the best. Everyone in the business knows that theft is always a possibility. It's in our contracts, for heaven's sake. But you said these contracts were different."

"Help me to understand that. Maybe, for example, your uncle took out extra insurance on this particular show you were planning."

"That would stand out too brazenly. For example, do you remember the twelve works stolen from the Isabella Stewart Gardner Museum that I was telling you about? That was one of the biggest art thefts in history, and those paintings were completely uninsured. Well, the collection was insured against damage, but not against theft. Part of the reason was the rapidly rising cost of art back in the '80s. And part of it was the increase in art robberies at that time, too. Both things coupled together made theft insurance more expensive than most museum or gallery's operating budgets."

"Okay, compared to value –"

"Which is subjective, when it comes to art," Lacey interjected.

"Compared to subjective value, art in general has relatively little security and almost no insurance. I've been researching art theft for the last few days and it seems that not even the insurance companies are fighting to stop these crimes. When I looked it up, I found out the FBI's art theft division is headquartered here in DC – but there are only sixteen special agents on their task force. That's pretty small. Did you meet any of them when you called the FBI about the disappearance of the Iniquus art works from your warehouse?"

Lacey shook her head. "They spoke to Mr. Reynolds, my lawyer. Why?"

"Just wondering if you had a description of the agents. Wondered if maybe any of them have floated into your path since your part in the Iniquus case was put to rest. So we're left with possible fraud and possible theft. What do you think about a combination of the two?"

"How do you mean?"

"It's a pretty odd setup, don't you think? The team working on this is up to something complex. They've got someone pretending to be you who is setting up a gallery opening. And there is a whole file on the show, including catering receipts. There are printed invitations. There's a location. They've made reservations for the artists' agents at some very nice hotels. Pricey. Why?"

"They're making copies of the work – the forger who's doing them is really talented. I can't tell which ones were fake and which ones are the real deal simply by looking," Lacey said.

"When we were in the warehouse, you were wiping one of the paintings with a chemical. Why?"

"All of the paintings are oils. Acrylics dry very quickly, but oils can take months to cure, and then sometimes they're varnished. But that last step is up to the artist. It looked to me like the forgeries of the paintings where the original artist chose to use varnish had been painted first, and the last ones to be forged were of the paintings that weren't varnished, which makes sense. The room was set up with de-humidifiers, fans, and warm temperatures to encourage the quick drying process of oil on canvas. What I was doing with the cloth was testing to see if the painting was dry or not. On the real painting, the one that had been allowed to cure properly, I wouldn't have picked up any pigment. I was reassuring myself that what I thought I was seeing was in truth what I was seeing."

"You're confident then that you saw fake paintings. And when we looked in the crates, we found what we think are the originals."

"Right. I think they're the originals, but I didn't test them for dryness, and without the right equipment—even with the right equipment—that's not my bailiwick. I don't know that I could tell one from the other," Lacey said.

"So what are they doing? Are they making the fakes to sell as the real deal? Are they going to give the fakes back to the artists and try to pass them off as the originals? Why go through all of the effort to have an impostor Lacey involved?"

"You've got me. These works are very valuable. The receiver will almost certainly know the work is illegal, so the buyer isn't going to display the work to visitors who might recognize it as stolen. Unless, of course, they're sending it to parts of the world where that wouldn't be a problem."

"Like where?"

"Oh, I don't know. Somewhere outside of North America. Money and distance would be an illegal collector's best friends."

"Okay, I have another possibility. What about posing the fake paintings in a gallery show, stealing the real ones, and then contacting your gallery to ransom the real ones?"

"That's a lot of work and an unnecessary extra step. Why not take the originals and ransom them? Why would you need fakes hanging up? Like I told you, we don't have insurance to cover theft, so what would they get?"

"Your uncle has money – millions."

"*Great* uncle. I can't imagine he'd care. Remember, it would be the artists' loss, not the gallery's."

"So let's say they thought your uncle might be willing to cough up some money   say a million dollars or so—to save his reputation. Could you see him doing that?"

"Going back a few months, I really don't know. Could have gone either way. He might have told them to go jump in the lake, or he might follow through for some reason. But he got caught up with the Iniquus theft in November. He ran off to his vacation home in Bali and moved all of his financial resources offshore. I don't think he plans on ever coming back – so I can't see how they could extort money from him. And if they succeeded in killing me, which is what they've been trying to do, how could they extort money from me?"

"You're referring to your uncle's money?"

"No, my own. I inherited a great deal of money. I work for pleasure, not necessity. And I lead a simple life by choice, not necessity."

Deep leaned back in his chair and crossed his arms over his chest. Lacey watched carefully to see how he took in the information that she was an heiress. In fact, she was worth a lot more money than her uncle was. But her wealth seemed to pass right through Deep's consciousness. He didn't put any emphasis on it at all as he worked to figure out the scam. Lacey wondered what had been on the computer screen that made him look so fierce earlier. But she trusted that Deep was progressing forward in a systematic way and not simply dumping things on the table in a jumble, which she appreciated. Order amidst all of this chaos was appreciated.

"Okay, go back. On the flash drive, there are signed contracts with the artist's agents."

"Signed by whom?" Lacey asked.

"Your uncle."

"What if the signatures were forged? That artist from the warehouse could probably do it."

"I put them through a program I have that identifies the differences between known signatures and unauthenticated signatures."

"How did you get a copy of a known signature?"

"I had one on my computer from when Iniquus was investigating their art theft."

"Oh, yes, that's right." Lacey pulled her hands back so she could wipe them on her pants.

"The software authenticated his signature. The contracts state that the Bartholomew Windsor Gallery will be handling the show. It enumerates the ways in which the art pieces will be marketed, including a cocktail party for the agents that will, according to these contracts, be tomorrow night. It says that they will not be housed at the Bartholomew Windsor Galleries, but will be at a rented space in a more accessible and affluently inhabited part of the city, and they give an Alexandria address."

"That's what the man was talking about at the warehouse. So that means it's still a go. And the pieces were insured for their whole amount?"

"There's no indication that your uncle followed through on purchasing the theft protection insurance. But other contracts showed proof of insurance. For example, there was a contract for each of the paintings that was listed in the catalogue, price paid in full."

"What? Before the show opened? Before they were publicly offered? All of them? That's unheard of. Who bought them?"

"Eastern European businesses, all of them. And each of the art pieces is insured."

"Against theft?"

"Against damage."

"Oh." Lacey rolled that tidbit over in her mind. "That makes all the sense in the world."

Chapter Thirty

Lacey

Tuesday Night

Deep leaned farther across the table. "Tell me."

"Well the theft insurance is so costly it would almost be a wash by the time all was said and done. But short-term damage insurance is comparatively inexpensive. Especially if it's for an abbreviated time, such as for the time a show is supposed to be up, through shipping a piece to its new location. So, let's say two months. With insurance in place, you could put up some counterfeits, and then do something that would cause them damage. It would have to be enough damage that an expert witness couldn't prove they were fake, though."

"Something like what?"

Lacey searched the ceiling, thinking it through. "Couldn't be the normal things that might cause damage: smoke, water, vandals. That's why the damage insurance isn't as much— there's a slim chance things like that would happen."

283

"I don't know about smoke, but fire would certainly take care of the problem."

"It would if they could get it to burn enough to destroy the canvases, but you'd have to do it in such a way that no one could accuse you of arson. So, like, you couldn't pour gasoline everywhere and pitch a match. But yes, that would work."

"Alright, so let's run that scenario. We've burned up the fake paintings. Nothing left but the nail they were hung from. We'd still have the original paintings."

"Yes, that's the really interesting part. See, if the corporations own – No, that might not work if they got insurance money."

"Go on with that thought." Deep leaned in.

Lacey stalled while she took a sip of water. No, she couldn't see how that would work. "Nothing. I was going to say, if the paintings had a contract and had been paid in full, they wouldn't have been stolen. They could hang them in their offices or living rooms without any danger of Interpol getting involved – or whomever."

"What if they'd already shipped the authentic paintings to the buyers, and it was your uncle who had signed the insurance contracts?"

"Then the companies would be fine—they could enjoy their art. My uncle would be the one who committed insurance fraud. If he paid the artist and agents, he'd be out a little over half a million in commissions and another million and a half in insurance claims. He'd walk away with about two million dollars, as long as no one was the wiser. If somehow the foreign buyer was involved, and really, I can't imagine all of these pieces being sold the way they were unless they were pre-selected. And that's what I'm imagining happened here, since my uncle handed me a list of art that he wanted me to gather." Lacey shook her head. "It seems so unlike him. I shouldn't say that, because he did steal the Iniquus art. To tell you the truth, I still don't understand how that happened, either. Do you think he became mentally unstable? Do you think maybe something was going on with his finances that I might not know about? Why would he sign those contracts?"

"A million and a half is a good pay day."

"But my uncle doesn't need the money. He lives luxuriously on his interest. He doesn't even need to tap into his principal. So why in the world would he do something so criminal?"

"He was being blackmailed."

"Over his homosexuality? That can't be all." Lacey considered Deep for a long moment. He'd braced himself and his eyes had lost all traces of the merriment that she usually found there. "You know why he was being blackmailed, don't you?"

"He was a pedophile, and he had sex with pubescent boys." Deep said it so softly that Lacey thought she had to be mistaken.

She jutted her head forward. "What?"

"Lacey, one of the thumb drives is full of photographs that includes your uncle involved in some very disturbing contact with teenaged boys."

Lacey jumped up to race forward. Her only thought was that she needed to protect those children. As she left her seat, her hand reaching out for the doorknob, her vision dimmed. The next thing she knew, she was looking through a long tube, listening to a distorted voice from far far away.

It got closer each time the call went out. "Lacey. Lacey. Lacey, sweetheart, open your eyes."

Lacey reached up a rubbery arm and hooked it around Deep's neck. "I'm going to be sick."

Deep immediately propped her up and leaned her over a trash can. He supported her weight with one arm and scooped her hair from her face with the other. It seemed he had a lot of practice with puking girls. Lacey's stomach heaved, and she made horrible gagging sounds, but nothing came up. Finally, she was simply dangling there, panting. Deep eased her back over to her chair and handed her a glass of water.

"You have to eat under stress or this happens."

Lacey looked at him incredulously. "Are you crazy?" Her voice was a hoarse rasp. "Seriously, are you completely off your rocker? You mean if I had eaten a sandwich earlier, I wouldn't have fainted when I found out my uncle, my only living relative, is a monster who attacks children and rapes them? What?"

"No. I don't know why I said that. I'm sorry. It's how my family deals with stress. Something bad happens, then you make a meal and the family gathers and somehow, somehow that makes things better." Deep crouched beside her chair. His hands covered his face; his head tilted toward the ceiling. "Those images were sickening, Lacey. I'm trying to deal with what I saw."

Lacey moved her mouth to say something to comfort him, but all of her words were lost in the sobs that rolled up her throat. She felt dirty and horrible. No wonder Deep looked that way when she came down the stairs. No wonder Deep had closed the lid and protected her from actually getting those images into her head. He had seen them, though. He had gone through them so she wouldn't have to. He'd been the warrior, though it was her war. It was hurting him. That was plain as day. It kept getting worse. Everything kept getting worse.

"Come on, up you go," Deep whispered in her ear. He pulled her arm around his shoulder and walked her up the stairs. "You need warm water and a dark room."

Deep sat her on the toilet while he started the bath water. He went out of the room and came back in with lavender jar candles and rose-scented bath oil. The room softened around her, becoming an island of calm. She pulled off her clothes— he wasn't going to undress her like a baby, not again—and climbed into the tub. She was only mildly surprised when he undressed too, picked up a hairbrush, and climbed in behind her. She leaned into him while he brushed her hair in long strokes.

She closed her eyes. Slowly Lacey felt some of the revulsion and shock from downstairs ebb. She turned her head to rest her ear on his chest and listen to his heart beat. If only they could stay this way wrapped in the warm cocoon of scents, the world shut away by the door. "Is this what you've done for your other girlfriends when they were freaking out?"

He paused. "I don't know what to do, Lacey. I've never been in a situation like this before. I've never had to grapple with all the feelings I'm going through. Right now, I'm trying to guess what might soothe you. I'm doing my best."

She turned up her chin to offer him a kiss and whispered, "Thank you."

Chapter Thirty-One

Tuesday Night

Lacey lay under the covers, her naked body tangled with Deep's. She wanted every bit of her skin to be in contact with his. In a world that suddenly seemed filthy, Deep was pristine. To her, he felt like the strength of goodness personified. Her heart was filled to overflowing knowing that he was there with her. Yet gratitude and shame made strange bedfellows. The shine and warmth of her feelings for him juxtaposed with the cold ash of dishonor. If she were an artist, she'd try to catch the starkness of the contrast in some medium. To get the thoughts and sensations out of her body and onto a canvas, so it no longer hurt her.

They lay there, whispering in the dark.

"You said Higgins was on an FBI task force for Violent Gangs. Do they protect minors?" Lacey asked.

"The case I worked on with Higgins had to do with human trafficking. Running girls—especially under-aged girls—is one way that gangs have diversified."

"I thought you said you didn't think this was a gang. You thought it was a family."

"Gangs usually find girls here in America. Runaways. Kids who've gotten caught up with drugs. But, yeah, this seems like a family deal. Sometimes they're involved in human trafficking. After seeing the pictures with your uncle, I think that's why Higgins is involved."

"Where do criminal families find these children?"

"Asia, India, Eastern Europe. I worked a case once involving a girl from the Czech Republic. She was lured over to the US and held as a sex slave. Strike Force rescued her. We know that there are families out there who specialize in hiring girls as maids or nannies—sometimes even as models—to lure them to the United States. When they get here, their handlers take their papers and threaten the women and children who have fallen into the con. They tell them the horrible things that the US government would do to them if they were found by the authorities. Or worse, they threaten to kill their family back in their home country – their moms and dads, their sisters or brothers. It's a hell of a shackle. And they'll do whatever they're told to do."

"Do you think that's what happened to the boys in the photos?"

"Maybe." He squeezed her tightly against him and kissed her hair. "We can't sit on this. We need to take this to Iniquus. There are children being exploited. We have to get them help."

"Yes, absolutely. Yes. The children are our priority."

"Good. Okay. I've been thinking about this since I saw the photos. I'm really not sure what to do. So I'm going to lay out my thoughts and ask you to weigh in."

"Alright." Lacey untucked herself from his arms and sat upright with her legs crisscrossed. She wanted to be able to study his face, even if it was only illuminated by the dim light put off by the digital clock.

Deep reached down to the end of the bed and dragged the throw cover up, tucking it around her, protecting her from the chill in the January air. "When dealing with criminals, sometimes you have to be creative. Do you remember Al Capone?"

"The mobster?"

"Yes. They couldn't get him for his mob crimes, so the feds went after him for tax evasion. The judge gave him eleven years in prison. It got him off the streets, which was their only real goal."

Lacey wrinkled her brow. She didn't understand where Deep was heading with this. "Okay."

"There are only sixteen special agents assigned to art. And this operation looks like it's getting a lot of attention. We're going to assume Higgins was in the bar sitting near you on purpose, because from the YouTube videos of him moving you out of the bar, it looked like he was leading you to a car outside with two other agents in it. Those agents knew who you were—you can see it in their faces."

Lacey nodded. She completely agreed with that assessment.

"Higgins is on Violent Gangs. That's the thing catching me. Gangs aren't going to play with arts cons. Families would, but still, there are too many resources in place for an arts con. I'm going to assume that Steve is FBI, too. Call that a gut feeling. We've been back and forth about his role, but I think he is. He was deep undercover if he was living with you. Again, that's a hell of an expenditure of resources for him to be in place for an arts con."

"Do you think they were going after my uncle? But he's been in Bali since November. Over two months ago."

"I think they're going after the family. I think this has more to do with the children than the art. The art would be a good means to catch them and get them off the streets."

"Like Al Capone."

"Exactly. Now, let's walk through some other ideas. And remember, we are speculating. Based on a small amount of evidence, true. But speculation isn't fact."

Lacey nodded.

"Your uncle is sexually gratified with teenaged boys. He seeks them out through some service. The service provider takes the pictures, planning to use them somehow in the future. What are your uncle's assets? His reputation, his affiliation with the Assembly, his wealth, and his gallery. So they wait to figure out how best to use their photos. And somehow, this art con comes up. And then you get involved. It's a hell of a lot more than just a matter of your uncle handing over the collection to you. Because right afterward, he sends you fake correspondence claiming that the show is off. When did he hand you the show—before or after your accident?"

"As soon as I got back to work after the accident, he gave me the acquisitions list. And he sent me the letters claiming the show was off from Bali. He wanted me to keep the gallery open and running, but the show was a no-go. Our plan was for him to resume running the gallery as soon as his lawyer arranged for the charges to go away. But from my perspective, I had no hand in the show."

"You never communicated with any of the artists or their people?"

"No, I'd made absolutely zero progress. I never actually made contact with anyone. I did some research in preparation, but Uncle Bartholomew said not to move forward yet. He said he had to get some things organized first."

"And when did he email you, in relation to the Iniquus art incident?"

"Uhm, he had flown to the islands to play golf, he said. And then I emailed him letting him know someone had stolen the Iniquus art from our warehouse. Then, hmm. I'll have to look it up, but I'd guess it was a week or so later."

"He was in Bali? And it was about the time that the hacked Assembly files were released to the press and the members were getting arrested?"

"Yes."

"So if he were in Bali, perhaps he didn't realize that such a huge shakeup was happening to the Assembly here in the States. He probably still thought that he had connections that would make all of his problems go away."

"Or perhaps he knew his goose was cooked, and he was never planning to come home. Maybe he sent me the email saying the show was over because he didn't want me to assume that because I was in charge of the gallery, that I was now authorized to develop the show. I'd start making inquiries that could derail their plans, and confuse the people who had been interacting with the impostor. But who really cares about the art? How does this affect the children?"

"Here's the thing. If this is FBI, and this is their sting, they already know what's going on. We'd accomplish nothing by taking these photos to them. And if we take them to the wrong person, perhaps the one-in-a-million special agent who's got his head screwed on wrong, then we could warn them off and blow the arrest. If we hand it to Iniquus, well, same outcome in that Iniquus would be required to move forward and present what evidence we have in hand to agencies that might be involved. I don't know who the bad guys are here, and that makes me worried about moving forward."

"So what do we do?"

"Exactly. What do we do?"

Lacey pulled her knees up and wrapped her arms around them. She sat in the dark and silence and prayed. *God, help us to make the right decision. Help us to help those children.* And though she hoped for it, as she had so many times in the past, there was no aha moment. No cosmic voice whispering in her ear.

Finally, Deep said, "I think for now—at least for tomorrow—we need to keep investigating on our own. See what we can turn up. That might be absolutely the wrong thing to do. That's why I need your opinion. We don't have the benefit of a crystal ball."

"I am so out of my league. I'm really not the person to talk to. Maybe Lynx? She might be able to sort this out with you."

"She's asked me not to call her unless I want Iniquus involved. So that call would put wheels in motion."

"Why were you asking me so many timing questions?" Lacey asked.

"I'm trying to figure out how and when they placed the lookalike Lacey. And it seems to me that everything centers on your car accident."

Lacey's blood turned to ice.

Chapter Thirty-Two

Wednesday Morning

Once again, Deep was first out of bed. Once again, Lacey followed the scent of coffee down the stairs. Once again, Lacey found Deep in the living room with his brow furrowed as he stared at his laptop. Lacey's stomach tightened. What new horror would today bring?

When her foot left the last stair, Deep turned toward her. "Have you ever heard the name Zoric?"

"Is that a first name or last name?"

"Last name. Bogdan Zoric."

Lacey shook her head. "Can you give me a context?"

"Maybe from the gallery? Maybe from your uncle's social circles?"

"Bogdan Zoric? No, it's a unique name, so I think I'd remember it. Why are you asking?" She balanced her elbows on the back of the sofa and leaned her weight forward to give Deep a kiss.

"According to this article in the Washington Post, Leo Bardman's name was a fake. His driver's license was a counterfeit. The Washington PD turned to fingerprints and came up with a picture from Zoric's Slovakian passport and visa; it was a match."

"Huh." Lacey made her way through the living room, moving toward the kitchen and some coffee. She desperately needed a shot of caffeine to rev her brain. Deep looked more like himself this morning, she thought, as she pulled the gallon of milk from the fridge to doctor her coffee. She was glad. That cloud in his eyes yesterday had unnerved her. Lacey realized how much she depended on Deep being the solid one. It gave her space to be the emotional mess. Someone had to be the adult, and Lacey had been glad to hand that role to Deep. "Can I bring you a fresh cup of coffee?" she called from the kitchen.

"Yes, thanks."

Lacey moved back into the room, balancing the mugs on salad plates. She was sure there were coasters somewhere around, but she didn't care enough to go looking for them. As the dishes rattled against each other, Deep watched her progress.

"Bogdan. Bardman," Lacey said, handing over the mug with the black coffee. "They sound similar. Bardman sounds like an English surname, but the guy didn't look English. You've seen him. He was tall, with wide, high cheekbones. I would have guessed Eastern European rather than English. Slovakia? He did have a heavy accent."

"You didn't mention an accent before," Deep said. "What. . ."

Lacey's brow pulled tightly together, and she stared at the floor. Anything Deep was saying to her were simply vibrations in the air, indistinguishable from smell or light, just fumes and waves oscillating the atmosphere. Finally, her head came up until she was focused on Deep. "Radovan. I'm fairly sure he was Slovakian."

Her hands were shaking uncontrollably and the creamy beverage sloshed over the rim. Deep took the plate from her hands and put it on the floor.

Lacey pinched her nose and turned her head to the wall, tucking her other hand under the elbow. She felt like someone poised to jump off the high board. Terrified of the trip down.

She went quiet again, her eyes shifting along the floorboards left then right like she was trying to read the cracks. Then she sank onto the sofa and looked at Deep, her lips rolled in tightly.

"I want to hear what you started to tell me. Bardman had a heavy accent . . ."

"I didn't think about his accent. With everything that was going on, the blood and the bubbles, the screaming and the camera flashes, black cars, scary men . . . I didn't realize until I just said it that he had an accent."

Deep waited with what seemed to Lacey like infinite patience as her confetti thoughts came to rest. She shook her head. "I don't know what to do," she told the floor. "It seems. . ." She searched out Deep's eyes. She was lost and looking for a speck of land on the horizon—some dot of hope she could navigate toward.

Deep shifted over and took her hands. "Don't try to put it all together. You don't need everything to connect. Let your thoughts come up." He pulled her over to sit against him and wrapped one arm around her, then put his notebook and pen on the side table. "Close your eyes, and when you're ready, say the thing that comes to mind."

Lacey rested her head back, shutting her eyes the way Deep had asked her to. Her mind was jangling with impressions. She tried to grasp at just one. A single thought that she could pull like a thread from the tangle. "I met Steve when I killed a deer," Lacey said. "I've never killed anything before. I feel terrible for killing the deer."

Lacey could feel the wiggle of Deep's arm as he put those words on paper.

"At the bar, there were two sets of men. The guy with the black car who grabbed my ankle—he was right outside the door. The news said he was a special agent with the FBI. You said you recognized him. His name is Higgins, and he fights gangs and sometimes human traffickers." Lacy reached up and pushed her hair behind her ears. "You said you thought Steve was trained. If Steve were trained and lying to me, and if your friend Lynx says he looks too clean, then Steve Adamic probably isn't his name. Just like Leo Bardman wasn't that guy's name, either. I thought that Steve being trained meant that he was a good guy – maybe even an FBI agent. But he didn't have to be. He could be a bad guy. He could be a criminal. In my mind, you know, I thought that Steve might have been undercover, like you were saying last night, and somehow protecting me while he figured out a crime. But that's really weird that he happened to be driving down the road behind me when I killed the deer. And right after that, he started showing up in those pictures."

Her eyes blinked open, and she looked at Deep.

"Please tell me you're a good guy."

"I'm a good guy," he said. "But you're not going to believe that until everything shakes out. I understand that. It's smart. You're smart not to trust me because I say you should."

"It's not completely that I don't trust you. You're right, though. I spent months trusting a guy who said he wanted to marry me. He acted like he believed that. It felt awfully real to me. It's not so much that I don't trust you as much as it is that I don't trust myself. I obviously have been showing poor judgment." Lacey pushed to sitting. Her thoughts were too angst-filled to allow her to be comfortable. "And that doesn't reflect on you. It's my deficit. I don't want my lack of judgment to get you killed." Her voice was crawling up an octave with each word out of her mouth. "I can't let that even be a possibility."

"Wait. Woah." Deep twisted away from the notepad, turning so they were almost nose to nose. "How did we get there? That's what Lynx would call a 'ginormous synaptic leap'. What canyon did you cross? Getting me killed isn't a function of you not believing that I'm a good guy, which is what I thought we were talking about. Now you're saying that my being in danger is a function of my associating with you? There's a big hole in this story if you think that's the case."

Lacey sat mute.

"That isn't the first time you've made this reference. Way back when this whole thing was unfolding, I said, 'All those months — you didn't call me until you were in danger.' And you responded, 'I didn't call you all those months because I

302

was in danger, I didn't want you involved.' What danger, Lacey?"

Lacey swallowed and stared. Finally, she forced herself to blink. Just one blink. Then another. Blink.

Deep put his hand on her knee, and it pulled her out of her lost place. "Start with one thing. Something small that doesn't scare you," Deep said.

Lacey swallowed and nodded. "Sometimes as part of my job, I go to people's houses to hang their art and make sure that it's properly positioned. An investment piece could become damaged by sunlight or room traffic. I offer to do that as a concierge service when we sell a piece."

"Okay, good. Has anyone taken you up on that offer lately?"

"Yes, Radovan did." Lacey's muscles banded, pulling her limbs in tightly, making her stiff. Even her lips became tight and thin. "Radovan Krokov has bought several pieces from us. He likes male nudes."

"Good," Deep encouraged. "When did he buy his last painting?"

"September." Lacey was able to push out the words with what little air her lungs would hold. She tried to focus on her breathing rather than the fear tingling up her spine. The more she said, the more dangerous things became for Deep.

"And you went to his house to hang the painting."

Lacey squeezed her eyes and nodded.

"Were you coming home from his house when you had the car accident?"

Lacey nodded again.

"You're having a traumatic response right now. Go as slowly as you need to. Is this a reaction to the accident?"

Lacey twitched her head.

"Something that happened in the house?"

Lacey sat still as if petrified; she stopped breathing. She was the beat of her heart and nothing more.

Deep took her icy hands in his. "Did someone hurt you, baby? Or did someone do something that wasn't alright with you back at the house?" Lacey could tell that Deep tried to modulate his voice to the same tone he had used for his other questions, but she sensed the wolf-snarl running under his words.

"No one hurt me there that day," she managed.

"But somewhere?"

"On a different day," Lacey said.

"Let's start with the house. Did something happen at the house that made you feel that you needed to get away fast?"

"Something was happening at the house. I don't fully understand what I was seeing, but I believe it was part of a murder."

"You saw a body?"

"No, but I know that Radovan died." She took in a faltering breath and screamed in her head to get herself together. Lives were at stake, children's lives. "This is what happened. My uncle gave me a key to Radovan's house. Radovan was supposed to be away on business. But when I got there, the door was already unlocked and the stove was on. At that point, I assumed that it was the help."

Deep pulled the notebook into his lap and quietly took notes.

"I called out, but no one answered me. I went in the kitchen, looked in the pot, and wondered if I should turn off the element. I decided to leave things be and if no one was there when I left, I'd turn the stove off and leave a note."

"Okay, pot on the stove, no one home."

"Radovan's painting had been delivered but hadn't been hung. I was there to find a good place for the piece, taking into consideration the aesthetics and any environmental issues. The only constraint was that the piece had to go in a public room. So I was downstairs looking around when I saw two men coming up to the door, which was fine. My first instinct was that they were the gardeners—that's how they were dressed. They wore green coveralls, and they had masks over their faces. Dust masks. No, not dust masks. You know—the kind of masks that gardeners wear when they're spraying pesticides. It goes over the face and has a motor for purifying air that clips to their back belt. And they were wearing goggles like they were spraying for weeds."

"What did you do?"

"Well, nothing at first. The door was still unlocked. They didn't jiggle the handle or anything. They walked in like they knew it would open."

"Were they wearing gloves?"

"Yes, gardening gloves. So they came in and weirdly, that's when they turned on their respiratory machines. They had buttons on their throats and when they pressed them, you could hear what they were saying to each other despite the masks on their faces. Something about those buttons frightened me — didn't seem right for a gardener. I moved back into the corner by the buffet table. I could see a little of what they were doing because Radovan has an antique hall mirror in there that's at least twelve feet high."

"Okay, so you're hiding in the dining room. What did the men do?"

"The guy said, 'Check the birds.' And the other guy said, 'Canaries in the coalmine.' And they both laughed."

"Does Radovan have birds?"

"Yes, he had a pair of peach-faced love birds. They're beautiful. I wonder what happened to them after his death." Lacey paused for a moment stuck on that thought, then she continued on. "Radovan had a tree in his gaming room, and the birdcage hung there. Usually he left the cage door open, and the birds were allowed to fly around. I was trying to convince myself that that was a normal thing to say. "canaries in the coalmine.' See, when guests come to the house, we have to be careful not to let the birds fly outside."

"What happened next?"

"One guy says to the other, 'I'm going to go upstairs and make sure everything's good. Why don't you clear that stuff out of here?' Then someone was on the stairs and someone was making a lot of noise in the games room."

"Okay, good. Then what?"

"Nothing much. Really, still simply odd. But I was very scared. I had never felt that way before."

"What way is that?"

"Like my lungs were filling with air, but not. And like my heart was beating, but not. I was having trouble keeping myself focused. I was praying really hard. I wanted these people to leave, because I didn't know what was going on." Lacey remembered that her fear had tasted like a bright copper penny, metallic on her tongue.

"And what did they do next?"

"The guy came down the stairs, and he's laughing. He said something like, 'The maid's going to have a nasty surprise.' And the other guy responded, 'So a done deal?' 'Good and done,' the first guy said, and they laughed again. They seemed to be enjoying themselves, whatever was going on. Then the one guy says 'Make sure to vacuum that whole area. I'm taking the rocks out.'"

"'I'm taking the rocks out?'"

"Yes."

"What does that mean?"

"He took the pot off the stove and went out the Florida room door to the side garden. I was having a hard time. I was getting dizzy. All I could think was I had to get out of there right then. I stood up and pulled my keys from my pocket. Obviously, I wasn't thinking very clearly. I got as far as the front door when I heard the guy right behind me, shouting, 'Hey!'"

Lacey watched Deep swallow hard. His jaw had set, and that combat focus returned to his gaze.

"I turned around and the guy was right there in front of me. I could see his eyes, even with the goggles. They weren't angry or menacing or anything. They were confused. He looked at me and said, 'Danika? What are you doing here?' And I inexplicably smiled and waved and went out the front door."

"He let you go?"

"At first. I ran to my car, which I had left out front so I could get to my tools. I jumped in and took off. And that's all I remember. I was in the car, struggling to calm myself and catch my breath, and then Steve was there, calling my name."

"But that's not the end of this story."

"No." She shifted uncomfortably. "It's not."

Chapter Thirty-Three

Lacey

Wednesday

"**G**o back," Deep said. "Danika? He called you Danika?" The name had slipped out and hung there in the air like a fly ball, and Deep was directly underneath it, waiting for its slow descent into his glove.

A lie formed on the tip of Lacey's tongue, but she stopped it before it dripped out. Deep told her she could unfold her story at her own pace as she grew to trust him – but not to lie. It seemed to her in that moment that Deep would never forgive her if she broke that covenant. She also thought about her other pledge—that she wouldn't be putting her life alone in danger by revealing it, but Deep's too.

"This is why you scare the hell out of me, Lacey. I don't know you. I don't know what you've done in your life. Who you are. All I know is that I'm in it like quicksand. I'm not going to pull myself free from how I feel about you. I don't

311

even want to. But it sure would be nice if I knew what the heck I've stepped into."

Lacey pressed her clenched hands to her forehead.

"There—tell me that thought," Deep said.

"Maybe it's time for me to go to the FBI."

"I agree. Maybe it is. That's your call," Deep said. "The men and women over at the FBI are stellar. You can trust them."

"That's not really true, is it? I mean, if I'm one of the pieces in some ongoing game, I can't really walk up to their office and say – hey, I want my life back the way it was. They couldn't do that, could they? They can't unwind what they were doing. So what would they do with me?"

"Depends. If they thought you were in danger, they'd probably put you into the witness protection program."

"Which means what, exactly?"

"They'd give you a new identity. Move you to a new location. You'd have a handler as a contact point. And you'd have to keep your head down. No communication with anyone who's been in your life up until this point."

Lacey brought her hands to her throat. "For how long?"

"Could be for always. I don't know what's going on here. If they catch the criminals, put them on trial and send them to prison, it could take a few years to get to that point. Or it could be forever."

"And I'd be nearby, so I could help figure everything out?"

"I imagine if the FBI covered up the accident and had eyes on you in the bar and a waiting car outside, they have a darned good picture of what's going on. They're getting all of the evidence together to bring everyone in. Crime solving on TV looks like a bullet train, but in reality, it's more like a battleship in the ocean. It takes a long time to maneuver around and to get from Point A to Point B."

"And I couldn't contact anyone from my life – not even you?"

"I'd be out of the picture until things got resolved."

Lacey bit off one nail after the other until Deep covered her hand and brought it down to her lap, wrapping it gently in his. "If Steve is working for the FBI undercover, and his name is even really Steve—wow, this is a lot for me to wrap my brain around—then he was making up our relationship. I mean, I was sleeping with him, thinking I was in a maybe-forever kind of relationship with him. We were making plans, talking about children. What kind of good guy would do that? That seems like psychological rape. He was sleeping with me as part of his job? He was screwing me as a pretense to get me to cooperate or get some evidence or something? Do you think he has a wife and family that he went home to when I thought he was travelling for his job? 'Hi, honey, I'm home. . .'" She cupped her hands over her mouth and swallowed hard. "I think I need to vomit." She twitched her head to the left then the right, looking for the closest trash bin. Her stomach reseated, and her gaze settled on Deep. "Oh dear, do they do that? Is it possible?" she whispered.

"It's possible. But you can't jump to conclusions. We're only speculating."

"Seems like it fits together." Lacey's eyes had lost their focus as she churned the ideas around.

"It does," Deep agreed.

Lacey stood up and paced, angry tears forming in her eyes, and she swiped at them. Back and forth, back and forth, she moved across the living room.

"Lacey . . . "

"I need you to not talk to me right now. I need to be alone." Lacey stormed up the stairs and burst through the bathroom door. Hot water—that's what she needed. That had helped her so much last night. Maybe it would work its magic again. Yes. Lots and lots of hot water. She pulled off her nightclothes and stepped under the stream, twisting back at first from the searing heat of the shower. First one arm, then the other, one leg, then the other. As her skin warmed and she acclimated to the temperature, Lacey finally moved to stand under the shower head. She reached for the washcloth and soap and began to rub her skin. She tried to scrub away the memories of Steve's hands on her. He was one hell of an actor—or probably it was more like she was one hell of an easy target. So desperate. So desperate to be loved. How was it that she had missed that she was being used for some damn reason or another? A pawn in a chess game. It felt awful to have been used. Manipulated. Endangered.

They do that? They sleep with people to achieve whatever ends they want? They lie about loving someone and make promises? That seemed so wrong. Setting someone up like that to be hurt so badly.

Was she hurt? Hurt . . . She was angry. That was for sure. Would that work its way into pain? She didn't really miss Steve. Didn't really want to talk to him or check to make sure he was okay. And not just because of the revelation that he was playing both sides of some fence, either. From the moment he had stood her up at the bar, and she had to claw her way through the trash to safety, she was done with him. That was clear as a bell.

If things had gone the way they should have: that she went home, called the police, and they had taken her statement, and then Steve had shown up at her door, Lacey was pretty certain she would have shut it in his face and moved on with her life. It wasn't even the part where she found herself rolling in kitchen waste. It was at the bar, when she looked at her phone and there was no message. Any positive loving feelings she might have conjured up for Steve drained away as the minutes ticked by without a word from him. Somehow, that wait had been the turning point in their relationship. She was already done with that page in her book before Leo Bardman stepped into her personal space and mistook her for Danika.

Did it make her sad that Steve was not who she thought he was – not intellectually, but in her heart? The hot water sluiced over her back and shoulders, taking with it the stress that rolled off her skin. No, to be honest, the transition was painless and much easier than she could ever have imagined it. To be honest that transition happened last November, when Deep first stood under the high-vaulted ceiling of the gallery and extended his hand to her. She had just been waiting for Steve's health crises – first with his heart, then with his nephew, to pass so she could let him go without being heartless.

Deep. The mere thought of him steadied her. They had met because of a crime. He had reentered her life because of a crime. Could a relationship forged in stress and crisis survive once life settled down to banalities? She sure wanted an opportunity to figure that out.

Now, she asked herself, *can I trust my feelings for Deep? Or am I simply jumping from one sinking life raft to another, thinking this one might buoy me through my storm?*

Lacey took her time drying her hair and dressing again. She had left Deep mid-story, and she owed him the rest of it. She did. She owed it to him. If he was going to help her for no obvious reason other than that he wanted to help her, then she was going to trust her very first reaction on that amazing November day when her hand was in his and her heart said, "You belong here."

She went down the stairs to find Deep sitting quietly on the sofa, exactly where she had left him. She curled up next to him and offered up the semblance of a smile. Lacey had told the easy part. This next part, though. . . She'd have to power through it.

Deep pushed his computer out of the way as Lacey cleared her throat to launch herself forward in the story. "I was held in the hospital for a few days after the deer accident," Lacey said, playing with the hem of her sweater. "The doctors were worried about my vital signs. When the ambulance brought me in, they said that my blood hadn't been oxygenated properly for a long while. The doctors were worried about my heart and lungs, and were running tests to figure out why my bloodwork looked so poor. They thought I might have experienced some kind of systemic event that could have been the reason for my accident."

"You told them about the men in the house?"

"I didn't remember that. At that point, all I remembered was driving to Radovan's to hang the painting, and then I woke up in the car."

"When was it that you started to remember the men at the house?"

Lacey nodded, acknowledging the question. "I need to say this bit first. My uncle didn't come and see me at the hospital, but he came to my apartment. That's when he met Steve. Steve brought me home and took care of me, but you know that already. Now that I'm thinking back to that time, huh, that seems kind of off."

Deep tilted his head.

"My uncle came to my apartment to tell me that Radovan had passed. To me, Uncle Bartholomew was, as one would expect, grief-stricken, but he was also really agitated. Uncle Bartholomew was preparing his eulogy for the funeral and asked me to look it over. It was during this visit that I learned that Radovan had died in his sleep and was discovered days after his death when the maid went in. And I know from what Uncle Bartholomew told me that Radovan must have been dead when I was there at the house. He asked me if I had noticed anything unusual. I still had post-traumatic amnesia. Everything was black from the point where I arrived at the house and was staring into the pot of stone soup until Steve was calling my name. I thought Uncle Bartholomew was wondering if I had smelled the body or something. So I told him I had no memories in the house at all."

Lacey saw questions churning in Deep's mind, but he chose to start with, "Do you know how Radovan Krokov died?"

"Yes, he had a heart attack. He was only in his sixties, but he had a pacemaker. I wasn't surprised."

"Stone soup? What's that all about?"

"I told you—when I went into Radovan's house, there was a pot on the stove."

Deep waited for her to continue.

"Well it was a stew pot with a little bit of water simmering and a bunch of rocks."

"That's kind of weird." Deep said, his brow pulling together with concentration.

"Only because we don't know why they were being boiled."

Deep grinned. "Lacey, give me one good reason to boil rocks on the stove. Just one."

"Hot stone massages. And I know that Radovan got regular massages to help him with his circulation."

"But the man with the mask took them outside."

"Okay, maybe they were boiling them to get rid of weeds in the cracks or get them cleaned in some way. My gardener sometimes did that with the decorative stones in our rock garden when moss started growing on them. That would make sense, too."

"Still weird."

Lacey shrugged. "I can't see how it would make a difference one way or another."

"So you're in your apartment and your uncle came to tell you that his lover had died, and to ask you if you happened to smell him decaying upstairs while you were at the house hanging a picture of a nude man. And as nuts as that sentences is to say, that's not the part that made you say, 'Huh, that seems kind of off.'"

"That was about Steve's reaction. He was standing at the cocktail table, pouring my uncle a tumbler of whiskey. He was very focused on our conversation. His whole body was rigid with concentration. And when he looked at me, I thought he looked frightened for me. I didn't know Steve very well at the time, though, so I talked myself out of that thought."

"Did Steve bring any of this up later?"

"He asked me questions—what was I doing at Radovan's? Was I the only person there? How close was I to Radovan? Steve told me he was sorry for my loss. Conversational stuff."

"But you have more memories of that time now. Have they been filling in over time, or did they come back to you all at once?"

Blood drained from Lacey's face. "All at once," she whispered.

Deep came upright, leaned forward. "This is the number four. I know of three times they tried to kill you, but you said there were four. Someone came after you."

"It was my first day going back to work," she whispered, staring at their entwined fingers. "I closed up the gallery. It's a little creepy down there at night. There's that park across the road and the church at the end of the cul-de-sac; the street gets very dark and desolate at night. But that was the night of a full moon, and the air was warm and comfortable. The security guard had started his rounds, and I didn't feel like waiting around for him to walk me to my car. I went out by myself. I climbed into my car, no problem. I locked my doors and was clipping on my seat belt when someone rose up out of the back seat." Lacey breathed through an open mouth like a locomotive chugging up a mountainside. "He wrapped an arm around my neck." She pulled her cowl neck up around her chin.

"You're okay. You're safe." He looked her square in the eye. "It's okay to tell this story. No one knows you're here. No one can hurt you." He took both of her hands. "You're okay, Lacey, I promise."

Lacey nodded. She only half-believing Deep's words, though she tried. "I looked up and I saw the knife in the mirror. It was a big fighting knife like I've seen battlefield soldiers carry when they're on the news. He pressed the blade against my throat." She stopped to pant. "I shoved my head back into the headrest, trying to get away from it, and the man said, 'You recognize me, don't you?'

"'Yes,'" I whispered, "'you're the gardener.'"

He laughed, it wasn't a menacing laugh it was a true laugh like he'd heard a good joke. I remember that because, it gave me a little hope. "'You see why you won't be allowed to live.'" I didn't see at all. He went on, "'I was wondering why Danika would go into the house. It took us a few minutes to figure it out. But I called her, and she was nowhere near there. You thought you could fool me? You thought I was a dunce? Huh?'"

Lacey had fallen right back into the moment, vividly recalling every word, every nuance. She remembered how the car had filled with the smell of her fear. Her body trembled. She forgot that Deep was there. She forgot she was in Lynx's living room. In her mind, she was fully back in her car, smelling her fear.

I said, "'nobody cares. Let it be.'

"He was laughing again. 'Let it be. Hell no, I'm not going to let it be. Now turn on your car keys, put this thing in gear, and let's go. I'll tell you where to turn. No games. This knife stays at your throat. If you read any stupid women's magazine articles about causing an accident to save yourself, remember the knife is there, so you won't survive it.'"

Lacey fluffed her sweater, trying to release some of the heat that poured off her chest, then she pulled the whole thing off and sat there in her bra. She balled the soft mohair together and hugged it to her like it was a child's teddy bear. "I drove down the road. I couldn't think. I tried to pray, to say the 'Our Father,' but all I could think over and over was 'God is great. God is good. Let us thank him for this food.' Which is ridiculous. I knew it was ridiculous, but I couldn't get any other words out. Until suddenly, I heard myself talking. I said, 'Yeah? Well I know who you are. And more than that? I have absolutely all of it on video. I had my phone out, and I recorded everything. And I mean *everything.* Then I sent it to a friend who put it in her cloud. Could you torture me and find out who that friend is? You don't have to. I'll happily tell you her name, it's Claudia Schmidt. Why would I tell you? Because she's on a sailboat, sailing around the world. What does that mean to you? If anything happens to me, then Claudia will release that video to the world. What happens if I'm just fine? Claudia does nothing. No one's the wiser. Right now, everyone thinks Radovan died of natural causes. I'm fine with that. I never liked the man. I don't care how he died. Let sleeping dogs lie."

Lacey looked up to find Deep watching her closely. "That's when I realized they'd killed him. And I'd witnessed part of a murder."

"He let you go?"

"He said, 'Pull over.' And I did. He started to get out of the car. He reached up and pulled my hair so I couldn't move my head. 'Here's the deal,' he said. 'You tell anyone? And I assume you've told everyone. I start killing them, one after the other. One after the other. One after the other. And I can kill them in such a way that no one will ever figure out how.'"

"Crap," Deep muttered.

Lacey nodded.

Deep sniffed. "So things continue to get weirder and weirder."

Lacey nodded, again.

"Did you actually make a video? Who's Claudia Schmidt?"

"No, I didn't even have my phone with me at the house. I'd run out of battery, and it was recharging in my car. And I have no idea where that name came from. I don't know anyone by either name."

"Lacey?"

She slit her eyes at him. "I know that tone. Please don't ask me to eat something right now. It's not going to help."

Deep grinned. "You know me so well. Actually, I was going to ask you about the name Danika. It's interesting to me that he thought you were Danika at the house and that it took him some time to figure out that it wasn't Danika but you. That's significant."

"At the bar, too," Lacey said.

"How do you mean?"

"Leo Bardman or, what did you call him? Bogdan Zoric? At the bar, before he came up to me, he was staring at me as if he were trying to make a decision. Then when he approached, he said, 'Danika, you're in danger.' I think we have the first name of the dead girl. Danika. I should have put it together — they were mistaking me for the woman who was standing in for me. It's so obvious—a child's puzzle. But I didn't. The name and the person in the photos sat in two very different compartments in my mind."

"Don't fall into the trap of blaming yourself for not seeing something that in hindsight is so obvious. You see and hear and feel and experience so much information moment by moment. And you don't know what's significant until it's significant. Surely you made the connection between the men who killed Radovan and Leo being killed, right?"

Lacey nodded.

"And you put those together because of the name Danika. But you've had a huge amount of information thrown in your lap. There's a lot to sort through. It takes time – and sometimes, someone from the outside who doesn't have as much of an emotional involvement can piece things together more quickly. The brain is an incredible machine, but it also tries to protect you in weird ways that often are doing the exact opposite of keeping you safe. Now," he said, patting her leg. "Are you cooling down again?"

Lacey pulled her brow together.

"Here. Put your sweater back on, and come in the kitchen and eat something."

Lacey hadn't remembered she'd tugged it off. She shook it out to find the front, then pulled it over her head. As she pushed her hands through the arm holes, she said, "But Deep, I think—"

He was already moving toward the kitchen. "I'm not listening to another word out of your mouth until you eat."

"I—"

He held up a hand. "Nope. Not listening."

Lacey followed behind with a sigh of resignation.

They decided on soup and sandwiches. Lacey pulled a can of chicken noodle from the cupboard and opened the lid. She was going through the motions of stirring the pot on the stove, but her thoughts were far away. "Stone soup," she said, under her breath.

"Huh?" Deep slid in beside her to reach for a cutting board, so he could make the sandwiches.

"You're absolutely right—the stone soup is really unusual. I remember thinking so at the time. I wish I knew what that was about."

"I'd like to go by and look at the rocks. Are you up for it?"

Lacey wanted to say no. In her mind, Radovan's house meant danger. But as her mouth opened to respond, the image of Deep's face as he scrolled through the pictures of what her uncle had done to those teenage boys slid back into her consciousness, and Lacey said, "Let's eat quickly. This soup is warm enough." And she twisted off the element.

Chapter Thirty-Four

Wednesday

Deep made a few passes around the estate. Lacey swung her head back and forth, looking everywhere for anything. Anything that would give them a few seconds' warning and a chance to escape. The killer's eyes in her car's rearview mirror — in Lacey's mind, she saw them staring at her, menacing her, reminding her of his promise that he would kill her and all those she knew, one after the other. One after the other.

Deep maneuvered his car up the drive and parked it at an odd angle in the parking circle in the back of the house. Lacey could see that if they needed to escape, Deep would be headed out over the fields, where few cars would be able to follow them. The killer's pickup truck would be able to do that, no problem, she thought. But she also knew there was a road on the other side of that dip in the land. That direction was the quickest one toward freedom – well, toward the highway, at

329

any rate. That gave her a little confidence as she dangled her foot and lowered herself to the ground. Before she could step all the way down, Deep caught her around the waist to help her.

"Ready?" he asked.

"Sure. In and out okay?"

"Sounds fine. Which side of the house is it?" Deep pulled on a pair of leather gloves and took what looked like a brown paper bag from the back.

With a point of her finger, Lacey moved around to the side of the house to just outside of the Florida room, where Radovan had a Zen garden. The center was comprised of a rectangle of tiny pea gravel that was raked into gentle curves around three massive rocks. It was pristine, which meant that the gardener was still attending things. Lacey was momentarily worried that, having found the odd-looking rocks, the gardener would have removed them. But there they lay, lined up in a soldier-like row in front of the bamboo. They looked natural there as if they had been artistically added to the scene, creating an interesting juxtaposition of the smooth height and graceful sway of bamboo and the craggy density of the rock. If she hadn't seen them boiling in the pot, she would never think they were out of place here in this garden. As a matter of fact, they fit in so naturally that Lacey questioned herself. She walked around the interior of this walled area and searched for other rocks that could have been in the pot.

Deep stood out of her way. She was staring at the line again, hoping she wasn't making a stupid mistake, when suddenly he was at her side. He crouched but pushed on her elbows, forcing her to stand.

"I don't want to alarm you, but there's a car coming up the driveway."

Alarm didn't even come close to what Lacey felt in that moment.

"Calm." He smiled. "Calm. Breathe. The car has a single person in it. It looks like a middle-aged woman. She's driving a beat-up old Buick. Do you recognize my description?"

Lacey shook her head and strained to see the car coming up. "Are you sure? There's no one there."

"I saw her on the road. I'm a bit taller than you are. Did you find your rocks? Are these the ones?" Deep pointed to the soldier row.

"I think so. It was so long ago, there's no way I can be sure."

"Okay, I want you to nonchalantly move toward the Land Rover. We aren't trying to get away. That would rouse suspicions. Just head toward the car. I have you covered. Nothing bad will happen to you." Deep was kneeling at her feet, and Lacey leaned her thighs into his chest.

"You can do this, sweetheart. If she wonders why you're here, it's not a problem. You've been to the house before. Tell whoever it is that you're checking on the temperatures in the house to make sure that the art isn't being damaged. Make up some shit."

When Deep said that, Lacey looked down into his face. He was having a good time. How could this be a good time for him, when she was doing everything in her power not to pee in her panties?

The car moved into her view but was still a ways off.

"Where are you going to be?" Lacey asked.

"I'm going to blend in."

"Whatever that means."

"Wherever you are, I'll be your shadow," Deep said.

"Are you quoting some James Bond movie line or something?"

"Nah." Deep chuckled. "Lacey, you're going to do fine. Okay, do you have the phone I gave you?"

Lacey patted her pocket, then pulled it out.

Deep took it from her and played with the buttons. Then he tucked it into the waistband of her pants, leaving it sticking most of the way out. "That's eyes and ears," he started, but Lacey shook her head with non-comprehension as the car moved closer and closer.

"I'll be able to hear everything you say. If you say the word 'tapestry,' it means I'm to come and pull you out of the situation. Say 'tapestry.'"

"Tapestry." Lacey wriggled one knee in front of the other, then switched.

"If you see anything interesting or you want to record her face, just aim the phone that way. You'll be recording audio and video the whole time, and I can see that as well. If you get the chance, I want you to find out anything you can that might give us a clue as to what's going on. Got it?"

"Got it," Lacey said, putting on what she considered to be her game face. But that only made Deep chuckle again. He gave her a little push in the right direction. She took three steps forward and turned to say something to Deep, but he was gone.

Chapter Thirty-Five

Wednesday

"**M**iss Stuart, oh, I'm so glad you're here," the woman said through the gap made when she gave her car door a two-handed shove. She gripped the side of the Buick and the door handle and hefted herself out with some effort. Deep was right, this woman was late-middle-aged. She wore an oversized grey coat over her black maid's uniform with its crisp white apron showing in the opening. An orange scarf wrapped around the creped skin of her neck, and she tugged a hand-knit hat over her curls for the short walk from the car to the kitchen door.

She must have met Danika, posing as me. Lacey had no idea who this woman was. She walked forward, but made sure to keep her distance so the height difference between Danika and her wasn't as noticeable to this woman. Lacey wondered how observant she was. Would she discern, for example, anything was off about how she moved or the way she spoke?

335

"Hello." Lacey decided to try and keep her sentence short and sweet.

The woman pulled a wad of keys from her pocket. "The funeral home called me again this morning, ma'am, and I don't know what to tell them except that I would pass along the message."

"I'm sorry, did you leave a message for me already?" What in the world was going on?

"No, ma'am, with Mr. Winslow. Mr. Winslow told me you weren't to be bothered with such things. I'm sorry that you've taken Mr. Krokov's death so hard." She touched her fist of keys to her heart, then gestured toward the door.

Lacey moved that way, working hard not to let her eyes search where she thought Deep might be "blending." "My uncle is out of the country right now. He's actually been gone for months. Have you been in contact with him recently?" Lacey watched the maid unlock the door.

"No, ma'am, things had mostly settled down after the funeral. There were some additional issues after they exhumed Mr. Krokov."

Exhumed?

"Pity about the mix-up." The housekeeper continued as she pushed the door open, then held it politely open for Lacey. "It seems wrong somehow to bury a body and then dig him back up that way."

Lacey stood in the kitchen as the woman made her way in, shut the door, and turned toward Lacey to finish her thought. "I don't know why that struck me as spitting in the poor man's face. It was, after all, the scientists making things right, the way Mr. Krokov wanted them." She stopped and her eyes opened wide. "I'm so sorry. I didn't mean to say that out loud." She pulled her dress out to the sides and did some odd little curtsey-like thing that made her look even more embarrassed. She shrugged out of her coat and hung it on a hook in the pantry, then reemerged, wiping her hands down the front of her apron to smooth its already pristine appearance. Finally, the woman came to rest in front of Lacey, where she stood with her eyes pointed forward and her hands dangling by her sides like a soldier waiting for an order.

Lacey moved into the house that she had been through many times, but always in the capacity of her role at the gallery. She patted the housekeeper's shoulder as she passed by. Though her uncle and Radovan had been lovers for more than two years, she had never been invited there socially.

"Could you tell me what the funeral home needs? Perhaps I can help, since my uncle won't be back in the States for quite a while."

"The funeral director wants Mr. Winslow to be the one who picks up Mr. Krokov's jewelry that the university removed when his body was dug back up."

Lacey blinked. *What?* "Perhaps they would let me pick that up. I'll call to see. Do you have the phone number and the name of the person with whom I should speak?" Lacey asked.

The housekeeper bustled to the other side of the kitchen where she pulled a notebook from the drawer under the house phone. Opening the cover, she dragged her finger down the page, then stopped. "Here it is."

Lacey reached out and took the whole notebook from her hand and looked at the message, then tucked the spiral-bound book under her arm. "How are you doing in all of this?" Lacey asked kindly. Lacey felt like she was stretching the boundaries. Perhaps this wasn't the way Danika would have addressed the help.

"Everything is going along fine. It's sad though, the house being empty. Mr. Krokov was such a lovely man. And his birds—I miss their singing."

Lacey turned her head toward the game room and noticed that their cage no longer hung from the limb. "But you don't miss cleaning up from where they had flown about," Lacey said.

The housekeeper smiled uncomfortably. "That's true. They were beautiful, though. I thought perhaps you took them to your house?"

"Me?" *Uh-oh.* "Why would you think that?"

"Since they were part of your engagement present, I just assumed . . . That horrible day when I found Mr. Krokov." She stopped and made a sign of the cross. "I had come in to feed the birds. And of course they weren't here. I thought there was something off in the house, it smelled badly, and that's when I found . . . you don't need to hear this. I didn't mean to upset you." The housekeeper folded her hands in front of her and seemed to cave in a little.

"Thank you kindly. Here, let's go into the game room and sit." Lacey led the way, hoping to show that she knew the house, and she belonged here. *I was engaged to Radovan? He gave me those birds as part of an engagement present?* Lacey pitched back in her memory, trying to remember when the birds first showed up in the house. Certainly they were there in July. She had been hanging the painting in his bedroom, and downstairs Radovan had been getting after someone for leaving the door ajar. He was afraid the birds would fly away.

They moved farther into the house, into the open room that held the seating and gaming areas. A cover was draped over the billiards table. Lacey sat and flipped quickly through the book of notes passed back and forth between Radovan and the housekeeper—her name was Agatha.

"Please continue. You know my Uncle Bartholomew is very protective of me, and I don't believe I know the whole story. Or maybe I was told the whole story, but these past few

339

months have been a fog. You'll forgive me if I seem a little off." Lacey made a gesture with her open palm toward the love seat, and Agatha looked a little taken aback, but sank down anyway to the edge of the cushion. Her big red hands gripped the ends of her knees. Lacey moved to sit kitty-corner to her on the couch. "So, you found my dear Radovan. And then what happened?"

"I called the office number for the police and told them my boss had passed away in his sleep. They sent an officer and a medical examiner's assistant." Agatha gestured toward the notebook, and Lacey handed it back. "Here. The medical examiner's person was Jennifer Kyte, and she called his doctor."

"Which one? Did you jot it down?" Lacey asked, mentally crossing her fingers that he had had more than one.

"Yes, this one. Dr. Brad, the cardiologist."

Lacey reached to take the notebook back. She thought there was probably some very good information in there. "Why did they do that?"

"I wasn't trying to snoop. I wasn't listening in, but I was in the room and all."

"Of course, Agatha, there is nothing that you did that was wrong. It's me. I'm afraid I've been so depressed, that my mind's not working as it should. It would be a kindness if you could help me retrieve my memories of what all has happened since Radovan passed."

"Yes, ma'am. Well the police called Dr. Brad and asked them if he'd sign the papers."

"Which papers are these?

"The one's that said Mr. Krokov died of natural causes, so they wouldn't have to do an autopsy."

"Yes, of course, well, he had the heart condition. This was somewhat expected, certainly. I hoped for more time with him before he left me alone in this world without him." Lacey sighed and tried to play the part of grieving fiancée.

"Yes, ma'am. I had called you immediately, but since you didn't answer, I called Mr. Winslow since he and Mr. Krokov were such close friends."

"Which was perfect." Lacey nodded her approval.

"Mr. Winslow said he'd handle things, and everyone—the police and the medical examiner lady—went away. Then the funeral home sent the hearse, and Servepro came and cleaned everything up. They took the bedding and mattress with them, and they had to cut a square out of the carpet. But Mr. Winslow said that made no never mind since it was under the bed. Then he had a new boxed spring and mattress delivered the next day. I made up the bed with fresh sheets and covers."

Lacey felt her stomach turn over. She fought against the need to be sick. If they had to cut out the carpeting, it meant that parts of Radovan had seeped through the mattress. It was too much. She needed to change the subject for the moment.

Lacey got up and walked under the massive fichus tree and put her hand on the trunk. "And the birds weren't here the day you came in to take care of them? They were gone?"

"Yes, ma'am. This is how I found things that day. As you can see, the cage is gone, their food was gone, even the birdseed and pin feathers that are so hard to vacuum up were gone. There was nothing for me to do as far as cleaning up after them goes." Her brow drew in with confusion. "I assumed that you had taken them to your house, since Mr. Krokov was supposed to have gone out of town, and you all forgot to tell me."

"No, I didn't take the birds out of here. I can't imagine . . . That's really very strange, Agatha."

"Yes, ma'am, if you say so."

"My uncle arranged for Radovan's funeral, and his burial, of course. He has more experience at this than I do. Such a sad day."

"It was, yes, ma'am."

"You know, I'm feeling rather poorly. Would you be kind enough to make me a cup of tea?"

Agatha jumped up with obvious relief and moved to the kitchen. Lacey used the time to search through the notebook, holding the camera to take capture the information on each page. Agatha had been meticulous about recording all incoming calls and what she did with each piece of information. Between the discovery of Radovan's body and his burial, there were many incoming calls that were routed to her uncle. Which made sense. That Agatha thought she was Radovan's fiancée, though—that was disgusting beyond words. Lacey wondered what Agatha thought Rodavan and her Uncle Bartholomew's relationship was.

Lacey moved around the room, hunting for anything that would give her information, anything that would explain the day that she found herself staring into the eyes of a killer. What she found was a series of framed photographs of Danika with Radovan. Why these very personal and very, *wow*, revealing photos were on such public display was a mystery. Lacey couldn't imagine why they were in the public room, other than that Radovan seemed to find some satisfaction with the display of the human body. At least, that had always been his taste in the oils he had bought from the gallery. These photos were a lot less artistic and a lot more pornographic in nature, and even though this wasn't her—it was Danika in the photos—Agatha didn't know that. Lacey showed the phone in her waistband each of the photographs. Lacey's face was a bright cherry red as Agatha walked back into the room.

Lacey spun the photo of Danika kissing the tip of Radovan's grizzly old-man's penis toward Agatha, then clutched it to her heart with a sigh and a shake of her head. "I miss him so." She hoped Agatha would interpret the revulsion on her face as grief.

"Yes, ma'am."

Lacey walked back to the sofa wondering if Danika had actually had feelings for Radovan or if he was somehow part of the arts scam. Or maybe a different scam. She remembered what Deep had said about criminal schemes, and how they were never straightforward. It seemed absolutely true. Every step they took shed light and cast shadows onto this knot of confusion. She didn't think there was a way to untangle these events, especially if major participants were missing — either dead, like Danika probably was, and Radovan definitely was, or permanently out of the picture, like Uncle Bartholomew. *Would even some of our questions get answered?* she wondered.

Agatha settled a tea tray onto the coffee table. She had prepared it with a beautiful china tea set, a little silver box with tea choices, and a delicate plate with cookies. "I'm sorry, ma'am, I wasn't expecting you today, so I don't have any pastries or chocolates the way you like." She stood in front of Lacey, waiting for her next directive.

"Please sit down again, Agatha. This is fine." Lacey leaned forward and prepared her cup. "Just a cup of tea, I think. Now, I see in the notebook that there's another doctor's name, a Dr.

Nadeer. I don't know that Radovan told me about him . . . her . . .?"

"Oh, he couldn't have. That's the one who's a scientist with the university."

"It says in the notes that you took that Dr. Nadeer had made arrangements with the funeral home and everything was taken care of. You left a message at my uncle's, but I don't see where he responded to you."

"No, ma'am, he didn't call me back. We spoke in person."

"He must have forgotten to tell me. Do you remember what Dr. Nadeer handled?"

Agatha tried to hide the odd look on her face, and Lacey thought she'd just made a big mistake. Agatha scooted even farther to the edge of the love seat. "If your uncle didn't tell you, ma'am, I'm not sure that I'm the one to say."

Agatha's eyes searched around the room, looking everywhere but Lacey's face. Lacey reached out her hands to calm Agatha, well to hold her in place since she looked like she wanted to bolt from the room. "Agatha?" Lacey put authority behind her voice as she'd learned to do growing up when she needed to control her mother or the help.

"Yes, ma'am, I'm sorry if you didn't know, but the university exhumed his body and took it away to the lab." She lifted her apron skirt and coughed behind the panel. She lowered and smoothed it, her gaze in her lap. "Your uncle didn't tell you?"

"I'm sure he did, but he also sedated me to get me through the first few horrible months. The doctor prescribed some pain medications for me, so that whole time is fuzzy."

"Mr. Krokov had promised his body to Dr. Nadeer for research. He had signed papers and all. Mr. Winslow's attorney—"

"Mr. Reynolds? How do you know this?"

"They ate dinner here. I was serving them. And, yes, ma'am, Mr. Reynolds was the one. He read over the documents and said they were legitimate. It was what they called a 'directive.'"

"Yes, that sounds like Radovan, wishing to support the sciences." *Actually, it doesn't sound like Radovan at all.* "The thought of him being. . ." Lacey gave a shudder. "I don't like to think of them experimenting on him," she said to cover the reflex. She offered a feeble smile. "Do you know what institute Dr. Nadeer works for?"

"No, ma'am. I heard them talking, but I don't know which university has his remains." She rubbed her hands together as if trying to wash away her responsibility. "Since your uncle is out of town, do you think you could go by the funeral home and collect Mr. Krokov's effects?"

***

Lacey could feel Deep grinning at her from the driver's seat, but her nose was stuck in the domesticity of the phone log. "Agatha, I would like cabbage soup and sausages for dinner." "Agatha, the birds would enjoy some fresh fruit." "Sir, I telephoned Miss Stuart, and she said she will be over in the morning."

"Deep, here's something really odd."

"Odder than crazy rocks, two birds that are MIA, and a body that's disappeared into the hands of some doctor when the family all thinks it's buried at the cemetery?"

"Agatha called me 'Miss Stuart.' She knew I was associated with Uncle Bartholomew."

"Well your uncle was dating Radovan, right?"

"Dating – that sounds too public. They were lovers. I don't think it was merely about sex, I thought they were actually in love. I didn't know Radovan was bisexual, that's for sure."

"How long were your uncle and Radovan together?"

"A few years." Lacey tilted her head and watched the naked trees fly by as they drove toward the city.

"Did you go over to Radovan's house frequently?"

Lacey flicked her attention back on Deep, tucking her hair behind her ears. "On occasion for work. But I've never met Agatha before. She knew me, though, so that means she knew

347

Danika as me. She knew Danika as me before the funeral, because she thinks that Radovan and I were engaged. And she also thinks I'm the subject in those photos." Lacey scowled, which won her a chuckle from Deep.

"Those were quite the photos to have framed and on display in the family room. I bet Agatha enjoys having to dust them."

"Shhh, that is *so* disgusting, I'm not paying even a smidgeon of attention to what you just said. Now, listen. Radovan was already dead the day of my accident. Therefore, if my logic classes aren't failing me, Danika was using my name and posing as me prior to his death. And not only that, but my uncle must have known and cooperated. When you speculated that this all began with the accident, that simply cannot be true. It doesn't fit the timeline."

"Agreed."

"Is this what you do all day in your job?" Lacey asked.

"My job has never looked anything like this before. Usually I'm fast roping into a hot zone, taking care of business, and fast-tracking it out of there. Or I'm hacking computers. This is more along the lines of what Striker and Lynx do. Each member of our team has a specialty, so when you put us all together, we've got the bases covered."

"Like a criminal crew?"

"Except for the criminal part." He sent her a grin. "You handled that well, though. And you got the notebook, which I think is going to be important."

Lacey focused on the highway sign. "Where are we going? This isn't the way to Lynx's house."

"I'm headed to the Smithsonian. I have a friend who curates the mineral sciences database. I've helped him out with a few software glitches. So I thought we'd pay him a visit. See what he can tell us about this space rock and why someone might be boiling it on the stove."

Chapter Thirty-Six

Steve

Wednesday

Steve's computer felt warm on his knee as he sat outside McDonald's with a large coffee. He was playing the video of Lacey's tackle and retreat at the press conference. The thing that he was stuck on was the roll. Whoever dove across the portico and into Lacey did two things that made Steve think that this was a rescue, and not an abduction. The guy hadn't taken her out at the knees, which could easily have hurt her legs and made her unable to walk and, based on the angle the guy was lunging in from, would probably have required orthopedic surgery for Lacey. Instead, he'd grabbed her around the hips. Second, he hadn't landed on top of her. Jumping on top of someone usually went a good ways into subduing them: they were winded, in shock, and demoralized. Landing on top of them was half the reason for making the tackle. Steve played that section again. Yup, the guy pulled Lacey tightly into his arms like he was tucking a football, then he rolled, taking the brunt of the force with his own body, flipping over, checking on her, and in a split second pulling her up and slinging her over his shoulder.

Who does that? Someone who's saving the girl. Someone who is protecting an asset. Someone who's had a ton of training. Steve considered and rejected the CIA, someone Black and Green had sent in. He went over the various people who'd been a part of this case. They were all trained and all capable, but this guy was practically defying human ability. Beyond capable. A highly trained, highly utilized special operative. The whole thing read like an Iniquus intervention.

He'd said that before. He pointed it out to Monroe right away that he felt Iniquus might be involved, and the FBI immediately signed a contract with Iniquus to find Lacey and bring her in to their protection. But had this been an Iniquus operator, then they would have notified him that they had Lacey in hand, because Iniquus would have been contractually obligated to move her through the system. Yet that's not what had happened.

How could this video be explained? Maybe Omega had grabbed her for some reason—maybe someone had hired Iniquus's competitors to go in and extract Lacey without causing her harm. Could be. But who would hire Omega? Her uncle? The Assembly was closely associated with Omega. But Lacey's uncle had been using her at every turn and in every way possible. Her uncle was largely responsible for Lacey's predicament. He was the seminal actor that brought her into the fray. *Who am I kidding? I'm the seminal actor that churned up this shit storm.*

"I've got to make this right, " Steve chanted through gritted teeth.

The guy who tackled Lacey is a good guy. He had to be.

Steve refused to believe, until he had proof positive in his hands, that Lacey was really dead. The thought of her dead sapped him of energy and his ability to think and process. Hope that he could find her whole and healthy filled him with energy and power. The only possibility that she was whole and healthy and walking into a dry-cleaning shop with a smile on her unstressed face, as far as he could tell, was that Deep Del Toro had grabbed her.

And he had something besides this tape to pave the path for those thoughts. Joseph Del Toro was supposed to be on a flight to Costa Rica last Friday, but he didn't claim his seat. There was no data showing that he left the country. None. And Lacey had called him.

So where would Deep go? Higgins had told Steve that Strike Force lived on campus in the Iniquus barracks; only Lynx had a home in her own name. India Alexis Sobado, aka Lexi, aka Lynx lived at 369 Silver Lake. And that was where

Steve was headed, on the off-chance that Deep was hiding out with Lacey at his teammate's home.

He drove through the neighborhood a few times. No lights were on at Lynx's house, but oddly, the drapes were drawn in the front room. He made another pass, moving forward at a crawl. He noticed the house had automatic lighting systems and probably had state of the art detection systems. He moved on by, turning a block up and over, and then parked.

Steve continued his search on foot, walking up the alley behind Lynx's house. Again, he saw no lights on, so he took a peek in the garbage can out back. He opened the lid and rifled through the trash. As his hand stirred through the debris, he only found kitchen waste. No telltale sign who was living here, or how many. And it certainly could be that Lynx was at home. A car with a woman driver moved very slowly down the alley. Steve stepped quietly into the shadow of Sobado's garage. He thought the car hesitated for a moment when it pulled flush with him, but soon it resumed its progress and turned left out of the alley. Steve let out his breath. Stepping back into daylight, he pulled the two paper napkins he'd grabbed with his fast food breakfast from his pocket and wiped off the goop. He threw the napkins away, then moved around the side of the house, checking the tall fence lining the sidewalk and wondering what the best way to breach her security might be.

As he got to Silver Lake, a middle-aged man with the authority and shoulder set of a cop was waiting for him. "Lose something?" he asked in a tone that said, *busted.*

"Yeah, my puppy. He jumped out of the car faster than I could grab his collar."

"And you think he's up on the top of this fence?" the guy asked.

Steve shook his head and offered a half-smile. *Shit.*

"Where was this that your puppy got out?" the man asked.

"Over on Sorrel. I live in the blue house."

"Hell of a long way for a puppy to make it from Sorrel to Silver Lake. What kind of puppy is this?"

"Husky," Steve said. This guy knew that he was full of shit. Steve was just trying to figure a clear path out of there before he was told to put his hands against the fence. If the guy frisked him, that pat-down would produce two guns and a knife, but nothing in the way of FBI identification. Steve thought for sure he was going to be on his way to jail for an attempted B and E. He needed to think his way through this. At that moment, the only plan he could conjure was to slug the guy across the jaw and run for it.

As that thought became more solid in his mind, a woman came out on the front porch across the street. She was barefoot and hopping from toe to toe with her sweater pulled tightly around her body. She cupped her hand around her mouth. "Dave," she yelled.

Dave didn't turn; he was still giving Steve the stink eye.

"Dave," she yelled again.

"Looks like your wife needs you. So, hey, if you see a husky pup, I'm in the blue house on Sorrel." Steve raised his arm in salute as he turned on his heels and walked slowly away, sweeping his gaze left, then right, intermittently whistling a come-here tune and calling, "Klondike. Klondike Mike, here boy," until he got to his car.

Now here he was sitting at McDonald's, once again at an impasse. He knew for damned sure he wouldn't be able to go back to scope out Lynx's neighborhood. He put his Styrofoam coffee cup into the cup holder and closed his computer. He clunked his head back against the headrest for a single, exasperated sigh, then dropped his chin to check the clock. He cranked the engine and put his car in gear. Time for the powwow.

***

Steve still wore the same jeans and boots he'd had on for the last few days when he got to Fourth Street, went up the elevator, and slogged into the FBI conference room. Higgins and Monroe had already claimed seats on either side of the dark shine of the mahogany conference table. A screen had been pulled down at the front of the room. Andersson walked in, looking smoothly professional in black pants and boots and a black turtleneck with her blond hair slicked back into a ponytail. Steve hoped she wouldn't sit next to him. It would only make his rumpled appearance seem worse in comparison.

"You look like shit," she said as she moved next to Monroe and pulled out the high-backed leather chair. "Have you been sleeping in your car?"

"I've been busy," Steve said. Though his answer made no sense, everyone left it be.

There was a tap at the door, then a tall, grey-suited man moved into the room with a determined stride, searched their faces, and arrived at the end of the table. "Looks like I'm the next to last one to the party," he said without a trace of joviality. He reached into his pocket and distributed a card to each of the others in the room. John Black. Everyone reached into their pockets and wallets and pulled out their cards to exchange. Mr. Black arranged each of the cards in front of him. He pulled out a small device that he held secretively in his palm. He used his phone to contact someone. "349LK9US7," he said. The video screen filled with the scene of a darkened office. The man sitting in front of the camera was merely a shadowy form.

Mr. Black gestured toward the screen. "This is my colleague, John Green, also CIA. Would everyone please take a moment to introduce yourselves?"

"Monroe, Human Trafficking, and I'm the task force liaison for this case."

"Higgins, Violent Crimes."

"Andersson, Arts."

"Finley, Terror."

Mr. Black remained standing at the end of the table. He obviously felt he was in charge of proceedings. "Mr. Green has asked that we gather so our counterparts in Eastern Europe could share some information and make sure that everything is going as planned. Ms. Andersson, if you would please begin with the transfer of art – just a brief overview at this time."

"Of course." Andersson cleared her throat. "The artwork was gathered by Danika Zoric, who was playing the role of Lacey Stuart. She procured all of the paintings from the Zoric family's wish list and employed a counterfeiter to produce copies. Tomorrow, Thursday, the fake paintings are scheduled to be moved to the Bartholomew Winslow Gallery's annex in Alexandria, Virginia in advance of the agents' arrival on Friday. Meanwhile, there are three Zoric family members, all females, who will divide the original paintings between them and take them on separate flights to Europe, each landing in a different hub city and travelling on to Bratislava, Slovakia.

This is also happening tomorrow. The first flight is scheduled for zero-seven-twenty hours. We have filed all of the flight information, and our counterparts at Interpol will be meeting the planes and watching the women while they travel. The original art will be confiscated in the United States and will not be placed in the baggage section of the planes when the women fly. Instead, we have had our own copies generated with a computer system. They are not of the same quality as the hand-copied pieces, but without the originals for comparison, we're hopeful that they will pass inspection, and the family will be none the wiser."

"And what is the plan from there?" Mr. Black asked, finally taking his seat.

Monroe leaned forward. "Our sources indicate that each woman will pick up two children to bring back with them on student visas Saturday. We expect six more children to enter the Zoric's prostitution system. We've arranged for them to be held at US customs—all nine, the children and their handlers—so we can follow the best route for the children's safety, and arrest the women for human trafficking."

"Age range of the children?" Mr. Black asked.

"Fourteen to seventeen, all females this time," Monroe responded.

"Very well. And the means by which they plan to destroy the counterfeit paintings?" Mr. Black sat rigidly in his chair as

359

if he were a soldier at attention. Steve had worked with Black on various cases over the last five years. Black was damned good at what he did, but he never looked like he'd had a rod welded to his spine like this before. Steve thought it was probably very telling how tightly Black was holding himself at this meeting. Steve needed to pay attention to these clues.

Andersson rubbed her finger under her lower lip. "We haven't yet discovered what they plan to do."

"Alright, let's change gears for a moment. I'd like Mr. Green to tell you what's going on in Slovakia because it's going to start playing out here in America, unless we can figure out a way to stop it. And let me pause here and say the arts sting has gone extremely well. If this continues and we're able to take the Zoric actors off the stage here in America, things will be a lot safer for our citizens. So kudos, and keep up the good effort. We're days away from realizing the results of years of hard work. Mr. Green?" Mr. Black's words were congratulatory, but his delivery laid the words out flat and cold in front of the special agents.

Mr. Green sneezed into a hanky and then see-sawed his elbow as he rubbed at his nose. "We understand that the Zoric family and the Krokov family have found a way to coexist and even offer each other a little mutual aid and crossover participation during various cons on American soil. However, that's in the US, and the picture is very different here in

Eastern Europe." He stopped to take a drink from his mug. His voice was artificially deep and mechanical as it moved through the voice alteration software on the video feed. "Both families are becoming more and more ideologically entrenched. Old wounds from the war are festering. The two families, in essence, are battling each other using various means to make their points. The Krokov family is working towards a firmer EU connection and western ties and is pro-American, while the Zorics are firmly attached with Russia and the Middle East. But don't let the Krokov's affiliation fool you—they are not the good guys in this picture. The Krokov and Zoric families both believe that terrorism is the best means to their own ends. Their politics and goals are outside of the scope of this meeting. Just know that the helpful attitude that the Eastern United States Krokov and Zoric families have enjoyed together is quickly imploding."

Monroe sat forward in his seat. "And this means their terrorism is headed to American soil?"

Mr. Black gave Steve a hard look pregnant with meaning. "The first moves have already been made." Then he focused back on Monroe to answer his question. "You understand that Radovan Krokov was murdered by the Zoric family. The Zoric family was ordered to remove him from leadership because Radovan's brother moved into a more aggressive role in Slovakia."

"There's been a mistake. Radovan Krokov died of natural causes. He had a heart attack," Higgins said, shooting Steve a bewildered look. Steve shifted uncomfortably.

"No," Mr. Black said. "He was murdered. I've brought Dr. Nadeer with me to bring us all up to date on that element of the case. He's sitting outside, and I'll call him in after our briefing. Mr. Green?" Mr. Black directed the conversation back to his colleague.

"The Zoric family has been killing off their enemies one at a time, and we don't know how they're doing it. The murders always look like natural causes—a heart attack, asthma, and etcetera." Mr. Green rolled his arm out to show how this was a continuation, like waves on a shoreline. "We can't understand how this is happening, except that they have developed a drug or poison—some sort of biological weapon that can't be found in the bodies after death. There is no sign of foul play. For example, there is no external asphyxia. There are no wounds present. Toxicology has turned up no poisons in the system. The Zorics have discovered another way to kill. Our concern here is that the Zoric family in America are puppets of the Zoric family in Eastern Europe. The Zoric family in Eastern Europe have extremely unfavorable feelings about the United States."

"The Eastern European Zorics are aligned with Middle Eastern terrorist groups," Mr. Black interjected. "As we all understand, the money derived from the cons and scams that take place through the American Zorics is funneled in large part toward funding those who are fighting against US interests."

"Exactly," Mr. Green continued. "Now, we have credible data that indicates that the US Zorics are trying out this new means of murder here in America, and if the vehicle for killing goes undetected, then they will start using it against our high-ranking officials. That's the chatter."

Monroe pulled his eyebrows in so tightly they touched. "Like whom?"

"That, we don't know. And we don't know how concerned we should be in that we don't know how they accomplish the murder. For example, how close does the murderer need to get to his victim? We just don't know," Mr. Green said.

Mr. Black bobbed his head in agreement. "It is imperative that we work on this from several fronts in the US. First, we need to understand how the people are dying, and we mean to do this by studying Radovan Krokov's death. Second, we need to interrupt the Zoric family's organized crime through imprisonment and extradition. And third, we need to stop the flow of children into the United States to be used in whatever capacity their handlers see fit. It all comes down to the next few days." Mr. Black rose from his chair. "Let's begin with the deaths."

Chapter Thirty-Seven

Wednesday

Deep circled the National Mall and turned onto Third Street, driving past the National Museum of American Indian Culture, then following the tourist buses down Madison before he cut over. "Maybe we'll be lucky and find a parking spot on the street," he said.

Lacey pointed at a minivan full of kids, pulling out ahead of them. "Our lucky day, apparently." As they waited with the blinker on, Deep leaned over and gave Lacey what she'd call a "very nice kiss, indeed." Which meant it was fine for public display, but still made her blood hum.

As they left the car and began walking back toward the Mall and the lineup of Smithsonian Museums, the wind whipped in from the river. Ice frosted the air, landing in their hair and on their shoulders. Lacey's nose was running from the bitter cold. She searched the pocket of the jacket Lynx had bought for her, but found no tissues. She dabbed at her nose with her wrist. Deep snagged a napkin from a hot dog vendor, calling out something in Italian to the guy hunched in the corner of his street-side stand; the guy laughed and waved.

Tourists filled the street with their cameras pointing in every direction, their excited shouts ringing back and forth. She and Deep dodged past the groups huddling on the sidewalks with their tour guides. In Deep's hand he was carrying the paper bag with their rock. It looked like he was carrying his lunch. Lacey felt stupid. Was Deep's friend going to look at them with a bewildered stare and wonder if they were pulling his leg? What exactly was Deep going to say about the rock in the bag? And had she actually found the right rocks? Stressed—Lacey was *hugely* stressed.

Trembling with cold and nerves, Lacey was happy when Deep wrapped his arm around her. He held her slightly in front of his body, using his back to protect her from the brunt of the icy wind. With him towering almost a foot above her and the expanse of his muscular frame, it wasn't hard for him to act like a human windshield. And Lacey could only feel appreciation. They took the stone steps up to the National Museum of Natural History two at a time and burst through the doors with a gust of wind.

Inside, they both expelled the outdoor air from their lungs in great big exhales. The warmth in the museum was inviting.

But before she could acclimate, Deep grabbed her hand and pulled her past the enormous elephant that stood guard in the rotunda. They skittered up the stairs to the second floor where Deep's friend, Augustine, waited for them next to the Hope Diamond. Deep hugged Augustine, and they exchanged kisses on either cheek.

"You have found a pretty rock that you wish for me to identify, my friend?"

Deep smiled. "This rock has a special history, so if it's alright, I'd prefer that you look at it in a private office."

"But of course, *mon ami*. This way." He gestured toward the back of the gallery, and the group of three moved forward. "It is a very valuable piece? You are afraid it will be stolen?"

"We think it's valuable, but not in the way that you're probably imagining," Deep replied. His hand patted the man's shoulder companionably as they walked down the hallway.

They entered a space set up with various microscopes and trays. Augustine sent Deep a quizzical brow as they moved to the counter. "Gloves, then?" he asked.

Deep's lips thinned into a tight line, and he nodded.

Augustine pulled out a pair of nitrile gloves. The gloves that Lacey had on hand at the gallery were white cotton; she'd never realized how ubiquitous these blue gloves were. Well, maybe not abundant in regular society – perhaps just for people in Deep's circles.

Augustine placed the evidence bag on a counter, reached in, and gently lifted the rock. After spending a moment looking it over, he sent a confused glance toward Deep. "Really? This is your mystery rock?" He shook his head with disappointment. "My friend, I was hoping that you were bringing me something truly extraordinary."

"What is it?" Lacey asked, unable to contain her curiosity.

"It is simply a rock that is formed by the compression of calcium carbonate skeletons from long-dead corals, or other calcareous organisms."

"Like sandstone?" Deep asked.

"In that both are sedimentary. This, of course, was formed in an ocean." Augustine reached out his foot to snag a rolling stool and dragged it over. Sitting down, he pulled out his gemologist loupe and examined the rock.

A colleague stood at the door and knocked. "What have you got there? It looks like live rock."

"Live rock?" Deep rolled the words around in his mouth. "Why would someone have a piece of this kind of rock? It's not very attractive."

"Ben," the guy in the doorway said, extending his hand first to Deep, then to Lacey. Neither one mentioned their names in return; instead, they offered up a 'hi' and a 'hello.' "So live rock—I guess the only place you'd find it is in people's aquariums. You've seen it, I'm sure. It helps make hides and habitats for fish."

"This is so," Augustine said. "Of course, this is true in the wild as well. And importantly in the wild it will contain numerous algae, bacteria, and small invertebrates, all of which are important for the ecosystem."

"Interesting," Deep said, leaning his hip into the counter and crossing his arms over his chest, watching Augustine scrutinize of the rock. "Do you think that if, say, someone wanted to use this rock, oh, I don't know, decoratively, or in a bird cage, or even in a garden, would they want to boil it first to get rid of those things? I'd imagine if someone didn't boil it first, then the decaying biological materials would smell really badly as they decomposed."

Augustine frowned and tilted his head back and forth. "I can't imagine using this rock in those instances, can you, Ben? It's not very attractive."

"Could it be something for birds? Filing their beaks, maybe?" Lacey asked.

"Calcium carbonate, which makes up this rock, is important to a bird's diet. It's the main substance found in eggshells. But calcium phosphate is found in their bones. You'd want a combination of the two, and you'd need to be careful that the birds weren't getting too much." Ben gave her a friendly smile. "I wouldn't give them a rock to peck on at will, I'd get a powder or liquid from the pet shop; something that can be measured, especially if you're talking about high-priced birds, like parrots."

"Or love birds?" Lacey wandered closer to Deep, and he put his hand on her lower back. It felt to Lacey like Deep was sending out a secret boy-signal, laying his claim. Both of the other men seemed to get the message and the atmosphere in the room subtly shifted. Lacey looked over at Deep, and without looking back her way, he lowered his hand to rub over her hip and thigh before he returned it to its place under her jacket in the small of her back.

"Yeah," Ben said. "I wouldn't do it. I don't think this has to do with birds."

"What about boiling it would make this significant, besides removing any live matter from the crevices? Does the calcium carbonate dissolve in boiling water?"

"No, it's insoluble," Augustine said, pulling the loupe from his eye, and laying the rock back on the tray where the four of them stared at it.

"Any other guesses why you'd boil this rock?" Deep asked.

The two scientists crossed their arms and stared at the rock, tipping their heads one way or the other. Finally, Augustine said, "What if you wanted to introduce this to a freshwater aquarium, and you didn't wish to introduce certain bacteria that might kill your freshwater fish?"

"Well, no," Ben countered. "You'd typically put river rock in a fresh water aquarium. Saltwater coral rock wouldn't look natural in a freshwater aquarium, would it? I've only heard of live rock being used in saltwater aquariums. Though in that application, you wouldn't boil them, right? The purpose for adding them is to introduce microscopic and macroscopic organisms to your aquarium to help break down the waste. Ammonia and what have you."

Deep patted Lacey. "Is there an aquarium at that house?"

"No," she said.

Augustine shook his head. "I have absolutely no idea. Hey, hey Paul." Augustine flagged the guy walking by the door. "Do you have a second?"

A guy in a mustard yellow polyester shirt and brown hand-knit vest stopped at the door. "What's up?"

"Why would you boil calcium carbonate?"

"You're bored?" Paul shrugged.

"Come on. Seriously. Why would you boil this rock?" Augustine held the specimen up for Paul's inspection.

Paul moved closer and ducked his head to get a better look at it. "You have a death wish?"

"Wait. What?" Deep shifted in a nanosecond from just a guy hanging out with a friend in the lab to a soldier, ready to drop behind enemy lines. "Why?"

371

Paul shrugged. "Apparently boiling this rock can be lethal, that's the takeaway I got from a story I heard at one of the Christmas parties this year. Remember guys? It was about Jones doing an experiment. He was boiling live rock as part of the protocol, and he nearly died, didn't he?"

The other men look blank faced.

"Come on, guys, Jones was telling us—do you remember what he was saying?" Paul swung his gaze from Ben to Augustine. "At the McVie Foundation's Christmas Party."

They shook their heads.

"Yeah, I can't remember what it was either, I was pretty wasted. Well, something happened in his lab," Paul said.

"What does Jones do?" Lacey asked.

"He's a marine biologist who focuses his studies on reef culture. Reefs, of course, are made up of this kind of rock along with live corals."

"Is he local? Could you perhaps call and ask if he'd see us?" Deep asked.

"Sure," Paul said. He pulled out his phone, searched through his contact list, and turned to murmur into his phone. They all waited in silence. Paul covered the receiver. "Dr. Jones says he can see you next month, if you could please send him an email."

"Would you tell Dr. Jones that this is a matter of some urgency, and I'm willing to pay him double his normal consultation fee if he can see us immediately?"

Paul got back on the phone and made final arrangements. He moved to a drawer and took out a pad of paper and pen. "Dr. Jones says he's flying in to DC now. I caught him between flights; he's on a layover in Chicago. He'll be back in his office in the morning, though. If you can go in around 10:30, that would work, and he can devote the time you need." Paul tapped his contact window and jotted down the information. "His office number, his cell number, his home number — just in case, and the address of his lab."

Augustine pulled the paper bag over to him. Before he put the rock away, he held it up to the light. "Really? If you boil this rock, it can kill you?"

Chapter Thirty-Eight

Steve

Wednesday Afternoon

"**D**r. Nadeer, would you please make your report?" Mr. Black stood at the head of the table and held the chair out for the wizened man with intelligent eyes and a spry step.

"I actually have very little to report, I'm afraid," he said. When he sat, he looked like a child at the adults' table, as the lip of the wood hit him at chest height.

Mr. Black moved a chair closer to Dr. Nadeer's, and he put his elbows on his knees as he leaned close as if to catch every last syllable and nuance of the doctor's words.

"The body of Radovan Krokov was exhumed, as you ordered, Mr. Black," Dr. Nadeem continued. "Unfortunately, the body had been preserved through the embalming procedures prior to autopsy. Embalming fluids make toxicology studies extremely difficult, if not impossible." He stopped to clear his throat and gather his thoughts.

Steve, too, scooted his chair closer.

"The subject presents as a male, sixty-six years of age, with prior cardiac history and a pace maker. The damage found to the heart is in line with a terminal cardiac episode."

"Have they continued to study the subject's toxicity?" Mr. Green asked.

"We have biopsied and examined the tissues. We are doing everything in our power to discover what could have entered the deceased's system to make a lethal encounter look like it was natural in origin. It would be extremely helpful to our team if we had a direction. Any behavioral clues prior to his death. Anything that he might have complained about. Did he have an upset stomach? Was he nauseated? Did he experience shortness of breath? Was he dizzy? Also, anything unusual in his environments, in his food supply; any special treats, for example, that might have arrived in the home. Was anyone else affected? Pets, even. We are really looking for a needle in a compromised hay stack. I'm sorry." Dr. Nadeer shifted his weight between his hips and turned to Mr. Black. "Since we last spoke, has any of this information become available?"

Steve's shoulders gave a sudden jerk, which he tried to hide with a fake sneeze.

"No. It has not." Mr. Black turned an assessing eye on Steve.

Shit, Steve thought—pretty much the only thought he'd been having all day long.

Mr. Black paused for a long moment. Black's focus on Steve didn't waver as he spoke. "Doctor, I would ask, at this juncture, if you wouldn't mind stepping outside of the door and having a seat in the reception area. Please let our receptionist know if there's anything he can get you to make you feel more comfortable. A cup of coffee, perhaps."

Mr. Black cupped his hand under Dr. Nadeer's elbow and steered him to the door. Stood there and made sure that Dr. Nadeer had settled, offered him a smile, and shut the door.

He walked unhurriedly back to the table where the meeting participants looked at him expectantly. "Finley," he said, "why don't you tell us what you're sitting on."

Steve cleared his throat. "As I reported to you in September, there is a possibility that we have a witness."

Mr. Black sat down again at the head of the table in the chair vacated by Dr. Nadeer.

"Why are you qualifying this information? What is the witness's name?" Mr. Green asked.

"Lacey Stuart—the *real* Lacey Stuart."

Mr. Black nodded and brushed his hand over his neatly crossed leg as if removing a crumb.

"And the word '*possibility*'?" Mr. Green continued.

"Miss Stuart was at Radovan Krokov's home the day prior to the discovery of his body by the housekeeper, Agatha Bowling. This would have been during the timeframe between Radovan Krokov's death and the discovery of his body. I know these pieces to be a fact. I received a call from Danika Zoric telling me that her cousin Musclav Zoric was going to shoot Lacey Stuart." Steve paused and wondered if that was enough information.

"Because?" Mr. Green prompted.

Steve sent a questioning glance at Mr. Black, but Mr. Black sat stone-faced.

"From what I can gather," Steve explained. "Lacey was in Radovan's home for some reason associated with the art gallery. Musclav saw her and addressed Lacey as Danika. He allowed Lacey to leave. Once she had driven away, Musclav followed up with a phone call to Danika to verify that it was indeed her." Steve's heel beat a steady tattoo into the carpeted floor, jiggling his body. He had guarded this story so tightly that saying it out loud in a room with so many people felt perilous. HE didn't know whether Black wanted him to share this or not. And he couldn't understand Mr. Black's posture. It certainly didn't give him clues about showing his hand or holding his cards close to his vest. Steve swallowed and continued. "Musclav hadn't expected Danika at the house. And, of course, Danika was not there. Musclav told Danika that Lacey had seen his face, and he needed to kill her. Musclav went after Lacey in his truck, causing Lacey to have a car accident. When I arrived on the scene, Musclav was preparing to shoot Lacey, but I talked him out of it." Steve's throat grew sticky as his subconscious tried to grasp his words and hold them away from the other agents. "I explained to Musclav that it would ruin whatever they had going on up the road if she were killed. Musclav left. I helped to keep Lacey safe until rescue could arrive."

Andersson pushed a bottle of water from the center of the table toward Steve. He hadn't even noticed the bottles sitting there. He gratefully untwisted the top and took a long slug.

"And you were close enough to the scene of the accident, why?" Monroe asked.

"I was following up on information from Mr. Green." Steve nodded toward the silhouette on the video screen. "CIA had received word that the assassination had taken place and that the cleanup crew needed to make a final sweep, and then all would be pristine and complete. I was hoping to gather any evidence that needed to be swept. But I obviously had already missed that opportunity, and I diverted to save Lacey Stuart."

"Did you know Miss Stuart?" Mr. Green asked.

"I had not yet met her in person, but of course her name and likeness were being used by Danika Zoric. Keeping track of what Danika did in the guise of Lacey Stuart was part of our ongoing casework with the Zoric family in our efforts to monitor the terrorist funding provided by the Zoric family, as well as our work supporting the rest of the taskforce agents in their efforts. We know, for example, that Danika began using the persona of Lacey Stuart at the same time as the Zoric family focused on Bartholomew Winslow and began blackmailing him."

"With what information?"

Monroe cleared his throat, indicating that he'd take that answer. "His homosexual relationship with Radovan Krokov. Taking a step back. The Zoric family became aware of and thus interested in Bartholomew Winslow because he was in a romantic relationship Radovan Krokov, Boss of the East Coast United States branch of the Krokov family. His relationship with Krokov gave the Zorics ammunition against Winslow because Winslow was a prominent member of the Assembly, and, of course, that organization is extremely homophobic. The Assembly went so far as, for example, to convince the parliament in Uganda to put anyone found to be involved in a homosexual act to death. Winslow maintained a great deal of power and produced a great deal of income through his association with the Assembly, and if the Assembly felt that Winslow had misrepresented himself and his dedication to Assembly beliefs, then that might have negative repercussions."

Mr. Green's silhouette took up almost the entire screen as he leaned toward the camera. "By repercussions, you mean . . ."

"Much of the Assembly's power lies with their law enforcement and judiciary connections." Monroe continued. "Something might occur such as a false arrest, sentencing, and imprisonment. It has been our experience that those whom the Assembly actively opposes have shortened life expectancies, especially in our penal systems. Winslow would do whatever it took to keep his homosexuality quiet – his life depended on it. To continue, we know that once information about Bartholomew Winslow and his connection with the arts community filtered back to Slovakia, the family there made a list of art they would like to have for their homes."

"In this case, Finley, why do you think that Winslow didn't simply bring this information to Radovan and have him handle it?" Mr. Black asked.

"From my understanding," Steve said, "Winslow was not aware of Krokov's crime connections."

"Go back to your word 'possibility,' please," Mr. Green rasped through the voice-altering software.

"Lacey Stuart was at the home. Lacey Stuart spoke with Musclav Zoric. These are facts. But subsequent to this interaction, she was in a car accident, and she suffered from traumatic amnesia. She says the last thing that she remembers is leaving the gallery to go and hang a painting for Radovan Krokov, and then she remembers me helping her at the accident."

"And that's when you extended your undercover role to playing the role of boyfriend to Lacey Stuart and informant to the Zoric family?"

"It is." Steve's muscles bunched in his calves, causing him burning cramps. He welcomed the pain – a small penance.

"Since the time of her accident," Mr. Green continued, "has the real Lacey Stuart mentioned anything about the Krokov estate?"

"No," Steve replied.

Mr. Black leaned in. "Have you considered having her hypnotized to see if she could recall any intel that way?"

"I did not, sir," Steve said. "I thought I would have the opportunity for her to work with some of our psychiatrists and learn what happened at the house once she was in protective custody. We needed her to continue with her normal life until this Saturday in order to keep the sting in play. Last Thursday night, however, we were tasked with removing Lacey Stuart from the area. We planned to put her in a safe house and begin the process of putting her in our witness protection program. This is why she was at the scene of Bogdan Zoric, aka Leo Bardman's, murder. I was supposed to meet her at the bar, but I was detained. I sent Higgins in to watch her until I could make my way there. Lacey ran from the scene." Out of the corner of his eye, Steve saw Higgins drop his head.

"You haven't found her?" Mr. Black twisted his chair so he was staring directly at Steve.

Monroe interrupted. "From the point where Bogdan Zoric was knifed down in the bar, we have been looking for both Lacey Stuart and Danika Zoric."

"You've lost track of both women?" Mr. Green asked.

"Possibly," Monroe said.

Mr. Green grunted. "There's that word again."

"We believe that one of the women was killed. Her body had not yet been identified by the medical examiner."

"When did this happen?" Black asked.

"Perhaps Monday—that was the night her body was found," Monroe responded.

"And they don't have her identified yet? This is a priority, a matter of national security," Mr. Green bellowed.

"Yes, sir, but we can't convey that to anyone, can we?" Monroe slipped a pen from his pocket and started rolling it back and forth in his fingers. "They have what they need in terms of records and samples, but there was a four-car traffic accident with multiple fatalities, so their lab is backed up. We've been promised an answer tomorrow."

Mr. Black pinched his chin between his thumb and index finger. "So tomorrow we'll know if the murdered woman is Lacey or Danika and from that—"

"*If* it is even Lacey or Danika. We believe it's one of them, but we don't know as fact that it *is* one of them," Monroe said.

"What is being done now about the search? If you have the possibility of one body, that leaves one of the women in the wind. We needed both women. We can't let one of them slip away." Mr. Black scowled at Monroe's twitching pen.

"The night Lacey ran, she contacted one of the Iniquus operatives. It seemed expeditious to include Iniquus in our search, so we contracted them to locate her. We have our own agents also looking for them."

Mr. Black typed a note to himself into his iPhone.

"We have a *potential* witness who could *possibly* give Dr. Nadeer the information he needs to narrow his search and find out how the Zoric family is becoming such efficient assassins, but either we can't find her or she's dead," Mr. Green sputtered.

"Yes, sir," Monroe said. "That's correct."

Andersson, sitting next to Monroe, had not shifted a single muscle since she'd passed him the water, Steve noticed. As if she thought her lack of movement would mean that eyes would slide past her, and her involvement in this fiasco would go unnoticed. But now that there was a moment of quiet, she stretched out her neck. "On a positive note. Everything is going according to script on the front of the arts con. We feel that we'll be able to recoup the original works. And this should also lead to significant arrests for Monroe's Human Trafficking Task Force." She smiled brightly.

Mr. Green rasped from the video screen, "I'm not interested in the arts con, and I'm not particularly interested in their prostitution rings. It's not insensitivity on my part. Shutting down this family means another crime network is gone from our streets. And I appreciate that shutting them down also means that they won't be raising and funneling money into terrorist activities. But my focus is on, and must remain on, stopping the political assassinations. And too, if it is discovered by the Krokov family that the deaths in their family are indeed Zoric murders, this will destabilize the hard-won and very tenuous peace here in the East."

"And here in the West, as well," Mr. Black said. "It is of the utmost importance that the Krokov family never find out that their US boss was *probably,*" Mr. Black took a moment to send a scathing glance at Steve, "murdered instead of the victim of a heart attack." His gaze scanned the task force members. "If that happens, we all understand it's not just Eastern Europe that will blow up, but that violence will break out right here in the streets of Washington. We will have our own little war on our hands, and the bodies will pile up.

Collateral damage will be high. Right here in the seat of democracy. Right here under our president's nose. Does that sound like a good idea to anyone?" Mr. Black's fist came down onto the mahogany conference table with a loud thud. "I want that woman found. And I want that woman found now. If she can tell someone that a murder took place, then she's our loose cannon. The only weak link while we figure out how this is happening. We need to handle this."

"Woah there." Steve jumped up. "By 'handle this,' just what are you saying?"

Chapter Thirty-Nine

DEEP

Wednesday Morning

"**O**kay," Deep said as they moved into Lynx's kitchen, after returning from the museum. "I'm going to put something in the oven for dinner. Why don't you sit at the table and keep me company?"

"I need to be doing something to move us forward." Lacey shucked her jacket, then reached out for Deep's.

Deep watched her move into the dining room, where she hung their coats on the backs of the chairs rather than in the closet. It seemed to him like she was trying to claim the space as a place where she could be safe and where she belonged. He hoped she felt that way here. Hoped he could make her feel welcome. Hoped he could keep her safe. He was anxious to talk to Dr. Jones tomorrow. "Alright, how about you look through the notebook and see what you can find?"

Deep watched Lacey pull her feet onto the dining room chair, curling herself up as she carefully turned the pages over. He went back into the kitchen to make his old Marine days' faithful tuna noodle casserole.

Salad fixed, fruit cut, casserole in the oven, Deep noted that if he planned to be here much longer, he'd need to go get groceries. He also noted that his R and R week was all but done. Strike Force would be down range until their task was accomplished. In planning, they'd given it a two-week window. Expectations were that he'd be jumping a transport back to the sandbox to join up and lend a hand. While his downtime had been figured into their operation, his team needed his skillset to accomplish the job. How was he going to leave Lacey? Where was he going to leave Lacey? He only had through the weekend to figure everything out. Monday, he'd be wheels up.

Lacey got up and went upstairs. While she was gone, Deep thought he'd start a fire in the fireplace to cheer things up a bit.

"Hey, Deep?" Lacey called down the stairs. "Do I have time for a quick shower?"

Deep moved to the bottom of the stairs to answer her when he spotted the folded piece of yellow legal paper with two pieces of junk mail on the floor under the mail slot. He bent to pick it up.

"Deep?"

"Uh, hang on." Deep opened the page and read:

Just to let you know, some guy lost his puppy in the neighborhood. He cruised the neighborhood about four times before he tried to find the little guy on foot. I talked to him over near your back fence. He seemed really determined to find the puppy. If you see a lost puppy, let me know. Also, we've been having trouble with raccoons in the trashcans. I'd be careful what you put out there that might attract them. –

Dave

Deep scanned over the information again. Someone had made the house. He and Lacey had to get out. *Now.* Deep moved back to the kitchen, where he grabbed some Windex, rags, and garbage bags and made his way up the stairs.

"Deep? Shower?"

"Lacey, sweetheart, someone's scoping the house."

She stiffened; her smile fell away. "What? I don't understand what you said."

"One of Lynx's neighbor's left me a note—he's seen someone casing the neighborhood. I promised Lynx we'd leave immediately. So, here's what we're going to do . . ."

Lacey pulled the note from his hands and read it over, shaking her head. "You got that someone found where I'm hiding from this note?"

"Lacey." Deep tamped down on the urgency and modulated his voice to keep calm. He'd found a cadence and sound quality that kept people from panicking. It was the voice he used when he had precious cargo under his wing, and he was trying to get them out of the hot zones. He'd found that a combination of voice quality and short lists of actions kept their heads together.

But he'd also had to stick enough of them with Lorazepam and hike their dead weight out of the shit, too. It didn't always work.

"Lacey," he repeated, to get her eyes off the note and onto him. "What I need you to do is gather all of your things and put them in a bag. You need to be thorough—every wrapper, every price tag, every *thing* that wasn't here when we arrived has to go. Trash, toothbrush, everything. Put the trash in one of these bags, and put the things Lynx bought you in another. I need you to strip the sheets and blankets on both of the beds and put them in to wash on the sanitary cycle. The washer is downstairs in the basement. Did you see the door in the kitchen to go down there?"

"Yes, but I—" Her eyes wandered back to the note, and he could tell she still wasn't on board.

"Lacey, we have to be out of here in the next five minutes. Okay?" He pushed the bags into her hands and turned her toward the middle guestroom.

"What are you going to do?" she asked.

"I'm packing my go-bag, and removing fingerprints. After you get the sheets, I'll fold up the bedspreads and take them with us."

"We can't take the quilt. Lynx's grandmother made it for her."

"I swear we'll give it back in good condition."

"Her *grandmother* made it for her. It's hand-stitched." That thought seemed to have some kind of distressing hold on Lacey. Sobs filled her voice as she hugged the trash bags to her chest.

She needed to be concentrating her efforts full-steam ahead. "Okay, then take the duvet and quilt, fold them, and put them in the very bottom of the quilt chest in Lynx's room. Actually, mix them into the stack that's there. Okay?"

Still seeming bewildered by the sudden change of events, Lacey started to move past him into the room he had given her their first night together. "Lacey, honey, really, I need you to put the accelerator down." Deep took her by the shoulders so she would look him in the eye. "We need to clean and go in the next five minutes. Every minute we're here puts you at greater risk. We don't know who was here. We don't know why. We don't know if they left eyes and ears in place," Deep said. She nodded and seemed to be on board.

Moving now with his own concentrated effort to the front room, he began spraying down the surfaces. His prints wouldn't matter; he was worried about Lacey's. Lacey, as far as he knew, wasn't being sought for a crime—she was trying to stay under the radar while she tried to figure out how she fit into this whole weird scenario. So his cleaning was more for Lynx than for Lacey. He didn't want to bring any heat Lynx's way. He checked his watch and gave himself four minutes to put his car in reverse.

Lacey was out of breath as she pulled the car door closed. Deep had put their gear in the back hatch along with his computer. He'd already downloaded the information from the thumb drives and sent it to a file Strike Force maintained on the Darknet, allowing them to encrypt and hide information while they were working their cases. If for some unknown reason something happened to either Lacey or him, the team would know to look on there for his notes and evidence files. So he figured the information, at least, was safe. He'd also concealed the thumb drives in a covert zippered pocket in the BDUs he was wearing. He needed to make sure the pictures of the kids, if nothing else, got into the right hands.

Dinner had been pulled from the oven and set to cool on the counter, and he sent a message to Lynx about the game change (and another to Sarah, to tell her to come get the food he'd made and use it for her family's dinner). Now he and Lacey were driving a circuit to lose anyone who might be on their tail.

"Any idea where we're heading?"

Deep swiveled his head toward her. Her eyes were wide and trusting, but he could see that this extra dose of intrigue was hitting her hard.

"I'm going to tool around for a little while." He sent her a smile. "You still haven't eaten. I know a pretty good place near Annapolis. Do you like seafood?"

"Whatever you want." She combed her fingers through her hair. It was the kind of preening move he'd seen bitchy girls make at the bars. The kind of girls that looked down their noses at you as if they ruled the world. But he knew that wasn't at all the way he should interpret Lacey's move. On her, at least in this context, it looked like she was trying to calm herself down. Food. That would help. He moved onto the highway and headed for I-50.

"I think you'll like this place. It's right on the Chesapeake Bay — so it's chilly, but they've got these big rock fireplaces that make things nice." He reached out for her hand, then pulled it to his lips for a kiss. "Cheer up, Lacey. I love you.

Everything's going to be fine. We're changing locations, that's all. Tomorrow, we'll go see this Dr. Jones guy, and then we'll have some new information, and you can decide what to do from there."

Lacey bit her upper lip and nodded.

"What?" Deep asked.

"You said you loved me," Lacey whispered.

"I do. I've been saying that since I tackled you." He chuckled. The 'I love you' had slipped out, and Deep hoped she didn't feel he'd pushed too far, too fast.

"You've been talking around it since you dove in front of a speeding bullet to save my life. How can I ever thank you enough? How could I possibly repay you for that?"

"That's not a debt, Lacey. Seriously. You don't owe me anything."

"No, it doesn't feel like a debt to me. You haven't asked me for anything. As a matter of fact, you keep asking me for what I want. That's really kind of special, you know? A gift, really. A gift that you keep giving." She paused. "I like that you're not making decisions for me – that you trust my judgment." She sent him a confused smile, as though her lips didn't know whether they should go up or down. "And my integrity . . ."

She was quiet for a long time. That last little bit had sounded to Deep like she was trying to work things out in her own head and wasn't looking for a conversation. The radio was off in the car, and they drove in silence. Deep thought she needed some integration time for herself. At least she didn't freak out when he said he loved her. That had to be a plus.

He was coming off the ramp to drive toward the restaurant when she said, "Love. It's such a strange word. It covers everything for my feeling about vanilla ice cream to I guess . . . no, I don't guess. Huh."

"What's that?" Deep asked.

"I was going to say it covers everything from my feeling for vanilla ice cream to you. But that can't be right, can it? There should be a different word for what I'm feeling. Something that's precious and beautiful. And not at all delicate. Sturdy. It should be a sturdy word, something that won't be weathered or wilted or abraded. Something that will stand the test of use and time. That's how it feels to me, like . . . Oh, you know, like a church pew from a renaissance cathedral."

"In Italy." Deep raised an emphatic brow.

"An Italian cathedral. Yes, of course."

"Weathered wouldn't be bad. I've seen some things that I thought grew more interesting if not more beautiful through use. The sharp edges rounded. The finish becoming soft as satin. More distinctive and interesting to look at. I wouldn't

395

mind becoming weathered with you, Lacey." He pulled into the parking lot and turned to her.

"That's so sappy." She laughed with tears in her eyes.

Deep leaned forward and kissed the tip of her nose. But his heart contracted hard when he pulled back and saw the look in her eyes. He saw the same thing there as the day they had met. "You are home. You belong here."

Chapter Forty

DEEP

Wednesday Night

Deep lay on the king-sized bed with his arms crossed behind his head, staring at the ceiling. He thought they were pretty safe here for the night. The hotel was a good-quality chain. Not so expensive that the employees were falling all over themselves to impress you by using your name, not so mainstream that he questioned their security. A "just right" in the Goldilocks hunt for a hideout.

This would have to be their last night on their own. When Lacey came out of the bathroom, he'd need to talk to her about heading in to Iniquus, probably right after they talked to Dr. Jones in the morning. Having the pictures of the children and not actively searching for them and bringing them to safety was a huge stone in Deep's gut. And too, there was the ongoing arts con.

The art should be going into place in the Alexandria gallery annex right about now. Something bad was supposed to happen Friday evening after the agents were photographed with the art pieces they represented. Deep had looked up the building on Google Maps. The rented space sat on street level in a high-dollar neighborhood. Over it were seven floors of apartments. In order to make sure all of the paintings were destroyed; the conspirators would have to pretty much obliterate the whole show space where the oils were hung. Deep couldn't imagine anything other than explosions or fire that would do that, and that meant all of those people who lived above, and all of their stuff, their photos, their family treasures, could be destroyed as well.

There was a restaurant around the corner from the space. And from what Deep could tell, that meant the kitchen shared a wall with the gallery annex. Last summer, his teammate Randy had headed to the West Coast to LA to pick up some evidence – a CPA's computer. When he got there, he discovered that the whole block had come down in an inferno when the gas stove blew in a neighborhood eatery at just the wrong time of day. The morning traffic jam kept the responders away for too long. By the time the LA fire crew arrived on scene, it was an issue of containment and cleanup. Too late for anything else.

As he lay there with his sock feet stretched out in front of him, a steady thumping began on the wall behind the king-sized bed. Deep sent a knowing smile in that direction and went back to his thoughts.

Washington had its issues with gridlock. But not in the timeframe they were looking at. The destruction would have to take place between the Friday night event with the agents and the Saturday show opening, if Deep followed what the counterfeiter had said on the phone.

If he were asked to come up with a plan to take out the space, Deep would cause a gas explosion in the kitchen of the restaurant and make sure that there was an accelerant left against the annex's side of the wall. There were plenty of things that would make sense in that space—the bar set up with plenty of big plastic gallons of alcohol, for example. Add in something like mineral spirits or some other things that might be used around the paintings, and that space could blow big.

Even if that's not how this was going to go down, in order to keep the insurance claim clean, he'd guess the destructive event would originate in one of the buildings on either side of the annex. And whatever that event was, it would have to be huge to ensure success. That certainly wasn't information he could sit on. He couldn't assume that the FBI knew about the impending strike and was taking action. No. If Deep had learned anything in his career, it was never to assume.

Of course, Lacey would have to make her own decisions about how she wanted to move forward, but for him, he planned to return to the mothership with as much detail about this whole intrigue as possible—as soon as possible.

Deep was trying to focus on a plan, but his thoughts were interrupted by the velocity of action from the room next door. Someone was hitting the mattress hard, and in a cadence that meant the guy surely couldn't keep it up for much longer. Every once in a while, the noise would stop and the murmur of a man's directive would come through the thin wall board. Ah, the joys of being in a hotel. Could be worse, Deep thought; it could be a screaming infant. Screaming infants usually went on for hours, if not all night long. No guy he knew had that much stamina. So hopefully this would be short-lived.

The door to the bathroom opened and Lacey emerged with a billow of steam. She was wrapped in a towel. Her skin looked warm and pink, and inviting. She focused over Deep's head at the wall. Deep peeked up to make sure the painting above him wasn't dancing with the vibrations. The last thing he needed was the ribbing he'd get from the guys if he couldn't make it over to the landing-zone Monday because he was held up by a concussion from a picture in a motel room. That didn't even make a good bar story.

"Sounds like someone's having fun," Lacey said.

"The guy's got stamina, I'll give him that."

"It's been going on for a while?" She quirked a funny little smile.

"Since you went into the bathroom."

Lacey stared at the wall. "You're kidding, right? They've been going at it like that since I started my bath? That poor girl's probably sending up smoke signals from her girly-parts."

Deep looked at her, then burst out laughing. He crawled to the end of the bed with mischief in his eyes. "I've studied human anatomy, and I don't remember learning that particular body part. Can you show me what girly-parts look like?" He gave the bottom of her towel a little tug.

Lacey squealed and held the towel tighter around her. "Shhh. Stop, they'll hear you."

"Me shhh? I've been listening to them thumping the wall for the last forty minutes."

The woman on the other side began moaning and begging loudly, "Oh baby, give it to me. Give it to me."

The pink of Lacey's skin turned a bright shade of red that made Deep laugh even harder. But he was thankful that the couple next door seemed to have hit their crescendo and were on their way down. At least the bed had stopped thumping against the wall.

"Our turn," Deep said, pulling Lacey into his arms.

"Oh, no. No, no, no." Lacey said in a scandalized voice as he fell backward onto the mattress with her in his arms.

"Why are you saying no, beautiful?" Deep asked as he tucked her hair out of her face.

"Because you're going to get all competitive and see if you can't go at least five minutes longer, and maybe put the bed through the wall instead of simply banging it into the wall. That's why. 'Be all you can be?' Isn't that the Marines motto?"

Deep spun until he'd pinned Lacey underneath him, and though she had said, 'Oh no,' her legs had wrapped up on either said of his hips, and she had let her towel fall open. He kissed her nose.

"That's the army. The Marines' motto is 'Always faithful'," he said softly. "And I do my best to live that motto." He kissed her chin. "But when a girl says no, it means no." He kissed her lips very lightly. "Do you want to rethink your answer?" Before she could respond, he kissed her lips again. "Besides, that guy was having sex like an army infantryman. They throw on a pack and hump their way to their destination. Usually it takes a long, long time, and it's damned boring. That's not how I was trained, ma'am."

"And just how were you trained, Marine?"

"I'm special ops. I home in on the target, I get it into my sights, right? Then I work with skill and efficiency to make sure my mission is completed satisfactorily."

"Satisfactory? Not exemplary?" Lacey asked with a little pout.

"I don't like to brag, but I have a number of shiny medals that they've pinned to my chest that say I'm one of the best of the best."

A coy smile spread across Lacey's face. "I'd agree with that." She strained for another kiss, but Deep kept his mouth out of range.

"I'm sorry, but you said no."

"It's a lady's prerogative to change her mind," Lacey said.

"Then say the magic words."

Lacey batted her eyes like Scarlet O'Hara and offered up a perfect Cupid's bow smile. "Pretty please, with sugar and cream on top?"

Chapter Forty-One

Thursday Morning

Deep and Lacey pulled up to the 1960s-style brick utilitarian building.

"Lacey, when we're done here, we need to take some time to regroup and make some big decisions."

Lacey looked over at him and tilted her head.

"We're going to have to move on our intel. Figure out somewhere safe for you to go. . ."

"Okay." Lacey's heart gave her a weird little knock. Deep's words sounded like he was done. Ready to wash his hands of this problem. *Her* problem. Her. He was ready to wash his hands of her. She was a burden that needed to be sorted and stored on a different shelf.

She got out and looked up at the sky. For the first time in days there was an expanse of blue, though the sun was only a dim globe. Lacey stomped her feet to keep her toes from freezing as the chill crept up from the sidewalk and through the soles of the tennis shoes Lynx had bought for her. Even with their grip soles, her heel slipped out from under her on the icy surface, and she flailed to keep herself upright. Deep was laughing as he caught her around the waist to steady her. She grabbed hold of the door handle as she came upright and waited while Deep moved around to the back of the Rover to gather the paper bag with the live rock, then came around toward her. With an arm around her waist, they started up to the glass doors, where they could see a figure waiting for them.

"Hello. Hello. I'm Dr. Jones." The man's enthusiasm was a little overwhelming as they moved into the lobby. Lacey wished she'd had a moment to adjust to the new environment before being bowled over with the man's big personality. "I understand that you want to talk about live rocks and boiling water. So interesting." He set off at a trot down the corridor, and she and Deep hurried along behind him. Lacey wondered whether Dr. Jones had swigged a pot of espresso for breakfast. Normal people didn't have his kind of energy.

He was thin and a good six-foot-five, towering over Deep. The hem of his pants hit above his ankles, showing one blue and one brown sock. The cuffs on his shirt and lab coat didn't quite make it all the way down to his wrists. He was elastic, and his movements were expansive. He reminded Lacey of one of those performers at Disneyland she'd seen on TV, dancing on stilts in the parades.

Dr. Jones burst through the doors and stretched his arms with a wide flourish. "My lab," he said, then stood in the center of the room. A self-satisfied grin spread wide across his face.

Lacey moved into the space and gasped. "Dr. Jones, this is spectacular."

The room was long and thin, like the professor. On the two longest walls were a series of aquariums on two levels. The upper aquariums held various configurations of coral and marine fish, and underneath were tanks that looked like they held sea weeds. The scenes in each aquarium were glorious, and for Lacey it was like walking through a living arts gallery. Incredible beauty — the movement of the water, the oscillation of the anemone and other sea creatures, the brilliant flashes of fish.

Lacey exhaled. Amidst the reefscapes, the stress in her body seemed to gain weight and substance that could now be identified by gravity and pulled down her spine and her limbs until it puddled on the floor. Lacey stepped forward. "Dr. Jones, this is simply exquisite. It must feel like you're on vacation every time you come to work," she said with a smile.

Dr. Jones was now rocking back and forth on his feet like a Jack-in-the-box that had sprung out and was dancing on its coil. He laughed. "Yes, that's exactly right. I have the best job in the world. They pay me to play. Isn't that marvelous?"

Lacey smiled at the infectious joy that Dr. Jones exuded. While over the top, he didn't feel manic to her, just like he somehow had learned to embrace happiness. Like a marine sciences joy-guru. Lacey smiled at the thought. She wondered what it would be like to live or work with someone like him. Would it wear off on you, or would it wear you down? She looked once again at Dr. Jones's mismatched socks and thought they probably reflected more of his distraction that morning than color blindness or lack of aesthetics, because whoever arranged these tanks did so with a flair for color and texture. She pointed at a crazy-looking fish and smiled up at the professor.

"That's a pajama fish—one of my favorites. It looks like he was drunk when he was getting dressed." Dr. Jones laughed. And indeed, it was a bizarre combination of polka dots and stripes and colors. It even had red eyes.

"Are these corals?" Lacey pointed at the bright bursts of color in the tank.

"Those there?" Dr. Jones asked, moving closer to peek into the tank. "No, that's a common mistake. People think that they're corals and even call them soft corals. Those are Palythoa, which are related to coral, but they are not actually corals."

Deep joined them in front of a massive aquarium that held an amazing garden of bright colors. Florescent orange, acidic green, neon purple in variations of tiny passion fruit-like flowers all mounding in soft pillow structures on the skeleton of rock. The rocks in the tank looked exactly like the rock that she and Deep had stolen from the Zen garden at Radovan's home.

"They're beautiful, aren't they? This animal is very popular with salt water aquarists," Dr. Jones said.

Deep leaned over the top of the open aquarium. "They look like the flowers you'd see in a science fiction movie."

"They do, don't they?" Enthusiasm and energy rolled off Dr. Jones as he spoke about the animals as if they were his children, and they had accomplished something spectacular. "Those Palythoa are extremely dangerous. You wouldn't know it by looking at them, but they produce the second-most deadly toxin known to man."

"Deadly?" Lacey asked.

"Yes. Oh, yes." Dr. Jones nodded emphatically. "One gram of palytoxin can kill one hundred *million* mice. Yes, oh yes, deadly. On contact, even in the smallest amount it can have an effect. It can, for example, cause a tingling sensation, and it can give someone a metallic taste on their tongue. Exposure can make you feel like you have the flu. With an increase in toxic contact, it increases blood pressure and decreases respiration. If exposure continues, it can put you into a coma, and at high enough doses, it will kill you. High enough doses, mind you, are miniscule."

Lacey and Deep both squatted down to see into the aquarium and the tiny flowers that glowed beneath the specialized aquarium lights.

"As a matter of fact," Dr. Jones continued, "we know that ancient societies would harvest the palytoxins to put on the heads of their spears, darts and arrows to kill their enemies. Of course, they wouldn't have wanted to put it on their weapons when they were killing their food supply. As the blood stream carried the poison into the body of the animals to effect the death, it would poison the muscle tissue, rendering it dangerous to eat."

"Huh." Lacey put a steadying hand on the aquarium's shelf. "It reminds me of that scene in Wizard of Oz where Dorothy is dancing in the poppies, relishing their beauty, when in fact they were dangerous."

"But only to make Dorothy sleep. If I remember the movie correctly, the good witch cast a spell, and it snowed on Dorothy, which negated the Wicked Witch's spell. That's not possible here."

"People have aquariums in their homes that hold the second-most deadly poison in the world?" Lacey asked, rising to her feet.

"Known to man. We're discovering new and wonderful things every day." Dr. Jones slapped his hands together and rubbed them, looking thoroughly pleased. "But yes, right in the homes of saltwater aquarium owners. And it's not an uncommon experience that hobbyists will run into problems. For example, they'll be fragging. Now, fragging is short for fragmentation. If an aquarist wishes to share a fragment with a fellow aquarist, or he wants to sell a piece, or he's trying to propagate the species in his or her own tanks, they go through the fragging process. It's really quite easy, let me show you."

Dr. Jones went to the back of his door and hung up his lab coat, switching it out for a rubber apron. He slid rubber gloves all the way up his arms and over his shoulders like sleeves. He pulled an elastic strap over his head that held a full-face visor in place. Reaching into the tank next to Deep and Lacey, he pulled one of the flower-covered pillows out of the water. "Now this is Zoranthus, but I still use protective precautions. Zoranthus is similar to Palythoa and can secrete a little bit of the palytoxin, but not nearly as much as a Palythoa." He moved with the specimen to a stainless-steel lab table.

"It can stay alive outside of the water?" Deep asked.

"Oh yes, but you don't want to leave them out for long. You take them out, you do your thing, and put them back in. Certainly, you need to work within a fifteen-minute time frame. Okay, you two, you need to stand back at least three feet. This guy is tiny, but it can squirt water pretty darned far."

Deep pulled Lacey by the hips well back from the table.

Dr. Jones turned the Zoanthus over. "You see, I've attached the colony to a plug with some epoxy, then the plugs are inserted into the prepared holes in the live rock. It allows the hobbyists to rearrange their tank for the visual balance of color and texture. Typically, aquarists have other things in their tanks for variety and to make them attractive. Of course, sometimes an aquarist needs to move the animals around because the specimen don't all get along. Then it's better to move them away from each other. Sort of like when siblings fight, you have to move them to opposite sides of the sofa to keep the peace." Dr. Jones chuckled as if he'd cracked a good joke.

Lacey smiled politely and nodded her head.

"This is a coral scalpel," Dr. Jones said. "I simply remove the fragments that I wish to move or propagate, like so. Now that I've removed the fragment from the mother colony, I'm going to put the plug right back into the water. See?" Dr. Jones walked back to the tank and maneuvered the plug back into a hole in the live rock. Dr. Jones stood back and looked, then reached in again, and with his hand dangling in the tank he said, "Get right down where you can see what I'm doing."

Lacey and Deep squatted down to eye level with his hands.

"I'm sticking it back in a hole. Safe and sound." He stepped back to look at the tank. "I think it goes better there. Now," Dr. Jones turned back to the work table, "with this little frag, I'm going to affix it to this plug with a dab of epoxy, give it time to set, and then I'll put it on this shelf I have set up in the corner of the tank so I can keep it isolated. Not really necessary, but it's a step I like to take."

"Why are you wearing a face shield?" Deep asked.

"Well, I am fragging Zoranthus, not Palythoa, *but* it always pays to be cautious. Zoranthus can still have enough palytoxin in it to cause a great deal of agony." Dr. Jones washed his gloved hands in the sink, then pulled the gloves off, hanging them to dry, then he washed his hands. He put his safety wear back in its place and donned his lab coat again. "I want you to see this."

Dr. Jones covered the room in a few long strides. He turned his computer around and played with the keys, then turned it so Deep and Lacey could see the screen. "The guy in this photo was fragging Zoranthus and a miniscule amount of water squirted him in the eye, and this was the result."

"Jezzis," Deep breathed out.

Lacey stared at the picture of an eye that looked inhuman. The tissues of the upper and lower lids were so inflamed that it looked like long blisters on either side of the eyeball. The

413

eyeball itself was bloodshot, and the pupil had taken over the iris. Lacey's body responded by pulling in tighter and bracing. *All that from a squirt of water off a tiny frag?*

"This is not an uncommon experience." Dr. Jones flipped through other like photographs. "It's important to always take precautions."

"Understood, sir, but that's what can happen to you if you come into dermal contact with the substance. What happens if you were to ingest it?" Deep asked.

"You die." Dr. Jones got a funny little look on his face that basically said, *Are you crazy?* "Well, if it's a small enough quantity, you'll wish you would die. There are some stories of people falling ill from eating crab with palytoxicity, and they've become very ill. but survived. But I can't imagine a circumstance in which you'd actually ingest the toxin other than through an unfortunate instance with sea foods."

"What would happen, for example, if you were to boil a piece of the live rock that had held Palythoa plugs?"

"Oh, no." He shook his head emphatically, then stood with his hands on his hips like a mother scolding a child. "You never, ever, *ever* want to boil a rock that had had Polythoa or Zoranthus on them. Never. Don't even pressure wash them."

"And why is that, sir?" Deep asked. "Well, first, let me ask you—are there good reasons to want to clean the rock either through pressure washing or boiling them? Legitimate mistakes that people would make in handling them?"

Dr. Jones reached up his sleeve and scratched his elbow. "Often times, you'll see a hobbyist begin with freshwater and advance to become a marine hobbyist. Freshwater hobbyists will boil their rocks to sanitize them. If you're moving from one kind of system to another, one might carry forward the habits from the last system. And as to the reason why one should never pressure wash or boil live rock – imagine, if you will, that the toxin is aerosolized. It's in the atmosphere, floating around in combination with the air. How could you render yourself safe? It's on your skin. It's in your airways. Your lungs oxygenate your blood, so now the blood circulating in your body is poisoned. Awful. I mean *awful*. Highly toxic. Deadly. There was a guy I talked to once who was boiling his rocks, and he almost took out his whole family, including his German shepherds."

Lacey reached for Deep's hand and twisted her fingers with his. "The toxins would kill animals? Like birds? The birds would be like canaries in a coal mine?"

"Absolutely—birds have relatively fragile systems. If there were birds in the environment, they would succumb to the toxins very quickly." Dr. Jones moved toward his desk at the back of the room and planted his hips on the edge.

"And what would happen, if, say, a person walked into a kitchen, and she put her head right over a stew pot with five or so rocks boiling in it?" As Lacey trembled, Deep moved to rest his hands on her shoulders.

Dr. Jones shifted his gaze to the ceiling, rubbing a hand over his chin while he contemplated the question. "Hard to say." He focused back on her. "It would depend on several things. For example, what was the toxicity level on the rocks? And how long had they been boiling? If they had been boiling for hours and hours, it could be that most of the toxicity had already entered the environment and dissipated, reducing the concentration over the pot. But if the toxicity levels were there, it would feel a bit like being very frightened. Like a panic attack. Breathing would become difficult; the heart would be straining. And here's an interesting little caveat. One of the problems with being poisoned with palytoxins is that the person understands that something very bad is happening, but they don't act like they do. There's a kind of euphoria that happens. So they might think, 'I need help, something's very wrong.' But they don't act on it. Or they act counter to their best interests—they do the thing that they know might endanger them more."

Lacey tilted her head. "Like stand up and walk out the front door in plain sight?"

"I beg your pardon?" Dr. Jones asked.

416

"Oh, sorry, I was thinking out loud."

"You cannot imagine how potent this poison is and how little it would take to make you very sick. It even happened to me. Not boiling it, mind you. Let me tell you a story so you can fully understand how potent and dangerous this toxin is."

Dr. Jones eased farther back until he was sitting on his desk. His long legs bent at the knee and crossed at the ankle, making him look like a frog in mid-jump.

Deep pulled Lacey's hand and had her sit on a wooden desk chair close to the professor. He pulled a lab stool over for himself, sitting beside her.

"So one day I was looking at my tanks. That one there." He pointed at an aquarium.

Lacey twisted in her seat to see the one he'd indicated, and then swiveled back.

"I saw a little piece of rock with a small Palythoa colony in there. I remember putting it in there as sort of a place to put it down, and frankly, I had forgotten about it. So I'm walking it over to another tank one where I kept my Palythoa collection along with other specimens, and as I walk it over—and this isn't broken off, I wasn't fragging, I just had a piece about the size of a silver dollar in my hand—I notice that there's a little slime on it." He rubbed his fingertips with his thumb. "It's like clear mucus that runs out of your nose when you've got a cold coming on, a little thicker maybe. Same thing. Only not."

417

Dr. Jones continued his tale with a faraway look in his eye. "I didn't think anything of it. I'd touched Palythoa with my bare hands quite a lot ever since I was a teen. At this point in time, I was doing what I do. I move things from tank to tank all the time.

"Now, I go home, and I have a terrible night. I felt like I'd been in a car accident. I ached. And I mean *ached*. It was far worse than the flu. It was as if someone beat me all over my body with a bat. My wife was sleeping next to me, and I was trying not to moan and wake her. I knew she would freak out if I told her I thought I was dying. I remember very clearly that I thought I might. Just. Die. And, at the same time, I didn't feel like I wanted to do anything about it. Remember that for a minute."

Lacey nodded and leaned onto her crossed knee.

"So the next morning, I feel better. Tired, but better. I no longer thought I was going to die, and I was really pleased that I was able to shake off whatever bug was going around. I decided I felt well enough to go in to the office." Dr. Jones hung his head and shook it slowly back and forth. "The first thing that hits me when I open the door? The smell. Oh my gosh, that smell, awful. I walk over to my tank and see it's cloudy. Cloudy plus smell means disaster. Disaster." He shook his hands like the heavens themselves were opening.

Lacey wondered if this guy spent a lot of time on a stage—his gestures seemed perfect for the theater but overwhelming in the laboratory space. Lacey wasn't used to loud. And she certainly wasn't used to exuberance. She sunk back against Deep's chest, and he dropped a kiss into her hair.

"The whole tank was dead. Everything was so healthy and magnificent the night before. Every last organism in the aquarium was dead. Fish. Everything." Dr. Jones shook his head in disbelief. "It was devastating."

"It was the Palythoa you moved into the tank that caused the problem?" Lacey reached out a hand and put it on the professor's knee like she was sympathizing with a death in his family.

"It was. And that's when I remembered the slime on the piece as I moved it. And I thought back, and yes, my symptoms were exactly that of palytoxin poisoning. Thank God I didn't actually die – I just wanted to. And that informed my future research. It turns out that palytoxins are transdermal. That's something we didn't know before. We assumed that the toxin entered the human system through an opening. But since it can pass through a dermal barrier, the poison doesn't need to enter into a cut or what have you. You can get some on your skin, and it can enter your blood system. Also, we had assumed that the toxicity came from the flesh of the animal. But no. It's the secretion. That was a new finding, too. Amazing and so, so dangerous."

"I'm sorry that you experienced this," Lacey said. "So that leads me to think, if I were writing a book or making up a plot for a killer in the movies, could they do something like add the palytoxin secretions to someone's personal hygiene products—put it in their hand lotion, for example—and kill people?"

Dr. Jones sent her a strange glance. "Why did you say you were here?"

Deep said, "We were over at the Smithsonian talking to Ben, Paul, and Augustine, and they were trying to remember the story you were telling at a Christmas party about almost dying and boiling live rock. They must have confused the two stories. We were there showing a piece of live rock to Augustine."

"Yes, the boiling, it should never be done. And yes, I guess you could poison someone by placing the mucus from a Palythoa with a high toxicity level into someone's body lotion. You'd have to know they would use the lotion. You'd be risking killing someone by accident, someone else picking up the bottle, using the lotion, and being poisoned. That would be very risky." Dr. Jones stared at the ceiling, thinking this idea through. "Well I suppose this is fiction, so the author could do as they wished with the outcome."

Lacey tucked her hair behind her ears. "I'm wondering from what you've said what would have happened if you had woken your wife. If she had called an ambulance, are there anti-palytoxins available like they have for snake bites? An anti-venom, if you will?"

"Yes. Yes. That's what I wanted to tell you when you brought up Dorothy and the Wizard of Oz. When I was poisoned I was sure that I was going to die. And I could have. But I didn't want to do anything about it. A very interesting effect of the toxin. Remember how Dorothy was being poisoned and she simply wanted to lie down and take a nap? She wasn't worried about it. She didn't try to fight it."

Lacey nodded.

"Let me begin with the first part of that question about waking my wife up. I was feeling toxic euphoria, so it would have been a hard fight to get me into the emergency department. I probably wouldn't have given my consent to go in the ambulance. If I got there, I would have presented as a man having a heart attack."

"The tests would prove that true?" Deep asked.

"Absolutely. I have a colleague who is no longer able to work, he had such a bad case of palytoxin poisoning. He actually had a heart attack, and they believe a stroke. It affected his brain so badly that he had to learn to speak again after the incident. Do the doctors have something to counter it?

The plain answer is no. And what's worse, if they used the normal drugs and protocol for someone who was having a heart attack or coding, the victim would not respond to their efforts. As a matter of fact, the CDC this very week came out with new guidelines for palytoxin poisoning, which say watch, and wait, and hope for the best. That's pretty bad when the CDC doesn't know what to do."

"You'd go to the hospital, then what?" Lacey asked.

"There is no bloodwork that would show up under normal scrutiny. No toxicity screening for palytoxins at all. So there's no way they'd find it. I'd say that 99.999% of doctors have never heard of it. None. And even if the person is conscious, and they know exactly what happened, the doctor has no way to fix it. They can try giving a respiratory treatment like they would for an asthma attack, but that's kind of like throwing a life preserver with no rope attached out toward a drowning person in a stormy sea and hoping for the best. There is nothing, absolutely nothing that can be done to stop that poison from following its trajectory. In a healthy person, they've got a shot at survival as long as their exposure was really limited, like mine. I touched the plug for maybe ten, maybe fifteen seconds. But if there's any kind of underlying health condition, heart, lungs, age-related fragility, low muscle density, low body weight, fatigue, alcohol, recent illness, anything that increases the efficacy of the toxins, then there's nothing that can keep that person from dying."

Lacey sat there in complete silence, processing the information.

Finally, Deep cleared his throat. "I had a question about all of the organisms that died in your tank. Was that an effect of this particular colony being highly toxic, and that you placed it into an environment that was not acclimated?"

"Well, yes. Probably. Hard to tell." He stuck his finger in his ear and scratched. "Palytoxin is believed to be an anti-predation defense. Normally, though, it doesn't affect the neighboring colonies. Why this one did has not been proven, but I would hypothesize that it was the sudden introduction to the level of toxicity in this particular colony. Not all Palythoa are toxic. Various studies have shown they actually have a wide spectrum of toxicity levels. For example, *Palythoa mutuki* was non-toxic; the *Palythoa heliodiscus* was—" Dr. Jones stopped and whistled— "off-the-charts toxic. Hugely dangerous."

"And the silver dollar-sized piece you were moving?" Lacey asked.

"Was *Palythoa heliodiscus*, unfortunately," the professor replied.

Deep rubbed his thumb back and forth over his lower lip. "Someone with colonies of any of these Palythoa, including the *Palythoa heliodiscus*, could frag the colonies and almost farm them?"

"Not almost—they do. That's a whole industry, fragging and growing colonies for reef shops and marine aquarists."

"Huh," Deep said. "Dr. Jones, if I were to show you a sample of live rock that's been outside in the weather since last September, is it possible that you could tell if there had been any Palythoa colonies attached?" Deep lifted the paper bag from where it sat by his foot, and pulled out the piece of live rock from Radovan's garden.

"Should be. Once a colony is growing it's pretty hard to get rid of the traces. They populate the tiny crags and get into the open areas. Let's see here." Dr. Jones picked up a pair of regular-length rubber gloves and pulled them on before accepting the rock from Deep.

"Rubber gloves even after it's been out in the rain for months?" Lacey asked.

"I was scared straight by that near miss. I take precautions now whenever anyone mentions Palythoa. I *do not* play with palytoxins. How about you go wash your hands over there?" Dr. Jones lifted his chin toward a sink in the corner that housed a wall medical kit above it and a high tech eye-wash station.

Lacey remembered that yesterday, Augustine had been wearing protective gloves when he alone had handled the rock. She wondered, as Deep went to scrub, if he had held the rock long enough for any toxins to have absorbed into his skin. And if he had, could they still be deadly?

Chapter Forty-Two

DEEP

Thursday, Lunch

Lacey and Deep walked across the parking lot to the quaint bistro, which was placed oddly out in the middle of nowhere. Deep had chosen this particular restaurant because it would be darned hard for someone following them to blend and observe from anywhere around here. The building had been an old gas station. Converted into a Swiss chalet, it sat alone at the corner of two busy rural highways and was surrounded by winter fields, which stood empty and wide. Deep's team had used this location on several occasions to pass or collect information. He was confident that he had chosen a safe place, and they could sit here for a while and come up with a plan.

"Who did Dr. Jones remind you of?" Deep asked as they reached the door.

Lacey looked up to catch his eye, and they both said, "Doc from *Back to the Future*," at the same time. Then Lacey held her hand up for a high five.

Deep slapped her palm, then held on to her hand, lacing his fingers with hers. "What?" he asked. "Pop culture and high fives? Who are you?"

"Just learning to blend." Lacey slowly skated her free hand out to show she could go with the flow.

The lunch crowd had already thinned by the time they stood in front of the hostess's podium. Deep asked for their most private seating. With his hands resting possessively on Lacey's shoulders, he winked at the waitress to let her know they wanted to be alone. He hoped that would keep her from popping in and out. He needed the waitress to bring their food and let them think. He needed to tell Lacey that time was up.

"That's darned terrifying," Lacey said as she picked at her food.

"Which part, exactly?" While Deep had ordered a big fat steak, Lacey had opted for the harvest salad, and that worried him. He couldn't seem to convince her that carbs, fat, and protein were her friends in stressful situations. Her body needed something to run on besides roughage. She had countered that this was what she normally ate and was still only able to maintain her weight with the benefit of weekday workouts with her kick-boxing trainer. Kick-boxing, that explained the moves he'd seen when she was battling Higgins at the door of the bar. He wondered if she took that up after the knife scene in her car.

This really wasn't the right time for her to be worried about her figure, though. She didn't see what he saw; she had been dropping weight since he'd grabbed her last Friday morning. Visibly shrinking. Fear burned an enormous number of calories. Trembling, nightmares, and worrying required a big bowl of Ben and Jerry's or something with more calories than lettuce. He wondered if he could get her to eat some cheesecake if he ordered it for himself with two forks.

"I stuck my head over the steam of aerosolized palytoxin." Lacey said.

He shook his head as if bewildered. "And lived to tell the tale."

"While Radovan did not. Now that I have that information, so much of the scene at Radovan's house on the day of my accident makes perfect sense." Lacey held her napkin poised on her finger while she spoke, then dabbed at the corners of her lips before replacing it in her lap.

Somehow, that action completely charmed Deep. "Why don't you tell me how you're interpreting the scene with the new information?" Deep sent a searching gaze around the room to make sure they couldn't be overheard, tucked as they were over here in the corner, away from the last of the diners.

With his back to the wall and an exit through the kitchen nearby, Deep felt in control of the environment.

"Alright. I arrived at the house and the door was unlocked. It must have been unlocked when whoever went in to start the stone soup had been there. The men were dressed in gardeners' jumpsuits, garden gloves, eye protection, and respirators, so their skin was covered and they were protected from any toxins in the air."

"And they checked on the birds first thing, right?"

"'Canaries in the coal mine.' They must have been dead, showing that the toxicity levels were high enough to kill them. When I talked to the housekeeper, Agatha, she said the birds were missing."

"If you think about it," Deep said, "they couldn't really leave the birds there, could they? The police might have seen two dead birds and thought that there was some kind of gas that killed Radovan instead of the heart attack. The bad guys couldn't remove the birds and leave an empty cage because that would make the police wonder why there was an empty cage. Which also might lead the investigators to ask some questions and have them take a closer at the body. Order an autopsy, for example."

Lacey nodded. "Not that that would help. You remember Dr. Jones said there are no toxicology tests to show palytoxin poisoning. Okay, let's see — the birds were dead, and the one guy goes upstairs, confirms that Radovan is indeed dead. I know from hanging a painting up there that his bedroom is directly up the stairs, so the steam—well, the aerosolized toxins—wouldn't have had far to travel from the kitchen. It's basically a straight line if the doors are open. I was in the dining room feeling like my body was out of control from fear. But in reality, I had put my head over the rock soup and breathed in the toxins. The guy takes the rocks outside and puts them in the garden, because who in their right mind would want to travel with those rocks in the same car? Even if they were in the trunk?" Lacey took a sip of water. "And then I'm there all out of breath, heart jackhammering, and not really able to think or care about my decision making as I stand up and walk out the door."

"Absolutely," Deep said. "It all fits into a nice neat little package once the idea of palytoxins is thrown in to the equation. Even the part where you felt so bruised at the hospital – though truthfully, that could well have been from the accident. It explains why the doctors held you longer to test why you weren't properly oxygenated, and why they didn't find anything abnormal in your system."

"But why would anyone do that? Kill with palytoxins?" Lacey asked. "It seems there are simpler ways – a pillow over his head or something."

"That's the million-dollar question." Deep's phone vibrated in the Strike Force pattern. That meant it was Lynx, and that couldn't be good. "Would you excuse me for a minute? I need to take this call." Deep wiped his mouth, laid his napkin on his chair, and went outside to sit in his car.

"Deep?" Lynx's voice came over the speaker.

"Oh, crap."

"Yeah. I'm sorry. Titus Kane called me in for a briefing."

"Okay. Tell me the story."

"When Lacey first disappeared from the bar, the FBI hired Iniquus to find her." Her voice was soft with concern and support. "The case was handed to Panther Force; the contact's name is Higgins."

"Yeah, I know the guy. He was the one at the bar that grabbed Lacey's ankle."

"Higgins along with his FBI task force and Panther Force were all out looking for her. When the woman's body turned up, the case was put on hold pending identification of the victim. No point in the Panthers beating the woods for a girl that was already on ice. We both know it wasn't Lacey. I wasn't pulled into the inner circle yet, so I didn't know any of this until thirty minutes ago."

"If they turned the contract back on, they must have an identification. Is the deceased's name Danika something?"

"Right. That's right. Danika Zoric. She's a naturalized American citizen who came to the US thirteen years ago at the age of twelve to live with relatives."

"Titus's crew is back on the hunt?" Deep asked, checking his mirrors, just in case.

"With no good trail, so General Elliot lent me to their team. And, of course, now I'm duty bound to move forward."

"The FBI initiated the contract. Do you have a particular task force assigned? That would give me a lot of information."

"FBI, joint task force. But get this, General Elliot got a call last night from John Green in the Eastern European office, CIA. He flagged the case – this is classified status orange."

"*What?*"

"I know. Any ideas what that's about?"

"Vaguely. My guess is this has to do with coral reefs. Is there a warrant out for Lacey's arrest?"

"Nope. She's wanted for her own protection. What's this about coral reefs?"

Deep decided to ignore her last question and hold that information. "Who's providing that protection? Are we? For how long?"

"Good questions. That wasn't part of my brief. Not part of my need-to-know."

"If Lacey and I walk into Iniquus, say we go to the interview room, so she can share some information – it's still her choice, right? She could walk right on out?"

"That depends, Deep. If this is a matter of national security, which it well could be now that we know the CIA planted their flag, then they could hold her indefinitely with no access to a lawyer," Lynx said. "National Defense Authorization Act."

"What's Iniquus's position about handing over people under those circumstances?"

"You've got me," Lynx said.

"This is really an extremely important point. I'll come in and share what I know, which is quite a bit. But if Lacey is about to lose her choices about her life and her freedom, there is no way in hell I'm bringing her anywhere near that crap. They'll slip her away, and she'll go black. Can you check policy with General Elliot, please? And can you fax it to my car? I probably need this in writing rather than a he-said-she-said."

"With a signature?" Lynx wasn't being sarcastic; she was being thorough. Little details like this could make or break a case.

"Yes, please. I'd like to bring Lacey in so she can tell them what she knows. But that's her decision. I'm not bringing her against her will. And since she hasn't got a warrant out for her arrest, I can do anything I want to help her get wherever she

434

wants to go." Deep checked his watch. Lacey would be wondering what was going on.

"True. Is that the direction you're thinking of going?" Lynx's voice took on a sharpened edge of concern.

"It's not up to me."

"Deep, look, I'm going to go right now to talk to the general. He's probably still in his office because I just left there. I'll get you the information about Iniquus policy faxed to your car so you can make an informed decision. Whatever it is you decide to do, I'll give you one hour beyond my faxed dispatch to show up here at Iniquus and take the reins. With or without Lacey, that's on you. After that one hour, I'm going to have to spill. It's my job. And it's our duty."

Yeah, time was definitely up.

Chapter Forty-Three

Steve

Thursday

"**S**teve, good, so we're all here," Monroe said. Higgins and Andersson had already taken the extra seats in Monroe's small office.

Steve put his shoulder against the file cabinet and waited.

"Diving in then." Monroe flipped open his file. "The autopsy report came back and confirms that the murder victim is Danika Zoric. That leaves Lacey Stuart in the wind."

The next few sentences were lost on Steve as his body adjusted to the information. Monroe dropped that statement on the table like it was a pile of papers that needed to be filed away, but to Steve, it was the discovery of the light bulb. It was the Nobel Peace Prize. It was believing there really was a God who gave a shit about him, brought him a miracle, and laid it at his feet. The others might perceive this information like a data point that needed to be covered, but it was not.

Lacey was alive. Steve breathed in the warmth of the thought. He let the colors flood his system. He reveled in the sensation of Atlas's weight being lifted from his shoulders. Then, suddenly, his mind brought the moment of reprieve to a screeching halt. *Wait, you don't know that yet. No one said Lacey was alive.* All he knew was that Danika was in the morgue, and Lacey was not. The miracle, which presented like a holographic ball, disappeared from the magician's hand with a quick flourish.

The room spun around him, and Steve gripped the handle on the file cabinet, accidentally pulling out the drawer as he lost his balance, toppling himself over. Higgins reached out to right him.

"Sorry," Steve said. "I thought it was locked."

". . . eighteen hundred hours, just two hours before the arts reception begins." Monroe said.

"Would you repeat that?" Steve asked. "I zoned for a second there."

"We have a powwow, you and I, at Iniquus Headquarters at eighteen hundred hours." Monroe raised his eyebrows.

"Got it. Any word from them on Lacey Stuart?" Steve asked.

"Panther Force is the Iniquus group assigned to find her, and they're the ones who called the meeting to give us an update. So I assume we'll get our intel then. Everything's coming to a head. Let's do a quick round robin and find out where we are. Andersson?"

Andersson sat with her feet perfectly parallel and touching, and her hands one over the other on her knees; she was self-contained. "I'm happy to report that we have successfully removed the original paintings from Reagan International Airport's baggage department. They were packaged, brought in-house, and are being catalogued as evidence. The original oils were replaced in their tubes with our own fakes and are headed to London, Paris, and Brussels. The three women will be flagged as they deplane and placed under agent surveillance. All three have connecting flights to Slovakia. We anticipate that they will be returning Saturday evening with the children."

"What about the gallery show?" Monroe asked.

"The artists' agents should be arriving tomorrow throughout the day," Andersson continued. "The counterfeit paintings were put in place at the annex gallery this morning in preparation for tomorrow's cocktail party."

Monroe stuck a pen in his mouth, holding it like one of the cigarettes he'd given up some five years ago. "And they plan to destroy them how?"

Andersson shifted her tailbones uncomfortably. "We haven't been able to ascertain that yet."

"What's the plan, then?"

439

Higgins jumped in. "We have video surveillance on the annex. Once they've put out the lights Friday evening, we'll go in and gather the fakes. Our warrants are already signed. We'll patrol the interior with K9 to see if there are any explosives in place. Other than that, it's a watch and wait scenario. If any family members show up on Saturday, they'll be arrested at the annex. We have to wait until the Zoric women and children are in the air, though, so we know they won't be alerted to the situation. We need them back in America to make their arrests. We think these three women are the most likely to turn state's evidence. And we need that badly."

"Once they're in the air . . .?" Monroe asked.

"We round up the family," Higgins said. "We're monitoring phone calls and locations on all the players. It should be a clean sweep."

Monroe rocked back and forth in his chair, making the springs squeak. "From human trafficking, then. We've been working on a master list of names and locations where the children are housed and the johns who we believe use the services. We think we have all the children in the Zoric ring accounted for. With Pavle heading to jail and out of the picture, if the kids get sold, they might slip through our fingers. Our evidence is, unfortunately, mostly circumstantial. While rounding everyone up right now definitely isn't optimal to making the charges against the adults stick, it is what it is."

"If we can get the children to cooperate," Higgins said, "we'll have strong cases."

"The chances of that are absolutely nil if the Zorics have threatened those kids, saying their families back in Slovakia would be hurt," Monroe countered. "So, no guarantees. That's the way it stands for human trafficking." Monroe turned to look at Steve. "Finley, terror?"

"We don't know how Radovan died. Lacey Stuart is our only chance at gathering the information Dr. Nadeer has requested." Steve spoke as if he were a marionette with someone else pulling the strings that animated his mouth. "Our hope, too, is that once Pavle Zoric and his family are gathered up from the arts con, their family will no longer be able to provide money from America to fund terrorist activity overseas and will no longer pose a direct terrorist threat here in America." Steve nodded toward Andersson. "My take on all this is that it comes down to the arts sting to stop all the other crimes. I hope to hell the Arts Task Force can pull this off and make those charges stick."

Chapter Forty-Four

DEEP

Thursday, Lunch

Deep waited until Lacey had eaten the last bite of the cheesecake without mentioning what was going on. He knew that as soon as he told her what Lynx had said, she'd stop eating. He didn't want her passing out, like she did when she found out about her uncle's perversions. Deep had no plan of action, anyway, until he knew what Iniquus's position was. He'd never worked on a case where the person he was saving wasn't grateful and the bad guy wasn't killed or jailed. This was sort of like limbo, where it was the good guy—well, gal— that might get the bad guy's outcome.

He paid the bill with cash, and they walked toward the car.

"You've been awfully quiet since you came back from your phone call. Do you want to tell me what's happening?"

"Absolutely. I'm expecting a critical communication, then I'll share the information with you."

"This must be from Lynx," Lacey observed matter-of-factly, walking a quick-step to keep up with Deep's longer stride.

"Hopefully not." Deep fobbed the door to his car and scanned the area before he opened it. He moved in front of Lacey and popped the glove compartment open. There was a single piece of paper curled over itself. He pulled it to his chest and moved out of Lacey's way.

After shutting her door, he gave the area another 360. He stopped at the back of the SUV to read:

Iniquus is a company of high integrity. We take down the enemy wherever and however we can to preserve the rights and freedoms of our citizenry. If a US citizen holds the well-being of America in their heart, and they mean our nation no harm, then Iniquus will stand by that citizen and fight for their freedom. Iniquus policy prevents us from forming an alliance with anyone under any circumstance that would infringe upon an individual's right to autonomy. However, the United States is also a country made great by its laws, and even if we disagree with them, Iniquus must abide by the laws of our land.

General Elliot

Deep leaned back against the car and scrubbed a hand over his face. This was not what he'd hoped for. But, of course, it

444

was what he knew to be true of his company. That's why he'd given Iniquus his whole heart and soul since he took up his position as an operative on Strike Force. Deep could feel Lacey's eyes focusing on him through the back window. He didn't want to ramp up her stress levels before she even knew what was going on.

Pushing off the car, he went around to his side and climbed in.

"So your critical communication came in, and you're not happy."

"I'm not unhappy. This doesn't offer me any new information, that's all." Lifting the steering column out of the way, Deep leaned against his door so he could swivel toward her. "I told you we would have to make decisions when we were done with Dr. Jones. Now, here are some things you should know—"

"Deep before you go any further, I would like to ask you a question, please."

Deep raised his brows and inclined his head. There was something about Lacey that shifted. She had pulled her shoulders back, displaying her core strength. For a moment, Deep saw her as a six-year-old — when her father died and her mother sunk into her depression – when Lacey was suddenly on her own to face the world. The difference was, now she wasn't on her own. He would stand next to her.

"Can everyday people hire Iniquus?" she asked.

"I don't understand."

"Me. Could I hire Iniquus to represent my best interests? To consider the information that I know, to bring it to the right persons' attention, to be my liaison, so I know that what is happening is both well-considered but also properly handled?"

"Well, yes, we do private for-contract work all the time. That's usually us rescuing a kidnapped CEO or doing close protection work for foreign dignitaries, but I could see this falling into the scope of what Iniquus does."

"I would like to hire Iniquus to intervene on my behalf." Lacey lifted her chin like a punctuation mark, as though the decision had been made and there would be no discussion.

"Lacey that's cost-prohibitive, but I promise I'll do everything—"

"I'm sure I can afford it. I'm an heiress who doesn't touch her money — not the principal, not even the interest. I've wanted to live my own life in such a way that I could prove that I can take care of myself. Up until now, it's been about me proving that I could support myself on my skills and talents alone. But now, under these circumstances, it's about using my assets to promote my best interest. I promise you, I can afford an Iniquus contract without batting an eyelash."

Chapter Forty-Five

Thursday

Lacy stared out the window at the winter wonderland of tree branches glistening with icicles. The sunlight glittered the landscape, making their trip towards Iniquus Headquarters a fairytale trail.

Deep sent her a glance. "You warm enough?" he asked.

"Yes, thank you." Lacey was shivering, but not from cold—more from apprehension. She didn't know what was going to be happening to her in the next hours and days. Deep reached over and grabbed hold of the seat belt that crossed her shoulders and yanked it uncomfortably tight over her hips.

Lacey's brow pulled together. As she turned to him, Deep reached out and flipped a red light on his console.

The background music from the radio suddenly disappeared and the airwaves now sparked with the crisp

447

voice of a woman who communicated with military precision. "Echo Zulu, identify yourself."

"Deep, Strike Force, Code red. Code red. Code red."

"Copy. We have your GPS coordinates. Tracking vehicle registered as a 1994 black Land Rover Defender license plate Charlie, Tango, Foxtrot, three, niner, zero, zero, one. Over."

"Affirmative. Patch me through to Panther Force."

"Roger Wilco."

Silence filled the cab. Lacey didn't know what was going on. Deep didn't seem stressed. His face was relaxed. His left hand wasn't gripping the steering wheel. His right hand rested comfortably on his gear shift. "Code red," though that sounded extreme. Maybe it meant something different at Iniquus. Maybe Deep was just coming out of the shadows now and needed those Panthers to know they were headed in to the headquarters. But if this was something normal, why was she losing circulation from her seat belt holding her in place with such tenacity?

"Break break," hissed over the radio speakers from an unknown voice.

"Panther Force, Titus Kane. State the nature of your code red, Deep."

"I'm transporting Panther Force's precious cargo to Headquarters. We've picked up a tail. Requesting immediate support from closest available operatives."

"Roger wilco, we have you on the screen, and we're dispatching three operatives to your trajectory. The closest is twelve minutes out."

Precious cargo? That must mean her. Picked up a tail? Lacey leaned back and checked the side mirror. There was nothing there. They were on an empty road. There were no other cars either coming or going.

"Lynx here. You guys okay?"

Deep sent a quick glance Lacey's way. "We just had some delicious cheesecake. I was going to bring you a piece, but Lacey ate it all before it got wrapped up."

"Well good then. Thanks Lacey you saved me from a ten-mile run. I don't enjoy jogging in freezing temperatures. You holding up okay, Lacey?"

Lacey moved her mouth to talk but no words came out.

Lynx didn't wait for her to respond. "Deep, after you texted me your decision to change locations, I had a chat with Dave. He confirmed by photograph that the guy who lost his puppy in my neighborhood was Steve. That's who made my house. I'm sure you've been following counter-surveillance protocol when on the move. I'm wondering if Steve didn't leave someone in the shadows to plant a tracker on your vehicle."

"That's what I was thinking only more along the lines that Steve wasn't paying close enough attention and lead someone by the nose right to us," Deep said. "If I've got a tracker on my vehicle, I'm not going to be able to shake this guy." Deep's voice was conversational. A bad guy was tailing them, but Deep was acting like this was just a day in the life – a walk in the park. "Still," he said. "I'd like to get off this road. Icy conditions. Poor lines of vision. Can you reel me in?"

"Affirmative," Lynx replied.

"Titus here. Can you give us a description of the tracking vehicle?"

Again, Deep sent a glance over to Lacey. She stared back, her eyes held as wide as her lids would stretch.

"Black Chevy Silverado, 4x4, dual cab, single occupant visualized. Caucasian male, blonde hair, black coat."

"Roger that. You're going to have to stay on the road you're travelling. The first road with access is seven miles ahead on the left. That's the first we can get an operative to you, and the first you can get off of a secondary road. Is he up on you now?"

"Negative, I've lost visual."

"And you're confident you're being tracked?"

"Affirmative," Deep said.

Lacey knotted her hands tightly in her lap.

"You're heading up on the Potomac Gorge," Titus said. "There are some tight turns and some nasty sheer drops down toward the water with no guardrails. How are the road conditions? You said ice. Can you try to out run him?"

"Black ice . . ." Deep popped his gaze up to the rearview mirror as an engine gunned behind them.

Despite the tightness of her belt, Lacey twisted around to see out the back window. The enormous pickup truck had shown up out of nowhere and was sitting on their bumper. She felt their vehicle accelerating. Lacey was right back in that moment on the road where she was racing away from Radovan's house. The man's truck was suddenly so close to them that she could see his face. See his eyes as they caught on hers. It was the man from the house. The man from the accident. The man with the knife. The one who swore he would kill her and everyone. One after the other, after the other. Deep. He would kill Deep.

A scream tore its way up through Lacey's body. Shrill, earsplitting sound filled the cab. Her lips vibrated as her cry moved through the Rover, filling every cubic inch of space with her horror. She was trapped and the killer right there behind her. She flailed her arms and legs as if to run away. She had to get free. She had to get out.

Deep's arm shot out, pushing her against her seat. "Lacey stop," he shouted at her as their car swerved over the road. Deep hunched his shoulders and gripped the wheel as he righted their course. He reached out to shift gears as they

451

rounded the turn. The truck roared behind them, and she felt a jolt as the Rover bucked forward.

"We're hit. We're hit," Deep yelled for the benefit of the team tracking their path. The Land Rover's back wheels slid to the right. The front wheels whined and scrambled as they worked to grab hold of the slick pavement, Deep worked the gears. His feet moving between the clutch and the gas. Lacey gripped at the door handle, pressing her back into the seat.

They righted for a split second when, BOOM, they took another hit to their back fender. This time the world spun out of control. It dragged her body up against the door and pinned her there. With a lurch, she was flung forward and back then forward again. The noise billowing around her was deafening.

"Deep. Deep," Lynx's voice called over the radio.

Lacey was dangling from her seat belt, her car door opened beneath her feet. She looked down and saw the world was still whirling, then she realized she was perched over the deadly waters of the gorge.

Chapter Forty-Six

DEEP

Thursday

Deep brought his head up. His vision was bathed in red. He reached up and wiped blood from his eyes. It hurt to breathe. The sound of his inhale came heavy in his ears. His heartbeat echoed against his eardrums. He was disoriented.

"Deep, report. Deep. . ." He heard his teammate's voice, and he tried to locate Lynx. He realized she was speaking from the radio. Deep opened his mouth and moved his jaw back and forth. His fingers brushed over his forehead where he found a gash in his brow.

"Lynx," he gasped. "We're over the ridge."

Laughter sounded above him. A heavy thud hit the back of the Rover and clanked its way across the roof. Deep watched a huge rock roll off the hood and out of sight. The Rover seesawed. Terrible screeches, metal against stone, wrenched the air. Deep gazed through the missing front windshield down into the gorge. They hung a good fifty feet above the river. "We need that help, stat."

Deep reached into the leg of his cargo pants and pulled out a bandana that he knotted over his gash so he could see. He reached out and grabbed the waistband of Lacey's yoga pants and started to haul her back into the cab. They tipped forward precariously. He froze, then very slowly lowered her to her original position.

"Lacey, you with me?"

Lacey whimpered.

She was conscious—that at least was good news. "Sweetheart, I'm going to have to leave you there. Your seat belt will keep you safe. I want you to close your eyes and focus on your breathing. This is very, very important. You are not to move. Not even an inch. Can you hear me?"

"Yes," Lacey said. Terror filled that one syllable to overflowing.

"I have air support headed in your direction," Titus said.

"We're dangling here, man." Deep wheezed, his own seatbelt cutting into his chest and abdomen, keeping him from dropping straight down into the water. "The rotor velocity will have us swimming."

"Roger that."

Another rock thumped against the car's roof and slid. Deep pushed back against the steering wheel as he assessed.

The guy above them wasn't going to wait until their cavalry arrived. Deep needed to act now.

With the windows busted out, Deep could see what lay below them. If they went down, there was no hope of survival, not in those treacherous rapids with water temperatures just this side of freezing. Deep tried to adjust the rearview mirror to see up the hill, but he couldn't get a good angle. As he searched for possibilities, he spied his jump bag. It had been flung loose in their tumble and wedged by Lacey's seat. Shifting his hips to the left to counterbalance his move, Deep reached right and slowly dislodged the bag, dragging it toward him. The Rover rocked. The screech of metal sliced the air, and Lacey screamed. Above him, Deep heard the guy calling out in some foreign language.

Bang. Another rock was flung down. This one landed on the rear hatch and pushed through the shattered safety glass, rolling into the cargo area. Deep flung his arms over his head to protect himself from the shower of shards. Lacey dangled out away from the splinters. As the Rover slid farther down, Deep braced his feet wide and clenched his jaw. They came to a bouncing stop.

"Deep, we're here. Let us know what we can do," Titus said.

"Support?" Deep gasped.

"Four minutes, man. Our guys are gunning it. We have EMS en route. We've contacted the PD and they're heading your way. We don't have their ETA."

Deep wiped his forearm under his nose, smearing snot and blood up his sleeve. He reached into the bag and pulled out a rope. As long as that guy stayed above throwing rocks, they might be okay for four minutes. Deep just needed to get the Rover tied in so if it slipped, it wouldn't go far. He had to buy himself those four precious minutes.

Deep stretched his foot outside of the cab and felt rock beneath his boot. Slowly, carefully, he moved his weight from the seat to that foothold. Deep tried to unlatch his seat belt but it had jammed. He pulled the tactical knife from his sleeve pocket and sawed through the webbing with his right hand. At the same time, he leaned out and gripped an exposed root with his left. As the belt gave way, Deep's full weight dragged him down, but he countered and pulled, maneuvering his body from the cab. He hoped somehow the guy above was too busy finding rocks to have seen him exit.

Deep stretched his neck to look up the embankment. So far so good. Wedging his arm under the root, he freed up both hands and tied his rope into a loop. He swung it out to lasso the wheel, hoping to get his line over the axle.

He missed.

Deep swung the rope to open the loop and try again. This time, the air split with a blast. The rock where his foot rested exploded. He hung from his elbow, while his feet scrambled under him searching out a new foothold.

"Deep," Lynx's voice yelled.

"High-powered rifle." He gasped, hunkering back into the side of the embankment.

"No shit. Are you guys okay?"

"Time's standing still out here."

"Three minutes. They're coming."

The rifle sounded again and again, but the guy's shots were missing his area completely. Deep focused down into the side mirror, toeing it gently until he could see that the shooter was aiming to Deep's right. He was gunning for Lacey. From his present positioned, Deep couldn't see her to check if she was alright. He desperately wanted to call out and have her confirm that she wasn't hit. But he held back, lest her voice help the gunman home in on her location.

Deep locked his jaw and steadied his nerves. He threw the rope again, and it wrapped over the wheel. He pulled the line taut, then reached out to secure it to the oak, standing sentinel just beside them. He pushed at the line and hoped it would buy them a modicum of safety. Then he pulled his pistol from his jacket. With a clear head and a steady grip, Deep wriggled his body, maneuvering around to face his target. The tight ledge where he'd crammed his boot crumbled with every move. Quickly, Deep realized how impossible it would be to get his shot on mark. He had to move.

The last reverberation of rifle fire gave way. Deep froze in place to listen, his body plastered flat to the embankment. Metal pinged against the macadam as the shooter dropped his spent magazine. The respite would last mere seconds while the guy reloaded. Leaping out, Deep threw his body against the sheer drop off and monkey crawled his way toward the oak. Pushing from tree, to root, to rock, to tree, he finally swung up against the side of the ridge. As the hostile brought an AR15 back up to his shoulder and molded it against his cheek, Deep leveled his sights. With a steady pull on his trigger finger, he emptied his gun.

Reloading on the move, Deep scaled upward to engage the shooter and keep him away from Lacey. *Is she still alive?* A blast of cold filled his core and for a moment he was frozen by the thought of Lacey dangling from her seatbelt. Dead.

Titus's voice broke through Deep's alarm. "Iniquus on scene. Hold your fire. Hold your fire. Iniquus on scene. Acknowledge."

Deep wasn't about to acknowledge and let the shooter know how close he'd crawled to the roadway. Titus's voice called again, "Iniquus on scene—"

Just then, the Rover slid away from its perch with a roar

"Clear. Clear" Came the shouts from above.

Deep didn't look up. His eyes fixed on his Rover dangling from one wheel by the rope. It swung out over the gorge then bounced against the rocks to arc out again. He followed the line to the oak that seemed to hold strong. That wouldn't last long.

"You okay down there?" someone bellowed above him. "Hang tight we've got rappelling gear."

The hell with that. Deep gripped at rocks and roots as he scrambled down. He slid out of control, grasping at handfuls of debris as the ice-covered grasses slicked through his fists and cut his hands. He made it under the car and grabbed the frame to stop the next swing. That's when he saw Lacey's shoeless feet dangling, unmoving, from the passenger's side door.

A whoosh and a grunt brought an Iniquus operative to his side. "Shit," the guy said, looking at the white socks, half-on, half-off, exposing Lacey's motionless heels to the frigid air. He reached up and depressed the button on his communicator. "This is Trip, Echo Force. We're going to need a med flight to stage away from the crash."

"Roger that, you should hear them coming in any minute now." Titus's voice came from the plastic box on Trip's shoulder.

"We need a technical rescue crew. Three ambulances. One for a DOA," Trip continued.

"Roger."

Deep felt the blood drain from his head. Could he something about Lacey that Deep couldn't see from his vantage point?

Trip reached out and punched Deep in the chest. "The guy topside took a fistful of bullets. He's Swiss cheese, man." He pointed at Lacey's legs. "This is going to be a trick." He unhooked his auxiliary harness and handed it to Deep.

Deep wriggled the apparatus into place. "Lacey," Deep yelled. "I'm coming for you, sweetheart. I need you to be very still." Deep refused to let his mind go to dark places. Places that Lacey couldn't come back from and live. "It's just going to be another short time, baby, and you'll be comfortable and warm." Deep buckled his apparatus into place and hooked into the secondary line Trip had brought down to him.

"How do you want to handle this? That anchor rope looks like it's wanting to fray. And I don't have anything to stabilize the vehicle in our gear."

Deep's eyes travelled up the embankment. "I need more slack," he called toward the road.

Trip said, "I've got one guy topside. We have another car coming in. Ten minutes from now this place's going to be crawling with help. But I don't trust that line you rigged up to last long enough. Not with all that weight."

Deep's practiced eye measured the scene. "Okay," he said. Deep worked his way to the back of the car and very slowly creeped in through the rear window.

"Shit, that's suicide, Deep," Trip called, reaching out to hold the car's frame to the slope.

Deep didn't disagree. If the rope gave and the car went down, his climbing harness wasn't going to help a thing. But as he slid forward, moving in through the back window, he could see Lacey's brown hair. Getting to her was the only thing that mattered.

Deep crept forward feeling his way more with intuition than anything else, just like he did in the Middle East when he was never sure if there was an explosive beneath his feet or a trip wire across his path.

The car lay almost directly sideways and the rear passenger door gaped open. Deep slid his leg over the seat from the cargo area, placing his foot on the car frame. Making his body rigid, he pressed his weight into his toes, freeing up his hands. He reached out and brushed the hair from Lacey's face. Her eyes were squeezed tightly shut. His gaze moved up her arms, and he saw that she dangled from quivering hands, her clenched knuckles were white on the steering wheel. Alive.

Thank you, Lord God, she's alive.

"I'm here, beautiful. Hold on for just another second. I'm going to get a line on you and get you out."

Somehow.

Chapter Forty-Seven

Friday

Lacey stood in the bathroom in Lynx's office at Iniquus, giving herself a last look-over before she headed to the meeting. There was no hiding the bruises and cuts on her face and body. Her wrists were wrapped in ace bandages, and Lynx had to help her dress and do her makeup.

She was in better shape than Deep was though. The gash on his forehead took fourteen stitches to close. They had had to shave his eyebrow to do it. They were lucky. Hugely lucky. No broken bones. No internal injuries, just stiffness and pain.

The other guy didn't fare so well. Deep had killed him. Shot him through the heart so many times that there was no heart left in his body when they took him away. That's what Trip said. Lacey didn't even know the bad guy's name. And never wanted to know it either.

She blinked at her reflection. It was Friday. Last Thursday she had dragged herself to Alexandria for a drink and some dinner with Steve, and her world had imploded. Today, maybe, she was going to start putting some pieces back together. Enough, perhaps that she could get a better picture.

A knock sounded, "Lacey, are you ready? It's time," Lynx's voice called out.

Lacey walked next to Lynx down the hall. Deep moved into their path dressed in his Iniquus uniform of digital gray cam fatigues and a charcoal gray compression shirt that show cased his muscular torso and made him look like a superhero. He was. A superhero. He took her breath away. Here was a man who loved her enough to put his life on the line time and again. Someone who put her well-being in front of his. It was humbling.

Lynx looked from Deep to her then back to Deep with an "I see." She turned her smile to Lacey. "Let me be the first to welcome you to the family."

Lacey sent a questioning glance toward Deep, who winked and bent to whisper in her ear. "You'll soon find that it's impossible to keep a secret from Lynx. Ready?"

Before Lacey had a chance to answer, the two operatives had started up the hall. The area they walked through had the feel of a fine-tuned machine. She remarked on the industrial black and grey colors both in the décor and the Iniquus attire. Neither Lynx nor Deep were talking. They seemed singly focused on moving her as quickly as possible from Point A to Point B. Wherever that was.

As they took an elevator to the fourth floor, Lynx made a call. "She's coming up now. Are we clear?"

Lacey almost rolled her eyes. This seemed so silly. When they had left the hospital for their hotel, Deep had explained that today she would be taken to a viewing room where she could see and hear everything that went on. Lynx would be sitting with her. But Lacey didn't have a full picture of why she was being led in such a clandestine, cloak and dagger way.

A very tall and very beautiful woman met the elevator with keys in her hands, and a smile on her face. "Ms. Stuart? I'm Leanne Burns, our owner General Elliot's personal assistant." She started to walk away, and their party of three followed.

Leanne unlocked a door, and they went down another hallway until finally, they came to a room that required a thumb print to enter, just like in Lacey's apartment building. Leanne pushed open the door, and they all moved inside. Lacey's interest was definitely piqued.

One wall was made of windows. A line of comfortable high-backed chairs with desks, which could be lifted into place or left to the side, faced the windows, providing the view. A buffet table spread across the back of the room. It was set with platters covered with glass domes – fruit, sandwiches, vegetables, nuts, coffee, tea, and bottled water. Very healthy.

"You and I will be in here at least in the beginning," Lynx said. "Deep is going to conference with the government. The FBI and CIA will be represented. We aren't going to let them know you're on premises until we understand their intentions. General Elliot will be in the room and will disclose that you have contracted with Iniquus."

"I have the papers for you to sign laid out over here." Leanne gestured toward a table. She looked at Lacey's bandaged hands. "Well, as best you can. I'll explain anything that you might have a question about. We've also assigned a lawyer to you, Sy Covington. He's on his way over to introduce himself." She checked her watch. "He can answer your questions, as well."

"Sy is brilliant," Lynx said. "I think you'll like him. He and General Elliot will both be sitting in the conference room. General Elliot will be representing both the government and their contract, and you and your contract. But Sy's job is to represent you alone. Between the two of them, they'll make sure that *all* of your rights are preserved to the best of our abilities," Lynx said. "I'm on your team. My job is to interpret what's going on for you and answer your questions as they come. And, if you ever feel uncomfortable and you wish to leave—" Lynx raised her eyebrows meaningfully, though

Lacey couldn't quite grasp its meaning, "—then it's my job to assist you to do just that."

Deep squeezed Lynx's arm, and they seemed to have one of their private mind-meld conversations. Finally, he said, "Thank you for that."

***

Lacey sat in her chair looking into the conference room. She was told that the wall was one-way glass. The agents would speculate as to someone being in here, but they would not be able to see or hear them, nor could they get to this room through any direct means.

"Why are you telling me that?" Lacey asked. "Do you think they're going to try to grab me and take me away?"

"I'm trying to lay any concerns you might have to rest. If they ask if anyone is watching, General Elliot will indicate that I am in here observing body language. Here they come. The older gentleman is General Elliot. You now know Sy, and Deep, of course. The next guy is the Panther Force Commander, Titus Kane. His force was tasked by the FBI with finding you. The next guy is FBI Task Force Coordinator, Calvin Monroe, CIA's John Black, and you know Steve Finley."

"Steve *Finley*, not Steve Adamic?" This was surreal. He didn't look anything like a software engineer. He looked . . . terrible, actually.

"*Finley*," Lynx said, and squeezed Lacey's shoulder with a look of sympathy.

Deep moved to the front of the table with a box and his laptop. Behind his head there was a screen. He took a moment to set up. The bandage over his eye made him look dangerous, like the kind of guy who enjoyed a good fight. He took Lacey's breath away.

Quiet descended.

"Gentlemen, we are here today with the common goal of keeping American streets safe. Over the last week, I have been involved, by happenstance, with a series of events that seem to be of importance both to the FBI and the CIA. My connection with this case is through Lacey Elizabeth Stuart."

Lynx said, "Wow, did you see that?"

Lacey turned her way.

"Steve. When Deep mentioned your name, Steve lit up with, gosh, I'd call it thanksgiving, hope, and overwhelm all at once. I thought for a second he was going to burst into tears," Lynx said.

Lacey didn't have the same angle of view that Lynx had, but she could see the side of Steve's face was splotchy red.

"I am here to talk about my week and my findings. Let's think of this as a three-ringed circus." A picture of a circus filled the screen behind Deep. He used a laser beam pointer to indicate the ring on the far left. "Ring One. Here we have a Zoric family member who had somehow lost favor and was killed." Deep pressed the button on the remote and the image was replaced with that of Bogdan Zoric lying in a pool of blood on the bar room floor. "Not quietly. Not privately. In fact, very, very publicly. And in such a way that by the time the photographs are snapped, and video footage was recorded, the only people who looked like they were involved was the dead man and this woman."

Deep pressed the button again and there was a picture of Lacey, pulling the knife from the dead man's back. "Lacey Stuart. She was grabbed by the FBI, Special Agent Higgins, as we see here." Once again, the image changed to show Lacey's ankle ensnared by Higgins's hand. "And she fights to save herself, here." A video showed Lacey's high heel stomping Higgins's chest. "She runs out the back door and is confronted by another group of men." The next picture showed a storm scene with four men in long black coats emerging from a car. "She runs to save her life." Deep looked pointedly at Steve, and Lacey could see that the splotches on his face became almost purple-red. "How did she get into this situation?"

Steve hung his head.

"That's shame," Lynx said, she turned her head toward Lacey. "You do know he's in love with you, don't you?"

"Deep?"

"Well, of course Deep is in love with you. But I was referring to Steve Finley."

"Oh," Lacey said with a frown.

"What you may not know about Ring One," Deep continued, "is that two pieces of information were passed to Ms. Stuart. First, before he was stabbed, Bogdan Zoric approached Lacey and addressed her as "Danika". Second, the murder victim slid a thumb drive into Lacey's bra. It's here in front of me, marked in Evidence Bag A."

"And since that scene at the bar, a woman named Danika Zoric has also been killed." Deep glared at Monroe. "Now, let's take a look at Ring Three." The circus scene was back on the screen, and this time Deep twisted in the other direction and pointed at the ring on the right. "The night that Bogdan Zoric was killed was not the first nor was it the last time that someone attempted to kill Lacey Stuart. She almost died in five different events. It began on a September day when Ms. Stuart went to Radovan Krokov's home to hang a painting. I will add here that Ms. Stuart almost died three times that day: once in the house just by being present, once when her car was run off the road, and the third time when Musclav Zoric held the gun to her head. It was only because of Steve Finley's quick and decisive action that day that Ms. Stuart lived. You will find eyewitness testimony on the flash drive marked in Evidence Bag B."

The assembled team offered Finley approving nods.

"Ah, let's not give Finley a medal too soon. He saved her life only to exploit it. We'll get to that in the Center Ring. The second day Lacey was nearly killed happened when Musclav Zoric climbed into the back of her car with the intention of slitting her throat."

Steve's face turned hard with a fierceness that didn't need translation.

"You didn't tell him about that, apparently. Is there a reason you kept it to yourself?" Lynx asked Lacey.

"Yes, well," Lacey cleared her throat. "We struck a deal, Musclav and I. I'd keep my mouth shut, and he wouldn't kill me."

Lynx nodded. "Sounds like a good deal to make."

"Lacey talked her way out of that situation," Deep continued. "The third attempted murder was our Ring One bar murder. The fourth, a sniper attempted to kill her at the press conference before Lacey could release any information to the public. And here we aren't sure who had her in their sights. It could have been someone from the Zoric family, but that's not a given. We have discovered that Lacey, in fact, had information of national import. It's possible that someone who was afraid of what Lacey would reveal at the press conference needed to make sure she could not then, or ever, share that information. Knowing what we now know," Deep stopped and stared hard at John Black, "It's possible that someone who lived in the gray world—where there is no black and white— might weigh the costs and decide that an American citizen needed to be eradicated."

John Black's gaze never wavered. His face gave no sign of acknowledgement, nor did it negate what Deep said. That was a blank that looked like it would never get filled in.

Deep placed other bags on the table. "Lacey and I were heading back to Iniquus Headquarters with the evidence we had gathered about that murder, when there was a fifth attempt on her life." Deep rubbed his fingers over the bandage on his head. "Musclav Zoric rammed my car off the roadway. But we survived. And we were able to retrieve the piece of live rock that you will find in Evidence Bag C. That live rock is the means by which we believe Radovan Krokov was murdered."

When Mr. Black and the FBI agents all leaned forward with attention, Deep stalled their interest. "I'll get to that in a moment. But first, let's look at the center ring. And if you thought Ring Two was busy, hold on to your seats, gentlemen. Wait until you see what's performing center stage. We have pedophiles, prostitutes, and human trafficking. We have Special Agent Finley deeply undercover, living with his unwitting asset. We have blackmail. We have forgers. And insurance fraud. We even have a woman who, with the aid of Special Agent Finley, is playing the role of Lacey Stuart to facilitate all of this. That, by the way, is chronicled in Exhibit A. We have action aplenty. It looks very clearly to me that you all used a law-abiding American citizen, without her consent, as a pawn. It looks like you have endangered her life many times over. And it looks as though she might have been marked for eradication because of information that she may or may not have possessed. Does anyone here in this room believe that Lacey Stuart has committed a crime?"

No one answered.

"That's an emphatic body-language 'no' from everyone," Lynx said to Lacey.

Lacey blew out a relieved breath.

"Does anyone believe that Lacey Stuart was harmed because of American government action?"

Again no one answered.

"And that's an emphatic yes," Lynx said.

Lacey nodded with tears in her eyes.

"Does anyone in here think that agents of the United States government are culpable of breaking the law as it pertains to Lacey Stuart?"

The men sat stoically silent.

"Again, that's a big yes," Lynx said.

"Before I go any further with my explanations, I want to understand the role that Danika Zoric played in this con," Deep said.

"Oh, good." Lacey kicked off her shoes and pulled her feet up under her hip, leaning forward with anticipation.

"We know she's dead. Why is she dead?" Deep asked.

Chapter Forty-Eight

Steve

Friday

"**D**anika." Steve came to his feet and shook his head. "She is a tragic figure and a criminal mastermind. She was an abused child who came to realize that the only way to survive was to serve the Zoric family and serve them well." He stopped to clear his throat. "Why she was killed, I don't know. Who killed her? I don't know. What I can tell you is that Danika's con was always blackmail." Steve spread his fingers wide on the table, and turned his head at an odd angle to look at the glass wall. His eyes closed, and he frowned deeply.

"Danika had, early in her teens, started visiting with Radovan Krokov. He loved her in his own way, they got along very well. By visiting with him, I mean she was sent to him for sex. Radovan was a bisexual man who, while he enjoyed Danika's youth and beauty, preferred the intellectual relationship he had with Bartholomew Winslow, Lacey

475

Stuart's uncle. The two men were lovers for several years. Officially, though, Danika Zoric was engaged to Radovan in June. She knew and was fine with the idea of Winslow being in her relationship picture. But she also shared the information of the two men's affair with Pavle Zoric, and the Zoric family began to exploit it. After she shared that information, she started calling herself Lacey Stuart. Radovan had a staffing change, and Danika was introduced to the staff as Ms. Stuart."

"Why did Danika play the role of Lacey with Radovan's help and obvious approval? Was Radovan involved in the arts con? Another con?" Sy asked.

"Since both players are dead, we may never know. As far as we can tell," Steve replied, "Radovan had nothing to do with the Zoric cons. Danika was a peace offering between warring families."

"Huh," Lynx said. "John Black was sending off definite shut-your-mouth vibes when it came to mentioning warring families. I wonder what that was about."

"However," Steve said. "Danika calling herself Lacey Stuart outside of that relationship is knowable. It all had to do with her procuring art for the Zoric family. While we're not sure why Radovan went along with her Danika using a new name. We do know why Winslow went along. He was being blackmailed and would do whatever he was told to do."

Deep stepped in. "We know that Winslow was supposed to gather art for the art heist beginning last summer in preparation for a show tomorrow, but after the car accident—when you jumped in to save the day, Steve. Some new con got under way." Deep's derision was an undercurrent. Not exactly blatant – he was still professional—but there was a wolf-growl undertone that made every single man in the room shift warily. Lacey didn't need Lynx to interpret that. Deep leaned his weight onto his fists on the table. "Was it Danika Zoric who masterminded that?"

Steve cleared his throat. The glance he cast toward the window begged Lacey to listen and forgive. "No. It was mine," he said quietly.

"You must have had a good reason—in your own mind, at least." This time it was Lacey's lawyer, Sy Covington, who spoke.

"We were going after the Zorics for funding terrorist groups."

"And trafficking children," Monroe added.

Steve sniffed. "Our goal was to take out the East Coast Zoric family. To get to that end, I helped Danika develop a bigger con, one that pulled in a greater number of the family members. Danika's goal was to steal the art for the family. I helped her figure out a way to get a million dollar-plus payday from the insurance to both support the family and give to the groups that they sponsor, and to place all of the blame elsewhere."

"On Lacey Stuart," Sy said.

"Yes." Steve pointed toward the evidence bag. "If those are the photos of Danika wearing Lacey clothes, then you'll see how the plan worked. We staged Danika in pictures that would place Lacey in the right place right time to be culpable. "Things were moving along just fine, until they weren't. Danika and Leo Bardman, were doing something on the side. Pavle Zoric decided to get the women, Lacey and Danika, under his thumb in advance of tomorrow's opening. The plan was that Lacey would be charged and be found culpable. And of course, we'd step in and protect Lacey."

"The Zoric's plan changed," Monroe said. "They didn't want to take any chances that there would be a big investigation, so they decided to remove Lacey from the equation all together."

"By that you mean she'd be killed," Sy said.

"As soon as I realized she was in danger. . . well, imminent danger, I moved forward to pull Lacey out."

"And what exactly was this plan?" Sy asked.

Steve could feel the strength of Deep's anger like a blaze of heat from where he stood at the top of the table, though to look at him, he was perfectly contained and participating in a business meeting. Steve swallowed. "The Thursday night that

Bardman was killed, something triggered Bardman to act. Bardman wanted Danika to run away with him and leave that life. He believed, and I agreed with him, that Danika's life was as disposable as Lacey's. Pavle Zoric saw Danika as a liability and didn't want her around. She had been skating on thin ice ever since she had found out that the family had murdered Radovan. You see, Danika actually loved Radovan in her own way. And here I will digress to explain that the whole point of murdering Radovan, by whatever means they did, was to ensure that it looked like a natural death and no one would know it was a murder. Danika knew it was a murder. And Danika was acting disloyal. She was a threat." Steve focused on the rock. His mind whirled, trying to understand how that could possibly have had anything to do with Radovan's murder. "The Zoric family and Krokov families are in opposition, and a murder would create a war between the families."

Monroe added, "Pavle Zoric came up with some scheme to threaten Danika into submission and to take Lacey hostage until after the arts con was over and then both women would be killed. We know bits and pieces. You know bits and pieces. The end result was that Bardman went to the bar to save Danika and warn her that the family had decided to kill her. But it was Lacey at the bar. Danika was with Steve. Bardman warned the wrong woman."

"You were telling us how you planned to remove Lacey from the environment," Sy said.

"Yes," Steve cleared his throat. "I invited her to dinner at a nice restaurant in Alexandria. I planned to drug her drink, so she'd pass out. I'd call an ambulance, which was actually the FBI's transport. We'd remove her in a very public way. I needed to stay involved in the con. I was going to say that she suffered a stroke and was in a coma. That her relatives took her back to Georgia. Lacey would be in the witness protection program."

"But things went bad," Monroe said.

"That's a gross understatement," Deep replied. He gave Sy a significant look then let his gaze scan the other men. "I think we need to take a break."

"Can I talk to Lacey, please?" Steve asked.

No one responded.

"Please," Steven said, again. His voice had taken on a plaintive tone.

"You understand that Lacey Stuart is a free agent. She will leave here freely. She will *go* where she wants and *do* what she wants," Sy said.

Steve's brow came together. "Yes, I . . ." He looked over at Monroe, confused. Monroe shrugged and shook his head. Steve turned to Mr. Black.

John Black's face was hard as stone. "We'll need to discuss this."

"No. We won't," Sy said.

Steve watched Deep send a text message. After a moment, the phone buzzed in reply. Deep's lower jaw extended in a snarl, but he said, "Follow me."

***

"Lacey." Steve was visibly shaking. He had been waiting for her in a small meeting room down the hall. It was big enough for two chairs and a table, and a little standing and maneuvering room.

Lacey walked in and stood against the opened door with her arms crossed over her chest.

"Lacey," he stammered. He felt like his world was imploding. Lacey's eyes were so cold and distant. His Lacey was not in the room with him. He needed to find her and bring her back.

Lacey leaned her head against the door, and Steve felt too tall. He needed to be eye to eye with her. He pulled out a chair and sat down. Fell into the seat.

Lacey leveled her gaze on his. "You're a good guy, doing what he thought was the right thing for America. Thank you for that."

Hope sparked in his chest. He opened his mouth to say something, anything that would right this, but she held up her hand to stop him.

"But you're also a bad guy who used me to get where you wanted to go. You endangered my life. And my life is every bit as precious as any of the other lives you were trying to save." She stopped and pulled her brow together. "The biggest hurdle for me to jump is that I really do believe you loved me, Steve *Finley.*"

"Love you. I love you. Everything I ever said to you about my feelings was the absolute truth."

"And yet you thought you could simultaneously love me and endanger my life? Not just my reputation or my job, but my actual existence. Who would accept that kind of love in their life? I want to feel safe. I want to feel cherished. I want to feel like I belong. I don't want to ever wonder if I'm the trade-off in some kind of con."

"Lacey, please, I'll make this up to you. I will make this better. I love you. I want to marry you and raise a family. I will do whatever it takes. Whatever you want." He realized his hands were gripped as if in supplication, and he knew that he was a drowning man who had risen from the depths of the water and taken his last breath of air.

"If you think I ever want to see you or speak to you again," Lacey raised a derisive brow. "You are seriously mistaken. I can't even stand here next to you. I'm breaking out in hives. Do you see this?" Lacey showed him how her arms above the bandages were covered in welts.

"Lacey, please," he whispered.

"I'm going to say this as clearly and plainly as I can." She folded her arms over her chest. "You saved my life, and for that, thank you. But from that point on, you've endangered me. For months, you treated me as someone who was disposable, someone who didn't matter. I was a castaway to be used in a con. But I do matter." Her gaze sizzled with angry sparks. "I don't ever want to see you or speak to you again. Not now. Not ever."

"Lacey, you have to understand. These people are dangerous."

She turned on her heels and started walking away.

"You can't go back to your life the way you were living it," he yelled after her in desperation.

"Oh yeah?" She threw over her shoulder. "Watch me."

Chapter Forty-Nine

DEEP

Friday Evening

The hotel room was luxurious. Deep had decided to take Lacey to the Jefferson Hotel for "the first night of the rest of my life," as she called it. Tonight, it felt like they needed a celebration. A beautiful setting and a sense of pampering.

Lynx had brought Lacey over earlier and stayed with her. They watched movies and ordered room service. Deep had stayed in the war room, where he laid out everything they knew about the palytoxins, the arts con, and the children. While the pictures of the children were vile, Monroe was ecstatic—they had the evidence they had so desperately needed to keep the kids safe and put the children's handlers in jail for a very long time.

While Deep moved through the evidence trails back at headquarters, Panther Force had deployed to the businesses that shared walls with the gallery annex. The Iniquus operatives and K9 Zorro found an explosive attached to a gas line with a dial-in detonator.

With Deep's tasks complete, General Elliot pat him on the back and told him to go finish up his R and R. He had two days left before his next mission.

When Deep arrived at the hotel room door, Lynx opened it with her coat and purse in her hands. "Thought that was you in the elevator," she said. "I'll check in with you later." And before he could say a word, she was off down the hall.

Deep walked into the room and softly shut the door. Lacey was curled around a pillow on the bed. She glanced up at him. He had the same reaction he had the moment she slipped her hand into his way back last November at the gallery. He had been thrown end over end. His whole world had shifted. His perspective and purpose. He'd found his heart, and she was everything brave and good and wholesome.

"Hello, beautiful."

"Hi." Lacey smiled at him with sleepy happiness. "What happened?"

"Things are blowing up for the Zoric family." Deep bent to take off his boots. He removed his weapons and laid them on the top of the highboy, then crawled onto the bed.

Lacey pushed herself up to sit cross-legged, hugging the pillow to her chest. "The children?"

"The FBI is sending out a team tonight." Deep checked his watch. "Another hour, and they'll start the arrests. The children have a group home ready for them, complete with psychological help and medical attention." As he said that, Lacey's face crumpled.

Fat tears rolled down her cheeks as she shook her head back and forth. "Thank, God for that."

Deep reached out and cradled her face in his hands, using his thumbs to wipe her tears. "You're so amazing to me, Lacey. So smart, so brave; you have such a loving heart." He set his jaw and looked her straight in the eyes. "I have to keep you safe, sweetheart."

Lacey's eyes popped wide as she jerked herself from one emotion to another. She settled on one that he read as fear. "What does that mean? Are you sending me away to the protection program?"

"I would never do something that involves you without your permission. You understand that, don't you?"

She nodded. Her eyes were focused and intelligent.

"Iniquus would like to develop a new identity for you. Name, birthdate, social security numbers—a whole new identity. If they do this, you will have to give up who you were before and not go back to it. It will be a legal change."

"I think that's okay. Just some new numbers to memorize, right?"

"Yes. New address, too. New bank accounts, credit cards. New job. We have a department that handles the changes, and Sy Covington can help you maneuver through your finances."

"I just need to give them the go-ahead?"

"They already started on an alias package for the time being. While you make your decision and the slow government machines turn their wheels, we need to keep your identity hidden."

"New identity? A new name. Who came up with my alias? Do I get to choose?"

"I came up with the temporary one. You will come up with the permanent one."

"What did you call me? Helga Longbottom?" She smiled and tipped her head.

Deep nodded. "Yes, do you like it?"

Lacey swatted him with the pillow, which he easily plucked from her hands. He rolled into a ball and settled back, tucking it under his head. He reached out and pulled Lacey into his arms and stroked a hand through her hair. "What do you think of Grace Elizabeth Del Toro?"

She lifted herself to look him in the eye.

"Grace sounds a lot like Lacey. You can say Gracey, for example."

She knotted her brow and mouthed the names. "I prefer Grace. I like Grace very much."

Deep gently brushed her hair from her face. "I picked Grace because it describes you so well, and then Del Toro, because I thought you might like to try it on and see how it fits."

She smiled self-consciously.

"I called my mom in New York, Long Island. She's inviting you to go stay with her as long as it takes until it's safe for you to be back in DC. I thought we could fly up on tomorrow. If you wanted."

"How long are they thinking it will be until I'm safe?"

"The FBI believes it'll be a number of months. My mom is thrilled because she knows I'll be up there seeing you all the time, so she'll get to see me, too." He stalled. "I'm a little worried, though."

Lacey frowned.

"My mom is a *mom*. A full-throttle mom, if you know what I mean."

Lacey shook her head.

No, how could she know what I mean? "Let's just say that you'll get twenty-five years of normal mothering in a few short months. And, every time I see you, you'll have gained at least ten pounds. She equates love with eating."

Lacey whispered, "What did you tell her about why I was coming?"

"That I wanted her to get to know you."

"Because . . ."

"I plan to marry you." Deep came up on his elbow so they were eye to eye.

"I see." She tilted her head with a funny little confused look on her face.

He reached out to plant a kiss on the tip of her perfect little nose. "I'm going to wait to ask, though, because I have a strict 'no means no' rule." He laced their fingers together. "If you were to say no, well, I'd have to go and mope my life away."

She smiled. "What if I were to say yes?"

"Then I'd be the happiest man in the world. But Lacey . . ." He paused a beat to make absolutely sure she heard and understood what he was saying. "This is my role to play. I know you like control – but not about this. I get to make it all sappy and romantic. I want to surprise you, so you'll cry."

"You want me to cry?"

"Only with happiness. And that's not where you are right now. Right now, you're in shock. Traumatized. And scared. I'm going to ask you to marry me. But everything in its right time. Right now, it's time for you to get a little mothering. It's a time for healing, and pasta."

Lacey curled around him. "That sounds really, really nice." Her contented sigh made him smile.

Deep leaned down and kissed Lacey with the conviction he had always felt when it came to loving her. In his arms, she was exactly where she belonged.

This is not
THE END

Please follow Deep Del Toro and the Iniquus family
as they continue their fight for the greater good.

Would you like a sneak peek at the next book in the Iniquus
chronology?

Book Two, Jack be Quick:

Jack Be Quick

Chapter One

Suz - 11:15 p.m. Sunday, February 13th
Suburban Hospital, Bethesda Maryland

Suz perched on the edge of her vinyl-cushioned hospital chair to study Jack's face. He was pale beneath his tan. His bruised and unshaven skin lay slack over the chiseled angles of his jaw and cheek bones. His mouth hung slightly to the left, following the tilt of his head as his lips slid open and hung loose.

Balanced on one hip, a good two feet from his face, Suz could smell smoke clinging to the black ebony of his hair. She brushed her hand down Jack's bare arm, stopping to dance her thumb lightly over the IV and tape.

"Here you are again," she whispered. "Here *we* are again." She lifted her gaze and let her focus take in his little corner of the post-op. They were the only ones there. It must have been a slow night for the emergency surgeons. They were probably in a back room somewhere, sipping coffee and playing Angry Birds, waiting for the next car accident, or gang beatings, or special operative who felt compelled to jump off a building. . .

Her eyes scanned over the room with its beeping machines and bright lights. It hadn't been bad this time. Well, not life threatening. Something to do with the meniscus in Jack's knee. When the surgeon tried to explain about the cartilage tearing from a massive impact and twist, he pointed to the images on his tablet. Suz's stomach jumped at the sight. With a sour face, she shook her head, pushing the photos away. She didn't need to know the details. She didn't want to know them. Deep down, in a place that she hadn't yet acknowledged, Suz understood that these kinds of details weren't going to be her burden to carry anymore.

The two points that got through her resistance were that Jack was going to be okay, and there was a three to four-month recovery time.

She laced her fingers into Jack's and while she squeezed to hold him tightly, his fingers hung unaware. Three to four months. Jack would turn that into a week maybe two. He couldn't sit still. He certainly couldn't lay still in a hospital.

Suz's mind drifted back to just a short time ago when he was fighting for his life after being shot in the thigh and through his chest, collapsing a lung. A covert mission that had gone very badly, jeopardizing his whole team. No one had come out of that one unscathed except for Blaze, their communications officer. She remembered how she had waited for the surgeon's report, waited for the "I'm sorry. We did everything we could. . ." She had pulled herself into the fetal position on the hard, plastic, waiting room chair. Her head rested in Jack's teammate's lap as she sobbed, and Blaze offered up what comfort an alpha male could offer up — which meant he pet her like she was a puppy and dropped a brotherly kiss onto her hair every once in a while. Jack and his friends were much more comfortable fast-roping into the fray than dealing with emotions.

"How in the world did we end up together, Jack?" It was the ubiquitous question that she had been asking herself since they started dating almost four years ago.

Jack mumbled something as if in response. Suz had been in this position too many times, watching him come out of his medicated stupor, to pay much attention. His work as an Iniquus special operative assigned to Strike Force put him in constant danger. And he loved it. Loved the adrenaline rush.

Suz preferred yoga and meditative quietude. Adrenaline was something she tried to avoid. She looked down at her hand so small against his bear paw. She was five-foot-two, and he was six-foot-five from his bare feet to top of his tight military haircut. She weighed in at a hundred and ten pounds, and he doubled her without an ounce of fat, just pure heart and muscle. A mountain of muscles. Unconquerable. Unless of course it's your job to jump off of three-story buildings as they exploded somewhere in the far reaches of the world. He'd have to be more robot than human to be able to do that and not end up here in the surgical wing.

Suz knew little other than what he had texted her from the ambulance. Apparently, as he flew off the top of some building — somewhere that required a plane to evacuate him and eighteen hours of airtime — he landed on the roof of a car which collapsed, absorbing the impact of the fall, and he walked away – hobbled away.

His last text said: **I'm home for a once over at Suburban Hospital.**

That text struck her as the nail in their coffin. She couldn't. She couldn't keep doing this. For someone who sought to be peaceful and centered, Jack brought life-or-death energy to their relationship on a daily basis. He loved it. She hated it.

"Jack be nimble," Jack mumbled. ". . .quick."

Suz leaned in, her ear hovering just above his mouth, trying to catch his words. "What? What are you saying, Jack?"

"Jack jump over. . . candlestick." Suz made that up. She thought it might be what he said – but nursery rhymes? Could be. People said awfully weird things while sedated.

"Thank you, Lynx. . ."

That last one was clear, and it hurt. Lynx's name was on his lips, not hers.

Lynx was Strike Force's newest teammate, Lexi Sobado. She was fun, kind, unduly attractive, as smart as they come, and Trouble with a capital T. Lynx had a way of magnetizing the bad guys to her, and then the Strike Force team of good guys would have to save her life, time and again.

Lynx was supposed to work in the office doing their intelligence and wasn't supposed to be a field operative like the others. Yes, for sure, where Lynx went, trouble followed. Suz scowled. That was really unfair of her to think. And not any more true for Lynx than the other team members. Jack had been in danger since before Suz and he started dating back when he was still a SEAL in California. His life had been on the line long before Lynx had shown up. *This is a stupid thought process.* Suz twisted her copper colored curls into a make-do braid. She was just looking for a bad guy – someone to blame for Jack's wounds and her misery.

"Jack jump. Jack. . . candlestick." Jack breathed out.

"What candlestick?"

"Jump."

"Jack, did you jump over a candlestick?" Was that code for something? Maybe the dynamite that blew up the building as he stood on the roof? Not that she actually knew why the building had blown up.

He lifted his free hand inches off the mattress and made a gesture that she read as jumping over.

"Why did you jump?"

"Lynx," he said.

Frustration painted over Suz. Jack never gave her a straight answer about his missions. It was as if he lived a parallel life. It was one of the things Suz hadn't been able to work through. She stared at the engagement ring glittering on her right ring finger – the "thinking spot" until she made up her mind to say yes. Or to hand it back.

Could she marry someone and not know what happened during most of his life? Their only reality as a couple turned out to be the short, sporadic bursts of time they were together. That just didn't sit well with her.

She had heard the soldiers laughing back in California "Are you married?" "Not overseas I'm not." Jack wasn't like that. She trusted Jack because he deserved her trust – but that many secrets wore at a relationship. Made it threadbare and fragile. And then it ripped, leaving ragged edges, that were all but impossible to mend.

In that moment, Suz needed an answer. Just one clear answer. "Lynx told you to jump. And you did. You jumped off a building. And then it exploded. Lynx was on this assignment with you? I thought she was here in DC."

Nothing.

Suz tried again. "You jumped, and you're alive because Lynx told you to."

Nothing.

"Come on Jack. I need to know this. How would Lynx know the building was going to explode? She was in Washington, and you were. . ." Suz had no idea where Jack had been. She frequently didn't even know he was leaving. They needed him – he ran toward the enemy. There were plenty of bad guys out there. Plenty of hostages that needed rescuing. Plenty of CIA or FBI or DHS or any other government agency who signed private contracts, preferring to use mercenaries over their own folks, especially in politically delicate areas of the world. Yes, there was plenty of extremely lucrative work for the operatives at Iniquus. Suz hated that money. She'd rather Jack were poor and home. And safe.

"Jack?" Suz shook his shoulder. "How did Lynx know you needed to jump off the building before it exploded?"

Jack pulled his hand towards his head and tapped a finger to his temple.

"She figured it out?"

"Psychic," Jack said. Maybe. Suz wasn't sure; he had barely mumbled. He had merely twitched his lips.

Suz plopped her bottom back in the chair. She felt as if she had just opened the door on a stranger using the bathroom, and she wanted to shut it as quickly as she could. If it were true, it wasn't something she was supposed to have seen. Suz shook her head and convinced herself that Jack was out of his mind on drugs, and she didn't really know what he was muttering.

"Jack be quick! Jack jump!" His body jerked and his hand landed on the brace that locked his leg out straight.

The hum of the ice water pump that cooled Jack's angry surgical site filled the sudden silence.

A wash of cold doused Suz's body, leaving her trembling and sweat-covered – because this time, Suz had heard the voice of someone leaping to their probable death. If Jack had missed the car roof, if it weren't engineered to absorb impact energy, he'd be dead.

She couldn't do this.

She lived in terror. All the time. Terrified. Every single time her phone buzzed, she was sure it was *the* call. Jack was dead. Or worse, Jack was injured to the point that he wished he were dead and now would live in a broken body with no adrenaline surges to electrify and power his system.

Jack scraped his teeth over his lips and Suz reached for the moistened washcloth that she had been using to dab his mouth. "My world is so vivid, Suz." He had tried to explain. "You can't imagine how bright the colors are, how meaningful every nanosecond is when you're in survival mode." He tried to help her see why he did what he did. Even when she felt willfully blind to the pictures he tried to paint, Jack was always patient with her. She couldn't imagine him ever raising his voice or his hand to anyone. There was nothing about Jack that was violent. She knew intellectually that he had killed people. But it didn't make sense to her. Jack was a gentle giant. A reader. A thinker. A devoted would-be fiancé, waiting patiently for her to decide to say yes.

Suz bit her bottom lip to stop its trembling. She was tired of crying. Bone tired. Wrung completely dry. She didn't understand why Jack chased those adrenaline highs. Her system didn't brighten with fear; her system crashed under heavy cotton-filled emotions, buffering her from the moment, keeping her hidden inside of her body. Her limbs became dull and heavy. Her thoughts slowed. She vibrated with anxiety and inability like she was doing now. And this was no way to live.

Suz disentangled her fingers from his – when she tucked her fingers up into the web of Jack's hand, her joints

503

stretched too far apart as the distance splayed her palm. The difference between them was physically painful. They didn't fit comfortably together.

She lay her forehead on the cool sheet by his elbow. "I love you. Oh my god, I so desperately love you." Her words tumbled out in sobs. "I can't do this anymore. I can't, Jack. I'm so sorry."

Like what you've read?
You can get your copy now.

Readers, I hope you enjoyed getting to know Deep and Lacey. If you had fun reading In Too Deep, I'd appreciate it if you'd help others enjoy it too.

Recommend it: Just a few words to your friends, your book groups, and your social networks would be wonderful.

Review it: Please tell your fellow readers what you liked about my book by reviewing In Too Deep on Amazon and Goodreads. If you do write a review, please send me a note at FionaQuinnBooks@outlook.com so I can thank you with a personal e-mail. Or stop by my website www.FionaQuinnBooks.com to keep up with my news and chat through my contact form.

Let's stay in touch!

For new release notifications, free offers, gifts, and sneak peeks for members only, please sign up for our Fiona Quinn mailing list. We don't want to leave you out of the fun!

Join Fiona Quinn's www.FionaQuinnBooks.com

Also:

@FionaQuinnBooks on Twitter

Fiona Quinn Books on Facebook

Fiona Quinn Books on Pinterest

Acknowledgements

My great appreciation ~

To my editor, Lindsay Smith

To my Beta Force, who are always honest and kind at the same time.

To my Street Force, who support me and my writing with such enthusiasm. If you're interested in joining this group, please send me an email.

To H. Russell for creating the Iniquus Bible – so I can keep all the details correct

Thank you to the real-world military who serve to protect us.

To all of the wonderful professionals whom I called on to get the details right. Please note: this is a work of fiction, and while I always try my best to get all of the details correct, there are times when it serves the story to go slightly to the left or right of perfection. Please understand that any mistakes or discrepancies are my authorial decision making alone and sit squarely on my shoulders.

Thank you to my family.

I send my love to my husband, and my great appreciation. T, you live in my heart, you live in my characters. You are my hero.

And of course, thank YOU for reading my stories. I'm smiling joyfully as I type this. I so appreciate you!

Copyright

Canadian born, Fiona Quinn is now rooted in the Old Dominion outside of DC. There, she pops chocolates, devours books, and taps continuously on her laptop. For more, please visit her bio at http://www.fionaquinnbooks.com

Made in the USA
Middletown, DE
18 November 2020